THE WATCHING II
WHISPERS OF RETALIATION

J.A. LOPEZ

CONTENTS

DEDICATION PAGE

There is one person I need to thank above all others, my husband and partner in crime, Rolando. He is the constant force that pushes me forward in all my endeavors. His belief in me is never ending, and I am so grateful to have him in my life. Love you!

A SPECIAL THANKS

To all of my beta readers Monique L., Gina B., Jilly S., and Michelle F., whose attention and imagination was greatly appreciated. You all got the story I was telling! Love ya!

Also, to Kyle Markham, and his terrific talents in graphic arts and formatting.

Next, my heart goes out to all of you who purchased my first book, The Watching a Paranormal Romance, and have been looking forward to this second book in the series. Thank you so much for taking a chance on me. Please enjoy your ongoing relationship with all of the characters, especially Willie, who I know has been a favorite for some of you. You will be pleased to know, he has a much bigger story line in this second book. FYI Willie is also my favorite, he was patterned after my dog Obi, who had passed away after I finished my first book. He was always by my side, and I miss him terribly.

I am introducing some new characters, in this second book, that I hope you will enjoy. So, find a comfy chair, grab a beverage of choice, and settle in as Kayla and her friends are swept away again, as more supernatural happenings come into play.

Thanks again, and as I always say, HAPPY READING!

J. A. Lopez

CONTENT WARNING

This is an adult book of fiction, which contains themes and depictions that may be distressing or triggering to some readers. It contains scenes of alcoholism, crude language, instances of graphic violence, sexual graphic content and physical abuse, including rape. There are also some cringe worthy scenes that the reader my find upsetting. Reader discretion is advised.

CHAPTER ONE
A NEW HOME

At midnight, Michael and Tarsula sat in the kitchen of the townhouse quietly. Tarsula placed her hand over Michael's, "sorry things didn't go according to plan. That little fuck Peter needs to be stomped out like a bug. He's not human, killing Basheba and Coletta with ice picks that came from his fingers. What kind of shit is that?"

"Tarsula, I don't give a rat's ass about Peter, my concern is with Kayla. I'm still trying to comprehend the fact that she is still alive. Do you think Peter can raise the dead, does he have that much power?"

"I'm not sure Michael, was he the one that killed your mom and dad? We don't know? You were busy running after Kayla, and quite frankly, I thought your mom could kill Peter all by herself. I guess I was wrong."

"So, how do we get Kayla? That's all I really want. We need to take her Tarsula, find a place to hide her away, as soon as possible. It pisses me off knowing she is spending so much time with that shit head, Peter."

"How about here, at the townhouse?" Tarsula interjected.

"No, I want her away from this town, but close enough, that we can hide her away quickly. An isolated place where others can't meddle in our affairs. I think it's time to purchase some real estate."

Tarsula smiled, "let me contact my agent Ted Grith, and see what he may have available."

"Thanks Tarsula, but I don't want to use an agent here in town,

I'm going to find one on my own. This property needs to be special for Kayla, breathtakingly beautiful, just like her."

The next evening, they had an appointment with a realtor, two towns away. Far enough to roam about freely and not be recognized. Michael had his mind set on buying another property. He thought about his previous home, which was now reduced to a pile of charred wood and ash. It was difficult to lose everything, including his painting of Isabella which was irreplaceable. The new residence that he wanted to purchase had to meet certain requirements. It needed to be large and impressive, a place where Kayla would be comfortable. Isolated, away from prying eyes and neighbors. Last and probably the most important thing, NO CLIFFs! The land needed to be flat and solid.

Arriving at their destination Michael parked the car, and they made their way into the real estate office, where Courtney Stein was waiting for them. A woman in her early thirties, medium built, with strawberry blonde hair and gold framed glasses. She stood up from her substantial desk covered with papers and introduced herself. After all the necessary introductions, Ms. Stein got down to business.

"Okay Mr. Blaydon, I understand you are looking for a remote house rather isolated, with over ten thousand square feet of living space, is that correct?"

"Yes, I have a habit of throwing elaborate parties. I'm afraid they can get loud and out of hand at times, I wouldn't want to disturb my neighbors." Michael looked over at Tarsula with a wicked grin.

"Well, that's very considerate of you Mr. Blaydon. I love parties, maybe if I find you that perfect house, you'll invite me to one. I have a few properties I could show you. However, there is one that I really think you will love. We can see it now or tomorrow morning if you're available?"

"I must be frank with you Ms. Stein; I don't have much free time during the day. The showings will have to be in the evening. Would that work within your schedule?"

"Well, I'm usually here until eight or so, and please call me Courtney. Looking at your paperwork I didn't see a set budget. What is your price point Mr. Blaydon?"

"My budget is open; I just need to fall in love with the house," responded Michael.

Courtney was elated, thinking about the large commission that could be hers. It also didn't hurt that Michael was gorgeous. With her busy schedule and lack of free time, meeting single men was almost impossible. Michael was every girl's dream come true. Tall, blonde, muscular, with a killer smile, and unique eyes. Not to mention his sexy English accent. Courtney pushed her hair back behind her left ear, as she gathered up her papers, along with her car keys. "Alright Mr. Blaydon, if you're ready to see the first property I'll be happy to show it to you both. We can go in my car if that's okay?"

"We would rather follow you, if that's alright Courtney. I can get a better feeling for the area if I drive myself. What's the square footage and price of the property?"

"It's roughly sixteen thousand square feet. The price is ten million five, is that alright? I know it's up there in price, but I think it's a good deal for what you're getting. I hope it will have everything you're looking for in a home. If you don't mind me asking Mr. Blaydon, what is your occupation?"

"First, call me Michael. Mr. Blaydon sounds so formal. I dabble in the stock market mostly, but I've been lucky enough to come from old money. So, that price won't be a problem. Ten million five sounds pretty reasonable, for a house of that size. What is it haunted?" Michael started to chuckle, as did Tarsula, helping herself to some hard candies from a jar on Courtney's desk. Courtney looked down at the floor, trying to think of what to say.

Michael grew silent. "Oh, come on Courtney, you've got to be kidding me, it's haunted?"

"Well, the manor is old and stories about the place have been going around for years. I'm sure it's just rumors. I mean, I've never seen a ghost have you Michael, Tarsula?"

"No, I can't say that I have." Michael answered, looking over at Tarsula who shook her head no and continued to crunch the candy in her mouth. "Let's go have a look at it. If it suits my needs, you can consider it sold. That would make us both winners tonight. I'll have my dream home, and you will receive your substantial commission."

"Well, I would be lying, if I said I hadn't thought about that." Courtney replied, as she felt her face get flush. "However, aside from the money, I will do my best Michael to find you the most perfect place haunted or not. Should we get going?"

"Yes, you lead the way. I can't wait to see this first property," Michael acknowledged with anticipation.

As they drove, houses and shops were replaced by farms and woods. Everything seemed darker without a single streetlight. The roads seemed to go on forever as they drove through the night. Courtney constantly checked behind her, making sure Michael was following. They spoke over their cell phones making small talk. She was thinking about her commission and hoping the house wasn't too large and isolated for him. "Here we are, Jesus I almost drove past the driveway. It's narrow, but it opens further down." The graveled road soon changed to blacktop as the cars approached the house. The outside landscape was lit up by pathway lights and spotlights, which illuminated the front of the property and the surrounding land. There were enough parking spaces in front for numerous cars. This house reminded Michael of some of the mansions he had visited in England. Very large and grand, spacious and opulent, old but well taken care of.

"It looks good!" Michael yelled, looking over at Courtney as they got out of their cars. "What do you think Tarsula?"

"It looks adequate. Are there any bakeries close by?" Tarsula asked, always thinking about her obsession with baked goods.

"I'm not sure Tarsula. I must admit, that's a question I've never been asked by a potential buyer before. Let me check into it, if not, there's a grocery store a short distance away. Michael, shall we walk the grounds first? The land is a little overgrown in the back, but a good landscaper will help solve that problem for you." Courtney smiled, as they moved on, the crisp leaves beneath their feet rustled as branches reached out to them mangled and dead. The land could definitely use some T.L.C. Michael thought, as they walked around the property.

"Courtney, how much land is there?"

"Altogether, there are ten acres, of which six are woodlands surrounding the property. This house is known as The Stone Manor. Although it is actually an estate, because of the property surrounding it back there," Courtney announced pointing. "You'll find the caretakers' cottage, along with the family chapel. There's also a swimming pool and tennis court. Do you play, Michael?"

"No, the game never interested me. Are there any spots where the land gives way, shears off?"

"Absolutely not. I can assure you Michael there is nothing like that, not with this property. Why do you ask?"

"I don't want any of my party going friends falling off a cliff, now do I?" He looked at Tarsula who gave him a cunning smile.

"Oh yes, I forgot about your wild parties, no fear about that Michael, no worries. Let's see how you like the inside. From the things you have told me, I'm sure you're going to love it."

As they walked inside, Michael felt the house embracing him. The slate floor beneath his feet and the hand carved wood impressed him. The ornate mantels which adorned the fireplaces took him back to another time. When fine craftsmen labored over each intricate design for endless hours, a skill that has long since been forgotten. The manor was undeniably beautiful, the perfect place to take his beloved Kayla. Courtney continued describing the house and all its unbelievable details.

"There are ten bedrooms and six bathrooms on the second floor, with an additional two baths on this level. A huge kitchen with two islands, a spacious dining room, media room, a library...." But Michael wasn't listening, lost in his world, imagining Kayla by his side. As they climbed the stairs to the second floor, the floorboards squeaked beneath their feet. Michael felt the house was welcoming him, he smiled looking into each room. The top floor had been renovated to perfection. As he viewed the last bedroom at the rear of the house, he was amazed. It reminded him of his house in England centuries ago. The room where he first made love to Isabella, however on a much grander scale. It had a massive ornate fireplace and beams on the ceiling, on which a huge chandelier presented itself.

"I'll take it!" Michael blurted out. "Since I'll be paying cash, how soon can I move in?"

Tarsula and Courtney were both caught off guard. "Well, you're a man who knows what he wants. Since you're paying cash and the house is empty, I guess within the month." Courtney answered.

"Good, draw up the papers, I want to move in as soon as possible." Michael started to Chant with Tarsula, speaking to her telepathically. "We'll put the townhouse up for sale but keep the furniture. The furnishings will have a place in this new home, along with you my old friend."

"Michael, are you sure this is the house you want?" Tarsula Chanted back. "Maybe we should look at a few more, just to be sure?"

"No this is the one, this is the house I feel it," remarked Michael, with no doubt in his mind.

"Okay, if you feel that strongly I'm on board." Tarsula looked over at him and smiled.

Exiting the house Courtney turned to Michael and Tarsula. "I'll start the paperwork tomorrow, as soon as I get back into the office. This house is fantastic, one of a kind, I think you've made a wise choice Michael."

"Courtney, are there any coffee houses nearby?" Tarsula asked. "I could use a cup of something warm right now." Secretly hoping, they would also have some baked goods available.

"There is a restaurant along with a few antique shops, just ten minutes from here. You just stay on the main road, keep driving straight, it will take you right through the center of town."

"Thank you dear, you've been quite helpful." Tarsula grinned, wondering what kind of treats she would be able to indulge in.

As Courtney was getting back into her car, Michael ran over to her. "Courtney, would it be possible for me to keep the key just for tonight? I want to buy some items in town and bring them back here. I'll have Tarsula return the key first thing in the morning."
Her substantial commission flashed before her eyes. Never had she shown a buyer only one property and have it sold. Meeting Michael was a God send, rich and very easy on the eyes. In her head she was trying to figure out a way to see more of him. However, giving a key over to a prospective buyer was something she would never normally do. That said, just looking at his gorgeous face, it was hard to deny him anything. She handed Michael the key, making him promise to return it to her first thing in the morning. Courtney waved goodbye to them, realizing there was a ton of paperwork that she would need to get started on.

* * *

Michael and Tarsula followed Courtney's instructions, driving through tiny neighborhoods and acres of farmland. Arriving at the restaurant along with a few quaint local shops, that they were eager to go inside and browse through. Michael was focused on purchasing a huge four poster bed. The bed he would share with his beloved Kayla, along with a fur rug to be set in front of the bedroom's fireplace. White and soft with a thick pile, a rug similar to the one Isabella lost her virginity on centuries ago. He just wanted to hold Kayla again, caress her. However, there was only a feeling of isolation now. Being so far away from her town, so far away from her body.

Tarsula tapped him on the shoulder. "Michael are you alright? I can tell you had drifted away there for a moment. What's on your mind?"

"The one thing that's always on my mind, Kayla. She's mine Tarsula. As soon as the house is in order, I will take her, whether she comes willingly or not."

"Yes, Michael she will be yours, I have no doubt. Let's do some shopping and get something to eat. Everything will work out in time my dear boy."

After making a few select purchases, such as a fur rug for Michael's bedroom. They headed towards the restaurant. They were seated at a booth towards the back, the perfect table for two, as they tried to blend in with the locals. Coffee cups in hand, they waited for their food to be brought over.

Tarsula started to Chant, telepathically shouting, which she did when she got excited. Michael could hear her in his mind. They communicated with each other this way all the time. Using only their minds to have complete conversations. "Michael, don't look now, but Bradford Cummings just walked in. What a sick fuck he is! What the hell is he doing here?"

"I don't know, but I can smell him." Michael was part werewolf, and his sense of smell was always acute. "No need to shout Tarsula, I know that son of a bitch is heading this way."

Seconds later Bradford stood before them. "My dear boy, how odd meeting you here. So sorry about your mother and father. Tarsula, so lovely to see you."

Tarsula looked at him with repulsion. "Mr. Cummings."

"I must say, I was very happy I left your party when I did. I heard the festivities came to an abrupt halt." Bradford commented, making a sarcastic sad face. "I hear that house of yours burnt down to the ground. Such a beautiful home, what a shame. Oh, by the way, how is your fiancé? What was her name, Katie?"

The waitress arrived with their food. "If you'll excuse us Bradford, we would like to enjoy our meal. I wish I could say it was nice seeing you, but we all know that would be a lie." Michael didn't want to hear another word, come out of Bradford's mouth. He looked over at Tarsula, a smile formed on her face, as she thought.

If Michael doesn't like you, he will definitely let you know.

Bradford Cummings had a seat at the bar. Keeping an eye on the two of them, drinking a cold beer and waiting. The thought crossed his mind to follow them. Would that bring him closer to Michael's beautiful fiancé? Standing near them, he was able to latch onto their scent. Tracking them would be a piece of cake, he thought. His mind was racing as the bartender engaged him in polite conversation. He finished off a second beer watching, as Michael and Tarsula got up to leave. Paying for his bar tab and exiting the restaurant, Bradford walked quickly to his car. Opening the door and getting in, he lowered the windows. Turning his nose up into the air while driving, tracking Michael and Tarsula to their car. He began to follow them, as Bradford grew more excited, eager to see where they were going.

Michael eventually turned off the road, was this where he was living now? Bradford needed to see more. Pulling over onto a grassy area, Bradford's eyes glistened with a yellow glow as he stepped out of his car. Walking into the woods that flanked both sides of the long driveway he started to run. Avoiding trees and jumping over anything in his path. No need for a flashlight, his vision was perfect, in pitch black darkness. The trees gave way to an opening, and beyond that point stood The Stone Manor. Bradford smiled, wondering if Michael's fiancé was inside. He remembered her face, her body. He walked back to his car thinking. Since he no longer had Michael's mother Sasetta to hunt with, she would do just fine.

* * *

Tarsula walked around her new home. Trying to figure out where all the furniture would go. It would take a few days to pack up the townhouse and more than a few trucks to move everything there. She walked into the expansive living room, which was empty except for the fur rug, that Michael had just purchased and was sitting on.

"How do you like the rug, Tarsula? I had a rug like this a long time ago. We laid upon it, the first time I made love to my Isabella." Tarsula smiled. "I like the rug, but it looks silly in this large room.

Shouldn't we have gotten a larger size?"

"Oh no Tarsula, this rug is not going in here. It's going in my bedroom, in front of the fireplace."

"I see. I have a feeling that rug will be used for a lot more than walking on it."

Michael looked at her with a devilish grin. "I think we should leave now, get back to the townhouse. We both have a lot of packing to do." As they exited the house, Michael made sure the massive door was locked and then put the key into his pocket. The wind was out of control, it almost sounded like an old man groaning. Leaves swirled around them as they quickly ran to the car. Once inside, Michael sat there admiring his new home, he couldn't wait to move in.

"The house is beautiful Michael. I know Kayla will be quite impressed."

"I hope so Tarsula." Taking one last look, he put the car into drive and headed back to the townhouse.

Inside The Stone Manor, all was quiet for the moment, as the wind moaned through the trees outside. There was an eeriness to this place. Dark and foreboding, as moonlight shown through the windows casting shadows on the floors of the massive rooms. Suddenly, there was a slight sound coming from the second-floor landing. The faint squeaking of a floorboard, as if someone was pacing back and forth. Then, the sound of heavy boots coming slowly down the stairs, which resonated throughout the manor. The footsteps moved along the hallways, stopping at the entrance to the living room. Michael's rug that he had just purchased was thrown and landed in a corner. A sound of laughter could be heard echoing through the vastness. Then one word was whispered within the darkness, "Michael."

* * *

Emily and Simon were in the middle of their nightly walk with their dog Dino. Since the apartment they rented was directly across the street from a park, it made it very convenient. They always took him out together, walking him before dinner. Dino led the way, running ahead of them trying to find the perfect spot to relieve himself. As he did, Emily reached into her pocket to retrieve her house key. Now that Dino's mission had been accomplished, it was time to go home. Feeling for her key, it wasn't there, but she did find a sizeable hole where the stitching had come apart.

"Shit! Simon, I lost my key to the apartment."

"It's okay, I've got mine."

"I need to find it Simon; I don't want to leave it here in the park. Take Dino home it has to be on this walking trail. I'm going to look around, I'll just retrace our steps." At this point Emily was grateful they always carried a flashlight on Dino's walks. She turned it on, aiming it down and started her search, walking along the trail angry at herself for losing the key. Emily could hear a bunch of guys leaving the basketball court. The winners couldn't get enough of busting the loser's balls. They walked past her, laughing and joking around. It made her smile; boys will be boys she thought still searching the ground. Moving the light back and forth, a glimmer of metal caught her eye. "Yes!" It was her key lying on the grass along the trail.

Exiting the park, she heard something. A sound she couldn't quite put her finger on, a muffled grunting noise. Emily looked around and followed the sound. It was coming from behind a line of tall shrubs. She stepped off the walking path, moving slowly towards the bushes, pushing them apart quietly with her hands. There, hunched over a wild goose, knelt a very large canine eating its prey savagely. It suddenly stood up on two legs, looking right at her. Its eyes lit with a yellow glow which showed through the darkness. It had torn the goose's neck from its body. Holding it in its mouth, the goose's head dangled, swinging from side to side. Emily ran. She turned around to look behind her, terrified it was coming after her. Running across the street and up the stairs of her apartment building, she tried to get her key into the lock of the door. Her hands were shaking so badly Emily gave up, pounding hard on it with her fists. Simon opened the door, as she quickly ran inside closing and locking it.

"Simon, something is in the park!" Emily was breathing heavily trying to catch her breath. Her expression was one of pure fear, as tears rolled down her face. Simon wrapped his arms around her, telling her to calm down.

"Emily sit down." Dino came over to her, he could sense her uneasiness. Emily reached down to pet him, as she told Simon what she had just witnessed. "Em, maybe it was a black bear, they are known to stand on their hind legs occasionally."

"Simon, I'm telling you its eyes were glowing. It wasn't a bear; it was some kind of dog or a wolf. You've got to believe me!" Emily stood up and walked towards the window, wondering where it was. Was that thing still out there? "I'm not going to set foot in that park, ever again at night. We can walk Dino through town, where there are people around."

"Okay Em, I believe you, now calm down. I think you need a drink; it might help to calm your nerves. What do you say?"

"Yeah, make it a strong one." Emily sat there going over and over it in her mind. Could it have been a bear? No, I know what I saw she thought, picking up Dino and placing him on the sofa next to her as she sat down again.

"Here you are." Simon said, handing her a glass of brandy. Noticing she was still shaking he sat down next to her, putting his arm around her shoulder. "Em, just relax, you're safe. Should we call someone? Animal control or the police?"

"I don't know, maybe it was a bear. I mean it was dark." Emily was starting to doubt herself.

"Right, things can look different in the dark Em. Feeling better?"

"I guess, but I'm still not going into that park at night." Simon sat down beside her, kissing her cheek and putting his arm around her. Emily smiled, feeling better, sandwiched between the two guys she loved most in this world, Simon and Dino.

Bradford stood at the park's entrance. He was cleaning between his teeth with the quill of a goose. He watched from across the street, looking at the building Emily had run to. He smiled, turning the collar of his jacket up around his neck. I remember seeing her at Michael's party Bradford thought. If I'm not mistaken, she's friends with Michael's fiancé Katie or whatever her name is. What a fantastic happenstance. I will definitely find a way to meet up with her again. Hopefully, she will lead me to the prize I am searching for. Bradford walked down the street smiling, cleaning the blood from underneath his fingernails.

* * *

Later that night, Kayla lay beside Peter. She was dreaming of Michael once again, standing before him naked as his hand caressed her large round belly. "This child is mine, Kayla." He informed her, looking deeply into her eyes. He kissed her mouth exploring it with his tongue, as he fondled her breasts. Then licking her neck and making his way down her body, tenderly biting and sucking her nipples. Kayla stood there enjoying the feel of his touch. Getting onto her knees, she spread her legs for him. Michael came up behind her, penetrating her. Leaning into her, grabbing hold of her hips, he knew exactly when to slow down or speed up. Taking her on the verge of orgasm and then easing his thrusts, over and over again. It was as if he could read her mind, prolonging her sensation to come. Feeling his breath on her neck, he bit down into her shoulder, as her blood ran into his mouth. Michael's heavy breathing turned her on, as he licked the blood that had trickled down her back. Kayla was finally climaxing, she let out a scream of sexual fulfillment. It woke her up, along with Peter sleeping by her side.

"Kayla, are you okay?"

"I'm sorry I woke you, just a nightmare."

"Want to talk about it?"

"No, I'm fine. Try to go back to sleep sweetheart." Kayla said, kissing his cheek, and bringing the blanket up around her neck. Why was Michael still invading her dreams? She looked at Peter who had no trouble resuming his slumber, as Kayla stared at the ceiling. Did she still want Michael sexually? Even though she knew what he was, "NO!" telling herself. I am having Peter's baby. Turning over, she could still see Michael's face in the darkness of the room. Kayla closed her eyes praying. "No more dreams tonight, please." She slept soundly until…….. the alarm clock went off as Kayla and Peter tried to wake up. He rubbed her ass, then brought his arm around her, touching her belly.

"Time to get up Kay. Sorry you didn't sleep well last night. That had to be some kind of nightmare you were having. Do you want to talk about it now?"

"No, it's okay." Kayla got up putting on her slippers and robe, then proceeded to go downstairs. Putting the coffee on, the dream of having sex with Michael kept swimming around her head, it felt so real. Sitting down at the kitchen table, Peter walked into the room.

"Are you okay? I didn't even get my morning kiss."

"Sorry babe." Kayla got up, wrapping her arms around Peter kissing him. "There, feel better?"

"Yes. I forgot to mention it last night, but I have a teachers' conference coming up soon. It's a two-day thing. I'm not sure of the dates yet, I'll have to let you know. Will you be okay here alone?"

"Of course, between work and the stuff to do around here. I'll have enough to keep me busy."

"Good. Shouldn't Willie be coming for a visit soon? With any luck, he'll come the days I'm gone."

"Peter, how can you say that, he loves you. He follows you everywhere you go."

"That's my point, it gets to be a bit much after a while. I still can't figure out why he does that though?"

"Yeah, he's a little weird at times, I'll admit. However, I do miss him." Kayla thought of Willie and smiled.

Willie, a Voyeur Pixie was hatched from a willow branch after being summoned by Tarsula, a supreme witch. She taught him three commands Follow, Return, and Hide. However, she didn't realize

Willie was kind in nature. He turned against Tarsula, helping Kayla
and her friends, doing anything he could to keep them safe. Who
would ever think a five-inch tall brown fairy-like creature would
have such a big heart? He was taken by Zadoc, Peter's father an
extraterrestrial to live on a distant planet where he could thrive.
Every now and again Zadoc would send Willie down to earth in a
beam of light, to visit Kayla and Peter as he had promised.

Kayla chuckled, thinking about Willie. She cleaned off the
kitchen table contemplating the day ahead of her. Running upstairs,
she needed to get ready. The sun was coming up and it seemed like
the weather was going to cooperate today. Not so bad, with March
just beginning Kayla thought, hopefully spring will be right around
the corner.

* * *

Emly ran down the stairs of her apartment building and all the
way to her car. She tried to be on time these days, wanting to keep
in Sam's good graces. Starting her car, Emily checked out her face
in the rearview mirror. It showed a few more hours of sleep were
definitely needed.

Walking into the café, Kayla was already there. "Good
morning, Em." Emily walked past her taking off her coat and
hanging it on a hook. "It is a good morning, isn't it?" Kayla inquired,
noticing that Emily looked tired.

"Can I see you in the ladies' room." Kayla could tell Emily
needed to talk. She followed her, praying it wasn't bad news. "I don't
even know where to begin." Emily started, hoping that Kayla would
believe her. "Last night Simon and I went for our usual walk with
Dino. You know, at the park across the street from our apartment.
I made the mistake of putting my house key in a pocket that had a
hole, so I lost it. I told Simon to take Dino home. I wanted to look
around for it and I found it eventually. Trouble was, I also found
something else."

"What? What did you find Em?"

"Kay, there was this thing in the park. It had killed a goose and

27

was eating it." Emily felt nervous hoping Kayla would believe her.

"What kind of thing?" Kayla had a sinking feeling in the pit of her stomach that another nightmare was about to begin. Maybe Michael and Tarsula weren't done with them yet. "What did it look like Em?"

"It was some kind of dog or wolf; it stood up on two legs. Simon thought it could have been a black bear, but I don't think so. It had yellow glowing eyes Kay and when it stood up, it almost had the shape of a man."

Kayla could feel her body starting to tense up. Emily's description of this thing sounded like the beasts at Michael's party. Everyone's memories had been wiped out that night, thanks to Zadoc. With the exception of Peter, Sergeant Daniels, and herself. She stood there listening, telling herself to remain calm. "Emily let's hold on for a moment, it could have been a black bear. They do roam around and at times stand upright."

"What about its glowing eyes Kay?"

"Did you have a flashlight with you?"

"Yeah, but I'm not sure it was on when I saw it."

"Well, if it was, it could have hit the bears eyes making them seem to glow."

Sam knocked on the ladie's room door. "Good morning ladies, shall we start the workday please?"

"We'll be right out Sam." Kayla answered, as Emily threw her arms around her, kissing her on the cheek. "What's that for Em?"

"For always making me come to my senses. Love ya Kay."

"Love ya back, now let's get to work before Sam loses it."

CHAPTER TWO
BRADFORD CUMMINGS

Bradford Cummings was just getting home from a late night of hunting. After a few geese, a couple ducks and a cat, his appetite had been satisfied. He stripped off his clothes, throwing them in the corner of his bathroom and jumped into the shower. A lot of blood and a little bit of cat guts found their way down the drain. Standing there he tried to remember Michael's fiancé, how beautiful she was, her firm and curvy body. Bradford closed his eyes, grabbing hold of his cock, he stroked himself. Imagining what she would look like naked. Fantasizing about tasting her cunt, ordering her to suck him off, fucking her then turning her, into a she beast of his very own. Bradford stroked himself faster, getting ready to come. He let out a gruntle moan coming on himself and the tiled floor.

Stepping out of the shower, it was time to rest. He would head back to the park, across from the apartment building this evening. Sit on a bench and watch, waiting for the red head to emerge and follow her. Sooner or later, she would lead him to Katie. Sorry Michael, he thought, I will turn on the charm with that little fiancé of yours. Fuck her and turn her, like I did to your mom. Bradford let out a laugh that bellowed, loud and piercing. Thinking about it was getting him excited, he began to change. His legs became muscular and covered in fur. His feet were elongating, ending in black clawed toes. Bradford stood there naked, half man, half beast. Looking down between his legs, his cock stood at attention once again firm and hard. Bradford let out a sound that echoed through the house, a sound between laughter and howling. He grabbed hold of himself, jerking off once more.

* * *

At the end of the workday, Emily walked into her dimly lit apartment. Except for a few night lights, that were left on for Dino. He came to meet her at the door with his squeaky ball in his mouth ready to play. She reached down to pet him, taking the ball and throwing it. Pulling out her phone from her pocket, she called Simon. "Hey hon, where are you?" Concerned, it was getting late, and Simon wasn't home yet.

"Sorry babe there was an accident, it happened right in front of me, traffic is backed up."

"Are you okay?" Emily asked.

"I said, it happened in front of me, not with me. I should be home in fifteen minutes or so."

"Great!" Emily smiled, grateful that he was alright. "I'm going to walk Dino, but not in the park, forget that."

"Want me to grab a pizza on the way home.?" asked Simon.

"Yeah, that sounds good. See you soon, love ya."

"Love ya too, Em."

"Well Dino, it looks like it's just going to be the two of us walking tonight." Emily got his leash; they walked out the door and down the stairs. Dino ran over to a small patch of grass and relieved himself immediately. "Wow, you really had to go!" Emily remarked, patting his head. "Come on boy let's walk, it's a lovely evening. I want to get a coffee then we can go home." Spring will be here before you know it, she thought to herself. Soon Sam will be putting the tables out on the patio. Thinking about the warmer weather made her happy. They made their way down the street. Reaching their destination, she picked up Dino as they entered the convenience store.

"Hey Pauline, what's going on?" Emily inquired, making her way over to a small counter which was set up in front of the store, where you could make your own coffee. She placed Dino on the floor next to her, as Pauline walked over.

"Hey Em, quiet night." She reached down to pet Dino. "Hey, there Dino. I hate nights like this with no body coming in."

"Excuse me!" Emily pointed to herself and Dino, laughing at Pauline's remark.

"Sorry, you know what I mean. Where the hell is everybody? It's such a beautiful night, you would think there would be loads of people walking around town."

Emily smiled, setting her coffee down at the checkout counter, along with two coffee cakes to have with Simon after dinner.

"That will be ten twenty-five." Pauline looked at Dino and smiled. Emily reached into her coat pocket, pulling out a twenty. "Thanks Em," Pauline said, as she handed her the change. "See you again, you too Dino!" The door to the store opened, as a man held it for her to step outside.

"Thanks." Emily smiled at the stranger.

"My what a cute dog, may I pet him?" Dino growled, showing his teeth and barking.

"Dino! Sorry, he never acts this way."

"Do I know you?" he asked. "I'm horrible with names, but very good with faces, especially pretty ones."

Dino barked and growled again. "Sorry, I don't think so. Enjoy your night." Emily replied, looking at the stranger curiously.

"You do the same dear." Bradford smiled, as he watched Emily walk away. "Little by little," Bradford told himself. "These things take time."

* * *

In the morning Kayla arrived at the café early. She said a quick hello to Sam and Max making a straight line to the ladie's room, feeling sick to her stomach. It had finally arrived, morning sickness. The bathroom door opened as Emily walked in.

"Kay, are you alright?"

"Yeah, just a little morning sickness that's all." Emily watched as tears formed in Kayla's eyes and rolled down her cheek. Emily put her arm around her shoulder.

"Kay, don't cry, I'll get you some crackers and a ginger ale."

"No Em, it's okay I can deal with it, I'm just upset. I've been having dreams of Michael lately. I'm not sure if Peter is the father of this baby."

Emily gave her a wide-eyed stare. "You didn't mention any of this to Peter, I hope.

"No, of course not, but I've been thinking about last December. I had sex with both of them in the same week, only a day or two apart. I've been reading about it Em, a man's sperm can live in a woman's body for up to five days. I think either one of them could be the father." Kayla answered nervously, wiping away her tears.

"Kayla stop it, Peter is definitely the father. Michael is gone, he's no longer in the picture. Why are you doing this to yourself?" "You're right Em, Michael is no longer here. Peter will be the father to this child, absolutely. However, I've been having these strange cravings lately."

"What kind of cravings?"

"Very rare steak for one. You know me, when I eat meat, I always tell them to burn it. I hate seeing any pink at all. Now, I find myself wanting to lick the blood off the packaging of a pot roast, that Peter had made."

"Kay, I wouldn't be too concerned. Women have all kinds of weird cravings when their pregnant."

"I guess so, I'm sure you're right. Come on let's start the day." Emily hugged Kayla and smiled but also felt uneasy. Was it possible that she was carrying Michael's baby? Emily thought, could this baby be Michael's? She also had doubts, that this child was Peter's.

* * *

That evening when Kayla arrived home, the weather had changed. A light snow began to coat the sidewalks and bushes. The air was dead still as the flakes fell softly. Getting out of her car she just stood there. The moon was so bright it lit up the snow, giving it a look of small diamonds scattered across the front lawn. She placed her hand on her stomach, there was life growing in there which was her responsibility to care for. Whoever the father was, she was its mother. Thinking about it made her smile, knowing her child would be raised with love. Kayla tried to catch a snowflake on her tongue but was unsuccessful. It made her think of her late mother. There were good times growing up, running around in the snow with her mom Jennifer. She was a strong woman, who took care of Kayla on her own. In that respect Kayla would be exactly like her, strong and loving, doing whatever it took to raise this child right.

Walking up the front steps and unlocking the door, she could smell tonight's dinner. Peter was taking a roast chicken out of the oven. Placing it down on the top of the stove, he walked over to her. Kayla removed her coat, as Peter wrapped his arms around her.

"The chicken smells great! Did you throw in some of those small potatoes that I like?"

"Yes, I certainly did, along with some carrots. I have a surprise for you."

"A surprise, what is it?" Kayla asked, shaking the snow out of her hair.

"I was going to wait until after dinner, but I'll show you now." Peter took her by the hand and escorted her into the kitchen. The table was set with flowers and candles.

"Oh my God Peter, this is lovely. What's the occasion?"

Peter pulled an envelope out of his apron pocket. "The occasion is, that I love you with all my heart."

Kayla carefully opened the envelope. Removing two plane tickets to the Bahamas. "Peter, what is this, the Bahamas? These tickets are dated for next week. I love the gesture, but I can't just leave work whenever I feel like it. I have to clear time off with Sam."

"I already did, Sam thought it was a great idea for us to get away someplace warm. He said, the café had been on the slow side lately and was sure that Emily could handle working solo for the week. Quite frankly, I'm surprised Emily managed to keep it a secret."

Kayla was super excited, hugging Peter tightly; she kissed his mouth lovingly. Running her hands down his back she grabbed his ass, pressing her body against his and giving him a sexy look. Peter grinned, "What about dinner Kay?"

Kayla walked backwards, moving away from him and removing her blouse. Then playfully throwing it at him, she turned, running up the stairs to their bedroom. He ran after her thinking, I guess dinner can wait.

* * *

Michael and Tarsula were feverishly packing up. They had already found a buyer for the townhouse who did not negotiate on their price. However, they wanted some of the furniture thrown in as part of the deal. Michael agreed, whatever furniture was needed he would buy new. Michael's phone rang, picking it up, he saw it was Courtney.

"Hey Courtney, what can I do for you?"

"Hi Michael, I'm sorry to tell you this, but I have a few more papers that need your signature. Also, we never discussed having The Stone Manor inspected. I have a guy who is exceedingly thorough if you are interested? Would you be able to swing by the office when you get a moment?"

"Is tomorrow night alright? Tarsula and I are in the middle of packing, I would really like to get it done."

"Certainly, how's seven thirty?"

"Fine Courtney, see you then, bye."

"See you then Michael." Courtney grinned; in her head she had figured out a plan that would hopefully bring him closer to her. Michael hung up the phone. Looking at Tarsula he said, "I think our Ms. Courtney has a thing for me."

"So that's nothing new Michael, I know you do well with the female population."
Michael just smiled, rubbing the back of his neck with his hand.
"You know Tarsula, I'm going to need to feed soon. Our Ms. Courtney has been so helpful, maybe she can help me with one more

thing."

Tarsula laughed, as she cut herself another piece of chocolate cake.

* * *

As Peter took a shower, Kayla called Emily, thanking her for keeping the surprise. She also wanted to make sure Emily was capable of working solo for the week. Em acknowledged that all would be fine, now that she had full use of her right hand again, there shouldn't be a problem. Instructing her to have a great time and not to spend a second thinking about work.

Hanging up the phone, Kayla went to her closet in search of her summer clothes. She chose a couple of sundresses, shorts, and tee shirts, along with a few bathing suits. Searching the closet floor, she grabbed sandals, a pair of flip flops, and white sneakers. It was time to find the suitcases. Basement or attic, not remembering where they had been stored. Going down into the basement Kayla started the task at hand. Moving boxes around, old pieces of furniture and baskets, searching for them to no avail. Next stop the attic, pulling down the ladder Kayla climbed up. Looking around, noticing them underneath a small table in the corner, she pushed herself up. Walking to the table and glancing out the attic window, she could see into the neighbor's yard. The moonlight shone on an old tree stump that a cat was sitting on. Not just any cat, but a cat that seemed to have calico markings. "Bowie?" Not having seen him for a while, Kayla retrieved the suitcases, throwing them down quickly. Stepping down the ladder, grabbing her coat, she ran outside calling out to him, "Bowie"! Running into her neighbor's yard the cat was gone, but there was a need to search the yard just in case. Calling out to him again, Kayla suddenly stood quiet and still. It dawned on her, Bowie's eyes, his eyes were just like Michael's one golden amber, one sky blue. If Michael was capable of shape shifting into a hawk, why not a cat. Pulling her coat tightly around herself, she walked back inside quickly, as a cold chill went through her body.

CHAPTER THREE
GOODBYE MY LOVE

The next morning was dark, with intermittent rain. A day most people would rather stay in bed than venture out. Sam rubbed his eyes trying to wake himself up. He reached over to wake up Mary, gently rubbing her hip. "Time to get up, my love. I know it's hard to wake up on days like this, but we must. I'm going to start the coffee, come on." Sam walked into the kitchen, still half asleep. He poured the water in, measured out the coffee and turned on the machine. Sitting down at the kitchen table, he looked through some of his mail from yesterday, bills mostly. Getting up, he was sure Mary should have been up by now, but he didn't hear her moving around. Walking back to the bedroom she was still lying on her side under the blankets. "Mary sweetheart time to get up." There was no reply or movement. Sam ran over to her touching her face, she was cold as ice. "MARY! MARY!" Sam put his head down to her face, she wasn't breathing. Sam frantically ran to get his phone calling 911. Running back into the bedroom, he tried to remember the CPR classes he had taken in the past. Trying his best to breathe life back into his lovely Mary. The police were the first to arrive, followed by the paramedics. She had apparently passed away in her sleep during the night and was pronounced dead at six ten a.m.

To say Sam was struck with grief would have been an understatement. He watched as they placed her body onto a gurney, covering it with a white sheet and took her out of the apartment. Sam sat there numb for what seemed like hours, but in actuality, only a short amount of time had passed. Picking up his phone, he needed to call Kayla. Looking outside it was pouring rain, Sam felt the whole world was crying, for the loss of his love.

* * *

Kayla and Peter were having breakfast when her phone rang. "Hey Sam, what's with the early morning phone call? Couldn't it have waited till I got to work?" At first there was silence, then the broken voice of Sam crying hysterically. He could hardly get his words out. "Sam, are you okay? What's going on?" Peter looked up from his eggs as Kayla started to cry. "No Sam, no, my God I'm so sorry. I'm coming over, I'll be right there."

Peter stood up from the table. "What's going on?"

"That was Sam, Mary passed away last night in her sleep." Kayla could hardly get her words out. Choked up and thinking about what Sam must be going through. "I have to go to him Peter, call Emily and Max, I have to get dressed."

"We can call them from the car, I'm coming with you." Peter called in sick from work, his head was swimming, in his mind he wondered if he could still do it? Never trying it on a human before, but how could he get Mary alone to try? Peter drove, as Kayla made the phone calls to Emily and Max.

* * *

Sam answered his door distraught, looking like a beaten down man. His eyes were red and swollen from crying. Kayla threw her arms around him trying her best to calm him down. "Sam, sit down I'll get you some water." Kayla said, wiping away her own tears. Peter took a seat across from him, both of his hands were sweating, not sure how to go about suggesting what he wanted to do.

"Sam, remember the day at the café when I healed Emily's face?" Sam looked over at him, still crying and in unbelievable sorrow, he nodded his head yes. "What if I told you, I think I can bring Mary back."

Kayla handed Sam the water, looking at Peter, stunned.

37

Putting down the glass, Sam wiped the tears from his face with both hands. "Peter, did I hear you right? Did you say you could bring Mary back?"

"I said, I think I can. I've only done it on small animals, never people. I'd like to try it, for your sake."

Sam stood up with a glimmer of hope in his eye. Placing his arms around Peter he said, "if you could try, I would be eternally grateful. Please, please try Peter."

Sam dressed quickly; they were out the door in minutes. Peter drove, as Kayla called Sergeant Daniels direct line.

"Sergeant Daniels." he answered. Taking his first sip of morning coffee and trying to wake up.

"Sergeant Daniels it's Kayla; we need your help. Sam's fiancé passed away last night; her name is Mary Kovack. Peter thinks he can bring her back, but we need to know where they took her body. The funeral home or the morgue at Saint Paul's?"

"Alright Kayla calm down. I'll start at Paxton's Funeral Home. They would have taken her there if an autopsy was required, they have a pathologist on staff. It's more convenient to have everything done in one place. I know the owners, so let me reach out to them. I'll call you right back." Waiting for the call back from Daniels, seemed like forever, Kayla answered her phone on the first ring.

"Kayla, they took her to Paxton's. I've asked them not to touch the body, told them it was part of an ongoing investigation. I'm leaving my house now; I'll meet you there."

"Thank you, Sergeant Daniels, we owe you one. Sam, Mary is at the funeral home. Daniels said he would meet us there. Peter drive faster!"

When Peter pulled into the parking lot of the funeral home, Daniels was waiting for them. He got out of his car, putting his arms around Sam. "Listen guys, I think it's best if Peter and I go in first. As they started to walk away, Daniels asked. "Peter, do you really think you can do this?"

"I'm going to try, I've only used my light source on small

animals, never humans."

"Okay let's go in, and hope to God you can do it."

As they walked inside Peter turned to Daniels and said, "I've
put a call out to my dad, his light source is much stronger than
mine." Peter's father was from a distant planet not in our solar
system. They are known as Seekers sent to earth to observe and
report back their findings on humans. Their bodies contained pure,
white light enabling them to heal, amongst other things.

Walking in they were met by the funeral director Viv Paxton.
"Sergeant Daniels, it's so early in the morning, but death waits for
no one I'm afraid. How are you, and who is this?"

"This is Peter, I need him to take a look at the deceased Mary
Kovack. He's an important part of my investigation."

"Certainly, right this way." They walked down a flight of stairs,
feeling the temperature dropping as they descended and entered the
morgue.

"Viv, can you give us a minute with her, this investigation is
tricky. We don't want any information to leak out."

"Of course sergeant, I'll be right upstairs if you have any
questions."

Daniels and Peter walked in, closing the door behind them.
Daniels stood guard at the door as Peter walked over to Mary's
lifeless body. Hesitantly, he pulled the sheet off of her; her skin had a
blue tint to it, as she lay there in her nightgown.

Peter looked over at Daniels nervously. He didn't want to let
his friends down, especially Sam. "Here we go." Peter said, out loud.
Closing his eyes and dropping his chin to his chest. He could feel the
burning sensation, starting at his feet and working its way up and
around him. Feeling it circling around his thighs, hips and chest.
Until finally, going down his arms and coming out onto his fingertips.
Peter moved his hands above Mary, the light coiled around her faster
and faster. He did his best to keep the light force coming, to keep
it moving around her body, it took everything he had. After a few
minutes, his legs were starting to shake, as well as his arms. Peter was

on the verge of passing out. He had to stop; he wasn't strong enough to bring her back. Throwing his hands off to his side the light came off his fingers like icicles, that merely dropped onto the floor, as Peter fell to his knees. Daniels ran over to him, helping him up and sitting him on a chair. "I'm sorry sergeant, I can't do it." Most of Peter's color was gone from his face, as he sat there trying to catch his breath.

Daniels reached into his coat pocket, wrapping his fingers tightly around his crystal. The crystal Zadoc had promised him would become a beacon for help, if he ever needed it. "Peter, I have an idea, wait here." Daniels walked out the back door, onto a small grassy area, he held up his crystal to the sky. "Zadoc we need help, a much-loved woman has died, we need to bring her back. Please Zadoc, please hear me. Your son tried, but he's not strong enough." Placing the crystal back into his pocket, he stepped back inside. Peter looked up, as Daniels walked back into the room.

"What am I going to tell Sam?" Peter asked, with tears rolling down his face. "This is going to crush him even more."

"You're going to tell him the truth, you gave it everything you had, but it wasn't enough to bring her back." Daniels placed his arm around Peter. "Come on son, let's leave Mary in peace." They climbed the stairs slowly, both feeling horrible and defeated. Death had won this time, both men wiping the tears from their faces. Neither of them wanting to break the news to Sam, that his Mary was gone forever.

Viv walked over to them, as they stood in the hallway. They were trying to think of what to say to Sam. "There's a gentleman here to see you Daniels," remarked Viv. "I assume he is part of your investigation. He's waiting in the room there, at the end of the hall." Daniels and Peter looked at each other confused, as they walked down the hallway and into the room. There stood an average looking man around six two, his outerwear consisted of a long black coat, a grey hat, gloves and sneakers. Peter looked at Daniels. "Do you know him?"

"Not yet, can we help you sir?" Daniels asked, never seeing this man before in his life.

The man turned to them and smiled. "What are these things?" he asked. As he pointed to the variety of caskets, set out around the room. Peter and Daniels just looked at each other.

"They're caskets, coffins." Daniels replied, not understanding who would ask such a ridiculous question like that.

"What are they used for?"

"Who are you?" Peter inquired.

"Zadoc sent me. I was the closest Seeker to this death place." Daniels and Peter looked at each other. The stranger looked at them and grinned. "What? You were expecting to see purple robes and a body that glowed from within?" He partially removed one of his gloves. A hand made of pure white light peaked out. Placing his glove quickly back on, he extended his hand. "My name is Kranthar. Do I pass for one of you?" he asked, with a slight grin on his face. "We have been walking among you, for a very long time. Seekers have the power to turn off their light source, or to cover it with garments of clothing to fit in." Kranthar smiled. "Before I forget, Zadoc sends his regards. So, what are these casket things used for?"

"We bury the dead in them." Daniels spoke up, still not believing Zadoc had heard him asking for help.

"You put this box in the dirt, with humans inside? What grows from it? A flower, a tree?"

"Nothing, it's considered a resting place for the dead," answered Peter.

"In the dirt?" Kranthar couldn't believe what he was hearing. "That's very strange, humans are a very strange breed. Okay, take me to this woman." They walked back down together opening the door, Viv, Kayla, and Sam turned to look at them as they walked in.

"What is everyone doing in here?" Daniels asked. "Please go back upstairs, we need to continue our investigation. Kayla, please take Sam upstairs. Please Viv I am sorry, but we need a few more minutes, then we will all be out of your hair."

"Alright, but please make it quick." Viv answered, "I have other things to attend to."

When everyone had returned upstairs Daniels said, "go ahead Kranthar, quick as you can." Kranthar took off his coat, as Daniels and Peter watched from the door. He removed his gloves, the light coming from his hands was intense. Dropping his head down to his chest, a thick glowing light swirled around his body. It moved fast and with great force, spinning and turning. Kranthar laid his hands over Mary's dead body cocooning her in powerful light. Faster and faster the light source spun. Daniels and Peter watched in amazement, as Mary's skin lost its color of blueness and became a shade of soft rosey pink. Then her chest began to move, as breathing took place. Kranthar shook the light off his hands, which exploded off them, into shards of glass. Hitting both sides of the morgue's concrete walls, cracking some of the cinder blocks. A slight movement from Mary's toe could be seen, and then the twitching of a finger. Seconds later, Mary sat up gasping for air. She took a deep breath opening her eyes, frightened.

"Where am I? What happened to me? Peter, is that you?" Daniels walked over to her. "You're okay now Mary, you're fine." He reached into his pocket taking firm hold of his crystal, as Kranthar quickly put his gloves and coat back on.

Viv Paxton opened the door to the morgue. "What was that loud noise? I'm afraid you've all got to leave……" Viv let out a blood chilling scream, seeing Mary sitting up. "How is this possible? I checked her vitals myself when they brought her in!"

Mary looked horrified, realizing she was in a morgue. "How did I get here?" She jumped off the metal table she was sitting on. Freaking out. "Why am I still in my night gown?" Looking down at her feet she noticed the tag on her big toe. That's when she really lost it. Daniels took a sheet and wrapped it around her, trying to calm her down. Viv just stood there, in shock. In all of the years of working as a funeral director, none of the dead had ever come back. She was shaking, her legs were giving out, she had to sit down.

After removing the tag on Mary's big toe, Daniels, Peter, and Kranthar escorted Viv and Mary out of the morgue and into the vestibule at the bottom of the stairwell. Mary was still losing it, while Viv was in a daze, not believing Mary was walking beside her. Kranthar asked Peter and Daniels to cover their eyes. Removing his glove once again, a flash of light filled the vestibule. After a few seconds, Daniels asked. "May we open our eyes now?" Not getting an answer, Daniels opened one eye. Mary and Viv stood there looking at him confused. "Open your eyes, Peter." Daniels instructed, touching Peter's shoulder. They both expected to see Kranthar, however he was gone, along with any memories Viv or Mary might have had, as to what had just taken place.

Sam and Kayla were seated in the hallway upstairs. Kayla was looking at him, as Sam's mouth dropped open. She turned to look in the direction, as to what he might be seeing. Sam stood up and ran to Mary. "Mary! Mary! I thought I had lost you forever!" He held her tightly, as a river of tears ran down his face. "Peter, thank you, thank you so much." Sam said, wrapping his arms around him. Peter was about to tell him, that he had nothing to do with it. However, Daniels hushed him up, no one else knew about the Seekers. No one except Peter, Kayla, and himself and he would do everything in his power to keep it that way.

Viv walked over to Daniels. "Why is that woman wearing a nightgown? I'm having a hard time remembering anything."

"Her name is Mary, she walked right out of an assistant living facility. They've been looking for her for days. We got the call at the police station; someone saw her walk in here," answered Daniels.

"Oh, my heavens, poor thing."

"It would be a nice gesture, if you showed all of them out." Daniels looked at her and smiled.

"Of course, come on everyone, I'll walk you out. Don't worry dear, you're safe now." Viv said holding onto Mary's arm, as Mary looked at Sam totally confused. Sam took off his jacket wrapping it around her, while trying to think of an explanation to ease her mind.

Kayla got on her phone, calling Emily and Max. She told them what had happened. That Mary was alive. She told them that Peter was the one who brought her back, even though she knew, his father had sent down a Seeker to help. Neither Emily nor Max knew of the Seekers, that was a subject never to speak of.

Daniels ran to Viv's office; he needed to erase Mary from her computer hard drive. He sat down entering Viv's password. He had watched her enter it many times, when she was looking for a name. "Yes, there you are Mary." Daniels deleted her information. Then he quickly went to the file cabinet, not seeing a folder for her, he checked Viv's desk. Her file was there resting on a stack of papers. He grabbed it, putting it under his coat and went to join the group outside.

* * *

Back at the station, Daniels called downstairs to records. "Hey Beth, it's Sergeant Daniels, a death certificate may have been issued this morning, in wait of an autopsy. The name Mary Kovack, that's K O V A C K. If it's there, it was issued by mistake, by some miracle the lady pulled through."

"Okay Daniels, good for her. If it's here, I will remove it from the files and bring her back to the world of the living."

"Thanks Beth. Oh, and one more thing. Can you call the State Bureau of Vital Statistics and Registration. Just in case anything was sent over. We need to delete all info."

"I'll get right on it, sergeant."

Daniels walked outside holding his crystal in his hand. "I know you can hear me Zadoc, thank you so much for sending help. We are forever grateful to you, and the other Seekers." Daniels looked up at the sky, the crystal suddenly felt warm within his hand. Putting it back in his pocket, he let out a sigh of relief.

* * *

That evening Michael needed to feed. He was on his way to see Courtney hoping she would be alone in the office. After parking his car, Courtney met him at the door. "Michael, come on in, it's good

44

to see you. I'm sorry you had to come back, but the paperwork is never ending."

Michael noticed her attire seemed a bit provocative for a place of business. Her skirt was exceptionally tight and short. Also, her blouse was unbuttoned showing a peak of her bra and some cleavage. He followed her into her office as she closed the door. "Now, we can have some quiet. Would you like a drink? Since it is after hours, and I'm pretty much the only one who works this late."

"Sure, what do you have?" asked Michael. Courtney leaned over pulling out a few bottles from her lower desk drawer, exposing a lot more of her breasts and pink bra.

"Scotch or gin?" Courtney held up the bottles smiling.

A grin formed on Michael's gorgeous face. "Two of my favorites, scotch is fine thanks." Michael watched her pour the drinks. "So, where are the papers I need to sign?" he asked, as she handed him the scotch.

"Right here, there are eight pages. Here's a pen, sign on the bottom of each sheet next to the red arrow."

"Okay." He started to sign the pages, looking over at her. Courtney had crossed her legs letting her skirt ride up, her entire right leg was exposed to him. Michael grinned; he knew she was trying to seduce him. Signing the last page, he gave her back the pen, taking hold of her hand as she reached for it. Michael stood up and walked around the desk. Standing close to her, he looked into her eyes watching them glaze over. Since the shades were already drawn, he stepped away from her, locking the office door. He undid her skirt and let it fall off her body. Then Courtney was instructed to lean over the desk as Michael sat in her chair, his mouth inches away from her thighs. Finding the spot he was after, the back middle of her left upper thigh, he bit down as her blood filled his mouth. He feasted, wiping his chin now and again, not wanting to waste a drop of her vital fluid. Michael closed his eyes enjoying the taste of her feeding until he was full; her blood was satisfying. Courtney was instructed to put her skirt back on as he got up, sitting her in the chair and waited.

"Michael what happened? I feel kind of weird. It's not like me to zone out." She looked at Michael apprehensively, still feeling dazed and confused.

"It's alright Courtney, you must be overworked. You just closed your eyes for a brief moment, and you were gone. Don't worry, it happens to the best of us. So, the papers are signed. I guess I should be leaving."

" You know, I do feel a little lightheaded, I guess because I haven't eaten much today. Want to get a bite somewhere? What do you say Michael?"

"I say, Courtney you're a lovely girl and you are quite good at your job. Your sexy look this evening wasn't wasted on me, believe me I've noticed. Yet, my heart belongs to someone else. Let's keep our relationship strictly professional if that's okay?"

"Certainly, can't blame a woman for trying though." Courtney's face turned a lovely shade of pink. Feeling embarrassed that her plan to seduce him had failed. "I'm a little embarrassed Michael."

"No, don't be ridiculous Courtney. Maybe another time, another place."

"She's a lucky girl, whoever she is. Thanks for coming in Michael, have a good night."

"Yes, you do the same Courtney." Michael felt it was a very productive evening. He got two things accomplished. Papers signed and enough of Courtney's blood to sustain him for at least a week. What a perfect night, he thought, as he got into his car and left.

CHAPTER FOUR
MORE THAN JUST PASTA

On Friday night, Max and Jeanna were having dinner at their favorite Italian restaurant, Anthony's. They both had ordered the chicken parm with angel hair pasta. A bottle of wine, basket of bread, along with a small salad was brought to their table. Max couldn't stop talking about Peter and how he had saved Mary, even though that wasn't true. He knew Peter had healing abilities, but never did he think they were powerful enough to bring back the dead. It had opened Maxwell's perspective of the world he lived in. It made him a believer, that anything could be possible. That people should always keep an open mind. You never know what could happen, at any given day or time. Max poured the wine looking into Jeanna's eyes. "How's the salad?" he asked. Taking a slice of bread out of the basket and coating it with butter.

"It's good, fresh, but the food's always good here, you know that."

Max noticed a sexy expression on Jeanna's face. "What's going on in that pretty head of yours? Why are you looking at me like that?"

"Like what?" Jeanna answered, giving him a lustful grin. Max suddenly jumped, as Jeanna had taken off her shoe and was rubbing his shaft with her foot.

"Jeanna" Max whispered. "We can't do anything here, there are people all around us."

"So?" she whispered back. "The tablecloths are long, no one

can see what we're doing underneath them. Come sit in the chair next to me." Max moved over, as a wicked smile formed on his face. Eager to see what was going to happen, he let her take charge. Jeanna lowered her left-hand underneath the tablecloth, rubbing his cock. Max gave her a look, as she slowly unzipped his jeans. Slipping her hand inside his pants and underwear she grabbed hold of his cock. Slowly moving her hand up and down his shaft, as their dinner was being placed on the table.

"Are you okay sir?" the waitress asked. "You're breathing kind of hard."

"I'm fine, it's just that the food looks so delicious," Max replied. Jeanna held in a laugh and started to eat, leaving her left hand still stroking him. He was getting hard. She let go of his cock, taking hold of his right hand and bringing it under the table, guiding it to the zipper of her jeans.

"I want you to finger fuck me." She whispered in his ear, as she once again took hold of his almost erect manhood. Max pulled down the zipper of her pants, moving his hand slowly inside her jeans. He looked at her surprised, she wasn't wearing any underwear. He rubbed her pussy up and down, finding her clit he lingered there, loving the look on her face. Then moving the tips of his fingers in and out of her, feeling her wetness. Maxwell, held in a moan of sexual pleasure. He couldn't hold back any longer, coming in her hand. Jeanna took a napkin off the table, cleaning her hand and his limp dick. Now it was Jeanna's turn, Max placed two of his fingers in his ice water. Bringing his hand back down under the tablecloth, he ran his ice-cold fingers up and down her pussy. Jeanna almost jumped out of her chair, as he once again fingered her clit. Max proceeded to finger fuck her slowly, she was becoming extremely wet. He moved his fingers deeper into her, moving them faster and harder. She was coming, just as the waitress came over.

"Is everything okay here?" she asked.

Jeanna let out a…. "Yes! Oh baby!" The people who were sitting close to them looked over at her, including the waitress.

Max looked up from his chicken and said, "she really likes the food here." Jeanna smiled, as Max looked over at her and mouthed the words, "I love you."

* * *

Saturday morning, Sam drove Kayla and Peter to the airport. It was time for them to begin their vacation. Getting to the airport they had lots of time to kill. Leave it up to Sam, getting them there extremely early for their flight. After sitting around for a few hours, Peter ran to the men's room as Kayla took out a magazine that was bought from one of the airport kiosks, along with a few packs of gum. She scanned the cover. Some of the headlines were Fifty and Fabulous, How to Get a Man Out of Your Dreams and Into Your Bed and Ways to Spice Up Your Sex Life. "Alright then," Kayla said. She thought that the titles were silly, popping a piece of gum into her mouth. Doing her best, to get comfortable on the plastic chair she was sitting on. Peter returned, sitting down next to her. "Everything come out okay?" Kayla inquired. Peter smiled, gently pushing her with his hand.

"Excuse me, might I have this seat?" A woman was asking, as Kayla and Peter looked up at her. She looked to be around forty, maybe slightly older. Her head was wrapped in colorful material as was her body and she spoke with a strong Jamaican accent.

"Oh yes, sorry, please sit down." Kayla replied, removing their carry-on bags and smiling up at her. "Are you from Jamaica?"

"Originally yes, I'm going to see my sister in the Bahamas. Have you ever been?"

"No, it's our first time. I'm Kayla and this is Peter."

"I'm Barbara, but everyone calls me Babette. You're going to love the Bahamas. It's warm and the water is so blue. It's just beautiful. It's definitely a place to relax. How long are you going for?"

"Only a week" Peter chimed in. "We're staying at the Margarita Ville Resort. Have you ever been there?"

"No child, can't say that I have. It sounds wonderful though.

If you would like to venture out and have your fortune read, here is my sister's business card. Some say she has the gift."

"The gift?" questioned Peter.

"Yes, she can see the future, as well as the past. If you go tell her Babette sent you." Suddenly there was an announcement overhead. "Flight 17 traveling to the Bahamas, gate 15, we are now boarding."

Kayla took the card, putting it into her beach bag as they entered the boarding ramp. Both were thrilled to be going someplace warm, a place where no winter coat, scarves, or gloves were needed. Kayla looked around for Babette but didn't see her. Was she traveling in first class? Peter found their seats in coach, offering Kayla the one by the window. He placed their bags in the overhead compartment above their heads, as Kayla became more excited with each passing moment. They heard the announcement, to stay seated and fasten their seatbelts. Their week-long vacation was about to begin.

* * *

Sam was a man re-born, over the moon that he got Mary back. They were going to wait until summer to have their wedding, but decided to make it sooner, having set their sights on early spring. Sam had asked Mary to quit her job working at the hospital, wanting her to work at the café with him. After everything that happened, he felt the need to have her by his side always. However, Mary refused, loving her job working at the front desk at Saint Paul's.

After dropping off Kayla and Peter, Sam arrived at the café early, waiting for Max and Emily to show up. He cleaned off the menus and tables, then made his way to the kitchen. Standing behind the counter he started the large urns of coffee and hot chocolate. The bell above the door chimed as Max walked in.

"Sam how are you doing? I still can't get over the fact that Peter saved Mary. I had no idea he could do that!"

"Everything is okay Max, better than okay; Mary is fine and we're moving the wedding to the spring. When I thought I lost her, I realized how much I truly loved her. Know what I mean?"

Max put his arm around Sam. "Yeah man, I get it. I'm thinking of asking Jeanna to marry me. I'm waiting to save enough money to get her the perfect ring, one that she'll love."

"Max, if she loves you, she won't give a shit what the ring looks like. If it comes from you, she will love it. Listen to an old man, don't waste a moment."

Emily walked in on time and ready for work. This week would be different without Kayla, but she would give it everything she had. "Good morning gentleman." Emily walked over to Sam kissing him on the cheek. "So, how's things? You look good. Damn! You're almost glowing with happiness."

"I am happy, the happiest I've been in years. I can never repay Peter for what he did, bringing Mary back to me. From now on he eats here for free."

"I know Peter is something special, I owe him a lot too, he gave me my face back." Emily said smiling and putting on her apron. They were now ready to serve the morning customers.

* * *

Michael had gotten permission to move their belongings into their new home. Since he was paying cash, and the house was empty, the owner didn't have a problem with it. However, they could not take up residency in the manor until the day of closing.

Tarsula greeted the movers as they entered the townhouse. They began by covering all of the furniture with a cloth and then wrapping each piece with plastic wrap. All of it was carried out to the trucks carefully. Tarsula supervised, watching the men diligently. She was on her own in daylight hours. Michael had found a dark hotel room just outside of town, only coming out at dusk to lend a hand. It took six strong men and three huge trucks to accomplish the task. After two days, everything was packed up and ready to move, a one-way ticket to The Stone Manor.

Tarsula had asked Courtney if she could meet with the movers. Opening the door for them, allowing them to start unloading the furniture and boxes. Tarsula had marked everything, stating where each box should be placed.

Courtney agreed, knowing her huge commission was close at hand. Taking her cell phone, tablet, and car keys, she walked out of the office, got into her car and left to meet the movers. At least the sun is shining, Courtney thought as she drove. Turning on the radio her thoughts went to Michael. Feeling silly, her plan to seduce him had failed. Still, he was quite the gentleman about it all, which made her want him even more.

By the time she reached the manor, the moving trucks were just getting there. They had passed the entrance to the house twice. Courtney got out of her car to meet them. "Hello guys, just give me a second, let me get my stuff and I'll open the door for you." She reached into her car gathering her belongings. Opening the immense door, she walked inside. Followed by six muscular men all impressed with the size of the home and in need of a tour, showing them where everything should be placed. They decided to split the move into bottom floor, top floor. Once that was achieved, then they would place the items into the rooms Tarsula had designated.

Courtney walked into the enormous living room. She noticed a fur rug lying in the corner, thinking that was strange. Did Michael throw it there? She picked it up, laying it down towards the middle of the room. "Hello!" Courtney stopped and listened. "Hello!" Yes, someone was calling out to her from the foyer. She stepped into the hall, walking towards the front door.

"Hello, can I help you?" Courtney called out. Noticing a young woman standing in the foyer, holding a fruit basket.

"Yes, I live down the road aways, I saw the moving trucks. I just wanted to welcome you to the neighborhood. I'm Tina Abruzzi." Tina held out her hand.

"Nice to meet you Tina", Courtney stated, shaking her hand. "I'm not moving in, I'm the realtor. My name is Courtney Stein."

"Oh, I just assumed, I saw the trucks and all. When will the owners be moving in?"

"I'm working to get them in as soon as possible, hopefully in a few days."

"This house is fantastic isn't it, Courtney? I love all the unbelievable details; you won't find workmanship like this anywhere. I knew the previous owners. They kept to themselves mostly, but didn't live here very long, I guess because this place is haunted. I mean, you know about the rumors, I'm sure. Supposedly there's a vortex somewhere in this place," Tina announced looking around. "Where the dead can enter into our world, a passageway between our world and the next."

"Listen Tina, like you said, it's just rumors." One of the moving men walked over to them, he needed advice on some boxes that weren't marked. "It was nice to meet you Tina, but as you can see, we are a little busy right now. Do you want to leave the gift basket?"

"No, I'll come back another time. It was nice meeting you." Courtney watched Tina as she walked down to the parking area, got into her Range Rover and left. Making her way to the second floor she attended to the movers. "A vortex", Courtney said out loud, as she climbed the stairs. "Pure nonsense."

* * *

Kayla and Peter were enjoying the warm sunshine. Sitting around the pool with a tasty drink in their hands. It was hard not to think about the café, feeling bad, leaving Emily working solo for the week. Kayla placed her hand on her stomach; a small baby bump was slightly showing through her bathing suit. She put on a straw hat and sipped her virgin pina colada, as Peter jumped into the pool.

"Coming in?" Peter shouted, "the water's warm."

"Maybe later, I just want to enjoy the sun for now." Kayla reached into her beach bag looking for her sunblock cream and came across the card that Babette had given her. Looking at the address for Jilly Williams, it made her wonder how far away it was. Perhaps it could be fun? Something different, she thought, hoping Peter would go with her.

Coming out of the pool, he sat down next to her. Taking a towel to dry himself off, Kayla handed him the card. "What's this"?

Peter asked.

"It's the card Babette gave me at the airport. Her sister's name is Jilly Williams. Reader of tarot cards, tea leaves, and palms. What do you think Peter, want to get your fortune told?"

"Are you serious Kay? Do you really want to do this?"

"Why not? I think it would be fun. I'm not sure how far away this address is though."

"Alright Kay, we'll ask at the front desk in the morning. They have to know the area. If it's not too much out of the way, we'll give it a go."

Kayla wrapped her arms around him. "Really? Thank you, this is going to be so much fun!"

* * *

Courtney watched as the last of the furniture was taken off the trucks. It took most of the day, and a lot of patience. She signed the delivery slips, letting the tired men leave and head home. She walked through the house shutting off the lights and closing doors. Walking back into the living room the fur rug once again was bunched up in the corner. Maybe one of the movers kicked it, she thought. Picking it up and laying it down flat one more time, towards the center of the room. Collecting her things on her way out, it dawned on her. That she had forgotten to turn the light off in the living room. Closing the door, she walked back through the large foyer and down the long hallway stopping at the doorway to the living room. Courtney stood there staring, the rug she had just placed, was back in the corner bunched up in a ball. Turning off the light she ran down the hallway, through the foyer and all the way to her car.

Laughter resonated from the living room. Then the sound of footsteps could be heard, echoing down the long hallway and going slowly up the stairs to the second floor. A door was opened and closed with a loud bang.

CHAPTER FIVE

IT'S ALL IN THE CARDS

It was a beautiful morning, as Peter and Kayla walked through the lobby of the hotel; they strolled over to the front desk. A young man looked up from his computer. "Hello, how can I help you?"

Kayla read the gentleman's name tag. "Brandon, we would like to go to the address on this card. Do you know where this is? How long would it take us to get there?"

Brandon looked at the card. "Yes, I know this area. Maybe fifteen to twenty minutes. It's in a very touristy part of town. You know lots of souvenir shops, restaurants, tattoo parlors, that kind of thing. So, you're looking to get your fortune read? You believe in this stuff?" Brandon looked at them, like they would be wasting their money.

Kayla shrugged her shoulders and looked over at Peter. "I just thought it could be fun, something different," she replied.

"Alright, it's up to you. I can call you a taxi if you like?"

"That would be great, thank you Brandon." Peter answered, smiling at Kayla who was blushing, feeling silly about the whole ordeal.

In ten minutes, the cab was waiting outside for them. They waved goodbye to Brandon, as they walked outside and got into the back seat of the taxi.

Nassau was beautiful, as they took the scenic route. Driving along a cliff looking down at the deep blue water below. Eventually arriving in a town that was extremely overcrowded. Just as Brandon had said, this town was a magnet for tourists.

They got out of the cab, reading street names, and address numbers on the houses and shops. Finally arriving at the home of Jilly Williams. Kayla knocked on the front door, not seeing a doorbell anywhere. They stood there for a while. "Maybe she's out, we should have called before coming here." Peter said annoyed, he would much rather be lying in the sun than being surrounded by tons of people. They started to walk down the stairs, as Peter picked up his phone calling for a taxi, the front door opened. "May I help you?"

Kayla did an about face, running back up the stairs to the door. "Yes, we're looking for Jilly Williams. I got this card from her sister Babette." Kayla handed her the card.

"I see, please come in, and have a seat, I'll be right back."

Peter and Kayla sat down on a sofa, that had seen better days. The room was rather dark, which was odd because the sun was super bright outside. There were posters on the walls of different pentagrams and individual tarot cards. Also, the diagram of a palm, which was sectioned off showing the lines on the hand and what they stood for. Kayla walked over to it, examining her own hand lines.

Jilly walked back into the room. "Please if you'll follow me." Kayla followed as Peter stood up, he was stopped by Jilly's hand. "I'm sorry I can only allow one energy in the room at a time. Please wait here."

Peter looked over at Kayla, who raised her eyebrows and smiled. She followed Jilly into a small room towards the rear of the house. It was also dimly lit; with the only light coming from a single accent lamp sitting on top of a dresser. Kayla was asked to sit down at a table, which was covered with a fine black cloth. It had colorful flowers embroidered on it, with tiny sequins sewn here and there. Jilly lit a red candle in the middle of the table and asked, "what is your name?"

"Kayla, I met your sister at the…."

"Hush child, are we doing tarot cards or tea leaves?"

"I guess the cards." Kayla answered unsure, not knowing what she had just gotten herself into.

"Alright, forty dollars please."

Kayla reached into her purse, giving her the money. "Very good, let's begin." Jilly said, putting the money in her pocket. She opened a box, containing a set of tarot cards handing them to Kayla. "Please shuffle the cards Kayla, until you are satisfied. When you're ready, I'm going to lay the cards out on this table. It will tell me things that have happened, as well as things that will transpire." Jilly closed her eyes for a moment and sat very still. Then Kayla watched as she dealt the cards out in the shape of a cross. "First these are things that have happened, then we will proceed with things that will come about." She informed Kayla, as she turned over the first card. "The lovers card," two men fighting for your affections. Two extremely different men. Each wanting to possess you, but for very different reasons. I would say they are both infatuated with you, both deeply in love."

Kayla took a deep breath; she was telling herself to stay calm. As the next card was turned over. "The candle card", it showed two candles one lit, one not. "Lots of confusion with these two men. It seems that maybe one had your heart, the other your head. Do you understand?" Kayla nodded her head yes and swallowed hard. Jilly flipped the third card. It showed a flower, a tulip coming out of the snow. "This is the card of rebirth. Did you, or someone you know have a serious health issue? Where perhaps they had crossed over briefly to the other side and were brought back?"

Kayla just looked at her, stunned. She thought about Mary, but then remembered falling off a cliff only to wake up in Peters arms. "Yes, I think so, maybe. Can we please go to the future cards, if that's okay?"

"Yes of course, if that's what you wish." Jilly turned over the first card, it showed two hearts coming out of the ground. "The two hearts emerging card, two hearts beating together. Does that make sense to you?"

Kayla placed her hand on her stomach. "Yes, yes it does.

I'm pregnant with my first child. So yes, my heart along with my baby's, two hearts, yes. That's unbelievable! How could you know that?"

"No child. The two hearts are emerging, emerging into this world. The world of the living, two babies."

"What? No. I mean, I'm having my first sonogram next week. This is crazy, two babies?"

"Yes. Let me draw another card to clarify this." As she drew the next card, Jilly looked up into Kayla's eyes, with a perplexing look on her face.

"What is it, what do you see? Tell me!" Kayla demanded.

"The clarification card. It shows two birds of a different color. One white, one black. Sometimes this card denotes indecision. However, in this case." Jilly hesitated. "In this case, they represent the men I spoke of. Your babies could have two different fathers my dear."

"What! No, what are you talking about? That's insane, I don't want to hear anymore! This is insane!" Kayla got up and stormed out of the office. Running past Peter and out the door.

"Kayla! Kayla! Will you wait! What happened in there? What did she say to upset you?"

"That woman is nuts; I mean Brandon was right, this was a waste of time and money! Come on let's get a taxi and get out of here." Kayla didn't know what to do or feel. Could Jilly possibly be right? If there were two babies, could one be Peter's and one Michael's? Was there even such a thing? How could that be possible? She would bring it to her doctors' attention. Maybe there was a way to check the paternity of the babies before they were born. How would Peter feel if she did have twins, and one of the babies was Michael's? The thought of it terrified her.

There was silence in the cab, going back to the hotel. "Kayla, what happened back there? What did she say to you? Don't let her upset you!" Peter said, trying to console her, taking her hand and kissing it.

"You were right, she was a fake just trying to make easy money. She told me I was going to have twins. Twins don't run in my family. How about you, any twins on your mother's side?"

"No, I don't think so. Don't ask me about my father, I don't have a clue there. So, what if she's right? Would that be such a bad thing? We can handle it Kay. I love you, more than anything in this world and I will love our children. Whether we have one, two, or half a dozen."

Kayla smiled, as Peter wiped away her tears. If Jilly had only acknowledged twins, she would be over the moon with joy, but two different fathers. That would mean Michael's child was growing inside of her as well. Would it be like Michael, with the same traits? Drinking blood and shape shifting into animal form. If her prediction was true, how could she tell Peter only one of the babies was his. Stop it! She told herself, let's wait until we get home and see Doctor Kyle. Peter put his arm around her, pulling Kayla close to him, and gently kissed her cheek. "Twins Kay, if she's correct, I will be the happiest man alive."

* * *

Courtney got a call from the seller of The Stone Manor. He wanted to close on the property as soon as possible. If the money was there and all the papers signed, what was the hold up? She looked through her paperwork. Yes, everything was in proper order. We could close tomorrow if everyone is available. Courtney picked up her phone to call Michael. If he was on board, she would receive her commission check sooner than later.

Michael's phone rang; he picked it up begrudgingly. It was late afternoon and this was his time to sleep, since he had been awake for most of the night. Seeing that it was Courtney, he sat up and answered it.

"Hey Courtney, I hope this isn't about more papers to be signed."

"Good afternoon, Michael. No, it's not about papers for you to sign. I got a call from the seller, and he wants to have the closing tomorrow morning. What do you think about that?"

Michael got out of bed, he needed to think quickly, since he was only willing to venture out at dusk or later. "Courtney, I was hoping to close on a Saturday, when I would have more spare time. I mean, tomorrow would be fine except my daytime schedule is crazy. Do you think he would consider closing in the early evening?"

"Well, I certainly could ask him. I'll call you right back."

Michael walked into the kitchen. Opening the fridge, pouring the blood of a raw steak into a glass with some ice and a good amount of gin. He waited, hoping the seller would agree and they could be in their new home by tomorrow night. His phone rang, as he took his first sip.

"All systems are go Michael, does seven sound good to you?"

"That sounds great! Thanks for all of your help Courtney, I'll see you tomorrow."

"Great, we have a conference room here in the building. It has a large table where we can all be comfortable. See you tomorrow at seven. Goodbye Michael."

"Bye Courtney." Michael finished his drink and laid back down. "I'm coming for you Kayla my love," he said staring at the ceiling. "We can now be together. I hope you will come with me willingly and stop this foolish game of playing house with Peter, that little fuck."

* * *

Emily ran down the stairs of the apartment building. Since Kayla would be gone for a few more days she needed to be on time. Driving to work she noticed some of the trees were starting to bud. Spring was fast approaching. It was a time of renewal, and she was thrilled, knowing soon her winter coat and all of her cold weather stuff could be put away. Emily opened her car window a crack, feeling the air on her face was refreshing.

Bradford Cummings made it a point to get up early also, deciding to follow Emily to work. Allowing a few cars to get in front of him, so there would be no chance of her noticing his car. Bradford watched as Emily parked her car and walked over to the café. He was intrigued; did she work there or just getting a bite to eat? Sitting in his car for a while, watching the café, but not seeing her exit the building. She must work there he thought, Bradford wondered if Katie worked there also. Only one way to find out, to go in and have breakfast. The door chimed as Bradford walked in, sitting down at a table Emily walked over to him.

"Good morning, sir. Would you like to see a menu?"

"Yes please. You look so familiar to me; I know you from somewhere."

"Oh yeah, maybe I just have one of those faces. I'll come back when you're ready to order."

Sitting there Bradford looked around the café hoping to see Katie, but she did not appear.

Emily walked back to him. "Are you ready to order?"

"Yes, I know where I've seen you. I held the door open for you at a convenient store the other night. You had that adorable dog with you. Who, for whatever reason, took an extreme dislike to me."

"Oh, that was you? Sorry about that. My dog Dino never acts that way, he's usually very even tempered."

"That's okay, who knows what an animal is thinking right? What's your name, by the way?"

"Emily, and you?"

"Mr. Cummings. Nice to meet you, Emily."

"So, what would you like to order, Mr. Cummings?"

"I'll have The Hungry Man's Special." Bradford grinned, placing his order.

"How do you want your eggs cooked?"

"Scrambled. This is a rather large café, are you the only one waiting tables here?"

"For the moment, my partner in crime Kayla is on vacation. She should be back next week. Do you want some coffee?"

"Yes, that would be fantastic, thank you Emily." Bradford's mind was spinning. Kayla yes, that was her name, he thought. Next week you say, alright Ms. Kayla, enjoy your vacation. I'll be waiting for you when you get back.

Emily walked over to Max handing him the order. "Here you go, small world isn't it Max?"

"I guess. Someone is hungry this morning." Max said. Looking at the order for a Hungry Man's Special.

"Yeah, it's for that gentleman over there, Mr. Cummings." Emily laughed. "Who introduces them self by their surname?"

Max looked out into the front of the café. Why does this guy look familiar to me, he thought? Cummings, I've heard that name before, but where? Try as he might, Max couldn't place him, so he started cooking the Hungry Man's Special, still deep in thought.

* * *

Peter got up to answer the door as room service brought in their breakfast. The smell of bacon, sausage, pancakes, and eggs made his mouth water. Walking over to the bed, Kayla was just opening her eyes as he sat down next to her. "Breakfast is ready my love, I hope you're hungry." Peter remarked, stroking her arm. Kayla did her morning stretch. Looking over at the cart full of food, she smiled. "Who else is coming for breakfast Peter?"

He laughed. "Well, since it is all inclusive, I thought I'd order the works. I mean, you are eating for two now, maybe three."

"Alright Peter, let's not talk about that this morning." Kayla remarked, as Jilly Williams' words kept running through her mind. "I just want to enjoy the time we have left in paradise."

"You're right, I shouldn't get my hopes up until we see the doctor. Let's have breakfast." They took their plates outside to the balcony, which overlooked the blue ocean and white sandy beach.

"I can get used to this." Kayla said, looking over at Peter, who was thoroughly enjoying his breakfast.

"What do you want to do today?" he asked. "Anything you want, as long as it's not too dangerous."

"Actually, I would love to just lay on the beach this morning, before it gets too hot." Peter just smiled at her, as he poured himself another cup of coffee.

* * *

Tarsula hired one more trucking service to remove the last pieces of their furniture. Leaving a few special pieces behind that the buyer wanted as part of the sale. She had spoken to Courtney this morning asking if she could come by for the key to the manor. There were a few more items that needed to be dropped off and the moving company only worked until five. Courtney obliged.

Michael walked through the almost empty townhouse. He couldn't rest, knowing he would be in his new home tonight. Soon, he would live there with his beloved Kayla. Tarsula looked up at him as he entered the kitchen.

"What's wrong couldn't sleep, Michael?"

"No, I keep thinking about Kayla. It's all coming together Tarsula. In a few days we will have the house set up perfectly, then I will take her, one way or another."

"Yes, Michael. I told you it would all work out, in time things usually do." Tarsula smiled, as she finished off a pecan pie. "Well, I must leave you now Michael. I have to pick up a key from Courtney. The movers should be here sometime this afternoon, but I should be back in plenty of time to give them packing orders. Hasta la vista baby."

Michael sat at the island thinking. He needed a plan, a plan to take Kayla away unseen. Under the disguise of Bowie, he would be able to watch her house day and night. There had to be a moment when she would be alone. That is the moment he would make his move. He would have her, no matter how long it took. She was his and would always be his. He just needed to be patient.

CHAPTER SIX

HOME SWEET HOME

Kayla and Peter were back from vacation. Sam and Mary had picked them up from the airport.

"So, tell us all about it, was it fantastic and relaxing?" Sam inquired, looking in the rear-view mirror.

"It was beautiful," replied Peter. "Thanks for picking us up." Kayla could tell he was biting his tongue, wanted to tell them about the twin situation. He looked over at Kayla who gave him a look, like don't you dare. Kayla filled them in on everything except the Jilly Williams fiasco.

When they arrived home, Sam and Mary were invited in, but they declined. They were going to spend the day looking for a venue to have their wedding. Going inside the house it smelt musty, opening a few windows just a crack would help the matter.

"Happy to be home?" Peter asked. "I saw the look you gave me in the car. Don't worry I won't tell anyone about us having twins, until we know for sure, okay."

Kayla smiled. "Okay, let's wait until we see Dr. Kyle. I will believe him, more than some crazy fortune teller."

* * *

Michael and Tarsula sat in their beautiful new home. All the furniture had been placed according to Tarsula's instructions. There were many more pieces of furniture that needed to be bought, since the house was massive, but overall, it was ready for Michael's love Kayla.

"What do you think of the house Tarsula? I think it's pretty wonderful." Michael acknowledged with a smile on his face.

"That it is Michael. Now, we need to devise a plan to take her, I will help you anyway I can."

"I will go to her house tomorrow night." Michael informed her. "And every evening after that, there has to be a moment when she will be alone, then I will make my move. Hopefully she will still have feelings for me, if not, I'll put her into trance state."

Tarsula and Michael suddenly jumped up, hearing a loud crash coming from the kitchen. They ran over seeing a very large plate rack that had fallen down and laid in pieces on the floor. Along with some expensive dishes that Tarsula had just bought. "What the fuck Michael! These dishes were a small fortune! How the fuck did this rack fall down?"

Michael looked at her grinning. "Maybe it was the ghost Tarsula" he joked, as he started laughing.

"Michael shut the fuck up. That's not funny, look at this mess!"

"Come on Tarsula, it probably wasn't bolted to the wall properly. You know how these old houses are. Sooner or later, something is bound to go wrong. Let me help you clean it up." Tarsula ran and got a broom and dustpan, as Michael started to pick up the pieces of the plate rack. Looking at the floor something caught his eye in the corner of the room. It was shiny and almost the size of his palm. Michael walked over to it bending down and picking it up. It was a badge, a detective's badge with the number twenty-eight on the front of it. Interesting Michael thought, maybe the previous owner of the property was a detective and left his badge. He took it and laid it on the counter, then he walked back to Tarsula helping her clean up the mess.

* * *

Sam and Mary had spent most of the day looking for a place to have their wedding reception. Paul, Sam's good friend, had recommended Danmore Castle which was a unique restaurant.

It was also a catering hall for parties and weddings. Paul had gone there for his anniversary and couldn't stop talking about how good the food was. Sam had arranged a meeting with the banquet manager to take a look around. They took a private road up to the facility, driving up a small hill, as the grounds spread out before them. Rolling mounds of green grass flanked the road, reaching the top, Mary gasped.

"Oh my God! Sam it's unbelievable! It looks like it came out of a fairy tale." There before them, stood the most perfect medieval castle sitting up high on a hill. It was adorned with flags of many colors and patterns blowing in the wind. Mary had visions of a knight in shining armor, galloping past them on his trusty steed. "Sam, this is the place, I love it!"

"Okay hon, but can we afford it, and can they fit us in?" Sam replied. Looking over at Mary hoping it was within their budget and that there would be some dates still available. Parking their car, they noticed a woman walking towards them. Her red flowing hair showed brightly in the sunshine. She was very petite with green eyes and fair skin. Sam and Mary looked like giants compared to her.

"Hello, I'm Loren O'Brien," introducing herself, as she spoke with an Irish brogue. "You must be Mary and Sam." Loren extended her hand to both of them. "So, what do you both think of our glorious castle? Isn't it special?"

"Yes, I think it's wonderful. What do you think Sam?" Mary asked, hoping he loved it as well.

Sam looked up, as dollar signs flashed before his eyes. "I think it's great, but let's not forget that we are on a budget. I hope you will be able to work with us on that, Ms. O'Brien."

"Of course, we have all different packages. We'll find one that's suitable. Please call me Loren. Come inside, I think you will both be impressed." Mary and Sam followed her to the front entrance of the castle. They walked slowly onto the drawbridge, suspended across a crystal-clear moat.

"Does this drawbridge work?" Sam asked.

"Oh yes. Some of our brides wait inside and then have the drawbridge lowered, so they can walk across it to their nuptials. Which usually takes place in the meadow, if the weather permits. It makes quite the entrance. What do you think Mary?"

"I would love that." Mary answered, looking over at Sam with pleading eyes.

Loren continued. "The reception soon follows in here; this is the great hall."

Walking inside the great hall, it was immense. The stone walls had to have been at least thirty feet high. Their footsteps echoed as they walked around. Loren pointed out interesting and impressive facts, as they slowly took the tour. Stepping ahead of them, Loren opened a large wooden door. "What do you think of this?" she asked, looking at Sam for his reaction.

Sam's mouth dropped open; the room was filled with weapons. Every weapon known to man for battle. "Most of these weapons are reproductions. However, there are a few that are the real deal" Loren stated, looking at Sam for approval.

All Sam could think about were the guys from the Fish and Game Committee. Paul would definitely lose his mind. Especially with the variety of arrows and bows mounted on the wall, since archery was his passion. I bet he wasn't shown this room when he came here for dinner, Sam thought.

"I'm impressed Ms. O'Brien, so let's talk dates and money." Sam stated, looking over at Mary who smiled and kissed his cheek.

* * *

Emily and Simon spent Sunday night watching T.V. and eating popcorn. One of the cable companies was running back-to-back horror movies. Which Simon enjoyed, but Emily could take or leave. She would always cover her eyes; at what Simon called the good parts, and it made him laugh. Emily looked over at Dino, who was laying peacefully on his bed. He could sleep through anything. Even with a damsel in distress screaming at the top of her lungs and running from a chainsaw maniac.

Simon rested his hand on her thigh, he kissed her cheek and then her neck. Followed by unbuttoning the top of her blouse and kissing her lower neck and decollete. "I think someone is horny." Emily announced, standing up taking Simon's hand and walking him to the bedroom. Sex will be a lot more fun, than watching these awful horror movies she thought. "Come on baby, let's sixty-nine it." Simon coaxed. Taking off his clothes quickly and lying down on the bed. Emily undressed as Simon watched, just looking at her naked body gave him a partial hard on.

That's when they heard the sirens coming from outside, it sounded like they were directly in front of their building. Emily took a throw off the bed and wrapped it around herself, as Simon got up and quickly put on his robe. They both walked into the living room, looking through their picture window at something that was happening in the park across the street. There had to be at least five police cars, along with an ambulance or two.

"Something must have happened in the park." Emily remarked. "Simon, you don't think it was that bear, or whatever that thing was I saw that night, do you?"

"I don't know, maybe we should go down there, just to find out what happened. Let's get dressed."

Simon and Emily walked across the street to the park. The police had roped off the entrance, the park was off limits. Pauline walked over to where Emily was standing. "Hey Em, Simon." Emily looked over at Pauline asking her if she knew anything. "I heard some guy and his dog got attacked. They took the guy into the ambulance over there; however, the dog wasn't so lucky. Whatever this thing was, it ripped the dog apart."

Emily swallowed hard looking over at Simon. "Pauline, I saw something in this park a few nights ago, it stood up on its hind legs and looked right at me."

"What was it?" asked Pauline.

"I don't know, but maybe I should tell the police what I saw."

"Yeah Em, I think you should. I'm going home where it's safe, see you later guys."

"Goodnight, stay safe!" Emily shouted as Pauline walked away. Emily walked over to one of the officers standing at the entrance. "Excuse me officer, who can I talk to that's in charge here?" The officer pointed to a man who was sitting in the ambulance, with the gentleman that got attacked. The man was crying hysterically over the loss of his dog. Trying to get a statement from him now was nearly impossible. Stepping out of the ambulance, he walked towards the entrance telling everyone to please go home and not enter the park at night.

Emily knew him, it was Sergeant Daniels. "Sergeant Daniels over here!" Yelled Simon, waving his hands in the air.

"Good lord, what are you two doing here?" Daniels asked.

"Hey sergeant, I just want to give a statement about something I saw the other night."

Sergeant Daniels looked at them both curiously. "Emily, why is it that when something is going on you're always in the middle of it? You should be a reporter, always in the right place, at the right time. So, what did you see?"

"Well, I was in the park a few nights ago and I saw this beast thing. Simon tried to convince me that it was a black bear, but I didn't think so. It had dark fur and could stand upright on two legs almost taking the shape of a man. Its head looked canine, like a very large dog or a wolf."

Sergeant Daniels took a deep breath. What she was describing sounded like the beasts at Michael's party on that unholy night. He couldn't comprehend that this shit was starting to happen again. "Listen Emily, Simon, do me a favor and don't set foot inside this park until we know what's going on. Emily, I'd like you to come by the station when you can. I want to get a written statement from you as to what you saw that night. Okay?"

"Sure, I'll come by this week."

Daniels walked towards the crowd and made an announcement. "Alright everyone, there's nothing to see here! Please go home and do not venture into this park, especially at night. Come on everyone, go home. Please stay safe. Emily, Simon, have a good evening. Emily, I'll see you soon."

Simon put his arm around Emily, as they walked back across the street, he asked. "So, are you still in the mood to sixty-nine it?" Emily just shrugged her shoulders.

"Okay then, let me try to convince you." Simon said, as he grabbed her ass running up the front steps to their apartment building.

* * *

The next morning, by the time Kayla got to work Max and Sam were carrying out the tables and chairs arranging them on the patio. A sure sign of spring and the welcome thought of warmer weather. "Good morning gentlemen." Kayla called out, as she made her way into the café, followed by Sam and Max. "Hey Sam, I just want to remind you, I have my ultrasound this afternoon with Doctor Kyle my obstetrician. I'm leaving on my lunch hour, but I should be back quickly. Did you and Mary find a venue for the wedding yet?"

"Yes, indeed we did. There's a replica of a medieval castle about an hour from town. It's now used for wedding venues. Listen to this, it has a working draw bridge and a moat if you can believe that. There is also a room dedicated to weapons from mid-evil times to the present day. That room is off limits to the public, but you can still have a look inside. Paul and my friends from the Fish and Game Association are going to lose their minds. Anyway, the castle is set high on a hill with nothing around it but rolling green pastures and woods. It was a little expensive, but Mary fell in love with the place, so we had to book it. The wedding is going to be on May twentieth. Your invites will soon be in the mail." Sam was beaming with happiness. "I would like Peter to be my best man. I mean, he did give me back Mary, without him there would be no wedding at all." Max looked a little disappointed. He thought for sure; Sam would have asked him to be his best man. However, with everything that had

70

taken place recently, he understood.

* * *

Michael was sound asleep in his new four poster bed. He was dreaming of making love to Kayla in front of the bedroom's magnificent fireplace. She laid nude on the fur rug before him. Professing her love for him. "I love you Michael and only you. Make love to me and turn me, I want to be with you for eternity, give me immortality my darling." Michael knelt before her pushing her thighs apart, he would first satisfy her orally. Licking her wet pussy slowly, he inserted his fingers into her, as his tongue continued pleasing her. He lingered there licking her rapidly, stimulating her, Kayla was lost in sexual bliss. She screamed for Michael to bite her. He laid on top and began to fuck her. He kissed her mouth, then ran his tongue down her neck and bit into it. Her blood filled his mouth, sweet and nourishing. Michael continued to feed, as he felt her life force slip away. She died, just as Michael came inside her. Pulling out he waited, Kayla opened her eyes, staring up at him. Michael slit his abdomen; as the blood ran down, Kayla suckled at the cut feeding, she was now his forever.

Suddenly, Michael opened his eyes, he was awakened by bright sunlight coming through his bedroom windows. All the curtains somehow had become wide open. His face and chest were burning, smoking. Throwing a blanket over his head he screamed for Tarsula.

* * *

Peter met Kayla at the doctor's office. He was excited, loving the idea of having twins. Kayla on the other hand felt nervous and downright frightened. However, she tried to remain calm until she knew the facts. Kayla laid on the table, as Doctor Kyle distributed a cold gel onto her stomach. He placed a device, called a transducer onto her moving it back and forth. A picture popped up on the screen, as Doctor Kyle smiled. "Well, Kayla, Peter, congratulations you are both the parents of twins." Kayla started to cry, as did Peter, but for different reasons. Peter took her in his arms kissing her

71

overcome with happiness. Kayla was overwhelmed by the whole situation. Would she ever be able to tell him, he was only the father of one of the babies. If Jilly Williams was right, a part of Michael was growing inside her as well. A baby whose father was a creature known to drink blood, who could change into a hawk and lord knows what else, at the drop of a hat. Try to relax, she told herself. Maybe the baby would be normal after all, it could take after me. There was no reason to tell Peter. What good would it do? He is so happy. Kayla remained silent, knowing he would be an excellent father to both of the babies.

Doctor Kyle wiped the gel off of Kayla's stomach. "Do either one of you have any questions?" Kayla did, but she wasn't about to ask him with Peter standing next to her.

"So, Doctor Kyle you're sure were having twins?" Peter asked.

"Yes, two eggs or in medical terms ova, were fertilized by two spermatozoa, sperm. There's no question. I noticed two separate sacs meaning each baby will have its own placenta. I am positive you're having fraternal twins. Maybe by the next sonogram, we can get a clear picture showing the sex of the babies. Would you both like to know?"

Peter said yes, at the same time that Kayla said no. Peter looked at her surprised, that she didn't want to know. "Kay, I can't believe you're not curious as to what we're having."
"I'd rather be surprised." Inside Kayla's mind she couldn't believe Jilly Williams was right about the twins. Was she also going to be right, that Michael was the father of one of them? She was absolutely terrified.

* * *

Bradford had been watching Kayla's coming and goings for most of the day. He was hoping to find some kind of a routine, one that she followed regularly. A moment when she was alone. In his mind he knew how to do it, he just needed to wait for the right time. He laughed to himself thinking how mad Michael would be, if he found out what he was planning to do. Bradford looked over at the seat next to him. A roll of duct tape and strong rope was ready to be put into use, Miss Kayla would be his. He was getting excited thinking about it all. Looking at his hand on the steering wheel it started to change elongating and turning claw like. He opened the car window and took some deep breaths. Needing to calm himself down, his hand returned to normal, patience was not one of his virtues.

* * *

Michael and Tarsula sat in the living room just looking at each other. Neither could figure out how the bedroom curtains had opened. "Tarsula, do you think this house really is haunted?"

"Don't be ridiculous Michael. Could it be, you opened them to look outside and just forgot to close them?"

"No Tarsula, I never open the curtains you know that. Even if I did want to look outside, I would only open the curtains of one window, not all of them. I found something odd in the kitchen yesterday, a detective's badge. Wait here I'll get it." Michael walked into the kitchen and over to the counter he had placed the badge on, it wasn't there. He moved the small appliances around looking behind them, but it was gone. "Tarsula! Will you come here please." Tarsula walked into the kitchen eating a bar of chocolate. "Tarsula did you take a badge off of this counter? I put it here yesterday. I found it in that corner over there." Michael pointed to the corner at the far end of the room.

"Absolutely not. Not only did I not take it, I never saw it. I was cleaning off the counter tops yesterday. If it was here, I would have seen it and probably would have asked you about it."

The front doorbell chimed loudly throughout the house. Tarsula walked down the hallway and across the massive foyer to the front door. "Hello, what can I do for you?" Tarsula asked, looking at a strange woman holding a fruit basket.

"Hello, my name is Tina Abruzzi. I'm your only neighbor from around the area, welcome to the neighborhood; this is for you." Tina handed over the gift basket for Tarsula to take.

"Well, thank you. Where is your house exactly? I thought we were pretty much isolated here."

"Yes, well my house is a few blocks away. Not much happens around here. So, when I saw the moving trucks the other day, I couldn't believe someone was moving into the manor. This house is one of a kind, you don't find craftmanship like this anymore." Tina had walked into the foyer running her hand across the fine wood details of the wainscoting. "May I ask you something? Why is it so dark in here? It's a beautiful sunny day outside."

"My stepson Michael just had his eyes dilated, the light was hurting them, so we closed all the curtains," replied Tarsula. She was thinking, this Tina may become a problem for us.

Michael strolled into the foyer, his curiosity had gotten the better of him, wondering why Tarsula was taking so long to return. "Hello, I'm Michael and you are?"

"Tina Abruzzi, I came by to welcome you to the neighborhood." Pointing to the fruit basket Tarsula was holding. "Even though, I know our houses are quite a distance away. When did you move in?"

"Last night. Tina, do you know if the previous owner was a detective? I met him at the closing, but I wasn't aware of his occupation."

"No, I believe he was a surgeon. Why do you ask?"

"I found a badge on the floor; I thought he might have left it here."

Tina gave Michael the once over. She was attracted to him, wondering what he would be like in bed. Tina's husband was a whiz at finances, but a dud in the sheets. He would bypass foreplay and go straight to intercourse. He knew one position missionary, and even that wasn't very good.

"Well, that is odd," Tina responded, staring at Michael's handsome face. "Is your wife around I'd love to meet her?"

"I'm not married Tina, at least not yet."

"Girlfriend or fiancé?"

"Working on it," replied Michael, grinning.

"Do you know the stories about this house? I could come by at another time to fill you in."

"What, that it's haunted. Yes, we were told. However, we don't believe in such things. Isn't that right Tarsula?"

"Yes, it's all a bunch of bullshit." Tarsula replied.

Tina continued talking about the house. "I was told, that was the reason the previous owner wanted to sell this place in such a hurry. The activity was getting to him and his family." Tina explained. "There's a vortex somewhere in this house. A pathway between our world and the next. I guess they couldn't take it any longer and decided to put the house up for sale."

"Okay Tina, it was nice to meet you. Thanks for the fruit basket." Michael walked away thinking Tina Abruzzi may not be playing with a full deck. Tarsula opened the door for her to leave. "Have a good day, Tina. Oh, and by the way, Michael is a man who loves his privacy. It's the reason he bought this house, so let's not make this a habit." Tarsula remarked, closing the door and locking it. Hoping Tina got the hint, not to drop by again.

* * *

Peter's duffle bag was packed and ready to go. He was leaving in the afternoon to avoid the morning rush. The teacher's conference was a two-hour drive away. Booking his hotel room a day earlier, he could wake up refreshed, only needing to go downstairs to attend his conference.

"Peter, are you sure you have everything?" Kayla asked, looking through his bag.

"Yes Kay, I've looked through it at least six times, I have it all. Anyway, I'm only going to be gone for two days. If I forget something, it's no big deal."

Out of the corner of her eye Kayla saw a flash of light. "Peter, Willie's here!"

"Good, now at least you won't be lonely."

Kayla walked to the front door, as Willie flew through the

mail slot and landed on the living room floor. "Hello my friend, I've missed you little guy." Kayla picked him up gently and patted his head. Willie smiled at her, showing his black teeth. "Kay la" He replied, rubbing his tiny face against her cheek.

Peter walked into the living room. Willie flew away from Kayla and onto Peter's shoulder. "Willie follow?" he asked, holding tight onto Peter's shirt collar. "Oh no Willie, I have to leave. You are staying here with Kayla, alright? I'll see you on the next visit." Peter kissed and hugged Kayla goodbye. Willie flew to the window and watched as Peter left. Kayla could see the sadness on Willie's tiny face. She picked him up and placed him in the pocket of her shirt. He looked up at her "Willie hide?" he asked.

"No, how about some cookies, would you like that?" Willie nodded his head yes, as his bright red tongue came out and licked his lips. Kayla placed a chocolate sandwich cookie on the kitchen table. He bit into it as the cookie crumbs went flying. Kayla sat at the table watching him, totally entertained.

CHAPTER SEVEN
MICHAEL MAKES HIS MOVE

Michael had parked his car down the street, he watched as Peter placed his bag into the car and drove away. Was he going somewhere? He needed a better look. Changing into Bowie, he made his way to the back of the house, jumping up onto the fence. Michael could see clearly through the kitchen window, finding Kayla sitting at a table there. However, he did not see Willie, who was sitting behind the box of cookies. Michael sat there observing her as the sun started to set, suddenly Kayla stood up and decided to take out the trash. He watched, as she stepped outside, walking the trash can to the curb. It was now or never; this was the moment he had waited for! He quickly ran down the driveway, changing back into human form. Kayla turned to walk back to the house, stunned by Michael's appearance.

"Hello Kayla, miss me?" Michael smiled; Kayla was caught off guard as her eyes glazed over.

Willie went to the window just as Michael and Kayla were walking away, he became frantic. Not knowing what to do. "Willie follow," he told himself. Flying out of the mail slot he watched them, as Michael placed Kayla into his Mercedes. Willie knew he had to act quickly; he flew into Michael's car through the back window, which was opened just a crack. "Willie hide," he told himself, going underneath Kayla's front seat. He sat there with a snarl on his face and hate in his eyes for Michael.

Two of the neighborhood kids were going by on their bikes,

as Michael was walking around to the driver's side door. "Hey Mister, nice car. Hi Kayla!" They stopped their bikes looking at her wondering why she didn't return their greeting. She was always so friendly, asking them about their day and how they were doing in school. Now she just sat there staring, with a strange look on her face.

"Don't you kids have homework to do, or something?" Michael questioned, as he closed his car door and drove off so pleased with himself. She was his now, after all the waiting and wanting. He turned to look at her as he drove. Still not understanding how she had survived the fall off the cliff, remembering her dead body as it laid upon the rocks. No matter, she was here with him now, and very much alive. "Kayla, I know you can hear me. I told you that you were mine. I bought you a mansion, it's beautiful, it's what you deserve. I know we will be happy there. I'm going to turn you when the time is right, giving you eternal life. Don't you want that? Don't you want to be young and beautiful forever?" Michael inquired, looking over at her.

Willie was listening to every word Michael was saying. He stuck his tongue out at him, made a disgusted face, and gave him the finger. Sitting on the floor of Michael's car wasn't cutting it for him. He needed to look out of the side window, so he flew behind the back of Michael's seat. Landing in a netted pocket, which was perfect for Willie to hide in and not be seen. Also, it allowed Willie to see the surrounding areas they were passing through.

Finally getting to their destination, Michael parked the car as Willie flew out the back window. Opening the door for Kayla and giving her his hand, he instructed her to get out of the car and come with him. Chanting to Tarsula to quickly open the front door. Walking through the threshold Michael's trance was broken, as Kayla woke up. Seeing Michael and Tarsula she screamed, turning to run. Michael ran after her, as Tarsula stepped outside to watch. This gave Willie the chance to fly behind her and go inside the manor. He flew behind a huge floral arrangement on the side hall table. "Willie hide," he told himself, shaking and terrified for Kayla.

Michael grabbed her, holding her face and telling her to look at him. She refused, now realizing he would put her into a dream-like state if she did. Tarsula ran over, she placed her hand over Kayla's head and recited the incantation of the Sweet Dreams spell. Kayla immediately fell into a deep slumber. Michael picked her up and carried her into the manor, as Tarsula closed the door behind them locking it.

"Tarsula, I'm going to bring her upstairs to my, I mean our bedroom. I'll tell you what though, I'm going to need a drink real soon."

"What would you like Michael? I can make it for you."

"Scotch over ice. Thanks."

Michael carried Kayla upstairs, as Tarsula went to make his drink. Willie came out from behind the arrangement and followed him. He watched from the doorway, as Michael laid Kayla on the bed. Sitting down beside her, he brushed her face with the back of his hand. Leaning over her, he kissed her cheek gently. This was the perfect moment Willie needed, to come into the room and hide under the bed. Michael stood up walking out of the room, closing the door and locking it. Watching him leave, Willie came out from under the bed and flew to Kayla's side. He tried to wake her numerous times but failed. Flying to the window scared, looking for anything that might help the situation, but he could find nothing. The house was set on such a large piece of land, and it was extremely isolated. Willie returned to Kayla's side hearing the lock of the door being open, he flew behind the curtains. Peeking through, as Michael and Tarsula entered the room.

"How long will she sleep Tarsula?"

"Until I wake her and remove the spell. Does she seem different to you?"

"Different? In what way?"

"I don't know, a little rounder perhaps."

"Tarsula, are you calling the love of my life, chubby?"

"No, not at all. Just a little different that's all." She had noticed a change in Kayla but couldn't quite put her finger on it.

"Alright, remove the spell," demanded Michael. I need sometime alone with her."

"Yes Michael, right away."

After removing the Sweet Dreams spell, Tarsula left. Leaving Michael sitting on the bed stroking Kayla's arm and Willie behind the bedroom curtains. Slowly Kayla became aware of her surroundings. She jumped off the bed running for the door frightened, however Michael got there before her. "Where are you going my love? Why are you running away from me? I love you so much. You had feelings for me once. Do you feel nothing for me now?" He looked at her, waiting for an answer, with lust in his eyes.

"I don't love you Michael, I never did. As far as loving me, I know about Isabella. I saw the painting you had of her in the attic. You only want me because I look like her!" Kayla screamed, trying to get around him.

"How do you know about the painting? How did you get into the attic, that door was always locked?"

"When you locked me in your bedroom at the Christmas party, it didn't lock properly, so I was able to get out. I didn't want you to lock me in your bedroom again. So, I looked around hoping to find the key, and I did near the door. It turned out to be a skeleton key, I used it to open the attic door." Kayla knew it was Willie that had set her free and showed her the portrait of Isabella. However, she wanted to protect Willie at all costs, not wanting Michael to seek vengeance upon him.

"Kayla, you are more than just someone who resembles Isabella. You have her soul, you are the reincarnation of her."

Kayla tried to push Michael aside once more, but he grabbed her, taking her back to the bed. "Kayla! I've told you time and time again that you're mine! No one else will have you, especially that little fuck Peter! Do you understand?" Michael yelled, frustrated with her. He walked out closing the door and locking it. Kayla sat on the

bed and cried. Willie came out from behind the curtains. He flew
to Kayla, sitting down on her lap. At first, she didn't realize he was
there. Willie pulled on her shirt sleeve to get her attention.

"Willie? Willie! How did you get here?" she asked, wiping the
tears from her face.

"Willie follow," he answered looking up at her.

"Oh my God. I'm so happy to see you." Willie flew up and
landed on her shoulder. He touched her face with his small clawlike
hand. "Willie, do you know where we are? Can you get help?"

Willie hung his head down, they were so far away from town.
He didn't think he could find the way back to Kayla's house. The
corners of his mouth turned down, like he was on the verge of crying.
"That's okay Willie, we'll find a way out of here. You must keep
out of sight when Michael or Tarsula come around. Hide, do you
understand?" Willie nodded his head yes. "Okay good." Kayla
replied. They heard the key unlocking the door. "Willie hide!" Kayla
whispered.

Willie flew back under the bed, as Michael walked into the
room. "I've brought you something to eat. I hope you're hungry."
Kayla was hungry, very much so, eating for three now. Michael
placed the tray on a desk, moving the chair out for her to sit down.
The food looked and smelled delicious. A large portion of salmon,
rice, and broccoli sat on the plate. Along with a basket of assorted
rolls with butter. There was also a bottle of her favorite wine and a
glass. Kayla looked at the wine, she told herself she wouldn't drink
any alcohol until the babies were born. "Michael, do you have ginger
ale or something like that?"

"Kay, I bought you everything you love. Your favorite meal,
and your favorite white wine."

"Can I have some water instead?" asked Kayla.

Michael looked at her and thought, why doesn't she want to
drink the wine? She does look a little rounder than I remember. "I'll
get you some water, I'll be right back."

"Willie, here take this food." Kayla had placed a little of

everything on a napkin for him and placed it under the bed. Michael walked back into the room with Tarsula. "Hello Kayla, long time no see," Tarsula said smiling. Kayla did not answer her back but continued to eat her food.

"Kayla." Michael said, hoping she would look up at him, which she did. He watched as her eyes glazed over putting her into trance state. "Go ahead Tarsula."

Tarsula put her hands on Kayla's head, and recited the Truth Be Told spell. "What is your name dear?" Tarsula asked.

"Kayla Conrad." Willie stopped eating, hearing what was taking place.

"Go ahead Michael, she's all yours."

"Kayla, are you with child?" Michael and Tarsula waited for her response.

"Yes. I am." Michael was stunned; this was something he wasn't expecting.

"Who's the father of the baby?" Inquired Tarsula.

"Peter."

"What the fuck Kayla!" Michael was beside himself with anger. "Tarsula I want you to kill this baby before it's born. Do you have a spell for that?"

"Oh, I'm sure I can find one." Tarsula was relishing at the thought of killing Peter's baby.

"And also, Michael." Kayla replied.

Michael and Tarsula just looked at each other. "Did she just say Michael?" He asked Tarsula, not sure if he was hearing right.

"Kayla, did you just say Michael?" Tarsula repeated the question.

"Yes. I'm having twins. I believe one baby is Peter's and one is Michael's."

"Tarsula, could this be possible? She is having Peter's child as well as my own?"

"I suppose it can happen. If she was having sex with Peter and you at roughly the same time, and two of her eggs were released.

Peter could have fertilized one egg and you the other."

"Shit! So, I guess killing one of the babies is out of the question."

"We could kill them both, then you can start over. That's an idea," Tarsula suggested, with an evil grin on her face.

"Let me think about it. I'll let you know Tarsula."

Tarsula left the room and closed the door. Michael ordered Kayla to stand up and undress. He wanted to look at her body naked. He sat down on the bed as she stood before him. Her breasts were slightly larger, and her stomach protruded outward slightly. He wrapped his arms around her body holding her tightly. Michael got up and got a robe out of the closet, telling her to put it on. He picked her up in his arms and laid Kayla on the bed. He needed to think. Walking out of the room, he closed the door and locked it. Willie flew out from underneath the bed; he sat beside Kayla waiting for her to wake up. Then flew to the inside of her arm, lying next to her and watching. Willie's mind was swimming with thoughts of how to get them out of there, a plan was needed. If he only had some help, but no one knew where they were. Willie kissed her cheek, just as she was coming out of Michael's trance.

CHAPTER EIGHT

WHERE'S KAYLA?

Peter called Kayla's phone for the fourth time; she wasn't picking up. Maybe she's with Emily he thought, calling Emily's number he waited for her to pick up.

"Hey Peter, how's the teachers conference going?"

"Good Em, is Kayla with you? I've been trying to call her and she's not picking up."

"No, maybe she went shopping and forgot her phone. I've done that numerous times."

"Em, do you think you could go to my house and check up on her? I know it's a lot to ask.

"Don't be ridiculous, of course I'll go over, I'll take Simon with me. Don't worry, I'm sure she's fine. I'll call you back."

"Alright, thanks Em."

"Come on Simon, we're going to Peter's house."

* * *

Bradford Cummings sat in his car watching Kayla's house. He had followed her home from work one evening, wondering why she wasn't at the mansion with Michael? Did they breakup? He was watching and waiting for the opportunity to grab her. Kayla's car was in the driveway, so she had to be home. Unless someone picked her up or she went for a walk through the neighborhood. Bradford noticed a car pulling up to the house. It was Emily and some guy, they walked to the front door and rang the bell, waiting and trying to look through the windows. They walked down the front stairs and around to the back of the house, he lost sight of them. When they came back to the front of the house, Bradford noticed that Emily seemed upset. She was on her phone talking to someone. Did something happen to Kayla? Or was she still with Michael after all? Bradford put the car into drive, he was heading back to The Stone Manor.

* * *

Kayla woke up staring at Willie's tiny face. It made her smile, knowing what a true friend he was. She got up and ran over to the window, there was no way to climb down. Tears formed in her eyes thinking about Peter and how worried he must be. "There has to be a way out of here Willie. I just need time to think." Willie smiled at her and jumped onto her shoulder. Then the sound of the door unlocking could be heard, "Willie hide!" she whispered, with panic in her voice. Willie flew behind the curtains as Michael walked in.

"How are you feeling now that you've eaten, little momma?"

"What did you call me?"

"I believe you heard me. I know your body Kayla, every curve, every scar, every beauty mark. Did you think I wouldn't have seen the change in you? I also know you are carrying twins, and one of them is mine."

"How do you know all that?"

"I have a friend called Tarsula, remember? She wants to kill both of the babies, so we can wipe the slate clean and start over. After all I don't know which baby is mine and I can't stand the thought of Peter's baby inside you."

"Michael please, if you truly love me as you say, don't let her touch me. I'll do anything. Please!" Kayla was crying hysterically, frightened of what Tarsula might do to her. Michael walked over to her wrapping his arms around her trying to calm her down. "Listen Kay, I will make sure you and the babies are safe, as long as you do what I ask of you. After all, one of those babies is mine. I would hate to see anything happen to him or her. Now, I'm going to take a shower, and you will be joining me, right?"

* * *

Peter called Sergeant Daniels cell phone. "Hello Peter, is everything okay?"

"Sergeant Daniels, Kayla is missing. I'm at a teacher's conference but I'm leaving now. I have been trying to call her, but she's not picking up. I had Emily go to the house, Kayla's car is in the driveway and Emily saw her purse on the kitchen table along with her cell phone. You know Kayla, she would never forget her phone. I just know something bad has happened to her!"

"Okay Peter, let's not get ahead of ourselves. How long will it take you to get home?"

"A couple of hours."

"Will you be home by ten?"

"Yes, if I don't hit traffic."

"I'll come there. I've forgotten your address, text it to me. Let's not panic, okay?" Daniels suggested, trying his best to calm Peter down.

"Okay, I'll see you shortly. Thanks sergeant."

* * *

Kayla stood in the shower, as the water and Michael caressed her naked body. She no longer tingled from the touch of his hands. Once upon a time, Kayla craved having sex with him, like an alcoholic craves booze. Now, there was nothing but a dull numbness going through her. She braced herself, holding both hands up to the tiled wall, as he fucked her from behind. Kayla stared at the wall, trying to figure out a way to kill him and Tarsula.

Willie looked into the bathroom, but he did not watch for very long. He hated Michael and everything he stood for. He sat in the corner of the bedroom and cried, knowing he was mistreating Kayla. That was something he wasn't going to stand for.

Coming out of the shower. Kayla put on her robe, as Michael wrapped a towel around his waist. "You'll find some PJ's in the

86

dresser over there. Put on the black satin ones, they're my favorite. Tarsula also bought you jeans, tee shirts, and sweaters. We stocked up on all the essentials, everything a girl could want. Of course, we weren't expecting you to be pregnant. So, another shopping trip is in the future I suppose. If you're a good girl, tomorrow I will give you a tour of the mansion I bought you. I think you're going to love it." Kayla looked around the bedroom, she was wondering where Willie was. She spotted him hiding behind the open bathroom door. Kayla smiled at him; she could tell he was upset.

Michael put his pajama bottoms on. He walked over to Kayla, who was now wearing head to toe black satin. "I'm going downstairs for a night cap; I'd ask you if you want one, but I guess not in your condition. I'll have Tarsula make you a cup of decaf tea, don't worry, I'll drink some in front of you. You never know with Tarsula." Michael laughed. "Sorry Kay bad joke, seriously you're safe here. I've missed you; I'll be right back." Michael stepped out closing and locking the bedroom door.

Willie flew over to Kayla landing on her shoulder. His small, clawed hand caressed her face. Kayla and Willie heard a sound coming from the closet door. Walking over, they saw a fine mist was permeating from underneath it. It flowed into the room, as Kayla and Willie stepped back. The mist moved and swirled eventually taking the shape of a man. Something fell out of the mist falling onto the bedroom floor, a badge. Michael was unlocking the door, as Kayla picked up the badge and quickly threw it into the nightstand drawer. The mist fell back under the door, gone in seconds, as Willie hid himself once again.

"Here you are my love, a nice cup of tea." Michael placed the tea on a table, but he could tell Kayla was hesitant about drinking it. He smiled at her. "Alright Kay, I'll drink some myself, see, it's good." Kayla sipped the tea, while looking around for Willie. He was fast, she could never tell where he was hiding within the room.

* * *

Peter arrived home, he ran to the front door not bothering to

87

remove his belongings from the trunk of his car. "Kayla!" He looked everywhere within the house. "Kayla! Willie!" The house was dead quiet. Peter walked outside to wait for Daniels, he blamed himself for leaving her. Daniels car pulled into the driveway as Peter ran over to him.

"Sergeant! Kayla and Willie are gone! Willie came for a visit just as I was leaving. Now both of them are gone!"

They heard cars pulling up in front of Peter's house. Emily and Simon along with Max and Jeanna, parked their cars and ran over to them. Followed shortly after by Sam and Mary. "What's going on Daniels?" asked Sam.

"That's what we need to find out." Daniels replied. "Emily, when was the last time you spoke to Kayla?"

"At work today, she seemed fine, her usual self. Where could she be sergeant?" Emily started to cry, very upset her friend was missing. "I'm praying nothing bad has happened to her and the baby."

"Did you say baby?" inquired Sergeant Daniels.

"Yes everyone, we wanted to surprise all of you. Kayla is pregnant with twins." Peter acknowledged.

"Oh my God, twins Peter." Sam replied, as he wiped the tears off his face. "We have to find her sergeant!"

"We will. I'm going to put out a missing person's report, ASAP. The sooner we start looking for her, the better. Peter, do you have a recent photo of Kayla?" As everyone went inside, Peter walked over to a framed picture which was placed on the coffee table. It was a recent photograph, of Kayla smiling and looking beautiful, he handed it to Daniels "Come down to the station first thing in the morning Peter, we'll have her face plastered all over town. Someone must have seen something, see you tomorrow. Everyone try and get some rest tonight. Believe me I will do everything I can to find her." Daniels walked to his car and left, as everyone else stayed, not wanting Peter to be left alone.

* * *

Bradford comings sat in the woods watching the manor. He was hoping to catch a glimpse of Kayla through the windows. He needed to know if she was in there. With the cover of night, he made his way to the house. Cautiously looking through the downstairs windows, he saw Tarsula rummaging about the house, but not Michael, nor Kayla. They must be upstairs he thought, walking to the back of the house Bradford tried to peer inside. However, the windows were covered with thick draperies. Standing there for a moment and seeing nothing, he decided to go back into the woods. Totally pissed off that the night was a big waste of time. Starting his car, he drove home. "I'll get her." Bradford told himself. "Sooner or later, I'll get her."

* * *

Kayla sat in an overstuffed wingback chair, staring at the floor, as Willie hid behind the leg of the bed. "Are you going to sit there all night?" Michael asked. "The bed is a lot more comfortable. You know this is the time when I'm usually out and about, instead I'm here with you. Don't you want to lay down next to me Kayla?" Michael got up, walking over to her, he physically picked her up and placed her in the bed. Walking to the other side he climbed in, laying down next to her and placing his hand on her stomach. "I can't believe a piece of me is growing inside of you. It makes me horny just thinking about it." Michael whispered, in her ear, as his hand traveled down between her thighs. He caressed her there, as he licked and kissed her neck. Kayla removed his hand and turned away from him. "I guess you're tired, so I'll let you rest. Sex in the morning is always better anyway." Michael informed her, climbing out of bed and getting dressed. He walked out the door, closing and locking it behind him.

Kayla reached over, opening the nightstand's drawer. She picked up the badge she had found earlier. It was a detective's badge with the number twenty-eight engraved on it. Willie flew over to take a closer look. "This is a badge Willie, a detective's badge, it came out of that mist." Willie touched it with his tiny, clawed finger. Kayla placed it back into the drawer covering it with some folded sheets. She walked into the bathroom rolling up a towel and placing it under the bed. "Here Willie, sleep on this, and stay out of sight. Okay?" "Willie hide." He said, as he flew under the bed and landed on the soft rolled up towel.

* * *

In the morning, pictures of Kayla were plastered all over town. Many of the towns' people knew her from the café. Sergeant Daniels was combing the streets asking if anyone had seen her yesterday evening. It was getting late in the day, as he walked past a group of young teenage boys, all sitting on their bikes and fooling around. Daniels approached them.

"Did anyone of you see this woman yesterday?" They all shook their heads no, with the exception of one teenage boy.

"Yeah, that's Kayla, I know her. I kind of have a crush on her," he said, as his buddies laughed at him. "She's always so friendly with me. I saw her getting into a car with some blonde guy, he was kind of nasty. I thought she was acting weird cause when I said hi to her, she didn't respond, her eyes looked kind of funny too. His car was nice though, a Mercedes Benz, I think it was this year's model. An EQE 350 4 matic. I know cars, that thing is worth buku dollars. You don't often see a car like that around here."

"What's your name kid?" Daniels asked.

"Thomas" he answered.

"I'm Sergeant Daniels, you've been very helpful Thomas."

With that Thomas pulled out his cellphone. "See sergeant, I even took a picture of the car, look." Daniels took the phone, it was a great picture of the car, but more importantly it showed the license plate clear as day.

"I could kiss you kid." Daniels remarked, taking out his cell and forwarding the picture. He couldn't wait to get back to the station and run the plates, which he did. Turns out the plates had been reported stolen a week ago. The owner of the car was getting ready to leave for work, when he noticed his plates missing. Realizing, someone must have taken them in the middle of the night. Daniels placed his head in his hands and exhaled. At least now, he knew the make of the car and what it looked like. He would put out an APB, hoping the car would be seen by someone.

* * *

Kayla woke up in the middle of the night looking beside her, but Michael was not in bed. She jumped up running to the bedroom door, praying it would be unlocked. To her disappointment, it was locked up tight. She heard movement coming from inside the closet, the doorknob was moving. Willie woke up, hearing Kayla moving around the room. He flew onto Kayla's shoulder, as she stepped away from the closet door. The mist was back turning and moving into the room. Something was thrown in her direction. Kayla looked down; it was a badge. The same one she had previously placed in the nightstand drawer. She picked it up, running to the drawer and searching for it underneath the sheets, but it was gone. Turning around, she noticed the mist had taken form, into the shape of a man. Willie hid under her hair frightened. Kayla would have screamed, but having seen it once before, she was more fascinated than horrified. It moved closer to her, K a y l a; it spoke her name slowly, in a calm whisper. Did it just say my name? She thought, listening, it said her name once more.

"Who or what are you?" Kayla asked, as Willie peeked out from under her hair.

The badge she held in her hand suddenly vanished, as a face emerged from the mist. A face that seemed familiar to her. Kayla thought of the badge, it said detective number 28. She watched the face as it became more defined. "Detective Roberts, is that you?" It answered, "yes here to help."

"Detective Roberts? How is this possible? I saw what Michael did to you that day. He can change into a hawk detective; he was the hawk that killed you! Can you help get us out of here?" Willie flew up into the room, he was no longer afraid, realizing this mist thing seemed to be a friend of Kayla's.

91

"Look up," is all it said.

They heard the sound of the floorboards outside the room, Michael was coming. Willie hid himself, as the mist quickly left, exiting back into the closet. Kayla jumped onto the bed, pretending to be asleep as Michael walked into the room. He walked over to her, she could feel his eyes gazing at her, as he leaned down kissing her cheek. Moving to his side of the bed he got in, laying down next to her. He placed his arm over her waist, laying his hand on her belly. It took all the willpower Kayla had, not to push his hand away. Her thoughts went to Detective Roberts, what did he mean by look up? Kayla turned her head, to look up at the ceiling of the room. Not understanding what Roberts was trying to convey. She watched as the night turned into day, shining through a slight opening in the curtain.

Michael rubbed Kayla's stomach. "Good morning darling, let's go downstairs for breakfast. I'm sure you're tired of being in this room. After we eat, I'll give you the grand tour of your new home." They got out of bed and Kayla put on her robe. Michael unlocked the door, putting his arm around her as they exited the bedroom. Willie followed through the open doorway. The house was extremely dark since all of the windows were covered. There were lamps set about here and there illuminating certain areas.

Tarsula was sitting in the dining room, eating at an enormous table. Above her, hung a huge crystal chandelier, facets of light bounced around the room. She watched as Michael and Kayla entered; her eyes peering up, over her coffee cup.

"Nice of you to join us this morning Kayla, help yourself to whatever."

Walking over to the buffet Kayla fixed herself a plate, taking a little of everything offered pancakes, eggs, and sausage. She poured a large glass of orange juice, carrying her breakfast over, Kayla sat down at the opposite end of the table. Michael sat down next to her with a grin on his face. Thinking it was funny, that Kayla tried to sit as far away as possible from Tarsula. He was drinking something that looked like orange juice, except it had a red tint to it. Kayla suddenly felt the need to throw up, asking where the bathroom was. Michael immediately got up, taking her by the arm and out of the dining room. Willie came out of his hiding spot quickly, not wanting Tarsula to see him. He crawled under the dining room area rug, waiting for Kayla to return.

"Feeling better?" Michael asked, holding her around the waist as he escorted her back to the dining room table. They sat back down as Kayla felt a tug on her robe, she suspected it was Willie. Dropping her fork, a quick glance under the table confirmed her suspicion. There he was smiling at her patting his belly, in need of food. Michael got up walking over to the buffet, as Kayla kept a close eye on Tarsula, throwing pieces of her breakfast down to Willie. Sitting back down at the table, Michael's plate was loaded with food. He placed his hand on Kayla's thigh rubbing it up and down, while Willie watched wanting to bite him, as he ate his bits of sausage and egg.

CHAPTER NINE

TINA ABRUZZI

Tina Abruzzi woke up to the sound of her husband's alarm clock. Normally, Dominick would let her sleep, but this morning he was feeling frisky. Reaching over he fondled her tits, kissing her neck lustfully. Tina inhaled and exhaled deeply. Not because she was getting turned on, but because she was impatient to get it over with. She lifted up her tee shirt exposing her breasts and let him have at it. A moment later he was pulling down her underwear and laying on top of her. As he fucked her, Tina thought about Michael. Fantasizing, that he was the one making love to her, still seeing his handsome face and tall well-built body. She closed her eyes wrapping her legs around her husband's waist. With every thrust, Tina wondered what Michael would feel like inside her. When he was finished, which didn't take long, Dominick walked into the master bathroom to shower. Tina got out of bed walking herself into the upstairs hall bathroom, where she kept a variety of sex toys to finish the job.

Tina made up her mind, she would go to see Michael today but needed an excuse to go back to the manor. Walking downstairs to the kitchen Tina had an idea. She could say her expensive scarf was lost. Perhaps it had fallen off in the foyer, when she delivered the gift basket, yes that could work. Tina made the coffee as Dominick strolled into the kitchen. "Did you enjoy this morning? I could tell that you did, maybe tonight we can do a replay? I've got to run; I'll pick up something to eat on my way to work." Dominick kissed Tina on her cheek and left.

Sitting there, coffee cup in hand, she would leave Dom in a second, if someone offered her something better. Someone like Michael perhaps? I bet he could satisfy me totally, she thought. I'll run over later today. Hopefully he will answer the door and not that woman Tar,… Tar,… whatever her name is.

* * *

After Michael's tour of the house, he sat down in the living room with Kayla. He wanted to know what she thought about the manor. "So darling, what do you think? Is it everything you could hope for?" She did not answer him. Instead, she looked around the room hoping to see Willie, but he was very small and could easily hide himself. "Kayla! When I'm speaking to you, I need you to answer me."

"The house is nice, I suppose. It doesn't have an atrium though."

"An atrium," Michael responded. "Is that what you want, my love? We can put one in, after all we're going to be here for a very long time and I want you to be happy."

Kayla turned to face Michael. "Do you know what would make me happy? If someone took a stake and rammed it through your fucking heart!"

Michael became enraged. He grabbed Kayla by her shoulders, lifting her up and shaking her hard. "I would try to be nice to me, if I were you. That's if you want those babies of yours to ever see the light of day! You ungrateful little bitch!" Michael placed her back down onto the sofa, stepping away from her, trying to calm himself down.

Kayla noticed Willie out of the corner of her eye. She mouthed the word "hide" to him. He flew behind a silver tea set on the credenza, wanting to scratch Michael's eyes out for pushing Kayla around.

Michael took Kayla by the arm bringing her into the library. He held her face in his hands, as Kayla closed her eyes tightly.

"Open your eyes love" Michael insisted. "Open your fucking eyes." Kayla opened her eyes, as Michael put her into a trance state. "Now, take off your clothes Kayla." Michael walked over closing and locking the library door keeping Tarsula out and also without his knowledge, Willie.

Willie flew around the door frame to try to get into the room, but the door was solid. He flew up onto a wall sconce, hiding within it and waited.

Michael ran his eyes up and down Kayla's naked body. "You've been a very naughty girl, Kayla. I'm going to fuck you like a real man, not like that little boy toy of yours Peter." Kayla was in a deep trance; all of her protective walls were down. She could only feel the sensation of touch, not sure where it was coming from or by whom. Michael reached for her, cupping her breasts in his hands. Kayla's breath became heavy, as she became sexually aroused. "Get on your knees sweetheart, place my cock in your mouth, I need you to please me." This is how it should be Michael thought. Kayla giving me pleasure and loving me. Looking down at her, it didn't take long, for his cock to become rock hard. He asked Kayla to stand and then to sit down on the sofa. Bringing his hand down to her pussy, he fingered her, until she was wet. He sat down on a leather sofa and asked Kayla to straddle him, she followed his command. Moans of pleasure escaped from her lips. "That's my girl, see you really do love me." Michael loved watching her during sex. He sucked her nipples and fondled her breasts. Feeling he might come, he repositioned her. "Kayla kneel on the sofa, show me that lovely ass of yours." He stood behind her, penetrating her once again. Holding onto her waist and moving his hips with hers, he came deep inside her. Pulling out, Michael commanded Kayla to clean him off with her tongue, she placed his limp member into her mouth.

At that moment, unexpectedly Kayla awakened, as she came out of Michael's trance. Aware of what she was doing, she bit down hard onto his cock. Blood filled her mouth as she spit it out. Michael screamed! "You fucking bitch!" He picked her up, throwing her onto the sofa, bending over in excruciating pain holding himself. Kayla got up running to put on her clothes, as Michael attended to his badly bitten manhood. The head was bleeding profusely, with deep bite marks. He grabbed his underwear, wrapping it tightly around his badly bitten dick. Sitting down on the sofa, he would only have to endure the pain briefly, as his injury would heal within minutes.

He waited, and after the pain subsided, Michael put on his jeans and unlocked the door. Kayla made a run for it, but only got as far as the foyer. Tarsula and Tina Abruzzi turned to look at them. Kayla was shocked to see another person. "Help! Help Me!" she screamed. Michael quickly put her into trance state once again. "Kiss me Kay, like you mean it," he whispered to her. "Now, grab hold of my ass." Kayla placed her hands on Michael's ass and kissed his lips, like he was the only man left on the planet. "Now take my hand and follow me into the back room," he softly whispered to her.

"Wow, what was all that about? That's a lot of passion." Tina remarked, jealous and wanting some of that for herself.

"Oh, Michael and his fiancé, they're always fooling around." Tarsula replied. "I'm used to it."

Michael came back into the foyer. "Hello Tina, what are you doing here?"

"I thought I left my scarf here, when I brought over the gift basket. Was that your fiancé?"

"Ah yeah, we're always fooling around. She likes me to run after her, the damsel in distress kind of thing. It's our version of foreplay, kind of." Michael smiled and winked at Tina. He was turning on the charm in a big way.

"Well, that's different and a little kinky." Tina acknowledged, her face turning red.

"Sorry Tina, I don't believe your scarf is here." Michael commented, looking over at Tarsula.

"Okay, sorry for intruding Michael."

"No worries," Michael said, showing her the door.

"Might I have a look around? I'd love to see what you did

with the place. Just standing here in the foyer, I can tell you have impeccable taste."

"Sorry Tina, It's not a good time. My fiancé is in the back room waiting for me. She's kind of hot and bothered, if you know what I mean." Michael smiled, as he opened the front door for her.

Willie flew to the door where Michael locked up Kayla. Again, there was no way in. He sat down in a planter box, covered by plants, frustrated.

"Tarsula! What the hell! Why did you invite her in?"

"Oh, for Christ's sake Michael, I didn't invite her in, she walked in when I opened the door."

"We may have to do something about her if she keeps coming around. I'm taking Kayla upstairs. Try not to open the door anymore, at least for a while."

Michael walked to the back room. He unlocked the door, taking Kayla by the arm and bringing her upstairs. Willie followed, trying to stay out of sight. Michael laid Kayla down on the bed, he covered her with a blanket, kissing her forehead. Willie flew back in and under the bed, unnoticed. Michael left the room locking the door. Seeing Michael gone, Willie flew out and landed on Kayla's pillow. He watched her sleeping. Hearing a noise from the closet, he tried to wake her. Tapping her shoulder and pulling at her hair, as the mist entered the room. Detective Roberts took form but remained still, he was also waiting for Kayla to come too.

She opened her eyes slowly, noticing the misty form of Detective Roberts standing before her. "Detective Roberts?"

"Yes, here, look up Kayla, up."

Kayla looked up at the ceiling, not quite sure what she was looking for. Then all at once she saw it, the light fixture over the bed. It was forged from wrought iron, ornate and intricate. With naturalistic forms of branches, leaves, and vines, but the part that caught Kayla's eye was the center of it all. The branches and vines ended in a substantial point. Forming the shape of a spear, at least eight inches long. She looked over at the detective.

"Is it the spear, in the middle of the chandelier?" asked Kayla. Willie flew around the room getting excited.

"Yes, very heavy," he whispered. "I will loosen the bolts, the weight should bring it down, then direct it into Michael's chest, his heart."

The floorboard squeaked, as they heard Michael unlocking the door. Willie hid, as the mist fell back into the closet.

"Kayla, I'm glad you're awake. I came up to check on you. I've decided to forgive you for what happened downstairs. Lucky for you I heal quickly. Maybe you lost it for a moment, I'll blame it on your hormones, in your condition and all."

Kayla glanced up at the ceiling for a split second. Yes, she thought, it could be the perfect way to kill him. "Michael, I'm sorry for what I did downstairs. I hope you're alright, please forgive me."

"You're very unpredictable Kayla, that's one of the reasons I find you so attractive." Michael walked over to her, taking her into his arms. "I'll show you the grounds tonight. There's a caretaker's cottage, along with a chapel that you might want to see. It can be very romantic if you give it a chance."

Kayla kissed Michael's lips, with passion. He took the bait, kissing her back and grabbing hold of her ass. Kayla smiled at him, wanting him to think she had a change of heart. However, her mind was racing, thinking of ways to get him in the exact position, underneath the chandelier.

CHAPTER TEN

LIFE GOES ON

Peter needed to go back to work. He had been searching for Kayla day and night. Hoping someone would find her, but now came to the realization, he would only have his evenings to look for her. Leaving the daytime searches for Daniels and the police department, who were constantly combing the streets looking for her. Peter still had bills to pay and was becoming fearful of losing his job, and perhaps his home. Unfortunately, life wasn't going to stop because Kayla went missing. They posted Kayla's picture up all over town, along with an APB on the car that Thomas saw her get into.

* * *

At the café, Sam was working the tables with Emily. It was getting busy again, and though Emily was doing her best, it was a lot for one person to handle. That left Max, handling all of the kitchen duties. Sometimes things would get backed up, leaving Sam running back and forth between the front of the café and the kitchen.

* * *

Bradford Cummings walked through town, staring at the flyers of Kayla everywhere. She's missing? He thought, did someone take her, beating me to the punch? I didn't see her at Michaels house, but she could have been upstairs. Was Kayla being held against her will? Very interesting he thought, I may have to go back there and take another look around.

* * *

Later that night, Dominick came home tired from a long day at work. He walked into the kitchen as Tina was taking a lasagna out of the oven.

"That smells great honey. I know, I promised you a repeat of this morning's sex fest, however I'm exhausted."

"That's understandable, you work hard." Tina was thanking her lucky stars, that there would be no sex tonight. Putting the dinner on the table, her thoughts went to Michael and his fiancé. He definitely turns me on. Tremendously sexy to look at and probably superb in the sheets, she thought, as she served up the lasagna. Looking over at Dominick, she couldn't believe how unfair life was. She was stuck with this very overweight, short, balding husband. While Michael's fiancé was having the best sex ever with an unbelievably, magnificent looking guy.

"I went out to lunch with some of the guys from the office." Dominick said, trying to make conversation. "We ended up going to a café the next town over from work. The food was excellent. Only, I think they were short on help. It took forever to get our lunch, I guess a lot of the locals eat there."

"Oh yeah, what was the name of the place?" Tina asked.

"Perk Up, I think. It probably started as a breakfast place. There were pictures of some girl, posted everywhere. A very pretty girl, apparently, she's missing. It's rather sad, I do hope nothing bad happened to her."

"Yeah, well hopefully someone will find her. I guess she'll have a better chance of being found around here, than if it happened in a big city like New York. In small towns everyone knows everybody you know." Tina responded.

* * *

Michael walked into the bedroom as Kayla stood there in her bra and panties, he grinned. "Don't get dressed on my account, you know I love looking at you."

"Thank you, that's sweet Michael." Kayla wanted to stay in his good graces. Wanting him to believe, she came to her senses and was now going to be his. Walking over to him she kissed him. "How do I look?" Kayla was now wearing a short black leather skirt with a dark grey oversized sweater with large front pockets. These were some of the items that Tarsula had bought for her.

"Fantastic, always fantastic." Michael wrapped his arms around her. "Even with your rounded belly and larger boobs. Don't get me wrong, I'm not complaining about the boobs."

Willie was watching it all from behind the nightstand with a disgusted look on his face. He knew Kayla was faking it, but it left a sour taste in his mouth, as he stuck out his tongue and gave Michael the middle finger, using both of his hands.

"Alright sir," Kayla said. "Let's go downstairs for dinner." Michael gave her his arm, unlocking the bedroom door, as Willie followed behind them.

* * *

Bradford Cummings made the long drive back to Michael's house. He was curious if he was holding Kayla against her will. Parking his car in the usual spot, he walked to the edge of the woods alongside Michael's driveway. Looking over at the manor, the landscape was lit up. A side door to the manor opened, he watched, as Michael and Kayla stepped outside. Walking towards the back of the property, Kayla had her arm around Michael's waist. She didn't seem frightened or wanting to run away. They looked like two lovers going for a late-night stroll together. Bradford was confused, was she being held against her will or not? Why was everyone looking for her, if she was there by choice? Stepping out he walked towards the house, following them but staying out of sight.

Michael held Kayla's hand, kissing it occasionally. "This is the chapel, it needs work, but it would make a great summer house."

"A summer house, what's that exactly?"

Michael looked at her and smiled. "Sorry, I forgot you're not British. It's usually a room outside where people can sit and enjoy a summer's day. However, I'm afraid I would only be enjoying it, in the evening hours. Let me show you the caretaker's cottage, it's small

102

and very quaint." They walked together to the cottage. Michael unlocked the door and they stepped inside.

Willie had managed to find a window in the manor that was slightly open. He cut out the screen with his tiny claws. Flying towards the back of the house in search of Kayla. Flying high amongst the top of the trees to keep out of sight.

Bradford watched as they entered the cottage. Should he dare investigate? He desperately wanted to, approaching the window in the rear of the building, he peered inside.

"So, Kay, what do you think? Not bad right? It just needs a little cleaning up." Michael remarked, pulling a sheet off the sofa.

"I like it, most of the furniture looks new." Kayla stated, lifting up sheets and looking under them.

"Come here, sit next to me." Michael sat down on the sofa and patted the cushion alongside him. He placed his arm around her, bringing her close to him. "I'm glad you've come to see the light Kayla. I'm going to turn you, but I'll wait till you're ready. You will stay as you are, forever beautiful. You will never want for anything." Michael looked into her eyes, but he did not put her under his trance. He kissed her, as his hand started to glide up her leg, to the inside of her skirt. Bradford looked on, wanting to see what would happen next.

"No Michael not here, let's go back to the house, our bed will be a lot more comfortable."

Michael kissed her again, as his hand caressed her breast. "Alright my love, if that's what you wish. I have a surprise for you when we get there, I'm hoping you will enjoy it." He had visions, of making love to her on the fur rug in front of the fireplace. While Kayla had visions, of getting Michael into the exact position that was needed to kill him, underneath the chandelier.

Willie flew above the care takers cottage; he watched as a man looked into its windows. He didn't know who he was, but he was sure this guy was up to no good. Willie watched as Kayla and Michael exited the building, he had to let them know they were being observed. Breaking a small branch off a tree, he flew down, hitting it against one of the back windows. Bradford swatted at Willie, who flew around him continuing to bang on the window hard. Hearing the commotion, Michael and Kayla walked around to the back of the cottage, as Bradford's body began shifting. Willie flew up into the trees, but was fearful for Kayla's safety. Bradford was spotted, as Michael became enraged. He yelled for Kayla to go back to the house. She stepped back slowly watching in horror, as Bradford became a monstrous wolflike creature. Michael also started to change into something she had never seen before. He started to grow tall, his hands elongated, covered in fur, ears protruded off the top of his head. His eyes glowed with a tint of purple, as fangs emerged from his mouth and gigantic wings protruded from his shoulder blades. Half Vampire, half werewolf, Michael had morphed into his own being. Willie flew down pulling on Kayla's jacket, "follow Kay la, follow Willie." Kayla grabbed him, placing him in one of her front pockets and ran. Though, not back towards the house, she ran in the opposite direction through the woods. Bradford also ran, not willing to fight.

Michael Chanted to Tarsula to get Kayla, as he began to fight Bradford. Tarsula had just finished a box of chocolate, when she got the Chant. Running out the front door, she looked around but did not see Kayla. Tarsula stopped, bringing forth her third eye, it allowed her to see an overhead view of the property, as if she was standing in pure daylight. Seeing Kayla running through the woods. Tarsula, shape shifted into a large panther and ran after her. Bradford let out a loud howl, as Michael jumped on him. He fell backwards, hitting the ground hard, trying to get up quickly, but the creature Michael had turned into was larger and pinned him down. He bit at Bradford's neck, tearing off pieces of furry flesh. Bradford was able to get in one strong swipe across Michael's face, as Michael flew upwards, his giant bat wings taking flight. Bradford started to run; he needed to get out of there. Michael flew after him, he was planning his attacks from above. He plummeted, clawing and biting at Bradford's back and head. Flying up to the treetops he was ready to strike once more, but this time Bradford was ready for him. He reached up grabbing hold of Michael by his neck, picking up a rock and smashing it into the side of his skull. Stunned, Michael flew up into the dark sky, trying to recover from the blow as Bradford ran. The thought of chasing after him crossed Michael's mind, but his priority right now was Kayla.

Kayla made it to the road just as an old pick-up was going by, she jumped out from the darkness in front of it. The driver swerved to avoid hitting her, coming to a complete stop across the road and ending up in a field. Kayla ran to it, telling Willie to remain hidden. "I need a ride please! Someone is after me. Please!" The man leaned over and unlocked the door, Kayla jumped in. "Thank you! Thank you so much!" Suddenly, out of the corner of her eye Kayla saw it, as did the driver of the pick-up truck. It appeared as a shadow at first, coming from the woods. Darker than any black, Kayla had ever seen. A huge cat emerged from the shadows. "Drive! Drive!" She screamed, as the man put his truck into drive putting the pedal down to the floor. The truck remained stationary, as the back wheels spun, caught in a massive pile of dirt and mud. He quickly put the truck in reverse, hoping the wheels would catch.

"Jesus Christ lady, is that a panther? Where the hell did that thing come from?"

"Yes, hell would be correct!" Kayla answered back.

After a few tries, the wheels finally took hold, sending the pickup hurtling backwards. Putting on the brakes, he shifted into drive. As Tarsula jumped onto the hood of the truck. The good Samaritan told Kayla to hold on and buckle up, he floored it and then applied the brakes. Sending Tarsula flying off the hood and onto the road.

By this time, Michael was flying towards the truck, he could see Tarsula had changed herself into an enormous panther. That a girl Tarsula, he thought, as he flew past the pickup and then turned around and flew directly towards the truck's windshield. Michael landed on the truck, his talons cracking the windshield, as his enormous wings flapped. Kayla screamed, placing one hand over her face and one over her pocket, trying to keep Willie safe. The man panicked, horrified he screamed, losing control of his truck. He drove off the road and into a tree, as a branch came through the cracked windshield impaling and killing him instantly. Kayla also hit her head and was knocked unconscious, as a small amount of blood trickled down her forehead.

Michael and Tarsula changed back into their human forms, approaching the truck. He needed to be sure that Kayla was alright. Michael instructed Tarsula to watch her, as he changed again into a hawk, flying back to the manor to get his car. Willie peeked out of Kayla's front pocket, flying up to look out of the truck's side window. He could see Tarsula standing there. When her back was turned, he flew through the cracked windshield and into the tree above them. Coming back, Michael removed Kayla from the pickup, laying her down in the back seat of his car. He drove quickly away, as Willie followed trying to keep up. Willie was swift, but not as fast as Michael's Mercedes. However, he knew he could get back inside, through the open window and the screen he had cut out with his claws.

Michael lifted Kayla out of the car, bringing her inside and up to the bedroom. Laying her down, he got a wet towel from the bathroom. "Her forehead is cut." Michael said, wiping the blood off Kayla's forehead and face. "I think she'll be okay. How does it look to you, Tarsula?"

"She'll be fine. She may have a headache for a few days and quite a bump. So, that's what she gets for trying to run away."

"Yeah, hopefully she has learned her lesson." Michael looked at her lovingly and kissed her forehead. He could taste the small amount of blood that was left there. He moved away from her quickly, as the urge to bite her overcame him. Exiting the bedroom, the thought of changing her crossed his mind, but decided against it. It would happen soon enough when the time was right.

CHAPTER ELEVEN
THE SEEKERS JOIN THE SEARCH

Peter came home from a long night of searching with Sergeant Daniels. He needed a strong drink and a good night's sleep in that order. Approaching his house, he noticed two tall gentlemen standing on his front lawn. They were wearing hats, gloves, and long dark coats. Peter thought that was odd since it was nearly April, and the weather had been relatively warm. Parking his car, he walked over to them hesitantly.

"May I help you?" he asked, keeping some distance from them. The tallest of the two took off his hat.

"Hello, my son."

"Dad?" Peter ran to him, embracing his father Zadoc.

"We came in search of Willie. He did not come back to us, in the light." Zadoc acknowledged.

"He's missing along with Kayla, we've been searching for them non- stop for days." Peter said, on the verge of tears, "she's pregnant with twins, my babies. Can you help me find them?"

" I had no idea you were going to be a father, felicitations my son. My heart is with you always. However, our power is healing, not search and rescue I'm afraid. Still, I will do what I can to help. May we enter your home?"

"Oh, I'm so sorry, of course."

They walked inside. "Peter, I would like to introduce you to my friend and comrade, Azulon."

"Nice to meet you, Azulon." Peter extended his hand.

"The pleasure is mine Peter. Your father thinks very highly of you." Azulon replied.

"We came because Willie did not come back to us. We did not know that Kayla was also missing. The bond between them is strong, I'm sure they must be together," remarked Zadoc.

"Yes," Peter concurred, "I think so too."

Zadoc, put his hand on Peter's shoulder. "We have many seekers, here on your planet. Is there a photo of her, that I may scan?"

Peter looked at him strangely, not quite sure what he was talking about. "Yes, I guess." Peter handed him the picture of Kayla smiling.

Zadoc held the picture up to his face. A tiny beam of white light shown from his eyes. He moved his head, motioning up and down, as the light traveled along the photograph scanning it. "Alright my son, I have scanned her photo. Her picture lies within my brain waves, which I will send out to all of the Seekers telepathically. They will all know her face and will be able to search for her and Willie."

"You can do that? Look at a picture and send it out through your brain waves. Jesus! That makes my cell phone camera seem ancient." Peter said, looking down at his phone and shaking his head in disgust.

"Well," Azulon chimed in. "I'm sorry to say we are a lot more advanced than the people of Earth." Azulon was gloating with the knowledge, that he was part of a much more highly intelligent race.

"We must go now Peter, give me a hug son. I will let you know if any of the seekers see or hear anything. May we use your yard to beam back, our navigation system is set for that location."

"Of course, I'll walk you out." Peter, Zadoc, and Azulon stepped into the backyard. Zadoc asked Peter to stand by the house, as a beam descended from the night sky. Gone in a flash, as Peter stood there in awe, as to what had just taken place.

* * *

As time went on each person was missing Kayla in their own

way. Sam and Mary sat in their living room, going over the details for their upcoming nuptials. Sam was feeling a deep sadness, getting married without Kayla attending the ceremony. She was like a daughter to him, always there whenever he needed her. If there was a free moment away from the café, he would ride around looking for her. It was also hitting him hard, as to what Peter was going through. He owed him big time, bringing back Mary. Somehow, it didn't feel right to celebrate without them. Sam thought about cancelling the wedding, but everything was set and ready to go. Looking at Mary, she was beside herself with joy and happiness. He couldn't take that away from her. Sam felt stuck between a rock and a hard place.

Emily cried herself to sleep almost every night since Kayla's disappearance. How could she just disappear without a trace? Never thinking in her wildest dreams that something like this could happen in their town. Simon did his best to comfort her, as the days went by without a clue.

Max would go into work, upset most mornings. They needed to do more to find her, he thought. He truly missed Kayla, as the workday progressed, he would look up from cooking expecting to see her running back and forth as she did. He missed joking around and teasing her. Kayla always had a clever comeback putting Max in his place, she made the day fly by for him.

* * *

The next day, Kayla woke up with a major headache. Reaching up and touching her forehead, she could feel a large bump had formed. She remembered being inside the truck and going off the road, hitting her head on something. Was it a tree branch? Immediately, she looked around for Willie. "Willie," she whispered. "Willie, where are you?" Kayla lay back down staring at the ceiling. How long was I out for, she wondered?

Hearing Michael unlocking the bedroom door, she closed her eyes. He walked in carrying a tray of food, sitting it down on the desk. "Kayla, you've got to wake up now and eat something." He approached her side of the bed. "Kayla, wake up love." Kayla opened her eyes, mostly because she smelled the food and was hungry. Michael sat down on the bed, running his hand down the side of her face. Kayla looked in his direction, but not exactly into his eyes. Watching as Willie came through the open door of the bedroom, flying underneath the bed. Thank God, Kayla thought, he's okay.

"That wasn't very nice, running away like that." Michael informed her. "Now a guy is dead and it's your fault. I thought we had come to some understanding that this is your home now." Kayla started to cry, realizing that the man who had picked her up was dead. Michael put his arm around her shoulder trying to console her, she detested his touch. "I brought you some food, try to eat something, I'll check on you later." Michael walked out locking the door and placing the key in his back pocket. He thought it would be much more convenient than taking it on and off his neck numerous times a day.

Willie flew up landing on the tray of food. He began to eat savagely, very hungry, and not waiting to be asked. "Alright, don't be shy. Please help yourself." Kayla remarked sarcastically, sitting down at the desk, to also eat. Watching Willie eat was quite a show. "Where were you, Willie? I was getting worried." He looked up at her and stated, "Willie Return." Kayla laughed; he was the one bright spot in this horrible nightmare.

While they sat there eating, they could hear movement from inside the closet. As the mist traveled out, from underneath the door. It came into the room but did not take the shape of Detective Roberts. It crawled across the floor and out under the bedroom door. Kayla and Willie just looked at each other. The mist never did that before, Kayla thought, as they continued to eat. The mist made its way down the long hallway. At the top of the stairs, it dissipated, still moving but now invisible. It moved towards the kitchen, watching as Michael and Tarsula sat down for a meal. Michael's back was turned towards the doorway, as the string holding the key dangled from his back pocket. Detective Roberts smiled, laughing to himself.

He walked into the kitchen taking hold of the string and with great care, slowly removed it from Michael's back pocket. Holding it tightly, he placed it behind Michael's back keeping it out of sight. Even though Detective Roberts was invisible, the key was not. The detective needed a distraction, something to divert Michael and Tarsula's attention. Roberts reached over grabbing a pitcher, waiting for the right moment to throw it. Tarsula got up walking away from the table momentarily, as Michael sat there focused on his food. He threw it, hitting the wall, barely missing Tarsula's head. Michael stood up running over to her, as they both looked down at the pitcher broken on the floor. Detective Roberts was already traveling, going up the stairs and moving towards Michael's bedroom door.

Kayla and Willie heard the door unlock, Willie hid himself quickly, as Kayla expected Michael to walk in. However, she was confronted with the form of Detective Roberts telling her to leave. "Willie, we have to go! Hurry!" They went out into the hallway, as Detective Roberts followed behind, invisible once again. They silently made their way down the wide staircase. Kayla knew what spots to avoid that squeaked underfoot, having gone up and down these stairs a few times. At the bottom of the landing Willie whispered. "Follow Kay la, Follow Willie." She did without question, as he took her to the back of the house. There was a window he had previously used to leave and get back in. The window with no screen, thanks to Willie's tiny claws. Kayla felt unseen hands helping her up through the window and gently placing her on the ground outside. "Run, Kayla, Run!" Detective Roberts commanded. Kayla ran like her life depended on it, which it did. Putting Willie in her pocket and going through the woods, not stopping, making her way to the road. She walked just outside the wood line ready to hide, always vigilant of Michael's car. A Range Rover stopped on the other side of the road. It was the woman she had seen briefly in the foyer that day. "Hey, aren't you Michael's fiancé, need a lift? Come on!" Kayla hesitated, but she didn't really have a choice. Better her, than some strange guy with bad intentions picking her up. She jumped in, putting her hand over her pocket.

"I'm Tina Abruzzi, I didn't get your name that day at the house."

"Kayla, please drive, FAST!" Kayla was beside herself, frantic that Michael would find her and bring her back to the house.

"What's going on? Why are you walking, you must have a car? Why isn't Michael with you?"

"He was keeping me against my will, he's not who you think he is." Kayla replied.

"What do you mean?"

"Do you have a cell phone? Can I use it, please! At this point Kayla was shouting, half out of her mind.

"Oh, I get it, is this one of the games you play with each other? The damsel in distress kind of thing."

"Tina, I can assure you this is no game!" Kayla shouted, hysterically.

Kayla took her phone and dialed 911. The operator came on the line. "911 what is your emergency?" The operator's voice came through the car's dashboard.

"My name is Kayla Conrad, I was being held against my will! I'm sure the police are looking for me. I need help!"

"What is your location?"

"I'm in a white Range Rover traveling…. Tina where are we?" Tina looked at her GPS. Finally, realizing that this was not some game Kayla was playing.

"We're going south on route 78. Going into Pikes Valley now." Tina answered.

"Alright keep heading in that direction. Do you know your license plate number?"

Kayla looked over at Tina.

"They're personal plates," Tina seemed embarrassed. "They say, LADY LOVE." Tina rolled her eyes. "Dominick got them for me."

"I will send patrol cars to meet you."

"Yes, thank you." Kayla was half crazed, as tears rolled down her face.

Tina looked over at Kayla, who was constantly looking behind them. "Don't worry Kayla, help is on the way. There's no way Michael would know where you are, or what car you're in. You're safe now."

Kayla looked into her pocket, as Willie smiled up at her. Resting her hand over her pocket she was safe, they were both safe.

CHAPTER TWELVE
SHE GOT AWAY

Tarsula cleaned up the mess, trying to get every piece of glass off the floor. She looked over at Michael and said. "That pitcher was on the back island over there. Did you see anything Michael?"

"I was busy eating my food. What the hell! Maybe there is something going on in this house."

Tarsula sat back down to finish her meal. "That thing just missed my fucking head! Maybe we should just leave. Let's put this place back on the market. I'm sure there are other isolated places we can go to."

"Let me think about it Tarsula," he said, as he continued to eat his meal. When he had finished, Michael wanted to check on Kayla. "We haven't made love on that fur rug yet." Michael gave Tarsula a sexy grin, as he reached into his back pocket to retrieve the key. At first, he thought he had the wrong pocket, so he tried the other one. It wasn't there either, that's when the panic set in. "Tarsula, help me look for the key to the bedroom. I had it in my back pocket. Did I drop it? It has to be here, check the floor."

"Maybe it fell out of your pocket, shit! It must be here Michael! I thought you were wearing it around your neck for safe keeping?"

"I was, but it became a hassle taking it on and off. So, I put it in my back pocket. Let me retrace my steps, keys just don't fucking disappear."

Michael walked down the hallway searching the floor, going back through the foyer and up the stairs checking every step, nothing. He walked down the long hallway stopping halfway, noticing the door to his bedroom was wide open. Michael ran to it, looking inside he stood there stunned. The room was vacant. "TARSULA!" he yelled, noticing his key on top of the bed.

* * *

Daniels was looking through some paperwork when Officer Parker knocked on his door. "Sorry to intrude sergeant, but we just got a call from dispatch. It's the girl we've been looking for, Kayla Conrad. She called from a white Range Rover, license plate "LADY LOVE." Traveling south on 78, entering Pikes Valley. Daniels jumped to his feet grabbing his coffee, he ran to his car. Getting into his car he picked up his radio. "This is Sergeant Daniels, all patrol cars in the vicinity of Rt. 78 traveling south into Pikes Valley. Stop and detain, a white Range Rover, personalized license plate LADY LOVE." A tear came to Daniels eye, he couldn't wait to tell Peter that Kayla was found.

Tina and Kayla could hear the sirens approaching them from behind. Tina pulled over, as patrol cars surrounded them. They could hear the police telling them to stay in the vehicle with their hands up. They looked at each other frightened. Did they think Tina was involved in the kidnapping? A state trooper walked over to the passenger side, telling Kayla to roll down the window. "Are you Kayla Conrad?"

"Yes, this is Tina, she helped me escape. I need to speak with Sergeant Daniels. Is he here?"

"Step out of the car please, keep your hands where we can see them. Kayla come with me, Tina please wait here, next to your vehicle," the state trooper requested.

Sergeant Daniels arrived shortly after. "It's all good guys, great job," he informed the officers. "Kayla, are you alright? Who is that woman?" Daniels asked, pointing to where Tina was standing.

"Her name is Tina, she helped me escape. Also, look Sergeant Daniels." Kayla whispered, opening her pocket as Daniels looked inside. Willie looked up at him and smiled, "Willie Hide" he said,

115

with a huge smile on his tiny face.

"Jesus! The both of you were together all this time?"

"Yes. Sergeant Daniels, it was Michael, he kept me locked up in a room."

"Michael, I thought he was long gone. That mother fucker, excuse my language Kayla, give me a second." Daniels walked over to Tina. "I'm Sergeant Daniels, I want to thank you for helping Kayla."

"Sergeant, I can direct you to Michael's house. If you like, I know the address."

"Thank you Tina, but we can handle it from here. May I have your phone?" Tina handed it over to him. "This is my cell phone number, text me with the address." Daniels requested, handing her phone back. "Again Tina, thanks for your help, you're free to go." Tina and Kayla said their goodbyes, hugging each other tightly. Then Tina got back into her SUV and left. Feeling so happy, she was able to help Kayla escape.

Kayla got into Daniels patrol car. "We have to get Willie back to Zadoc." Kayla said. She took Willie out of her pocket, as they drove back into town.

"I think I can help with that," Daniels replied, going into his pocket and grasping his crystal tightly. He looked over at Willie sitting quite content on Kayla's lap, he smiled at the sight of him.

"Sergeant Daniels, someone else also helped me get away from Michael. It was Detective Roberts."

"Detective Roberts? What do you mean, Kayla?" Daniels questioned, with a confused look on his face.

"I know this is going to be hard to believe. He would come out of the closet; into the room Michael was keeping me in. Like a mist, and then he would sort of manifest out of it. Taking form with distinct features. He spoke to me, helping me."

"Well Kayla, if there is such a thing as spirits. Ghosts, that can help people in some way. I believe Detective Roberts would be that ghost. I have no doubt about that. Believe me, with everything that has been happening lately in this town, my mind is now wide open."

"Is Peter alright and my friends?" Kayla asked.

"They will be now, let me get you home."

Willie laid down on Kayla's lap, he had gone through some adventure. Kayla stroked his small head with her index finger, as he closed his eyes.

* * *

Michael told Tarsula that they needed to leave. If Kayla was found, the police would be there at any moment! "We have to leave Tarsula! We can return at a later date if you want, but for now we should go" he said, in a demanding voice.

"Alright, Michael. Just let me get a few things."

"We have the house surrounded, come out with your hands up!" Came the instruction over a megaphone.

"Shit! Well, that didn't take long. What's your animal of choice Tarsula?" Michael asked, knowing they couldn't step outside in human form.

"Black cat I think, and you Michael?"

"My Bowie facade will do, white cat with calico markings. Tarsula go and unlock the door, I don't want them breaking it down!" She walked over to the door unlocking it slowly. Tarsula looked over at Michael with a cunning grin. "Shall we" was all she said, within seconds they had become felines, watching, as the front door was thrown open. The police stormed into the house, as Michael and Tarsula ran out, right in front of them. One of the men in the swat team, actually bent down to pet Tarsula. She hissed at him, running to join Michael in the woods. Another shape shift was needed, Michael changed into a hawk, as Tarsula shifted into a falcon. Flying together, Michael knew a place to go. They flew to his father's house for seclusion and time to think, it was the perfect place for both.

* * *

Daniels drove Kayla home. She held Willie in her hand, as they walked into the house. Peter wasn't there, they both assumed he was

117

out looking for her.

"So, how do we get Willie back to Zadoc?" Kayla questioned.

Daniels reached into his pocket and pulled out his crystal. "With this, somehow Zadoc can hear me, if I hold it up to the sky."

"Come into the yard Detective, that's where Willie lands when he comes for a visit." she informed him.

They walked into the backyard as Kayla woke up Willie. "Willie, you have to go home now. Back to Zadoc, do you understand. Thank you for standing by me, you are a true friend. I love you." The tears started to flow as they always did, each time she said goodbye to Willie.

"Willie Return, Kay la." Kayla smiled, placing him against her face.

Daniels held up his crystal. "All is well now Zadoc, we found Kayla and Willie. He's ready to come back to you." With that, a beam of bright light shot down from the sky. Kayla kissed Willie, placing him onto the ground, he walked into the beam of light, and was gone. Kayla exhaled, knowing he was safe now. "I have to call Peter; he must be worried sick." Daniels took a seat in the living room as Kayla called him.

Peter was combing the streets, whenever he could, looking for Kayla. His cell phone rang. Looking at his phone, the call was coming from Kayla's cell, he quickly answered it. "Hello."

"Peter, it's Kayla I'm home. I'm here with Sergeant Daniels. He offered to stay with me until you get here. I've missed you so much, sweetheart. I love you."

Hearing Kayla's voice, Peter was overcome with emotion. "Kayla, I've been looking for you day and night. What happened to you? I was running out of places to search for you." Peter could hardly get his words out, as he got choked up. Tears ran down his face, he was shaking. "Kay, I'll be right home. Don't forget to call Sam, he's been worried sick about you. I love you so much."

"I love you too, I'll call Sam." Kayla started to cry. Sergeant Daniels walked over to her, putting his arms around her.

"It's alright Kayla, let it out, you've been through a lot. I'm just so happy you and the babies are okay. Congratulations."

"Thank you, Sergeant Daniels, for all your help, I really appreciate it."

"Glad I could be of service Kayla. I wouldn't be concerned about Michael, a swat team is probably storming his house as we speak. I know people in the court system. I will see about freezing Michael's assets. He won't be able to withdrawal money from any of his bank accounts." Kayla was listening to the reassuring words that Daniels was saying. Yet, deep inside she had a gut-wrenching feeling, that Michael would somehow come out of this unscathed.

* * *

Michael and Tarsula landed in the back yard of his father's house. Most people would think it was a large home, but it was modest compared to the over-the-top mansions that Michael was used too. Changing back into human form, they walked to the front of the house. A circular driveway with an ornate fountain came into view. The fountain was large with naked cherubs adorning it. Michael walked to it, knowing exactly what he was looking for, one of the cherubs was removeable. It contained a secret compartment under its right foot, in which a spare key was kept. He had used this key numerous times when visiting unannounced. They entered the house, knowing that this would be their sanctuary for a while. Michael was happy that he had decided to keep his father's property after his passing. Tarsula began to take the sheets off the furniture, as Michael walked into the master bedroom. A line of bookshelves covered the far wall. He scanned the books looking for one particular title. "Yes," he remarked out loud, pulling the book towards him. The book was not removeable. It released a latch, to reveal a panic room hidden behind the wall; Michael stepped inside. The room was spacious, it was almost the size of a small apartment. There was a bathroom, a bed, and a small kitchenet. Michael opened the fridge. Bags of blood had been stacked up, ready to enjoy, along with some essential food items. The cabinets were also filled with snacks, which would make Tarsula happy. However, Michael wasn't thinking of his stomach at the moment. Going over to the bed, he knelt down. There was a slit in the mattress that ran down the side of it. He smiled, placing his hand inside and pulling out a hand full of one-hundred-dollar bills, the mattress was stuffed with them. "Thanks dad," Michael said, standing up.

Michael's father came from Europe and believed in the old ways. When people didn't have much money and hid their life savings in and around their home. His father had bank accounts in Europe, but Michael had transferred the funds into his accounts soon after his father died. Now, Michael was considered a fugitive, since the kidnapping of Kayla. Would they freeze his bank accounts? Not allowing him to access his money. Maybe, if a court order was put into place. It really didn't matter he could always find ways to get money, but his father's stash would keep them both comfortable for some time. Michael returned to Tarsula sitting at the table in the dining room. "So, Michael what is your game plan sir? Do you still want her, after all the shit she's put us through?"

"Don't be ridiculous Tarsula, of course I want her. She's carrying my child, but we have to be smart this time, no more mistakes. I don't care who you kill, but she must remain safe."

"Well, now you're speaking my language, Michael." Tarsula smiled, as her eyes glowed red. I might have an idea. I'm going back to the café, disguised of course. Maybe there is a way, to kill her little band of friends all together. Maybe a party or a function where they would gather. I could dip my toe into The Cave of the Unholy. Have you ever seen the likes of them Michael?"

"No, Tarsula I can't say that I have. I don't care what you do, as long as Kayla stays unharmed, and she becomes mine again." Tarsula sat there with a strange evil look on her face. It was a look, of the devil himself. She was about to set loose, the demons of hell.

* * *

Peter's car pulled into the driveway; he ran to the front door as Kayla greeted him with open arms. No words were exchanged, both of them filled with too much emotion to speak. Kissing each other profusely, their arms hugging each other tightly.

Sergeant Daniels stood up. "Well, I think I should be going, what is it they say, three's a crowd."

"Thank you so much sergeant, for all your help." Peter walked over to him wrapping his arms around him, giving him a hug, overcome with gratitude.

"You're welcome, Peter, stay safe Kayla." Daniels walked to his car; his fingers wrapped tightly around the crystal in his pocket. He was always grateful for a happy ending.

CHAPTER THIRTEEN
WELCOME TO HELL, TARSULA

Tarsula needed to isolate herself. The room needed to be dark and quiet. An incantation was needed to separate her spirit from her physical body. In her rush to leave The Stone Manor, she had left most of her belongings, along with her books of incantations and spells. However, since she always excelled in the dark powers, bringing to mind all that was learned throughout the centuries was an easy task. Lucky for her, the incantation for astral projection was locked in her memory. Tarsula would proceed to the astral plane, where she was sure Hegate would help her, but she needed to get there first.

Walking through the house, she looked for the darkest bedroom, some concentration was needed. Laying down on the bed Tarsula made herself comfortable. Slowing down her breathing and repeating an incantation to herself, which allowed her spirit to separate from her physical body. She felt herself floating, floating away. Looking down at herself she looked peaceful and calm, serene. Her ghostly self was being pulled. Not up, nor down, but sideways quickly, very quickly, through a dark realm. Tarsula could hear people talking, many voices all speaking at once. They were stating their cases to someone. Arguing and pleading not to have their spirit descend or begging to ascend. Some of them wanted to give it another go and have their soul reborn, back on the earthly plane. Pandemonium, Tarsula thought, as she made her way through the crowd of people. She tried to look beyond them, something or someone was standing on a hill, above the hordes of the dead. Tarsula smiled, "I know those horns anywhere, that's Hegate!" She did her best to move towards him, her body freely floating above the ground.

"Hegate!" Tarsula yelled. "Hegate! Over here!" Tarsula waved her ghostly arms high above her head.
"Tarsula? What are you doing here? Did you pass? Did someone finally, find a way to kill you? Why are you transparent? People are mostly in solid form when they arrive here, they look as they did on earth."

"I had to separate my spirit from my body to cross over. I'm not dead Hegate, I'm here on business. I need your help to descend to The Cave of The Unholy."

"No Tarsula, I can't help you with that. The Cave of The Unholy is off limits. You will never return from there." Hegate scratched his third horn, protruding from the middle of his forehead.

"I need to talk to the demon Mantus, I just need to get into his realm. Just to The Wall of Human Suffering I can take it from there." Tarsula begged.

"Tarsula, if I send you there, you are on your own. I can't help bring you back. That would be Mantus's decision, to let you return or keep you there for eternity. I don't think this is wise. What waits below, cannot be trusted. However, the choice is yours to make."

"Alright then, just do it and stop wasting my time Hegate!"

"Fine, close your eyes." Hegate picked up Tarsula's ghostly body over his head, Tarsula screamed as he threw her down. In this case, no tear was needed to exit the astral plane, as her ghostly spirit fell through the ground. Falling into a place of darkness and fire. Landing on the dirt, small fires smoked around her. Tarsula got up, standing unsteadily on her feet. She tried to float, as she had done on the astral plane. However, she no longer had the ability to do so. The ground was hot beneath her, even in spirit form, she could feel its heat. Bending down she marked an X in the dirt, this would be her point of re-entry back into the astral plane. Tarsula walked towards

The Wall of Human Suffering in the distance. Fire and the smell of rotting flesh surrounded her.

Approaching the wall's gate she marveled at its grotesqueness. It was constructed with naked bodies and wrought iron. The bodies twisted and turned in endless agony, as the wall spread out before her. Immense in its structure, and as wide as the eye could see, never ending.

"Hello! I would like to enter! Is anyone there?" Tarsula noticed the horn of a ram lying on the ground, she picked it up and blew into it. The bodies on the gate began to cry out. Moaning and screaming in undeniable, excruciating pain. Tarsula tried to look past the bodies, as a form walked towards her. She had never seen a creature, like the one that approached. It had the head of a cobra, and the body of a bull, which was strong and massive. Its feet were hooved, while the arms were muscular covered in dark fur. Its hands were gorilla like, with rough skinned fingers, resembling the darkest of leathers.

"I'm The Gate Keeper, you cannot enter. Who, or what are you? I can see right through you." The keeper hissed as he spoke, his mouth dripping with black saliva.

"My name is Tarsula, I live on the earthly plane. I have left my body behind, to travel here in spirit. I need to see Mantus."

"No one sees Mantus, unless he calls for them. Even you, in spirit cannot enter his realm. You need to leave."

"I'm sure he knows of me. I have done some wicked things, I'm sure he would approve of. Let me in!"

The Keeper started to laugh. "Do you not hear the cries of pain and torture coming from inside? Most of these bastards are trying to get out, as you plead to come in." He hissed again, as his mouth spit at her.

"I want to make him an offer, a few more souls for his domain. I have a friend who can tear a hole in the ground of the astral plane. His name is Hegate, he can send down the Golden Rope for Mantus's army to ascend. They will be able to climb up it, take a look around. Wouldn't he like that?" Tarsula pleaded her case. "From there, I will be able to get them into the earthly plane without difficulty."

The Gate Keeper rubbed his long-scaly neck, "wait here."

Tarsula sat on a rock and waited. She looked up at the gate filled with bodies, some of them were headless, some were limbless. Yet they still moved, their bodies seemed melted onto the iron facade, with no chance of escaping. They were stuck there for eternity. The Keeper was coming back removing a giant key, made from the thigh bone of a virgin, which he wore around his neck. The bodies on the gate started to scream. "No! No! Please Stop!" He opened the gate, as some of the bodies were being torn apart once again. Arms and legs were being pulled off to one side of the gate, while their bodies were stuck on the other. Their screams were deafening. Tarsula placed her hands over her ears, but it did not lessen the sound in any way.

"Follow me Tarsula, Mantus is curious about your offer. I hope it pleases him, or you may end up on the gate." The Gate Keeper started to laugh and hiss at the same time. "Follow that path, it will take you to the Cave of The Unholy. If you get through to the other side, Mantus will be waiting for you."

"What do you mean if?" Tarsula asked, looking at him to clarify.

"The cave is the entrance to hell. Did you think it was going to be rainbows and butterflies Tarsula?" The Keeper turned and locked the gate once more, leaving Tarsula alone as she walked towards the path, to the Cave of The Unholy.

The path consisted of black ash. A variety of bugs ran across the ground as she walked. Tarsula did her best to try and float but was unsuccessful, she had lost all of her powers in this realm. Spiders and roaches crawled across her ghost-like feet, trying to crawl up her legs. Only getting so far, before falling back down onto the ashy surface. There were small piles of coal and fire everywhere and it reeked of burning oil and flesh. The opening to the cave came into view, black as pitch. Tarsula needed a light. Reaching down she picked up a branch and lit it, from one of the fires that covered the area. Walking slowly into the darkness, there was laughter and things moving about.

She came across a woman sitting crossed legged on the dirt floor, laughing hysterically. There were bones surrounding her, as she ate something that looked like a human foot. Her face was covered in blood, as her sharp teeth bit into the rotting flesh. Tarsula hurried along, as the floor soon became a stream of red. She looked up, headless bodies hung upside down from the ceiling, their blood oozing out of them. A man with a goat's head was flaying bodies and cutting out their organs. He threw a bloody liver at Tarsula and then made a hideous noise. It sounded like a mix of a goat's bleat and a human child laughing. Moving on, she had finally reached the graves of The Unholy Ones, they were familiar to her. Hearing stories about them throughout the centuries, but she had never seen them up close and personal. Their graves were numerous, an army of Satan's spawn.

Tarsula watched, as the ground of one of the graves started to separate. A hand protruded upwards. Fine boned, much like a skeleton, but covered in white opaque skin. A spotted bald head began to show itself, as it wiggled up from its dirty confinement. Standing before Tarsula now, it was tall and gaunt, looking down at her. Its head was the shape of an upside-down pear, wide at the top and tapering at the chin. One large eye was centered in the middle of its forehead and the nose was extremely small, almost nonexistent. Yawning, it exposed three rows of teeth within its mouth. Sharp and crusted with dirt. Serrated fragments of bone protruded from behind its neck and cascaded downward to the small of its back. Then this hideous creature spoke.

"How dare you walk into our domain spirit? Who let you in? Why are you transparent, not flesh and bone as you were on the earthly plane? How do I torture a ghost?" He spoke with a rough and gravelly voice.

"My name is Tarsula, I'm a witch on the earthly plane. I am still alive there, I have learned to separate my spirit from my body. I need to speak with Mantus. I have an offer for him, for all of you. A way to bring you all up into the earthly plane, a war on earth's people. Think of all the souls you could steal. All the new bodies to torture, doesn't that sound like fun?"

"Yes, it does, my name is Chaos. How many of us would be allowed to ascend?"

"Well Chaos, I love your name by the way, all of you!"

"All?" Chaos spread out his arms, wanting Tarsula to take notice of the massive number of graves in all directions.

"The more, the merrier that's what I say. Now take me to Mantus," Tarsula demanded. Even in spirit form, her eyes seemed to gleam with red evilness.

The stairs to Mantus's throne were many and steep, constructed of white alabaster. Tarsula started the climb, counting as she went. By the time she had reached the top, she had counted forty-five steps, there in front of her sat Mantus. His black horns were lit with fire. His eyes glowed with an orange flame. His massive upper body was manlike, but his lower half was that of a bison. Mantus, appeared strong and powerful, looking at her with disgust.

"I have never seen the likes of you before. Why are you here now, and transparent?"

"My name is Tarsula, I'm a powerful witch on the earthly plane. I am here only in spirit, to make you an offer."

"An offer of what? What could you possibly have, that I could ever need or want?"

"I think I can make an opening, a tear between your realm and the astral plane. I have a friend there who can help us. From there, it's just a jump into the earthly plane, another realm to conquer. Wouldn't you like to extend your domain, become the king of two realms. Take some of God's territory for yourself? Perhaps kill a few, think about it, new flesh to torture."

"That sounds quite tempting, but what do you gain from this

plan of yours. You must want something?"

"Well, there is a little something. There are a few people, I would like you to make them your priority, kill them first. Except for one, I would need you to protect a girl. She belongs to my stepson Michael; he's infatuated with her." Tarsula announced, rolling her eyes.

"When would you like to begin the annihilation? I suppose I could send Chaos and a small army for starters, see how it goes."

"Yes Mantus, Chaos seemed eager to explore new surroundings. However, I still need to contemplate things. A time when a certain few could be slaughtered together, to get it done quickly and thoroughly."

Mantus reached over the side of his throne. "Take this Tarsula." He handed her a horn which glowed in her hands, made of alabaster. "This is the horn of my realm, it can be heard from the astral plane, you'll need it to get back up. However, you will not be able to leave here unless the Golden Rope is thrown down to you, even in spirit form. On the day of the attack, when you are in the astral plane and are ready to bring up my men, blow it again. Once the tear is made and the Golden Rope is thrown down, I will send up my army. These humans will never know what's coming for them. Hell on earth! Literally!" Mantus laughed.

"Yes Mantus, earth will be ours finally. I will now say my goodbyes, until we meet again."

" I will have Chaos and The Keeper show you out."

Tarsula held onto the horn, as she stepped back down the long and steep staircase. Chaos was waiting at the bottom to escort her through the Cave of The Unholy. As they reached the entrance to the cave, they were met by The Gate Keeper, who took her the rest of the way. Once exiting the gate, it was locked quickly. Tarsula walked holding onto the horn, looking for the X mark she had made in the dirt. Finding it, she blew into the horn Mantus had given her. Hegate punctured a small hole in his realm. It was just big enough to send down the Golden Rope and maybe the horn to fit through.

Tarsula grabbed hold of the rope and was hoisted up. Seeing the size of the hole above her, she screamed, thinking she would not fit through it. Her ghostly image along with the horn, surprisingly emerged up through the ground of the astral plane where Hegate was waiting, he closed the hole up rapidly.

"Finally Tarsula, I wasn't sure you were coming back. How did it go?"

"Very well I believe, now, I have to get back to my body."

"Wait, did you see Mantus? What is the plan Tarsula?"

"To raise hell on earth, Hegate." Tarsula replied, as her eyes shown the color of blood. I will keep you informed once a plan is initiated. She handed Hegate the horn of the realms. "Keep this safe, until my return, now I must get back."

Hegate thought for a moment then asked, "You want to raise hell on earth? I thought there was only a certain few you had your eye on. Not everyone on the earthly plane, I will be inundated with souls. Are you sure, this is a smart thing to do Tarsula?"

"Don't be such a goody two shoes Hegate. Now I must get back to my body."

Tarsula closed her eyes concentrating. Her ghostly body was catapulted sideways through the darkness and beyond, flying back into her lifeless body on the bed. Tarsula gasped for air, as she sat up. Michael was sitting there waiting for her.

"Where did you go Tarsula? I would have called emergency services, but being a fugitive, I didn't think that would have been a wise decision. Besides, I know what you are capable of, like astral projection. So, where did you go?"

"Let's just say, I traveled to hell and back."

"What does that mean, Tarsula?"

"You'll find out soon enough, my dear boy. Now, let's get something to eat, I'm famished." Tarsula walked out of the bedroom, leaving Michael sitting there thinking. What did she mean, from hell and back? I love her, but sometimes her wickedness outweighs her common sense. Not allowing her to think straight. I hope she hasn't done anything foolish. Michael stood up, he would question her again, but at a later date. Through all the years of knowing Tarsula, she hated it when Michael questioned her about anything, always headstrong and determined to do as she pleased.

* * *

The café had gotten extremely busy, since the weather had started to warm. People were venturing out more. Shopping and stopping in for a coffee break or lingering over breakfast was quickly becoming popular again. The tables on the patio were usually occupied by ten in the morning. Leaving others to step inside and have a seat. The bell above the door chimed, as patrons came in or walked out. Emily and Kayla no longer did rock, paper, scissors to see who would wait the tables outside or inside. Whenever a table became available, whoever was closest to it, would take it.

"This is crazy today!" Emily said to Kayla, as she cleaned off one of the outside tables.

"Yeah, we knew it was going to happen Em, as soon as the weather changed. Not to change the subject, but I'm trying to figure out what to get Sam and Mary for their wedding, any ideas?"

"Hey, why don't we go in together for the gift. Then we can get something really nice for them. What do you think?" Emily asked.

"I don't have a problem with that. My problem is what to buy them, any suggestions?"

"No, let's ask Sam if they are part of a bridal registry, that way we're sure to get them something they really want."

"Good idea Em, problem solved." Kayla replied. She walked to the far side of the patio, to another group of people who had just sat down for a late morning bite to eat.

CHAPTER FOURTEEN
HEGATE'S DILEMMA

Hegate sat on a rock, thinking about Tarsula and her plan to unleash hell on earth. Mantus and his army would have to cross into my domain first, he thought. There would be too much blood shed on the earthly plane, too many souls coming here at once. As it is, I am overwhelmed at times. I cannot allow this to happen, but I'm going to need help.

Hegate stood up, "I need your attention! All of you that wish to ascend come forward!" Hegate watched as a group started to form. He knew some of the souls were not eligible to ascend, but were scheduled to descend, into a hellish afterlife for eternity. "I need an army of fighters, a witch by the name of Tarsula wants to tear a hole in this realm and allow the demons of hell to pass through here, on their way to the earthly plane! We cannot allow this abomination to happen! We must protect the earthly plane, the loved ones you have left behind exist there! Your wives, husbands, children, the family and friends you once knew! Join with me, and I promise to ascend your souls to the realm above quickly! Even those of you who are scheduled to descend, eternally banished to hell, you will get a second chance! I will see that you are reincarnated to live another life! Who is with me!" The roar from the crowd was deafening, as they stood strong. Hegate looked out among them. Hundreds of them, chanting Hegate's name. "HEGATE!, HEGATE!, HEGATE!"

One of the dead raised his hand. Hegate yelled, "quiet let them speak!" A hush came over the crowd.

"How do we fight without weapons?" someone shouted.

A man stepped forward. " We can take down the Barrier of Separation, use the metal as spears!" The Barrier of Separation, separated the dead into three categories. Heaven bound, hell bound, or those destined to be reincarnated. "The pickets are iron and pointed at the top. There is more than enough metal for all of us to have a weapon! I was a blacksmith in life, if we can gather some fire from the realm below? I'm sure I would be able to forge some weapons."

Hegate thought for a moment. "Is there someone willing to retrieve, the fire from hell? I can make a slight tear in our realm; sending you down and then bring you back up with the golden rope." A silence came upon the crowd. "I'll go, said the blacksmith, it was my idea. My wife and I just had a baby on the earthly plane, I will do anything I can to protect them. I died helping a frightened young woman, when I was attacked by a creature from hell. I lost control of my truck and was impaled by a large tree branch. I need to keep my wife and baby safe, even if it means going to hell and back."

"Alright then, we have a plan. Let's begin by taking down The Barrier of Separation." Hegate announced. "Belfar, you know the barrier and how it was constructed. Don't you?" Belfar was Hegate's right hand man. Short in stature, ugly as sin, but extremely smart. The immense barrier had been assembled like a puzzle, the pieces fitting together just so, strong and solid. Belfar was the only one who knew how to take it apart. However, the job was too much for a single man to accomplish in the time allowed. He would have to share the secret of the puzzle, so that everyone could help in taking it down.

Hegate watched, as his people on the astral plane banded together. The souls of the damned working close, with the pure of heart. His mind went to Tarsula, he knew she would not surrender easily. Once her mind was fixed on something, there was no turning back. He once regarded her as a friend, but could not allow this atrocity to take place. In his eyes Tarsula had crossed the line. If she wanted a battle she would have one, but not with the people on the earthly plane.

Hegate walked over as pieces of the iron barrier were being torn down. He picked up some metal posts, placing them on the huge pile that had been established. He continued to work with the dead, until the entire structure was brought down. Hegate found the blacksmith, walking over to him he asked. "What is your name sir?"

"Steven, Steven Clark."

"Well, Steven Clark, you are a brave soul. You will find everything you need down there, but work quickly if you are caught, you will remain there for eternity. Gather wood, branches, twigs, and light them on fire." Hegate handed him a metal bucket. "Place all of it in this. Once you are back, we will build a stone vessel to contain the flame.

Steven Clark smiled, picking up a shiny black rock off the ground. "Do you know what this is Hegate?"

Hegate looked at it in his hand, "a rock."

"No, not just a rock Hegate, it's anthracite. It is a form of coal, except it burns longer and hotter. There's tons of this stuff all over this place. Once we establish a wood fire, we add the anthracite. Small amounts at a time. Wait until the first layer catches and glows orange, then add another layer. That will give me the ability to start forging. Just by bending the top of a fenceposts, I can turn some of them into daggers or sickles, leaving others as spears, sharpening them at the top."

Hegate made a small tear in the surface of the astral plane. He asked for the golden rope, which was brought over by Belfar. Hegate and Belfar secured the rope and watched as Steven climbed down. The first thing Steven noticed was the smell, which took his breath away. Strong and pungent, the smell of death. There were bugs everywhere. He had to shake off each piece of wood, as bugs crawled up his arm, before placing it into the bucket. Then he lit it on fire. In the distance he could see the Fence of Human Suffering. He had heard stories about it, but never thought it was real. Suddenly loud screams could be heard, coming from that direction. Was the gate opening? A figure appeared running towards him, as Steven ran towards the rope, bucket in hand. He screamed up to Hegate, grabbing hold of the rope. "Pull me up! Hegate! Pull me up now!"

Hegate and Belfar pulled up on the rope, lifting Steven upwards. Barely escaping, being grabbed by The Keeper's dark leathered hands. The opening was closed as soon as Steven's body emerged, back into the astral plane, holding tightly onto the golden rope.

"Steven are you alright?" Hegate asked.

"Yes, what was that thing down there?" Steven asked, handing the large bucket of fire and wood to Belfar.

"That was probably The Gate Keeper. You had entered his domain, and I'm sure he wasn't happy about it." Hegate replied.

"Are those the kind of things we have to fight?" Steven asked.

"No, he cannot leave his realm. Yet, there are others who are just as bad, or worse."

"Okay, well that makes me feel better. Thanks a lot, Hegate," Steven responded sarcastically.

Most of the men worked together, collecting stones in order to construct a fire pit. While under the instruction of Steven, they got it done. A roaring fire took hold, using the anthracite to keep it going and increase the heat. Steven put together a makeshift anvil, using a large rock and some of the iron from the Barrier of Seperation, soon the forging of weapons would begin.

* * *

The Keeper met with the leader of Mantus's army, Chaos. The Gate Keeper spoke, "I saw an intruder on the land outside of the gate. He was stealing, gathering things off the ground. He came from above, from the astral plane. They threw the golden rope down to him and pulled him up before I could grab him."

Chaos thought for a moment. "Who tore the astral plane? Was it Tarsula?"

"I don't know, but you should mention it to Mantus. Is Tarsula trying to win our friendship just to plot against us?"

"I hope not for her sake, but I will talk to Mantus about it. Stay vigilant and keep me informed."

"I will Chaos, most definitely."

Chaos climbed up the many steps to Mantus. When he reached the top, Mantus was raping a woman spread eagle, naked, and chained to a concrete alter. She screamed in excruciating pain as Mantus's massive cock fucked her violently and without mercy. Chaos turned his back to them and waited for Mantus to finish. When he was done, Chaos approached him.

"Sorry for the intrusion Mantus, but I have some information you should know."

"And what might that be?" Mantus questioned, releasing the woman to one of his guards, who held her up, noticing she could barely stand.

"The Keeper saw an intruder today outside of the gate. He was gathering things off the ground, stealing bits off our land."

"Who was this person? Where did he come from?

"Someone tore a hole in the astral plane, they escaped with the golden rope."

"Do you think Tarsula had something to do with this?" Would she dare plot against us?"

"I don't know Mantus. However, we should keep a sharp eye on the astral plane for any more tears."

"I agree Chaos, I'm starting to have my doubts about Tarsula, let me know if anything occurs."

CHAPTER FIFTEEN

KARMA'S BITCH

Michael and Tarsula sat at a table eating. Both were quiet and deep in thought. "What's going on Tarsula? You've been awfully quiet lately; it's not like you to be so withdrawn."

"I've been thinking, we need to go back to the Stone Manor. I left everything there, items that can never be replaced, things that I need."

"We can go back tonight, it's been a while since we've been there. They can't watch the house forever. Tarsula if you drive, I'll fly ahead to make sure the coast is clear. I'll Chant you, whether to approach the house or not, sound like a plan?"

"Yes Michael, that sounds good, I'll be sure to make it a quick in and out."

When night fell, Tarsula got into her car, as Michael flew ahead of her, back to the manor. Tarsula parked her car on the side of the road and waited. Michael flew over his abandoned property. He looked down on his opulent home, that once held so much promise. The property stood vacant, with no one standing guard. He Chanted Tarsula, that the coast was clear.

Entering the long driveway to the manor, Tarsula remembered how excited Michael was when he purchased the home. Thinking he would live there forever with Kayla. However, now that the dream was over, she was overcome with sadness. She parked her car near the front door, as Michael landed a few feet in front of her. She watched him change from a hawk to a man in the blink of an eye. Even though she had seen him do this numerous times, it was still impressive. He pushed the massive front door open. The house stood silent as they walked into the foyer. Walking up the stairs, the floorboards creaked. This time, Michael did not feel the house was welcoming him, as before. Now, it was just the sound of old floorboards in an antiquated house.

Once they reached the upstairs landing, Tarsula turned right to her room, as Michael turned left, walking down the long hallway to his. Opening her bedroom door, Tarsula walked quickly to her closet. The first thing she needed was her Victorian Carpet bag, made from an oriental rug. It contained important spell books, candles, a mirror, and her wooden bowl, carved in the year 1530 during the reign of Henry the Eighth. It had traveled with her through the ages and was irreplaceable. She collected her things quickly, making sure no item was left behind.

As Michael walked into his bedroom, he looked around the room. Walking over to his fur rug in front of the fireplace, he picked it up and threw it, thinking what could have been. Kayla crossed his mind as he laid down on the bed, a bed that was to be shared by both of them. Michael closed his eyes, trying to imagine her lying down next to him. Lost in his thoughts of Kayla, Michael didn't notice a fine mist coming from underneath the closet door. It moved slowly across the bedroom floor, then turned invisible, crawling up the wall onto the ceiling. Ever so slowly, it moved towards the chandelier, as the bolts that held it up were being turned, by unseen hands. They were loosened and removed, and thrown onto the fur rug, bunched up in the corner. The last two bolts were not strong enough to hold the massive light fixture. It pulled from the ceiling, the sound of it falling startled Michael. The spear stopped inches from his chest, only being held in place by a few cables, as the mist floated on top of Michael's reclined body. A face protruded from within it; its features well defined. There were also others coming from the closet, the men Michael had killed in the past. Their spirits flowed towards him, all of them angry and yelling at once. Seeking revenge on Michael for cutting their lives short. They held him in place, keeping him from moving.

"Hello, Michael. Do you know who I am? Because of you, my children must live their lives without a father, and my wife without me by her side. My name is Detective Roberts, I am the one you saw fit to kill that day, outside the café. I had never seen anything like you. As I am sure, you have never seen the likes of me and my friends, at this very moment."

Michael screamed for Tarsula, who did not hear his cries for help. Suddenly the bedroom door was gently shut and held closed.

"How does it feel Michael, being kept in a room with no chance of escape? I'm sure Kayla could tell you all about it."

Michael knew there was no escaping in human form, so he started to shape shift, he could now morph into the creature he truly was. Fangs elongated, his hands turning into claws. Wings began to flap coming out of his back, trying to maneuver between the rungs of the chandelier.

"Now everyone!" Yelled Detective Roberts. A barrage of hands, along with Robert's own grasped hold of the chandelier plunging the eight-inch spear, which extended from the bottom, into Michael's chest. He screamed, a scream so loud it echoed throughout The Stone Manor. Michael's body started to cave in on itself, as it disintegrated, turning into a large pile of ash. Tarsula stopped what she was doing and ran over to Michael's room. Trying the door it would not open, she called out to him.

"Michael! Michael! Are you alright? Open the door, Michael!" She stood there listening, suddenly the door opened as Tarsula rushed in. A pile of ash laid underneath a massive light fixture. Tarsula walked over to the bed, she reached down picking up a silver necklace that she knew was Michael's. He wore it underneath his clothes often, unseen by those around him, except for her. A small heart pendant dangled from the chain. It was coated in red enamel and adorned with the most perfect diamonds that spelled out only one word, KAYLA. "Michael?" she sobbed, "how could

this happen? Was this an accident, or did someone do this to you?"
Something landed on the bed, it fell from the ceiling above her, a
detective's badge. Tarsula picked it up, she sat down on the bed
feeling weak and stricken with grief. She screamed, "Michael! I
should have stayed with you! Protected you! We should have never
come back here!" Tarsula's grief had turned to anger, "there will be
hell to pay for this! I will unleash unspeakable evil onto this world! I
will find out who did this, and they will pay dearly for their actions!"
She looked down at the detective badge, she still held in her hand
and threw it across the room.

Tarsula placed the necklace into her pocket and picked up a
key from the ashes, for Michael's father's house. She walked back to
her bedroom, unsteady on her feet trying to come to the realization
that her Michael was truly gone. Tarsula gathered her belongings,
making numerous trips back and forth, taking everything that she
needed. Getting into her car, she took one last look at the house.
Driving off and exiting down the long driveway to the street, crying
tears of sorrow and frustration. Tarsula sobbed, knowing she would
never see her dear friend again or ever return to The Stone Manor.
She drove, wiping the tears from her eyes, back to Michael's father's
house.

Parking her car, she walked inside and took a seat on the sofa.
Screaming and crying, the unthinkable had happened, Michael was
dead. She got up and poured herself a drink, feeling alone now, so
alone. The silence in the house was more than she could stand, it cut
through her like a knife. Tarsula walked back to her car and gathered
her belongings. Once that was done, she walked to the kitchen
with the intention of eating a box of chocolate. Pulling it out of the
cabinet and placing it on the table, she took a seat. Opening the lid
and staring at its contents. "Fuck!" Tarsula yelled, grabbing the box
of candy and throwing it across the room.

Standing up, a thought crossed her mind; it was time to visit
her friends at the café. Eavesdrop on their conversations. She wanted
them dead, especially Kayla and her babies. If it wasn't for Kayla,

Michael would never have purchased The Stone Manor and would still be alive. Tarsula's eyes turned red, as her evil thoughts started to consume her.

* * *

On Saturday morning, Kayla woke up to the sound of birds outside the bedroom window. Looking over at Peter, she wondered how anyone could sleep through such a racket. Placing her feet on the floor she did her morning stretch, looking down at her stomach, she caressed her belly. Pushing herself out of bed, she walked downstairs wanting a cup of decaf coffee and a chocolate-glazed donut, that Peter had brought home the night before. She was excited for the day to begin. Going to work for only a few hours and then having brunch with the whole gang. It's such a beautiful spring day, maybe we can all have brunch on the patio outside, Kayla thought. It has been a while since we have all been together. I know the topics of conversation will definitely be my twins and Sam and Mary's wedding in a couple of weeks.

Peter made his appearance in the kitchen just as the coffee was ready. He looked over at Kayla, disapproving of the breakfast she chose to eat. "A chocolate donut and decaf, that's very nutritious."

"You're the one who brought them home, anyway, the babies wanted it."

"Oh, I'm sure they were craving chocolate glazed donuts." Peter bent down and kissed her, then kissed his hand, placing it on Kayla's protruding belly.

"Did the birds wake you up?" Kayla asked.

"What birds? I turned over looking for you. I thought you had gone to the bathroom, but then I smelled the coffee, so I knew you had come downstairs. It's going to be a fun day today. All of us getting together, that hasn't happened in a while." Peter acknowledged, as he poured himself a cup of decaf.

"Yeah, I'm hoping we could eat outside on the patio today. Sam doesn't usually like to eat outside, but maybe we can convince him. Emily and I were talking about what to get Mary and Sam for their

140

wedding. Emily overheard Mary saying something about her washer and dryer being old to Sam. That they needed to be replaced. Emily and I were thinking, if all of us chipped in, we could get that for them. I know Sam is moving into Mary's condo, since he only has a few months left on his lease."

"That's fine Kayla, whatever you guys want to do." Peter bent down, kissing Kayla's cheek. "Listen, no more chocolate donuts for breakfast, okay? I'm going up to take a shower." Kayla waited till she heard him climb the stairs and the coast was clear. Walking over to the box of donuts, she popped another into her mouth. "Now you each have one." Kayla said out loud, patting her extended belly and laughing to herself.

* * *

Tarsula sat in the living room surrounded by her books of incantations, reading page after page. "I need something inconspicuous, a bird or maybe a squirrel. That will do for the outside, but I need something for inside. Something that would allow me to get close but not be noticed." Thumbing through the pages a sound caught her attention, a buzzing noise. She looked across the room, a horse fly was trying to escape through a closed window. "A fly, a fly on the wall, that's perfect! I will bring my book with me and then decide once I get there. What fun!" Tarsula packed up her tapestry bag of spells and decided she would head over to the café later that day.

* * *

Bradford made his way to the Stone Manor, looking at the house there was no sign of movement. He scanned the grounds and noticed there were no cars parked in front. Bradford slowly walked towards the back of the manor noticing doors to the basement. They had been chained and locked up tightly. Breaking the chain wouldn't be a problem, but it could not be accomplished in human form.

He took off his clothes and started to change. Tall and muscular, covered in fur. Kicking off his shoes, his hands and feet elongated. He reached down, taking hold of the chain, breaking it

141

in two. Shifting back to his manlike self, putting on his clothes and shoes, he walked down into the basement. Finding the steps inside that led upstairs, Bradford climbed, cracking open the inside cellar door. He peered out, not a sound could be heard. The door opened with a slight creaking sound, its hinges were rusty in need of oil. He stood there frozen, not moving, just listening. Walking out into a hallway near the kitchen he waited, expecting to see Tarsula or Michael running towards him, nothing.

Bradford walked around admiring the inside of the lavish home. Walking into the foyer he was met by the main staircase. Should he dare go up to the second floor? His curiosity was getting the better of him, so he climbed up the stairs, left or right? Turning right, he counted five bedrooms and three bathrooms all empty. Turning around he proceeded to walk towards the opposite side of the manor, entering four bedrooms and two bathrooms. There was one more room to explore, towards the rear of the house. Could this be Michael's room? Slowly turning the doorknob he entered, his mouth dropped open. A giant chandelier sat in the middle of a massive bed on top of a pile of ashes. He had seen this before, vamps that had been killed leaving this sort of thing behind. Could this be the remains of Michael? Was this an accident or done intentionally? A million thoughts were going through Bradford's mind all at once. Did Kayla have anything to do with this, he wondered? He went back outside, sauntering back into the woods to his car. Now that Michael was out of the picture, if that was Michael, taking Kayla should be very easy, with her protector gone. I'll just have to wait until the right moment. Driving away he grinned, making his way over to the café.

* * *

Later in the morning, everyone had spoken to Sam about eating outside, but it was Mary who finally persuaded him. They set up a long table on the patio and gathered around, engaged in conversations that were never ending. Mary talked about her up and coming wedding, her dress, the flowers, the food. While Sam talked

142

about the trip they were going to take to Italy, after their nuptials.

Kayla stood up, her hand placed softly on her belly. "I'd like to make an announcement!" Everyone at the table became silent. "Emily, you are my best friend. I think of you as a sister. We've been through a lot together. I'd like to ask you, if you would consider being the God Mother to my twins?"

"Oh my God Kay! I would be honored, thank you so much." Emily stood up, hugging Kayla tightly and kissing her cheek.

Kayla continued to speak, still with her arm around Emily's shoulder. "Sam, you have always been so kind to me, from my first day working at the café. You have been the father figure in my life. We would love it if you would be their God Father."

Sam stood up embracing Kayla, with tears in his eyes. "Kay, Peter, I was never fortunate enough to have a child of my own, so I think of you all, as my kids. I can think of nothing better than being God Father to your children. You and Peter are so special to me, I will gladly accept." Everyone applauded at the table as Sam took a seat.

"So, Sam, tell us about the wedding." asked Max. "I can't wait to see this castle?"

"Yeah, Mary fell in love with the whole scenario. Walking across a drawbridge out to a grassy field filled with flowers." Sam looked lovingly at Mary, whose cheeks began to blush.

"That sounds like a fairy tale. Where is this place?" Jeanna asked, looking at Max hoping he would officially pop the question soon.

"It's called Danmore Castle, about an hour outside of town. It sits high on a hill with a working drawbridge and a mote. The castle is a replica of course, but still very impressive to look at. I'm sure you're all going to love it, remember May 20th save the date." Sam announced.

Emily stood up raising her glass of iced tea. "Here's to Sam and Mary and to my God babies! Cheers!"

Everyone stood up, clinking glasses, laughing, and excited for the future, as a squirrel with red eyes sat there listening intently.

CHAPTER SIXTEEN

EVIL PLANS

Tarsula scampered off into an alley to keep out of sight, changing back into her old self. Making her way back to her car she thought, a wedding when everyone is in attendance, be still my heart. It's time for me to contact Hegate. May 20th, I will turn this wedding into a nightmare she laughed, she would never stop until everyone was dead.

Tarsula stopped her car a block away from Michael's father's house. She watched as a few police cars turned into the home's driveway. I guess they're looking for Michael, tracking him down to his father's house, she thought. "Well, you won't find him in there, assholes!" She said out loud, looking at the tapestry bag in the seat next to her, which contained her spell books. However, there were a few items she needed to retrieve, along with some money from the panic room. Lucky for her, Michael always confided in Tarsula. He never kept secrets from her, showing her the bookcase and which book would release the latch, if she ever needed to hide.

Stepping out of her car, she engaged her third eye, enabling her to see the house from a bird's eye view. Watching, as the police walked around the grounds looking into windows and knocking on the front door. There was nothing left to do but wait until the coast was clear. After some time, the police finally departed, she watched as their patrol cars exited the driveway. Tarsula got into her car, putting it in drive and slowly made her way back to the house. Once inside, she acted in haste, getting her belongings and stuffing large amounts of money into a bag. She had the idea, that perhaps her assets would also be frozen, for being an accomplice to a kidnapping. Now, all that was needed was to find a cushy hotel room somewhere and book it for a long-extended stay. She needed to relax and plan her attack on the much hated May wedding.

* * *

Bradford parked his car near the café. He watched as Kayla and her friends were having some kind of get together on the patio. As Kayla got up from the table to head inside Bradford became furious, even from this distance he could see Kayla was pregnant. She wasn't wearing her usual apron, and her shirt was clinging to her stomach. True, it had been a while since he really had a good look at her, but this, his interest in her dissipated at that very moment. He was no longer sexually attracted to her. "Fuck!" He yelled, from the comfort of his car, banging his hands hard against the steering wheel. Now Bradford would have to set his sights on another woman, one with a kick ass body that turned him on. Putting his car in drive he headed back home, searching the streets, just in case some unsuspecting woman caught his eye. He reached over to the front seat, picking up the duct tape and rope, and threw them into the back seat of his car. At this moment he was very upset, for things were not going according to plan.

* * *

Hegate sat on a hillside looking into his Crystal Ball of Souls. It alerted him with the names and times, when new souls would cross into his realm. He watched as the names scrolled before him. Michael Blaydon? He thought, isn't that Tarsula's friend? He arrived here very recently. Would he be able to talk to Tarsula, maybe talk sense to her. I know she was quite fond of him. He is on the list to descend, maybe I can cut a deal with him, but first I have to find him.

Hegate stood up and yelled out to the crowd. "I'm looking for Michael Blaydon! Michael Blaydon please step forward!" Hegate's voice echoed throughout his realm.

The crowd parted, as a handsome man stepped forward. Michael looked up at Hegate, he had heard stories about him from Tarsula, but to see him in person was intimidating. "Are you Michael Blaydon?"

"Yes, where am I?" Michael approached him terrified.

"I'm Hegate, keeper of souls and this realm. You're Tarsula's friend, aren't you?"

"I am, I was killed by, of all things a chandelier. Am I in hell?"

Hegate laughed so hard it shook the ground. "Oh, this place is heaven compared to where you're going. However, maybe we can make a deal. I'm sure you wouldn't like to be tortured for eternity, and I definitely can't get you into heaven. Still, there is an alternative, reincarnation."

"Reincarnation, to be reborn?" Michael questioned.

"I know Isabella, was your obsession, and then a woman named Kayla Thompson. The woman I placed Isabella's soul into. Kayla is pregnant with twins, one of those babies is yours. Her babies will need souls, soon. How would you like Kayla to become your mother?"

"Are you saying instead of going to hell, you would put my soul into my child that Kayla is carrying?"

"Yes, she would be your mother. She would love you, care for you, how does that sound Michael?"

Tears ran down Michael's face overcome with emotion. The thought of having Kayla back in his life was overwhelming. "What do you need me to do? I will do anything you want, just name it!"

Hegate folded his arms, smiled and said. "Michael, I need you to speak to Tarsula. She has this crazy idea of turning hell loose onto the earthly plane. However, they must cross my domain to get there. We cannot allow this to happen. She is expecting me to make a tear in the ground of the astral plane, enabling the Golden Rope to be sent down and allowing an army from hell to ascend."

"What can I do Hegate? Tarsula is head strong, set in her ways.

I can try to talk sense to her, but it has never worked in the past.
Once she has her mind made up, that's it."

"Alright then let's put our heads together, there must be
something we can do to stop this from happening. We need a plan
Michael, you must help me stop her, if you want to be reincarnated."

* * *

Tarsula had booked the Presidential suite in a five-star hotel
for two months, booking it for an extended stay. She needed time to
come up with a plan, it was time to summon Hegate. Taking out her
wooden bowl, she filled it with water and then pulled her crystal out
of her carpet bag. Sitting down at a desk, she began her incantations.
Holding the crystal between her palms as it began to glow. Placing
it into the bowl, she watched as it started to spin. A thick grey fog
appeared, rising up towards the ceiling as Hegate emerged. "You
summoned me Tarsula?"

"I just wanted to let you know I'm making a tear on the earthly
plane on May 20th. On the grounds of a place called Danmore
Castle."

"Why that date Tarsula?"

"We're going to start our attack in the middle of a wedding.
My little group of café workers will all be present, along with many
others I assume. I'm going to go there and unleash Chaos, and
his army of cave dwellers. I need to find a spot that will ensure the
element of surprise."

"I've told you Tarsula I don't think this is wise. I won't allow
this to happen!"

"Grow a set of balls Hegate, if you refuse to help me, I'll handle
it myself. I have all my spell books now and any items I might need.
If I can tear a hole in the earthly plane, I'm sure I can make a tear
in the astral. I'm sending you back now, there's nothing more to
discuss."

"Tarsula you need to come to your"….Tarsula ended their
conversation taking her crystal out of the bowl, watching Hegate
dissipate and then dumping the water into the sink.

148

Her next step was to check out the venue and look around. She needed to find a point of entry, somewhere fairly hidden. Tarsula rubbed her hands together, excited that her little group of café workers would soon meet their demise. Chaos and his army would begin at the wedding killing all, and then move from town to town, killing anyone who crossed their path. Looking at herself in the mirror across the room, her glowing eyes and body exuded pure evil.

* * *

It was early in the morning when Mary arrived at the bridal boutique, on a warm sunny day. She was there for her last fitting before the wedding. As she walked through the door, she was greeted by two of her closest friends, Gloria and Nora. Who worked with her at the hospital's front desk. They ran over to Mary hugging her, excited to see her in her wedding dress. They were there to also, try on their dresses for the happy occasion. Mary had decided on a champagne-colored cocktail dress. Its bodice was lace, which changed from the waist down, into soft chiffon resting just above the knee. It moved and flowed as she walked around gracefully. The dresses for Gloria and Nora were made of linen, plain and fitted, they would wear the colors of spring. One was pale yellow, the other a soft lavender, a cropped jacket in the same material and color completed the look. Their dresses were classy and sophisticated. Mary stepped out from behind the dressing room curtain, she was met with oohs and aahs. She laughed overcome with joy, not believing she would find the second love of her life at age 56. Nora and Gloria also looked stunning in their dresses, which fit them perfectly.

"So, Mary is everything set for next weekend? I can hardly wait to see this castle you've been talking about." Nora exclaimed, as she looked at herself in the full-length mirror, pleased with her own reflection.

"Oh, it's truly beautiful, you're both going to love it." Mary replied, beaming.

"I'm sure we will." You're so lucky to have found Sam, he's one

149

in a million," stated Gloria.

"Yes, he definitely is, that's for sure." Mary smiled, as the three of them stood in front of the mirror. She could hardly wait to marry Sam, and as they say, live happily ever after.

* * *

Sam, Peter, and Max sat in the tuxedo rental place waiting for their suits to be brought out. Sam's suit was coffee brown. He would wear a champagne-colored shirt along with a bow tie, that had a champagne and brown pattern.

Peter and Max would both wear a light brown suit, champagne colored shirt, with either a pale yellow or soft lavender bow tie.

Sam was the first to step out from behind the curtain. He put his hands up in the air as he did a spin. "So, what do you think guys, am I a treat for the eyes?"

Peter and Max laughed out loud. "Oh, you're a treat alright, come here let me straighten you out, Mr. G.Q." Max replied, as he walked over to fix Sam's crooked tie. Peter just smiled and shook his head, knowing that Sam never cared about fashion. A pair of jeans and a clean white tee shirt were all you could hope for, according to Sam. Peter and Max were next in line to try on their wedding attire. Peter's pants were a little long and Max wanted his jacket to be more form fitting, other than that, they were good to go.

* * *

Mary said her goodbyes and headed straight to the florist. There were a few things to attend to before the big day. Yellow sunflowers with baby's breath, all tied up in pale yellow and lavender ribbons, which would be placed throughout the venue. In pots, vases, and on all the tables. Mary's bouquet was a combination of sunflowers, lavender, and champagne-colored roses, with a touch of baby's breath placed here and there. Her bridesmaids would also carry sunflowers and baby's breath, decorated with long strands of yellow and lavender ribbons cascading down. As Mary walked into the flower shop she stopped for a moment. Standing there the pungent smell of numerous flowers surrounded her, she inhaled deeply, enjoying the scent that had greeted her.

Brian came out from the back, drying his hands on a towel to welcome her. "Mary, how are you? Have you made a decision on the gentleman's boutonnieres?"

"I've decided to go with your suggestion of the champagne roses, with a spray of baby's breath."

"Fabulous, you've made the right choice. You're so lucky to be having your nuptials at Danmore. I'm going to try and talk my partner into having our wedding there, but first he has to ask me." Brian smiled, handing a red rose to Mary. "That's for you love, no charge. I will be at your venue early on the 20th to set everything up, don't worry about a thing."

"I trust you Brian, so much so, that I'm going to write you a check for the remaining balance right now."

"Alright, let me total everything up and I'll be right back."

Mary walked around admiring the different flowers and smelling them. Standing near the store's front window, she saw Kayla and Emily walking by. Mary gently tapped on the glass and waved. They both did an about face, walking quickly into the store to give Mary a hug. "What are you girls doing around here?" Mary asked.

Kayla responded, "I'm looking for a dress to attend a very special wedding on the 20th. Most of my clothes are getting snug now and actually are becoming uncomfortable." Kayla grinned, placing her hand gently on her belly.

"Did you try Maxine's? I just came from there, I had my last fitting before the big day."

"No," replied Kayla, "but I will definitely check it out."

Brian came out from the back of the store with Mary's bill. "Oh, hello ladies."

"Well, we have to get going Mary. I guess we'll see you on the 20th," remarked Emily. They said their good-byes and left.

"So, Mary are you ready to break the bank?" Brian joked.

"I sincerely hope not." Mary responded, as she took out her

checkbook. "Okay, hit me with the damage Brian."

* * *

It was getting late in the day, but Bradford Cummings needed to hunt. He was craving something different, something gamey and wild. Getting into his car he drove to the outskirts of town, parking just outside of a wooded area. He took off his shoes, placing them on the front seat of his car. Stepping into the forest he walked, keeping his eyes open and listening intently. He spotted a small rabbit sitting in the brush ahead of him. That would make the perfect appetizer for tonight's dinner, he thought, as his mouth watered. Bradford took off his clothes, as he began to shape shift at will. Most times he would wear clothes a few sizes larger than he actually was, giving his body the room to expand, but not today. Today, he would enjoy running through the forest naked, being one with nature. Bradford's body started to shift, growing taller and more masculine, covered in thick brown hair. His normal hands and feet became extended, protruding outwards ending in sharp claws. His face turned canine, as a muzzle with a dripping mouth and sharp yellow teeth made its appearance. His ears sprang out from the top of his head, twitching in response to any sound. Getting down on all fours, he waited for his moment to strike. He ran, as did the rabbit, under a bush and into its hole. Fuck! Bradford thought, not even having an opportunity to give chase. Bradford looked around for a bird, a squirrel, something. Maybe if I go deeper into the woods he thought, still listening and watching the area around him, he stopped dead in his tracks. Did I just hear a gun shot? Are there hunters out here? Bradford stepped up onto a fallen tree to get a better look around, he didn't see anything, but he could hear the rustling sound of walking. Feeling uneasy, Bradford decided to head back to his car, but he needed to find his clothes first. Re-tracing his steps, searching the ground, where the hell were they? He was sure this was the path he had taken. His ears twitched, hearing men whispering as an arrow came out of nowhere. It hit Bradford, in the dead center of his chest. He let out a howl extremely loud and foreboding, realizing he was hit and hurt. As birds took flight and

152

small animals scurried back into their hiding places. Bradford lay on the ground in excruciating pain, badly wounded. A small group of hunters ran towards the sound and gathered round him.

"What the fuck is that thing? Is it a wolf or a very large dog of some kind?" Jim asked. He looked at his hunting buddies for an answer. "It's suffering, I didn't mean to hit it with my arrow. I was just taking a practice shot aiming at that bush there, that thing got in the way." Paul remarked, as they watched Bradford's chest slowly stopped moving. Paul had a sinking feeling in his gut that he had seen this kind of creature before, but where? Was it in a dream, or was there more than one of these things roaming around these woods?

"What the hell do we do with the thing, should we bury it or leave it for the other animals to enjoy?" Jim asked, scratching his head, still trying to figure out what the hell he was looking at. "I mean, I don't think wolves are prevalent around here. It seems deformed, the legs are too long, it's just weird."

"Let's just leave it, it's going to be dark soon and our cars are quite a distance away. I don't feel like walking around these woods at night." Remarked another hunter in the group, as they started to walk away.

"What about my arrow, these are expensive. They were given to me for my birthday, their silver tipped." Paul announced, not wanting to leave his prized arrow.

"Okay then, just pull it out," Jim remarked, not understanding Paul's hesitation. "Oh, for Christ Sake!" Jim reached down and pulled out the arrow from Bradford's chest. "Here, now let's head back." Paul stood there looking down at the beast, feeling badly that he ended its life. Even though it was, shit faced ugly, something about it seemed so sad. Paul stood there looking down at it, then walked away to join his hunting buddies.

* * *

The next day, Tarsula drove her car up the private road to Danmore Castle. She was meeting Loren O' Brien to talk about an imaginary party she wanted to throw. She was curious about the castle, but it was the grounds she was truly interested in. Parking her car, Tarsula stepped outside and looked around. This place is surrounded by woodlands, the perfect place to hide until the moment of attack she thought. Tarsula walked to the castle and over the drawbridge into a large entry hall. Ms. O' Brien walked towards her extending her hand in a welcoming jester.

"Tarsula, welcome to Danmore. I'm Loren O'Brien, nice to meet you."

"Thank you, I've seen pictures of this place, but to see it in person it's really something."

"Shall we go into my office; we have a number of different packages I'm sure one will suit your needs."

"Alright, but may I tour the grounds first? The area looks lovely and it's a beautiful day for a stroll."

"Of course, is it okay if you go on your own? We're short on help today and I really shouldn't leave the phone. Just come back inside when you're through."

"No problem, I would actually prefer that." Tarsiula said with a smile. "It would give me time to think." Tarsula went outside and onto the fields of green grass making her way to the woods. As she walked down the hill, a forest of trees stood before her. Going deeper into the woods, there was one particular tree that caught her fancy. It was a large old oak whose trunk was massive. She could split it, making it the perfect place to enter the astral plane, a doorway. Yes, that would work splendidly Tarsula thought, as a wicked smile formed on her face. Leaving the woods she took out a small pocketknife from her purse. She marked a tree with a giant X; this would be her point of re-entering.

After some time, Ms. O'Brien realized that Tarsula had not come back. She walked out into the enormous entry hall calling out to her. "Tarsula! Tarsula, are you here?" No answer, she walked over the drawbridge and onto a grassy knoll looking for her, once again calling out her name. Maybe she changed her mind Loren thought, as she walked over to the visitor's parking area. The only car in the lot was her own.

Driving back to her hotel room Tarsula's mind was racing. She would have to study her book of spells on entering different dimensions and realms. She knew she could do it, without Hegate's help. It was time to devise a plan, maybe a fog spell combined with the sweet dreams spell, she thought. I could cast it on the entire astral plane, then bring up Mantus's unholy army. That could work, everyone asleep, no one getting in my way. "It's brilliant!" Tarsula shouted.

CHAPTER SEVENTEEN
WHAT'S COOKIN

Emily came home tired from her long day of shopping with Kayla. Simon walked over to her giving her a hug and a kiss on the cheek. "How was your day with Kay, buy anything?"

"No, not really. Kayla and I went to Maxine's, she bought a dress for Sam and Mary's wedding."

Dino had heard her voice and came running over to her, carrying his red ball in his mouth. She leaned over to pet him. "Hey buddy, I'm a little tired to play right now." Emily picked him up kissing his doggie face. "What are we doing for dinner, Simon?"

"I'm going to make some pasta, I've already taken out the butter to soften for the garlic bread. If you can make the salad?"

"Deal, I'm glad to be spending a quiet night at home with my two guys." Emily kissed Dino again, putting him down on the floor and watched as he laid down on his bed.

Simon walked into the kitchen filling his pasta pot with water, then placing it on the stove to boil. Emily opened the fridge, getting together the fixings for the salad. Placing everything on the counter, she bent over to retrieve her large salad bowl from one of the lower cabinets.

Simon was checking out her ass. He came up behind her, placing both of his hands on her ass cheeks rubbing them up and down. "You've got a great ass," Simon whispered in Emily's ear as she stood up.

"Not tonight, I'm really tired Simon, it's been a long day. I just want to eat, shower, and sleep."

"Are you sure I can't change your mind?" Simon put his arms around Emily's waist, then pushed her ass into his crotch. "Come on Em, you don't have to suck my dick, you just have to lay back and enjoy it. What do you say?"

"Are you sure? I just have to lay back and enjoy it?"

"I promise" Simon said, smiling at her.

Emily walked over to the kitchen table, removing her tee shirt and bra, and sat down on the table topless. Simon picked up the softened butter from the counter and walked over to her. He opened the container, placing a small amount of butter on both of Emily's nipples. He playfully licked and sucked the butter off them, looking at her face, he could tell this was turning her on. He removed Emily's jeans and underwear, pushing her back onto the table he spread her legs, inserting his tongue into her wetness. Emily moaned, as Simon enjoyed the sound of her sexual groans. He lingered there for a while, till his tongue was replaced by two fingers, he fingered her slowly. Finding her clit, he rubbed it in a fast-pulsating rhythm. Emily's moans soon turned into screams, Simon watched as she came undone. "That was so good baby, come on." Emily whispered, as she took down Simon's pants and underwear, taking hold of his erect manhood, she stroked his shaft up and down, till he was hard. Bending over the kitchen table she spread her legs. Simon grabbed hold of her hips, as he penetrated her.

He leaned over her and whispered. "Oh god baby your so wet, you feel so good." Simon fucked her slowly, grabbing onto her waist. Emily cried out and whimpered, enjoying the moment. Fucking her harder, Emily reached down finding her clit, she rubbed it quickly on the verge of coming.

"Yes! That's it don't stop!" Emily screamed, her moans and groans had taken Simon to the edge. He was about to come, giving Emily a few more good thrusts, he let out a moan of release coming inside her.

Simon pulled out, cleaning himself off. "So, Em, how do you

feel now, still tired"? he asked, out of breath and spent.

Emily walked over to the stove, turning it off, and seeing that most of the water had evaporated. "Care to join me in the shower before dinner?" she smiled at Simon with a lustful grin.

"Alright, but I'm not sure if I can go another round right now."

"Don't worry" Emily remarked, grabbing hold of his limp cock, "let's just see what happens."

* * *

Kayla tried on her new dress for Peter. It was deep navy blue with an A-line cut giving her the room that she needed to be comfortable. Peter put his arms around her, hugging her gently. "You are more beautiful now then the first time I saw you." He kissed her, placing his hand on her rounded belly.

"How's it going with your suit?" Kayla asked.

"They have to take up the pants a little, but otherwise fine. Max was complaining his jacket wasn't fitted enough, so they're going to have to fix that. Sam on the other hand was perfect, his suit fit him to a tee. Go figure, it seemed strange seeing him in a suit though, know what I mean?"

"Yeah, I've only seen him in tee-shirts and jeans since I've known him." replied Kayla. He's not exactly the poster child for elegant dressing and yet, I love him so much."

Peter smiled, "I know what you mean, he's got a heart of gold. What's for dinner?"

"Can we do Chinese? I'm craving sesame chicken and some fried dumplings."

"Sure, whatever you want hon."

"What do you want Peter, the usual?"

"Yep, chicken and broccoli and a side order of pork fried rice."

Kayla walked into the kitchen, picking up her phone and placing the order, a flash of light caught her attention. Putting down her phone, she ran to the living room, as Willie flew into the mail slot and landed on the living room rug.

"Willie!" Kayla was overjoyed to see her friend again, he flew

158

onto Kayla's shoulder as she patted his small head.

"Kay la, Willie return." He said, as Peter walked into the room, saw Willie and did an about face.

"Pe ter, Willie follow!" he yelled, flying off Kayla's shoulder.

Peter sat down at the kitchen table as Willie flew around him. Neither one of them knew why Willie followed Peter religiously. Kayla thought it was cute, but it just got on Peter's last nerve. Kayla grabbed Willie mid-flight sitting him down on the kitchen table. Looking at Peter he smiled, showing him his black teeth. Kayla took some dishes off the shelf and started to set the table for dinner. Spoons, forks, and knives were placed on the table along with a stack of paper napkins. Willie took a napkin and hid underneath it. "Willie hide?" he said, lifting the corner of it and peeking out.

"Why does he do that?" Peter asked, looking over at Kayla for answers.

"I don't know, he must have learned it from somewhere, or someone. Maybe we should ask him?"

"Willie, who told you to hide?" Kayla looked down at him lovingly, waiting for his answer.

He looked up at her and said only one word, "Tar su la."

Kayla and Peter just looked at each other. "Willie, why do you follow Peter around?"

"Tar su la." Willie answered again, with an angry look on his face. He hated her and Michael for taking Kayla and mistreating her.

"Willie, I have one more question. Did Tarsula teach you the word return?" asked Kayla.

Willie nodded his head yes, looking down at the table.

"So, Tarsula taught him all of these things, but why?" questioned Peter.

"Maybe she wanted Willie to follow you, then hide so he wouldn't be seen, and then return to her?" Kayla replied.

"Okay, but why would she want him to follow me? What would she gain by that?" Peter asked, confused.

"I don't know why Peter, but if Tarsula was involved, I'm sure there was evil intent."

After relaxing for a while, the doorbell rang, Peter got his wallet to pay for the food. Kayla picked up Willie, keeping him hidden.

They all sat down to eat, as Kayla placed Willie's food on a small saucer from a child's tea set. Peter looked at him differently now, knowing he had been trained for some reason by Tarsula. He watched, as Willie picked up a massive piece of sesame chicken with his tiny claws. He took a bite, smiled and devoured it. Then asked, "Willie follow Pe ter?" he looked at Peter for an answer.

"No Willie, no more following, alright." Willie nodded his head, he understood, as he reached for another piece of sesame chicken.

CHAPTER EIGHTEEN
MAKING PLANS

Tarsula sat on the floor in her posh hotel room, surrounded by her books of incantations, and all her belongings. She needed to find the exact spells that would allow her to succeed in her mission. Knowing that she could tear the earthly plane with no problem but needed to educate herself on ripping a hole in the astral one. Since the astral plane was not her domain, this was going to be more complicated. Going over and over it in her mind, this was the only thing she needed help with. The fog spell and sweet dream spell were easy; Tarsula had done them numerous times before. Her plan was to split the huge oak tree at its trunk, walk through it, then tear a hole in the earthly plane unseen. Allowing her then to proceed forward into the astral plane. Once there, she would use the fog spell making herself invisible to those around her. This would give her the opportunity to then bring forth the sweet dreams spell, sending everyone around her into a deep slumber. Then using her powers and a certain incantation, that she would study repeatedly, allowing her to tear the ground of the astral plane. Sending down the golden rope, letting Chaos and his army to ascend. Permitting the cave dwellers to then run through, into the earthly plane, ready to attack. It's genius, Tarsula thought, patting herself on the back.

* * *

Mary had been watching the weather channel for a couple of days. With her wedding coming up she was praying that it wouldn't rain. According to the local weather guy, the day would be overcast with occasional breaks of sun. I can deal with the clouds Mary thought, as long as it doesn't rain on my parade.

Sam sat down on the sofa next to her. "Will you stop watching the weather, it's going to be fine."

"I hope so, I just want our day to be perfect."

Sam leaned over and kissed her forehead, "and it will be my love, relax."

"I settled our debt with Brian, everything has been paid for, so were good."

"Who's Brian?" asked Sam. Trying to figure out who in the hell he was, and why were they paying him?

"He's the guy doing our flowers, remember you met him once. He owns the flower shop over on Main." Mary was laughing to herself, realizing how little Sam knew about the wedding plans.

"Oh yeah, now I remember. Do you want some coffee, I'm going to make some?" Sam asked.

"Okay, sure."

"And turn that damn weather station off!" Sam yelled, looking at her with a huge grin on his face.

* * *

Jeanna stood in her bedroom trying on outfits, hoping to find the perfect one for an outdoor wedding. She tried on pantsuits, short dresses, long skirts, but nothing seemed quite right. She wanted something eye catching, but nothing too sexy, drawing the attention away from the bride.

Max walked into the bedroom seeing the stack of clothes piled high on top of the bed. "What's going on here?" he asked.

"I'm trying to find something to wear to the wedding, but nothing seems right." She picked up a few outfits waving them in front of Max. This one is too sexy, this is too matronly, this skirt is too short, and this dress is too long."

"OMG Jeanna! You sound like Goldilocks. Just pick something, you'll be stunning no matter what you wear." Max walked over to her, putting his arms around her. "If you're making such a fuss over what to wear for Sam's wedding, what are you going to do when you need a dress for ours?"

"Well Max, first someone has to pop the question." Max kissed her and lightly smacked her ass.

"I'm going to watch the game, just choose something already!"

Jeanna sat on the bed and called Emily, wanting to find out what she was wearing. Maybe, it would give her some idea of what to wear.

Emily was playing with Dino when her phone rang. "Hey Jeanna, what's going on?"

"Hey Em, what are you wearing for Sam's wedding? I've tried on just about everything in my closet and nothing seems right."

"Yeah, I know what you mean, I've been trying on a few things myself. I have a dress with yellow flowers that I never get to wear. I guess that's going to be the one. Try and keep it simple Jeanna, it's a wedding, not a fashion show."

Max re-entered the bedroom, as Jeanna continued her conversation with Emily looking through her closet describing the dresses she was thinking about wearing. Maxwell walked over to the line of shoes thrown about and scattered on the bedroom floor. He quickly removed a velvet ring box from his pocket, placing it into the toe of one high heeled shoe. Sitting on the bed he waited, until Jeanna's conversation was over.

Jeanna sat on the bed next to him. "So, I guess I'm going to wear this green dress, what do you think?"

"That's fine, like I said, you're beautiful no matter what you wear. Are those heels new, I haven't seen them before?"

"Which ones?" Jeanna walked over to the shoe pile.

"The black ones with the red sole," replied Max feeling nervous. Jeanna bent down and picked up her black pumps.

"You mean these? What are you talking about I wear them a lot, they cost me a small fortune."

"They're very sexy, try them on for me. I want to see how they look on you.”

Jeanna hesitated, but wanting to please him, she stepped inside the shoe for her left foot. “What do you think?’ Jeanna turned her foot this way and that, wanting Max to get the full look.

“I think I need you to put the other one on also.” he asked. Starting to wipe his sweaty hands off, on the front legs of his jeans. Jeanna exhaled loudly, feeling stupid. She placed her foot into the right shoe, but something would not allow her foot to go inside. Jeanna picked up the shoe, placing her hand down into its toe, pulling out the box.

Max stood up taking the box from her hand and got down on one knee. “Jeanna, I love you to pieces, you are the only woman I will ever want or need.” Opening the box, he exposed the ring to her. “Jeanna, will you marry me?”

Jeanna just stood there in shock; it was finally happening. He stood up as she wrapped her arms around him and covered his face in never-ending kisses.

“Is that a yes?” Max asked.

“Yes! Absolutely yes!” Jeanna replied, as tears ran down her face. “Oh my God Maxwell, I didn’t see this coming, how long did you have this ring for?”

“Not long, I wanted to wait and get you a bigger stone, but after speaking with Sam I decided not to wait any longer.”

“So, I guess I should be thanking Sam? I’m glad someone was able to finally talk some sense into you.” Jeanna couldn’t stop looking at the ring on her hand. She was overcome with emotion, still crying and still wearing the shoe on her left foot. Reaching down to take it off, Max grabbed her arm.

“Would you mind putting the other shoe on, take everything else off, but leave the shoes on,” he said with a sexy grin.

“Max, I thought you were watching the game?”

“I’m recording it,” Max replied, taking off his clothes quickly.

* * *

Mary had laid the open suitcases onto the bed in the guest

room. They hadn't been used in a while and needed some airing out. She was packing for two, God forbid she left it up to Sam, to bring what was needed. Doing her best to pack lightly, to just bring what was essential. On past vacations Mary always over packed, never using half the stuff she brought. Walking over to her dresser she lifted out a box, opening the lid it contained a negligee. It was made of a black see through material, holding it up in front of her, it didn't leave much to the imagination. Mary sat down on the bed wondering, if it was a little too much, too sexy. She folded it up gently, placing it back into the box. Not sure, she would have the courage to wear it or feel comfortable enough in it.

Sam walked into the bedroom just as she was placing the box back into the drawer. "What's that?" Sam asked. "Is it a present for me, a surprise?"

"In a way, I guess you could call it that." Mary looked at him with a smirk on her face.

"What is it? You've got me curious now." Sam came up behind Mary wrapping his arms around her. Hesitantly, she removed the box and opened it. Turning around, she held it up for Sam.

"Holy mother of God! Are you trying to give me a heart attack woman? Tell me you weren't going to put it back in the box and leave it there, not even giving me the chance to see it? You are a very sexy woman, Mary Hayes. I'll expect to see you wearing that on our first night in Italy. Promise me you'll wear it."

"You're sure, it's not too much for a woman my age?" Mary could feel the blood rush to her face.

"Are you kidding me right now? What's your age got to do with anything? A woman can be sexy and beautiful at any age, and you are both my love. I know you are trying to bring only the essentials, but that's an essential, you need to bring it. I love it, and I love you." Sam wrapped his arms around her once again, kissing her neck and nibbling her right ear. He gently tapped her ass, as he walked out of the room. Mary stood there and smiled; Sam was everything she could ever hope for. She took the empty box and threw it onto the bed. Then gently and with care, placed the negligee into her suitcase.

* * *

Sergeant Neil Daniels opened the door to his bedroom closet. Since he mostly wore a uniform, his suits had been pushed to the back of it. Pulling out his suit jackets, he wasn't sure if they were outdated. "Bonnie, can you come here for a minute, I need your opinion on something." Bonnie stepped into the bedroom, looking at the clothes spread out on the bed. "Do these clothes look outdated to you?"

Bonnie exhaled deeply. "You do know the wedding is this weekend and you're just doing this now?" She walked over to the bed looking closely at each jacket, picking one that she thought was the best option. "I think this grey jacket would be okay. Do you know where the pants are to this one?"

"I guess they should be in the closet, somewhere." Neil replied, as Bonnie shook her head and closed her eyes, upset with her husband's procrastination.

"Alright," Bonnie said, as she started the quest to look for Neil's pants. His closet was anything but organized. Shirts hanging partially off hangers and his shoes thrown this way and that, none of them making a pair. His clothes were crammed in there so tightly together, you could barely move the hangers along the bar. Finally, she pulled out the grey pants that went to the jacket. They were very wrinkled and in need of a good pressing, but they would do. "Found them!" She held them up in front of him. "That was like trying to find a needle in a haystack. Now where are your black dress shoes?" she asked.

Neil looked down at the mess of shoes, all over the floor of his closet. Bonnie just looked at him disgusted, walking out of the room with his grey pants and an iron.

* * *

Later in the week, the group was getting together at Clancy's Bar and Grill to celebrate Jeanna's and Max's engagement. Jeanna

166

had reserved a large table to accommodate the group. As they waited for everyone to arrive Max placed his hand on Jeanna's thigh and said. "Too bad they don't have long tablecloths here. Your little antics at Anthony's restaurant will be burned in my mind forever, it was epic." Max smiled, placing his hand higher on Jeanna's thigh. She laughed, taking his hand off her leg. "Yeah well, tonight we are meeting our friends, so let's keep your hands to yourself and away from my private parts. Okay Maxwell?" Max just smiled, placing his arm around Jeanna's shoulder.

Sam and Mary were the first to arrive, followed by Kayla and Peter. Bringing up the rear, Emily and Simon made their appearance, somethings never change Sam thought. Emily's punctuality was getting better, but could still use improving.

Jeanna showed off her ring, as everyone complimented her on how beautiful it was. They all told Max he had done a good job picking it out. Sam patted Max on the back, letting him know he was proud of him for popping the question and finally taking the leap into marriage.

There was a lot to be happy about. As food and drinks were brought over, toasts were made, and everyone was very excited about the soon to be wedding of Sam and Mary. With so much laughter and joking around, their table would become loud at times getting the attention of one particular patron.

Tarsula looked over the room, wondering where all the noise was coming from. At first, she scanned the bar area, no it wasn't coming from the bar. She looked over at the tables, nothing, until…. "fuck them" she said, under her breath, seeing them all having such a good time. Tarsula was just about to leave, but then, she decided to have a little fun with the group first. Sitting there thinking, what can I do to spoil their night, an evil grin formed on Tarsula's face. Taking a napkin from the table, she drew a tiny picture. Closing her eyes she began to whisper an incantation, rocking gently back and forth and waited. Seeing pictures in her mind, as to what was about to happen, she laughed quietly to herself.

Suddenly a bone chilling scream was heard from behind the bar, as a barrage of mice started to crawl out from the floor drains. Vickie, the bartender, jumped onto the bar spilling the customer's drinks.

"What the hell is going on over there?" Sam questioned, as he looked at Mary. The group looked over to the bar area, but couldn't understand what the commotion was about.

Most of the woman and some of the men stood up on their chairs screaming. "Something just brushed against my foot!" Jeanna screamed, picking up her feet. "What the hell is happening?" She made the mistake of looking down at the floor. Mice were everywhere. People were now jumping on top of tables, as their drinks and food hit the floor. "They're coming out of the floor drains!" They heard a guy yell, helping his girlfriend get up onto the bar.

Mary started to scream and shake. If there was one thing she hated, it was mice. The girls jumped onto their chairs, screaming and crying. Sam took a push broom that was leaning against the wall and started to push the mice away from their table. The owner called the police, as the chaos escalated. "Cover the floor drains!" Someone yelled out from the crowd. Plates were being thrown to the floor, along with glasses and silverware. People were throwing anything they could get their hands on, trying to scare the mice away.

Tarsula chuckled, watching the havoc taking place around her. She collected her belongings and slipped out the back. Laughing all the way to her car.

"We've got to get out of here!" Emily screamed, reaching out for Simon's hand as he kicked the mice across the floor, which was now a sea of rodents.

Simon turned around, his back facing Emily. "Em, jump onto my back I'll carry you out!" Emily put her arms around Simon's neck as she straddled his back. He held onto her, shaking the mice off that were trying to run up his legs. He ran towards the door stepping on mice, food, and booze. Peter, Sam, and Max followed suit. Slowly the bar started to empty out, as men carried out their ladies.

The police arrived, along with animal control. Everyone just stood around outside, not understanding what had just taken place, as Sergeant Daniels arrived. Every time the front door opened to let the police and animal control in, the mice ran out, causing the crowd of people to scurry.

Sam was walking through the crowd trying to get to Daniels, followed by the rest of his group. "Sergeant Daniels over here!" Sam yelled, waving his hands in the air.

Daniels exhaled loudly, and shook his head, he was not surprised this little group was in attendance. "Hey Sam, why am I not surprised to see all of you here, fill me in." Everyone started to speak at once, as Daniels raised his hand, asking them to speak one at a time.

Sam spoke first. "I'm not exactly sure, what happened in there. We were having a lovely time, just celebrating. When these mice started to come out of the floor drains, I've never seen anything like it. There were so many of them, they covered the floor."

Daniels looked over at Kayla and Peter, he had a bad feeling in his gut. Peter put his arm around Kayla's shoulder, they had seen that look on Daniels face before. The wheels were turning in Daniels head, they knew his thoughts were going to the dark side. Between the three of them, they had seen too much on the cliff that night, outside Michael's house. The others had their memories erased, that night thanks to Zadoc, Peter's father. Daniels looked at the small crowd that was still lingering about, telling them to please go home and let animal control do their job. Max and Jeanna, along with Emily and Simon, said goodnight. Sam and Mary hugged Kayla and Peter, before they walked away, leaving them with Daniels. "Come on you two, I'll walk you to your car, I think we need to talk."

When they got to Peter's car Kayla asked. "Sergeant Daniels, do you think Michael and Tarsula were responsible for what happened here tonight?"

Daniels looked at them both square in the eye. "I don't know, but for all our sakes, I sincerely hope not. However, what other explanation could there be. I've never heard of mice coming out of a floor drain before. I mean, maybe one or two at the most, but hundreds of them that's just unheard of."

Kayla looked at Peter and Daniels. "If this was the work of Tarsula, I'm sure this is just a taste of what's to come." Kayla stated. "Who knows what she's capable of Sergeant Daniels." Peter put his arm around her, he could feel her shaking slightly as he held her tighter.

"Listen," Daniels began. "Let's not get ahead of ourselves, maybe it was just an inconvenient happenstance. Sometimes strange things occur in normal life for whatever reason. This mice thing could just be a fluke." Daniels was trying to stay calm, but in his mind he had a feeling that Kayla was right, that there would definitely be more to come. "If either of you see anything out of the ordinary give me a call, you both have my direct line. Try not to worry, like I said before, we may be putting too much into this. Have a good rest of the night guys drive home safe. I'll see you both, at the wedding." Daniels walked back to Clancy's, he needed to see for himself the carnage that had taken place there. Walking into Clancy's, the guys from animal control were walking out carrying garbage bags full of mice.

Daniels brought his hand up to his forehead and rubbed, this was definitely not a normal part of life. In his heart he knew Tarsula was up to her old tricks. He walked inside throwing up a little in his mouth. There were tons of dead mice and some that were still running around. A horrible feeling went through his body, that Daniels couldn't shake, as the men kept shoveling mice into black plastic bags.

CHAPTER NINETEEN

WEDDED BLISS

Mary was still checking the forecast on the day of her wedding. They had called for partly cloudy skies, but no rain. She was grateful for that, since most of the wedding was taking place outside. She walked into the kitchen to make some coffee. Usually, Sam would wake up before her and make a pot. However, he had spent the night at Peter's house, not wanting to see the bride before the wedding. Mary placed two slices of bread into the toaster. Her plan was to eat light this morning and pig out later at the reception. She was about to sit down when her doorbell rang. Opening the door, there stood Nora and Gloria, she greeted them with hugs and kisses. They followed Mary into the kitchen putting a box of donuts on the table. "They're your favorite, we got them at the bakery you like." Gloria said. She opened the box showing off the treats. "See there's jelly, chocolate glazed and of course cream. I made sure the cream was French cream, not that yellow kind that you don't like." The slices of toast popped up just as Mary was placing a chocolate glazed into her mouth. "Well, I guess the toast can wait" Mary laughed, taking out the slices of bread from the toaster. She grabbed a couple of mugs, pouring hot coffee into them. Nora went into the living room, carefully placing their dresses on the sofa. They would all get dressed together and later make their way to Danmore Castle.

* * *

Everyone was waking up, for what they hoped would be the

perfect wedding day. Sam was making breakfast for Kayla and Peter, it was something he wanted to do, considering he had spent the night with them. Making a pot of decaf coffee he felt nervous, but happy. Never in his wildest dreams did he ever think he would find such a lovely woman as Mary. In his mind he kept thinking, he would have lost her if it wasn't for Peter, who brought her back to him. Peter the half human, half extraterrestrial, Sam had grown to love. He had opened his eyes, that there was more to this world than we could ever imagine.

"Good morning, Sam." Kayla announced, as she walked into the kitchen. "Something smells good."

"Morning there, little lady, I'm making breakfast. We have pancakes, eggs, and sausage, plus decaf coffee. Is Peter awake?"

"Thanks, but you really didn't have to do all this, it's your wedding day after all. You should be relaxing." Kayla said, looking at him and smiling. "Also, in answer to your question, between you and me, I think Peter would sleep until noon if I let him. He's definitely not a morning person."

"Hello there!" Sam exclaimed, as he watched Peter walk into the kitchen, rubbing his eyes and trying to wake up. "Come join the living." Sam smiled, looking over at Kayla and shaking his head.

"Sam made us breakfast wasn't that nice of him?" Kayla looked at Peter, as she devoured her stack of pancakes.

"That's so nice, thank you Sam." Peter was doing his best to come around, but it always took a little while in the morning to get himself started. "Today's the big day Sam, how do you feel?" Peter asked, as he poured himself a cup of hot coffee, hoping it would wake him up.

"I feel a little nervous, I'm not going to lie, but I don't have any doubts about marrying Mary. Thank you for what you did Peter."

Peter smiled and said, "you're welcome." Yet, he felt guilty about taking credit for Mary's return. Sitting down, holding his coffee mug, Sam placed a plate of food in front of him. "This looks fantastic Sam." Peter dove in, starting with his scrambled eggs. He looked over at Kayla, who looked back at him and grinned, Peter was slowly waking up.

* * *

Emily and Simon were waking up, to find Dino in the bed with them. Sometime during the night, he climbed into their bed and laid down between them. Dino was an Italian Greyhound and always in need of affection. Emily rubbed Dino's back and kissed him on his head. "Thank God you're a little guy and you don't need much room." She said lovingly, getting out of bed and putting on her slippers. Simon started to rough house with Dino, grabbing a toy and playing tug of war on the bed. "I'm making omelets and coffee, when you guys are done fooling around, get your butts into the kitchen!" Emily shouted thinking her usual thought, boys will be boys.

* * *

Jeanna woke up with her head on Max's chest. After last night's nightmare in the bar, with what Jeanna referred to now as, "Mice-Capades" she was hoping today would be perfect for Sam and Mary's wedding ceremony. She kissed Max on the cheek and down his neck. "Keep going down, don't stop there." Max instructed her, just waking up and already horny as hell. Jeanna lightly smacked his face, telling him to get out of bed. There was a lot to do today, and she didn't want to be late for the nuptials. She had been looking forward to this day for a while and could hardly wait to see the castle and the venue. In her mind she was hoping Max would love it enough, to have their wedding there. Jeanna took her robe off the bed and carried it into the bathroom, with every intention of taking a quick shower. Looking over at Max, he had the saddest look on his face, and she knew why. "Want to join me lover boy?" Jeanna asked. Max flew out of bed, taking off his clothes before he even got to the bathroom door.

* * *

Brian's van pulled up the road to Danmore Castle, full of flowers and ribbons to decorate the venue. It was a cloudy day, but the sun would make its appearance occasionally. He had his

173

best workers along for the ride with him, experienced with flower arranging and all things bridal. As the van crested the hill, the castle was something to behold. The flags outside had been changed to the colors of the day, yellow and lavender moving with the slightest breeze. They got out of the van and were greeted by Loren O' Brien.

"Hello nice to meet you. I'm Brian, with Flowers by Brian. I'm here to do Mary and Sam's wedding."

"Yes, of course, nice to meet you Brian. I'm Loren O' Brien, B R I E N", she grinned. Feel free to roam about the grounds. Let me know if I can be of any assistance to you."

"Thank you so much Loren, but I think we have it under control." Brian opened the back of his van and the decorating began. The first thing to start on was the arch where the nuptials would take place. It would be constructed and covered with sunflowers, baby's breath, and champaign roses. Also, a sprig of lavender was placed here and there to bring in some purple color. Two tall golden plant stands would be placed on both sides of the arch, topped off with large floral arrangements that contained the same yellow, champagne, and lavender flowers.

Next on the scene were the people from "Let's Party", a company that delivers tents, tables, and chairs for any occasion. Removing the chairs from the truck, they were placed in the field in perfect rows. On the back of each chair, near the center aisle, they placed a bouquet of sunflowers and baby's breath. All tied up with ribbons, of yellow and purple cascading down to the ground. Inside the castle, the tables were decorated with large mason jars containing the same flowers and ribbons. All of the jars would be placed on lavender tablecloths. Champagne colored plates and golden utensils completed the look.

The D.J. was setting up his table, next to the dance floor, making sure all was in order. He spun a few records just to make sure the sound was crystal clear. Loren turned on the Bose speakers so that the music could be piped outside and onto the field.

CHAPTER TWENTY
TARSULA'S PLAN

Tarsula was excited, the wickedness in her had been building. Now that she no longer had Michael to reel her in, which he would have to do occasionally. At this moment in time, she was free to do as she pleased. Tarsula parked her car at the bottom of the hill away from the venue walking through the woods alongside the open field, just out of sight. This plan is perfect, she thought, reaching the top of the hill and looking at the castle in all its glory. Looking out over the field of chairs and beautiful flowers, it made her sick to her stomach. "Stupid Fucks," she said under her breath. "Your time is coming." She looked for her tree with the giant X, turned and walked into the woods needing to find that very large oak tree. Her plan was to split its trunk, turning it into a doorway, letting her make a rip in the earthly plane unseen. Holding a notebook in her hands, all the spells and incantations that were needed had been copied into it. She continued searching for the tree, mentally going over all of the pages again and again. It needed to be done perfectly, precisely, Tarsula suddenly froze. There before her stood the mighty oak. A devilish smile formed on her face, as she ran towards it, clutching the notebook tightly against her chest. Soon it would be time to open the doorway, for the army of hell to pass through, and the wedding ceremony to start. Sitting on a rock she waited, eating a giant chocolate bar and a package of cookies. The anticipation was more than she could stand, waiting for the killing to begin.

* * *

Daniels and his wife were dressing quickly, they were running late, with no time to waste. Bonnie was ready, with just a few more cosmetic touches. Daniels threw on his suit jacket, placing his crystal into his pocket. "Neil, are you ready?" His wife asked, grabbing her purse. As Daniels was putting on his shoes, Bonnie realized that his suit jacket was torn at the shoulder. "Jesus, Neil your jacket is torn at the shoulder quick take it off, your dress shirt and tie will have to do." She took hold of his arm, quickly grabbing his keys, as they ran out the front door.

* * *

Sam walked out of the guest room, all dressed and ready to go. Kayla and Peter looked up as Sam walked into the living room. "Oh my God Sam, you are so handsome! Mary is going to lose her mind when she sees you" Kayla exclaimed. She ran over to him fixing his bow tie and the collar of his shirt. Peter walked over and shook Sam's hand. "Well, this is it; your big day is finally here. Kay and I are so happy for you and Mary."

"Thank you both, for letting me stay here and for all your help with everything." Sam had tears in his eyes, he was filled with emotion.

Kayla wrapped her arms around him and asked. "Shall we go?" Sam nodded his head yes. He was too choked up to get any words out, at this point. He was ready to start the next chapter of his life with the woman he loved.

The guests were arriving at the venue, their cars traveling slowly bumper to bumper up the private road. They were waved over by an attendant, to a large parking lot on the right side of the castle. Some of the guests had been there before, while others stood amazed at the sight before them.

Sam arrived with Kayla and Peter. They stepped out of the car, as the well-wishers patted Sam on his back, congratulating him on his upcoming nuptials. They made their way into the castle, crossing over the drawbridge where they were met by Loren O'Brien.

176

"Congratulations Sam, today's the big day, nervous?" Loren asked, looking at Sam with a huge smile on her face.

"A little, but that's normal right?" Sam replied, looking at Kayla and Peter.

"Everything looks beautiful Sam. Why don't we make our way outside, you don't want to see the bride before the wedding, shall we go?" They walked outside to the field decorated in yellow, lavender, and champagne, as a slight breeze blew through the meadow.

Emily and Jeanna were already there seated, waving their hands in the air, so Kayla and Peter could join them. Sam walked over to The Justice of the Peace, shaking his hand and still fighting off emotional tears. He looked out over the field at his friends and family. Everyone turned to see the draw bridge being raised up. The bride had arrived, coming in through a back entrance of the castle. The Wedding March began to play through loudspeakers above their heads, clear and calming. Everyone was focused on the drawbridge waiting for it to lower. Sam was experiencing a ton of emotions, from excited to nervous.

* * *

Tarsula could also hear the music faintly, it was time. She stood in front of the massive tree placing her notebook on a large rock, she needed her hands free, as the incantation took hold of her. She spread her fingers and moved her hands in a circular motion. A ball of electric energy formed, floating between her palms. Rolling and spinning, gaining power she laughed, throwing the massive fire ball with force at the oak tree. It split right down the middle, cracking into two equal parts. Next would come her second incantation, to tear a hole in the earthly plane, enabling her to step into the astral realm. Easy, Peezy she thought.

* * *

The drawbridge was lowered, as Gloria and Nora walked across it, followed by beautiful Mary. Sam and the others looked on, as the women made their way across the field. Mary was smiling and crying all at the same time, hoping her makeup was still intact. They reached the gathering of chairs walking down the middle aisle as everyone stood up.

Peter put his arm around Kayla and kissed her cheek gently. Simon took Emily's hand bringing it up to his lips. While Max's hand came around onto Jeanna's hip, giving her a quick kiss on the neck.

Love was definitely in the air, as Mary stood before Sam trying to wipe away her tears and look presentable. Sam smiled and took her hands into his, telling her how beautiful she truly was. This made Mary cry even more.

"Dearly beloved." The Justice of the Peace started. "We are gathered here today to witness the marriage between Mary Elizabeth Hayes and Samuel Parker Anderson."

* * *

Tarsula stepped into the astral plane without anyone taking notice of her, using a simple fog spell. She moved around the hordes of the dead. Now, came the moment to cast her sweet dreams spell upon the astral plane. Quickly she removed her crystal from her pocket, a tall narrow prism which stood at attention in her hand, it suspended itself upright unassisted. Suddenly it levitated spinning, usually the sweet dream spell was a party trick for Tarsula. However, this spell now had to work on a much larger scale, placing everyone into deep slumber. The crystal spun as a white vapor permeated from it, smelling of sweet jasmine. Tarsula ran to a hillside watching, as people started to lay down. Closing their eyes they drifted off to sleep, even Hegate was slumped over snoring.

Tarsula stood there waiting. It was time to make a tear on the ground of the astral plane. She then realized with all her excitement; she had left the notebook in the woods on a rock. This wasn't going to be so easy, since this was not her realm. Yet, she had recited the incantation numerous times and felt she would be able to recite the words perfectly without the book. She just needed to concentrate. Her voice echoed through the plane, as a small slash began to open at her feet. Quickly she needed to find the horn of the realms, the horn Mantus had given her. Looking around she saw it laying between Hegate's very large hooves. Tarsula ran over, carefully and quietly picked up the horn from between his massive legs. Running back to the slash, she blew into it and waited.

Soon, The Gate Keeper appeared below her. He looked up at her, telling her to throw down the golden rope. Chaos and his army were on their way.

* * *

The Justice of the Peace continued, "Sam, do you take this woman, Mary Elizabeth Hayes to be your lawfully wedded wife? To love and cherish from this day forward, in sickness and in health, forsaking all others till death do you part?

Sam smiled as a single tear ran down his face. "I do."

"And do you Mary take this man Samuel Parker Anderson, as your lawfully wedded husband? To love and cherish from this day forward, in sickness and in health, forsaking all others till death do you part?"

Mary looked at Sam, wondering how she got so lucky. "I do."

"May we have the rings please," the Justice of the Peace announced.

* * *

Tarsula threw down the golden rope as Chaos climbed up, followed by thirty of his best warriors. "Where are the others, Chaos? Thirty men do not make an army!" Tarsula exclaimed.

"Well, Mantus thought this would be enough for now. These are my best men, the humans won't have a chance of survival."

The army stood ready for combat. Tarsula gave the order to go through the slit of the earthly plane and remain in the forest. "Do not proceed till I join you." She said, not wanting to miss out on any of the killings. "All of you stay hidden. I need to close the tear in the astral plane for now." Chaos and his army followed Tarsula's command, they ran towards the earthly plane, waiting there in the forest for her arrival.

179

Tarsula lifted and pulled the golden rope up, placing it back where she had found it. She then turned to address the opening and walked right into Michael, standing before her.

"Tarsula, what have you done! Why is there a tear in the astral plane?" Since Michael wasn't human, he had awakened sooner than the others. Tarsula's deep sleep spell only put him out for a short period of time. Hegate was also awake, looking over at Michael's confrontation with Tarsula. They had devised somewhat of a plan, since Michael knew her well, he had his suspicions of what spells she would use. They were hoping to have guessed right, and that Michael would have the balls to go through with their scheme.

"Michael?" Tarsula wrapped her arms around him. "My dear boy, this is perfect, come and join us!"

"Us, Tarsula? What do you mean us?"

"I have brought forth an army from hell, with the orders to kill. There is a wedding taking place as we speak. That cook Sam is getting married today, we will destroy all who have attended their wedding. Join us!"

"Sam is Kayla's friend; she will be at that wedding. What the fuck Tarsula?"

"Micheal what the shit is wrong with you! You've gotten soft since your death, it's pitiful."

"You're right, my dear friend Tarsula what was I thinking, come here." Michael reached out his arms to her, she thought he had come to his senses, that he would join her. Instead, he grabbed hold of Trasula and threw her down into the tear of the astral plane, letting her fall, descending into hell and landing on a pile of dirt and ash.

"Michael!" Tarsula screamed, standing up and brushing herself off. "Send down the golden rope, let's talk about this! You can't leave me down here! Michael please!" Tarsula watched in horror, as Hegate also looked down at her, through the hole of the astral plane. A smile came across his face, large and gruesome, as he slowly sealed up the tear to his realm. Tarsual screamed and cried out for Michael.

Surely, he wouldn't leave me down here, in this realm, she thought. All of that screaming, brought forth The Gate Keeper, who ran towards her.

"Tarsula, why are you here and not leading the army, Mantus has provided for you?"

Tarsula tried to make herself invisible to The Gate Keeper. She was fearful of what he might do to her. Try as she might, her spells, incantations, and powers did not work in hell. Tarsula remembered her first time here, when she tried to float towards the gate but couldn't. She ended up walking along the hot ground, as insects tried to climb up her legs.

The Gate Keeper looked up. "The opening has been closed Tarsula, you have no hope that the golden rope will be sent down to rescue you." He watched, as she tried to conjure up a protective bubble around herself. The Gate Keeper laughed and hissed. "Your powers do not work here, this is hell. The one realm, where being a fucking witch means nothing!" The Keeper picked her up, flinging her over his shoulder, as she kicked and screamed out of her mind terrified. Tarsula fell off his shoulder, trying to get away. The Gate Keeper chuckled and hissed, grabbing onto her. "Now we have one more body to torture." He laughed, as he walked back to the Gate of Human Suffering holding on to Tarsula's legs, dragging her along the hot bug infested ground.

* * *

The cheers of joy could be heard in the forest, as Sam and Mary 's ceremony continued. Chaos looked back through the hole in the earthly plane, but he did not see Tarsula. Where the fuck was she? This was her idea, and now she was nowhere in sight. One of Chao's soldiers stepped away from the group, he was getting anxious, wanting to start the battle. Unseen by the others, he moved away from the shelter of the woods, out onto the field.

Jeanna was looking around over the grounds, imagining her wedding with Max taking place there. Her eyes rested on someone in the distance, he seemed out of place. She squinted her eyes, hoping it would give her a better view, but she still couldn't see well. Jeanna touched Kayla's shoulder. "Kay look over there in the distance, what is that, is that a person?"

Kayla looked to where Jeanna was pointing, it started to move, running towards them. It raised what looked like an arm, was it holding something? Suddenly, the sun moved from behind the clouds, shining brightly on the field. Jeanna and Kayla watched as this thing disintegrated, going up in flames. Kayla stood up and yelled at the top of her lungs, "RUN! SAM, MARY, EVERYONE RUN TO THE CASTLE NOW!" Kayla's thoughts went to only one person, Tarsula. What had she brought forth now?

Chaos looked out from the trees, he could see people running away, it was now or never. They couldn't wait for Tarsula, he gave the command to charge. The army ran up the hill, towards the wedding sight. Everyone in attendance was also running, some turning their heads screaming, horrified, not sure what these things were or where they had come from. People were falling over chairs, flower arrangements were pushed to the ground, as the wedding guests were thrown into a state of panic. Sam grabbed hold of Mary's hand, running with her. One of the creatures grabbed Mary's arm, Sam took one of the golden plant stands and smacked the thing in the head. It dropped to the ground, but only for a moment, getting up once again ready to attack.

Sergeant Daniels got his wife Bonnie into the castle, as he went out to help some of the older guests. Taking them by the arm, as he pushed them along, calling on his cell phone for backup. He had to stop a few times, when he needed to fend off one of Chaos's soldiers. One of these creatures had a woman by the neck, it had wrapped its skeletal hands around her squeezing tightly. Daniels picked up a chair, bashing it in the head, what were these things? Skeletal cyclopes armed with what looked like human bones sharpened to a point?

Paul and Ralph were trying their hardest to get everyone into the castle. Grabbing anything they could use to defend themselves.

Seeing the drawbridge in the up position, they ran towards the back, getting people inside. Sam needed to get to the room where all the weapons were kept. Running inside, the door to the weapons room was locked, he needed to find Loren. Sam searched the crowd for her. She was standing by the chain that worked the drawbridge, trying to keep it in the up position. He ran over to her, "I need the key to the weapons room, NOW!"

"If I give you that key Sam, I could lose my job!"

"Better your job than your life! Now give me the FUCKING KEY!"

She handed Sam the key, as Peter, Max, and Simon found the back door and ran over to him. They ran to the weapons room together. "Help me guys," Sam said, take as many weapons as you can hold and follow me!" They pulled weapons off the walls, anything that was low enough for them to reach. Laden with weapons, they ran out the back and were met by Paul and Ralph. Ralph was bleeding from his arm, while Paul had a gash on his leg and across his forehead. Sam handed both of them a weapon, making sure to give Paul the bow and arrows, since he was an expert marksman.

Peter, Max, and Simon had pulled off the wall, many weapons, one of them called a Flail. It was a metal rod which had a thick chain attached to it, a large metal ball with spikes hung off the end. Simon held the flail high, spinning the spiked ball in a circular motion, this would be his weapon of choice. He was sure it would cause some damage and break more than a few bones. The men at the wedding kept on fighting, along with the police who finally arrived. Pulling out their guns they fired at the cave dwellers, but the bullets did not stop them. The men in blue were falling like flies, dying on the field as the war continued.

Sam ran over to Daniels giving him a sickle for protection, the semicircular blade gleamed in his hand. Daniels checked his pant pockets looking for his crystal, they could really use the help of the Seekers right about now. Then he remembered he had left it in the pocket of his suit jacket. Chaos came up behind him, carrying a sharpened rib bone and was about to plunge it into his back. When suddenly, the sun made another appearance, Daniels turned to defend himself. He raised the sickle above his head, ready to strike this unholy creature. As the warmth of the sun shone brightly, Chaos disintegrated before his eyes, he was stunned, not understanding what had just happened. Looking around as the battle continued, soon more of the creatures met their demise, turning to dust before his eyes. He looked up at the afternoon sky, as some cumulus clouds came into view. The sun suddenly vanished, leaving the creatures to battle on. "It's the sun! Daniels shouted; they can't take the sun!"

The creatures looked up. The cave dwellers realized that their skeletal bodies had always been cloaked in darkness, in the dirty confines of the cave. Never seeing anything like this bright light above their heads. The sun was killing them off, each time it appeared. They had to return to the forest, needing the shelter of the trees to survive.

Everyone that remained standing ran towards the castle. Sam and Daniels stood on the hill looking towards the woods. They were quickly joined by some of the wedding guests and a few police men. They waited, not sure what was about to happen, holding their weapons tightly, ready to fight.

* * *

Hegate and Michael looked out of the hole into the earthly plane, standing in the forest stood Chaos's men. Why weren't they fighting? Michael stepped closer to the tear, hidden by the giant oak tree. They looked like they had been in a war, some were covered in blood, but otherwise okay. So, why did they retreat?

Hegate, made an announcement. "Everyone listen, we cannot leave the cave dwellers to remain on Earth. It is our time to fight! Once you cross over into the earthly plane, you will change into spirit form. You will no longer be, as you are here, the way you looked before you died. You will be invisible, spirits, this will give all of you quite the advantage to fight and not be seen. I need the strongest of men, to step forward with Michael and kill these cave dwellers once and for all. We have the weapons we forged from the Fence of Separation; it is time to put them into use!" A large group of men and women stepped forward willing to fight. One by one, they stepped through the tear changing into spirit, their bodies slowly dissolving into invisible apparitions.

Hegate watched from the hole, he was not allowed to leave the astral plane, being bound to his realm. Michael's spirit moved around slowly, feeling out what was left of Chaos's army. One of the creatures turned to see, a weapon floating above him, as Michael plunged it into its rib cage. He pushed the cave dweller hard. So hard, it ended up onto the open field just as the sun came out to finish the job. Michael's opponent turned into dust before his eyes. The spirits in the woods, dropped their weapons, they realized, they just needed to get all of Chaos's men into the sunlight. They stood waiting, close to the enemy, each spirit choosing a cave dweller he would push out into the daylight. As Michael looked around, he knew there were more spirits than what was left of Chaos's army. Now the ghosts could double up or even triple up if they wanted to. Grabbing hold and dragging the unholy ones out, into the sun.

The wedding guests stood on the hill, with raised weapons, ready for another attack. They watched as one by one the cave creatures were coming out of the forest. "What are they doing?" Sam asked Daniels. The cyclops skeletons were not walking out, they were being pushed out, but by what? The unholy ones were fighting, with something no one on the hill could see. Everyone lowered their weapons and watched as the sun came out, turning the army from hell into dust.

The men stood there silently watching, looking out over the meadow, seeing some people had died. Mostly seniors, who could not run fast enough and were caught by the unholy ones. Some police officers also lost their lives, as their bodies laid still in the field. Sam hung his head down and cried, as Daniels called for backup once again. They needed ambulances and vans from the coroner's office.

Loren O' Brien lowered the drawbridge, looking outside, you could hear a pin drop. Soon people were coming out from the safety of the castle. Mary ran to Sam, throwing her arms around him, his clothes were torn here and there, but he made it out relatively unharmed. Kayla, Emily and Jeanna ran to their guys kissing and hugging them. The boys were cut up and bruised, but okay.

Daniels looked up at the afternoon sky, upset at himself for forgetting his crystal. A sadness came across his face as he exhaled deeply. Kayla looked at Peter holding his hand tightly, feeling her babies slightly move within her womb. Placing her hand on her belly, she felt something on her right cheek, it almost felt like a hand. Just the gentlest touch going down the right side of her face and under her chin, lifting her head. Kayla jumped back. "Kay, are you alright?" asked Peter. Kayla stood there frozen, that was something Michael would always do to her. Running his hand down her face and under her chin, lifting up her head to make eye contact. "Yeah, I'm fine. I just got a chill that's all." Peter put his arm around her shoulder holding her close to him. More police, ambulances, and vans from the coroner's office had arrived. Everyone stepped into the castle and sat down at the tables. The room was filled with sadness and sorrow.

Sam and Mary sat down together, thankful to still have each other. Loren O'Brien walked over to them, she looked quite disheveled. Her hair was a mess, and her clothes had been ripped, with cuts on her face and legs. "I will refund your money. I don't understand what happened here. Will you be taking a honeymoon anywhere special?" she asked, still in a state of shock.

Mary answered, as she cried softly, "We're going to Italy, for two weeks."

She placed her hand on Mary's shoulder, before walking to her office in a daze, followed by an officer to take her statement. "For the life of me, I don't understand any of this." Loren stated, as she started to cry, trying to explain what had happened. The officer was listening, trying to make sense of what she was telling him.

Two gentlemen entered the banquet room of the castle, along with a few more policemen. One of them shouted, "may I have your attention please!" He waved his hands in the air, trying to catch the group's eye, "everyone, please!" The room became silent as he spoke.

" I'm a crime scene investigator, my name is George Hernandez, and this is Detective Mark Wilson. Were here to get statements as to what happened." Everyone started shouting at once. "Hold on please! Please, let's not all speak at once!"

Sergeant Daniels walked over to them introducing himself. "I'm Sergeant Neil Daniels." Hernandez and Wilson extended their hands, asking Daniels to please step outside. Nothing was getting accomplished with a whole room of half-crazed people yelling.

"So", Hernandez began. "Tell me what happened here Sergeant Daniels?"

"I'll try to fill you in." Daniels answered back. "The question is, will you both believe me?"

"Well, let's give it a go." replied Detective Wilson.

"As you can see, this was a wedding which started off normally, on a beautiful spring day. Halfway through the ceremony we notice something coming out of the woods, back there." Daniels pointed to the far side of the field.

"Something? What do you mean?" asked Hernandez.

Daniels took a deep breath, not sure how to find the right words. "At first we thought it was just a person standing there, but it was odd looking."

"Odd looking how?" Detective Wilson was hanging on every word.

"Its head was shaped weird, it was tall and thin, skeletal like. Oh, and it had one large eye in the middle of its forehead." Daniels looked down at the ground knowing they would think he was crazy, and he hadn't told them the best part yet.

"What is this some kind of fucking joke! This is a crime scene Daniels, it's not fucking Halloween, you expect us to believe that!"

Hernandez was low on patience and wasn't buying the tale Daniels was spinning.

Wilson spoke up. "Maybe he was wearing a mask?"

"All twenty-five or thirty of them, I don't think so. There was an army of them, and they were carrying bones sharpened at one end, to use as weapons." Daniels said, looking at both of them, but not able to read their faces. "Listen I know it sounds crazy, but I swear it's true! You can get a statement from the other officers that survived. Go inside and get statements from everyone in the castle, everyone's story will concur."

As Daniels was trying to convince Hernandez and Wilson, a police officer walked over to them. "Guys I think you need to see this." The three of them followed him down to the far side of the meadow. "There's at least twenty bones or more scattered across this field sharpened at one end. I spoke to Joe in forensics, he thinks their human bones."

"Jesus Christ, let's rope off the area. I want pictures taken of everything. What the hell are all these piles of dust everywhere? I want some samples picked up and analyzed."

"That's them," Daniels stated.

"What the shit are you talking about now, Daniels?" asked Hernandez.

"Their remains anyway, they seemed to disintegrate when the sun hit them." Daniels mouth was dry, as he gave them this last bit of information. He walked away from Hernandaz and Wilson, leaving them to figure it out for themselves. They already thought he was out of his mind, so why continue. Whatever he would say, would only fall on deaf ears.

CHAPTER TWENTY-ONE

ALL IS FAIR, IN LOVE, AND WAR

Michael and the spirits returned to the astral plane, as the rip in the earthly plane was sealed. Hegate had made a promise to Michael, that his soul would be reborn into one of Kayla's babies, which he would make good on.

Hegate spoke, looking down at Michael. "You did well, you will have your just reward."

"I saw her Hegate, Kayla, I touched her cheek. If I can't have her as my wife, having her as my mother will be more than I could ever hope for."

Hegate cocked his head to one side and asked. "So, Michael, would you like to have your soul placed into Kayla's daughter or son?"

Michael laughed. "When do I have to let you know. I mean that's a hard decision to make. Boys are always closest to their moms and girls are to their".... Michael stood silent, he just came to the realization that Peter would be his father.

"Hegate, any idea which child is mine?" Michael couldn't entertain the thought of his soul going into a baby, that was Peter's.

"Yes Michael, Kayla's baby girl is yours."

"Alright Hegate, place my soul into my daughter."

"Michael are you sure? Once the soul has been placed there is no turning back."

"Yes, Hegate, I'm sure. Where do I go until the birth happens?"

"Why, to hell of course." Hegate stared at Michael, with no expression. He saw the terror grow across Michael's face as his eyes widened. "Only, kidding! You will stay here until your soul is needed. Relax Michael, you have some time before the births take place. Now I must leave you, I have lots of souls to deal with."

Michael sat down on a rock, longing to be with Kayla again. A smile crossed his lips as he thought about nursing on her breast. She would be his again, one way or another.

* * *

After two weeks of interrogation from Wilson and Hernandez, there still was no answer as to what really happened. With everyone's story confirming, the same scenario, Sam and Mary were free to leave for their honeymoon. Peter and Kayla were driving them to the airport. "Kayla, I'm counting on you to have everything run smoothly at the café," Sam remarked.

"Don't worry Sam, I will keep everything under control. I will rule with an iron fist!" Kayla started to laugh, glancing over at him in the back seat.

"Thank you Peter, for taking us to the airport. We're so excited to see Italy!" Mary exclaimed.

"We wish we were going with you." Peter answered, looking in the rear-view mirror. "Please take lots of pictures."

"Oh, we definitely will." Sam smiled, taking hold of Mary's hand.

* * *

The next morning Kayla left for work early. The café was her responsibility now, for at least two weeks. Sam had told her deliveries were dropped off early in the morning and she needed to be there to open the service door and sign for the goods. She parked her car on Wicker and made her way to the café. Opening the door the bell sounded above her head, it seemed much louder today, since the café was dead quiet before Emily, Max or any customers had arrived. Kayla started to clean off the tables and put the chairs back where

190

they belonged. She began to make the coffee, when suddenly the back door buzzer went off. Pushing the door open, she was greeted by the first delivery man of the day.

"Hey, good morning, where's Sam?"

"Sam got married recently, he is off on his honeymoon."

"Wow, well I've got the steak strips that he wanted. They're leaking a little, so get them into the freezer right away." He walked over to the counter placing the box down. "All I need is your signature and I'll be on my way." He handed a clipboard to Kayla for her to sign. Pulling off her copy he said. "If you speak with Sam, tell him Walter says congrats."

"Okay Walter, thanks." Kayla closed the back door, walking over to a rack she picked up a tray placing the box of steaks onto it and carried it into the freezer. A small pool of blood had collected on the countertop, grabbing some paper towels, she began to clean the counter off and then stopped. Her mouth started to salivate staring at the blood, she licked her lips. Kayla exhaled, quickly cleaning it up and throwing the paper towel into the trash.

* * *

After a day filled with sightseeing, Sam and Mary were enjoying their honeymoon in Italy. Sam answered the door of his hotel room, as room service wheeled in drinks and a selection of cheese and crackers.

"Buonasera, I have drinks and La merenda. Snacks."

"Grazie, Buonasera." Sam replied.

"Is there anything else you would be needing?"

"Not right now, thank you. I mean, grazie."

"Molto bene, I mean, very good." The man smiled at Sam, as he took his leave.

Mary exited the bathroom; the appetizers and drinks had arrived. Some crackers, ham, an array of cheeses and fruit, filled a large platter. "So, Mary my wife, I know we were both tired after our long plane ride yesterday, but I haven't forgotten about that negligee. You know, the one you almost didn't show me. I expect to see it on you tonight." Mary smiled; she kissed him passionately. "Your wish is my command love. Let's eat, I'm starving." Sam pulled out her chair as they both sat down at the small table to eat. Everything tasted so much fresher than in the U.S., the fruit, the cheese, all of it. They could hear a church bell somewhere in the distance, as Sam poured the wine. He looked lovingly at Mary, feeling so lucky she was his.

"Well," Sam remarked, "this was a nice afternoon between the sightseeing and museums. It feels good just to sit down and not move. I want to rent a car and take a ride through the countryside tomorrow, see how the locals live."

"That sounds like fun" Mary said, putting some cheese and ham on a cracker and placing it in Sam's mouth. Taking a sip of her drink, she was thinking about later that evening, when she would have to wear the next to nothing negligee, looking over at Sam, she smiled.

* * *

After a very early morning full of deliveries, Kayla unlocked the front door, as Emily and Max arrived very much on time.

"Good morning boss," Max announced. "What time did you get in?"

"It was early, there was a ton of deliveries this morning that I needed to sign for." Kayla answered, breaking a bagel in half and placing it into her mouth.

"How did it go at the airport? Did Sam and Mary get off okay?" Emily asked, picking up a box to refill the napkin holders on all the tables.

"I'm sure they did; I only hope Sam is not thinking about the café and is able to relax. I mean, he is in Italy; that's a very romantic country. With all of the architecture, the food, the people. I know I wouldn't be thinking about work, not for a second." Kayla replied, as she emptied out some coffee grinds into the trash. Looking down, the bloody paper towels came into view from the strip steaks earlier. Again, Kayla's mouth watered, resisting the urge to pick up a piece of the paper towel and lick it. Kayla quickly bundled up the trash bag and ran it outside. Her mind was racing, what is wrong with me? She thought, I'm grossing myself out. Stepping back inside the café, it was starting to get busy, which Kayla was grateful for. It would keep her mind occupied and away from any weird thoughts she was having.

* * *

Sam and Mary sat down outside a small bistro later in the evening for dinner. Sam had downloaded an app, to translate English into Italian. It worked most of the time, however, there were moments when Sam would have to improvise. These were the moments that Mary cherished the most, watching Sam doing his best to impress her. A bottle of wine was brought to the table and poured into long stem glasses, as a large basket of bread and butter appeared. The bread was still warm to the touch, as they both took a roll, coating it with butter. Sitting under a red and green awning enjoying their dinner, it had been a perfect day for sightseeing, warm, but not exceedingly hot. Once dinner was done, the waiter came over and announced the mouthwatering desserts that could be had. Sam smiled and proceeded to order more than he should have. Even so, this was their honeymoon, the perfect time to overindulge.

Mary excused herself, a trip to the ladie's room was needed. Placing her napkin onto the table she walked inside and asked a young woman behind the counter, where the "gabinetto" was. The woman smiled and pointed down the hallway towards the rear of the restaurant. Opening the door to the ladie's room Mary stepped inside. The room was quite large for such a small restaurant, with numerous stalls, sinks and mirrors. After relieving herself, she walked over to the line of sinks to wash up and felt eyes staring at her. Mary turned her gaze, to a woman sitting there on a small stool, she assumed the woman was the bathroom attendant. "Buonasera" the woman said, as she smiled.

"Buonasera" Mary answered back, as she took a paper towel to dry off her hands.

"Are you Americana?" the woman asked.

"Yes, I mean, si." Mary was doing her best to communicate.

193

" I speak English, poco. I, how do you say, a little. Was that your nipote? Mi scusi, ah, grandson with you?

"My grandson?" Mary was trying to figure out who she was referring to.

"The little child, rosso hair, tessuto scozzese, ah, plaid shirt?"

"No, I'm just here with my husband, we don't have any children with us."

The woman looked down at the floor. "Scusi" was all she said, folding her hands on her lap. Her smiling face, suddenly took on an expression of sadness.

"Okay, well, Ciao." Mary said, pushing open the door and walking back to the table.

Sam stood up as Mary sat down. "I ordered some of everything. I figured we could try a little of this and that. What took you so long? I was ready to come in after you."

"I was having a conversation with a woman in the ladie's room. I think she was the bathroom attendant. Anyway, wow, everything looks delicious. I'll have to hit the gym when we get back home, to work off all this crazy eating." Sam looked over at Mary and smiled.

"Don't worry sweetie, with the two of us walking everywhere, we will both probably burn off the calories, and then some. Anyway, you look fantastic. Whatever calories we don't burn off, we'll burn off tonight. If you know what I mean." Sam gave Mary a sexy look, as he took another bite of his pastry.

* * *

The café was jumping as Kayla, Emily and Max tried to keep things running smoothly. Max was crushing it in the kitchen. While Emily worked the floor and Kayla did her best behind the counter. Suddenly Kayla heard the cries of a small child. Her eyes scanned the café, as a woman and a small boy walked quickly over to her. "I'm sorry to bother you, but would you happen to have a bandage back there? My son cut his finger."

"I'll do one better, let's clean it off first. I'll get the first aid kit." Kayla said, smiling at the child, as she reached under the counter to retrieve the kit. "Come with me." They walked over to an empty stool at the counter. The child sat down, tears streaming down his face, as he looked up at her and held out his hand. "Oh, that's not so bad." She sympathized, taking hold of the little boy's hand. "Now this is only going to hurt for a second." Looking at his finger, a small pool of blood crested at the tip. Kayla swallowed hard as she licked her lips and stared. It took all of her willpower not to place the child's finger into her mouth.

The child's mother spoke up. "Excuse me, are you going to clean it or just look at it?"

"Yes, I'm sorry." Kayla sprayed a disinfectant, applied the wound cream and bandage. "There you go, all fixed up. You're such a brave boy."

"Thank you so much," said the mom, taking her child's hand and walking away.

Kayla stood up, closing the first aid kit and walked back to the counter. She felt a sinking feeling in her gut. What in God's name is happening to me? An idea crossed her mind, could it be Michael's baby, but then the thought was quickly diverted, watching as Peter walked in. "Hey there." He said, as he leaned over the counter kissing Kayla quickly on the lips.

"Hey, what are you doing here? I thought you would be watching football."

"I was, but my team was getting slaughtered, I couldn't watch any longer."

"Want something to eat? I could have Max make you something."

"No, I'm okay. Actually, I came in just to see how things were going, without Sam running the show."

"Well, as you can see, we have it under control. Ye, of little faith." Kayla said grinning.

Emily ran over, putting her arm around Peter and kissing him on the cheek. "Hello sir, nice to see you. Here for lunch?"

Kayla chimed in. "No, he came by to check up on us. He

wanted to see if we could handle it without Sam."

Emily smiled, "Peter, Peter." She said, as she shook her head in a disapproving way. "You my dear man, should have a little more confidence in your wife and a pregnant one at that. She's known around here as The Boss Lady."

Peter laughed. "The Boss Lady. I've got news for you Em, that's her title at our house as well." Kayla leaned over the counter, giving Peter a gentle smack on his arm. "Well ladies this has been nice, but I'm going to go now. I feel I have overstayed my welcome. Kay, I'll see you tonight. Emily see you soon. Tell Max I said hi!" Peter shouted, as he headed out the door.

* * *

After dinner their stomachs were full, as Sam and Mary walked back to their hotel. The sun was setting over the tops of houses whose roofs were showing their age. Like a sinking, orange fire ball, it slowly went down behind the hills of the small village. Sam looked into Mary's eyes.

"Mary, if anyone had told me a year ago that I would be in Italy, with the woman of my dreams, I would have thought they were crazy. I am so lucky to call you mine."

Mary looked down at the cobble stones beneath her feet and smiled. "No Sam, I'm the lucky one. Some women never find love their whole lives, and I found it twice. I love you so much."

"Ditto Mary." Sam said, as he looked at her, watching the expression on her face change. He could tell she was deep in thought and there was something on her mind. "What is it my love? Is something bothering you?"

"It's just something I keep thinking about. Did you happen to see a child with red hair outside the café this evening at dinner?" Mary looked up at Sam, waiting for his reply.

"No, I don't think so. Then again, I was too busy looking at you. Why?"

"This is going to sound silly. Even so, remember I told you I was having a conversation with a woman in the ladie's room."

196

"Yeah." Sam was curious, as to where this conversation was going.

"She said, there was a child around our table with red hair. She thought it was our grandson. Isn't that weird?"

"Maybe he was from the neighborhood, or he was with another family." Sam answered.

"Perhaps, but it was the look on her face, a look of sadness. I can't get her expression out of my head."

Sam put his arm around Mary's shoulder as they continued their walk back to the hotel room. It was a short walk past stone walls and flower boxes, whose flowers cascaded downward scenting the air with sweet fragrance. Once back in their room the French doors were opened, as they stepped outside onto the small balcony. Sam came up behind Mary moving her hair to one side. He kissed the back of her neck, then brought his hand around her gently caressing her left breast.

"What are you doing?" she asked, as Sam continued to kiss her neck.

"Just trying to relax you." Sam replied, with lust in his eyes. Mary turned around hugging him tightly. They walked back inside, as Mary walked over to her suitcase lifting out the elusive negligee. Sam smiled. "Now, that's what I'm talking about."

Sam washed up quickly. Followed by Mary, who after showering, stood in the bathroom holding the see through number in front of her. She was having second thoughts about wearing it. Could she really pull it off? Or was Sam just being kind? Even as a young woman, Mary's body image wasn't the greatest. So, this feeling of inadequacy wasn't something new to her. Staring at her image, her once perky body now showed the signs of gravity, things had shifted downward. A knock on the bathroom door took her back to reality.

"Is everything okay in there?" Sam asked.

"I'll be right out, give me a second." Putting the see through number on, she called out to Sam to turn off the lights. He had seen her naked body before, but the whole idea of trying to be sexy made her feel ridiculous. She had hoped the darkness would hide her body somewhat. Slowly stepping out from the security of the bathroom, she could see Sam lying there on the bed waiting for her. The room was somewhat dark, however, the moon had cast a silvery glow of illumination around the bedroom. Mary made a beeline to the bed, wanting to cover her body with the bed sheets. Sam jumped off the bed, stopping her in her tracks. He laid his eyes upon her, just as a tear formed and ran down Mary's face, feeling silly and afraid of rejection. Sam looked into Mary's eyes.

"Mary look at me. You're unbelievably beautiful and so is your body. You're more than any man could hope for." Sam placed his arm around her, escorting her to the bed. He laid her down onto the softness of the sheets. Sam lifted up the thin fabric of her negligee and made love to her gently and slowly. "Mary, relax. You turn me on, please don't doubt that. In my eyes you're spectacular." Mary smiled. They made love to each other, forgetting their age or how their bodies had changed over the years, both feeling young again. Later, they would sleep in each other's arms, as this old saying popped into Mary's head. Beauty, truly is in the eye of the beholder she thought, closing her eyes and drifting away into deep slumber.

* * *

As May turned into June the weather was warming up. Kayla was starting to feel it, going into her sixth month of pregnancy and uncomfortable, the heat was an unwelcome sensation. Not to mention the constant kicking and movement of the babies. She could feel them shifting within her womb, placing her hand on her stomach, as she got out of bed to make the coffee. Going downstairs she thought of the day that was ahead of her, it made her tired just thinking about it. She rubbed her belly and sat down at the kitchen table.

Suddenly a thought of Willie went through her mind. He would be due for a visit soon and that brought a smile to her face, as Peter walked into the kitchen still half asleep.

"Good morning! You moved around a lot last night, couldn't

get comfortable?”

“I think the babies are having a wrestling match in here.” Kayla answered, pointing at her large stomach.

“Hang in there sweetheart, only a few more months to get through.” Peter smiled, encouraging her.

“Yeah, easy for you to say. You’re not walking around with two little people in your gut.” Peter laughed, wrapping his arms around her and kissing her cheek. He was excited, in a few more months they would become a family. Peter never thought he could love anyone, as much as he loved Kayla. However, his children that she was carrying would change all that. He would love them just as much and was so grateful he would soon become their father. Not wanting to wait, he decided to ask her again.

“Kayla, let’s get married. Let’s get married before the babies come. We can go to City Hall exchange rings, just the two of us, or the four of us.” Peter smiled, putting his hand on Kayla’s protruding belly.

“You want to get married, now?” Kayla questioned.

“ Yeah, why not?” Peter sat down at the table taking her hand, looking lovingly into her eyes.

“Well first of all, I was hoping we would at least have our friends there. Sam and Mary are still in Italy, I would like them both to attend. Also, what about your dad and the seekers, along with Willie? Even though, we would have to hide Willie somehow.”

“Really?” Well, you must have thought about this for some time. Okay. I’ll let you pick the date, I just thought it would be nice before the babies got here, that’s all.”

“I’ll let you know. Now, let’s have breakfast.” Kayla said smiling, as she got up from the table and poured the decaf coffee into large ceramic mugs.

* * *

In Italy, Sam and Mary rented a car and were traveling through the beautiful back roads of the Italian countryside, which was magnificent. Sam suddenly applied the brakes noticing a sign which read, "Ristorante/ Restaurant, Cantina/ Winery. He managed to make a quick turnaround, as Mary looked on confused as to what he was doing.

"I just saw a sign back there for a winery. I thought we could stop and have lunch. What do you think?" Sam asked, glancing over at her.

"That's a great idea; I am a little hungry."

Their car turned onto a long-graveled road. In the distance grapevines came into view as far as the eye could see. Cypress trees adorned the fields, distinctly famous in an Italian landscape. Sam parked the car alongside a terra cotta-colored building, decorated with flower boxes and thriving greenery. They walked around taking in the spectacular scenery holding hands. Walking inside the coolness of the building greeted them, it felt good to be out of the afternoon sun.

"Buonasera." A woman announced, coming out of the kitchen and walking towards them.

"Buonasera." Sam and Mary returned the greeting. "Do you speak English?" Mary asked.

"Yes, I do fluently. I lived in the United States for a short time. It's where I met my husband. But I missed Italy so much, we decided to come back and open this restaurant, "De Falco's.""

"Well, it's certainly beautiful." Mary replied, smiling.

"My name is Nina, my husband is the chef here." Nina reached out and shook their hands. "And speak of the devil here he is now." Nina called her husband over, "this is my husband Bruce."

"Very nice to meet you." Sam said, as he and Mary shook his hand. Bruce smiled, as he greeted them and then walked away towards the kitchen, placing an apron on over his head.

"Please sit down, I can sit you here by the window, it's one of our best tables." Nina placed a menu into both their hands and then walked away greeting other customers.

Mary looked out the window, as a small dog ran around outside. A scruffy little guy with white fur, black feet and ears. Mary smiled, as the dog abruptly stopped moving and just stood there still, looking at their car. Mary leaned over the table, wanting to see what made the dog suddenly stop in its tracks. That's when she noticed a small child, who emerged from the opposite side of their car. He had red hair, and was wearing a plaid shirt, he looked right at her and waved. Mary caught her breath, as she had stopped breathing for a second, getting up quickly from the table she needed to get outside.

"Mary, what's wrong?" Sam asked, following her outside. "Mary, wait! What's going on?" She walked quickly to their car, looking for the small boy. There was no sign of him, as the dog ran over to them. Mary leaned over to pet him, as Sam asked again, "Mary, what's going on?"

"I don't know." she answered. "Remember when I told you about the woman in the ladie's room? Who saw a child around our table with red hair and a plaid shirt."

"Yes, I remember. Why?"

"Well, I just saw a young boy out here, with red hair and a plaid shirt."

"Mary, maybe he is Nina's grandson. Or, he could be here with his family having lunch. Come on let's go back inside." Sam smiled, putting his arm around Mary's shoulder. Walking in Nina approached their table, as the restaurant was starting to get busy.

"Welcome back. Where did you go? I saw that you had walked out." Nina asked, standing in front of them order pad in hand.

"Nina, do you know a child with red hair? He's wearing a plaid shirt?" asked Mary.

"No, but the restaurant is getting busy now. Look around, perhaps a family has just arrived. I'll give you both a few more minutes." Mary scanned the room, getting up once again to look around. However, there was no sign of the child, as she sat back down. Sam looked at her concerned, as a waiter came over to pour the wine Sam had ordered. Mary smiled, taking hold of Sam's hand, a cold chill ran up her spine.

CHAPTER TWENTY-TWO

TO HELL AND BACK

Tarsula sat on a rock very hungry and in need of food. Since Michael had literally pushed her down into hell, she had spent most of her time hiding from The Gate Keeper. After losing all of her magical powers, she was left with nothing more than her instincts. Sitting there she wondered, if her mind could still Chant, but who could she call upon? Michael was dead, but there were others she had bonded with on the earthly plane. One was a warlock called Ramill. He was an old flame, and even though their romance was over, he had remained one of her closest friends.

Tarsula set her gaze upon a small stone lying on the ground, always finding it beneficial to stare at small objects when Chanting. The Chant came back to her quickly, she jumped up with excitement. It was Ramill, she could hear him clearly, as if he was standing right in front of her.

"My dear Tarsula, where have you been? It's been a while."

"Shit Ramill, I can't believe I reached you. I have been pushed into hell literally, by Michael."

"Did you say Michael? Michael Blaydon?"

"Yes, he is dead, but I'm very much alive!" Tarsula Chanted back quickly.

"How could he push you, if he's dead ? And how are you still alive if you have crossed over?"

"It's a long story Ramill, I'll fill you in at a later date. Is there any way you could get me out of here?"

"Are you Chanting me from hell? How could I possibly rescue you Tarsula? I mean my powers are strong, but I would need to find a way into the astral plane, and even then, how could I find you in hell?"

"I have a book, it's sitting on a rock outside a huge oak tree that I split. It's there in some woods surrounding a castle, here on the east coast. The spells and incantations are in that book, it would enable you to make a tear in the earthly plane and allow you to cross over into the astral. Once there, you would be able to tear the ground of astral plane, sending down the golden rope to me, then pull me up. What do you think Ramill? I'll give you anything! Anything you want!"

"Anything Tarsula?"

"Yes."

"I have loved you for centuries, even though as the years have gone by, you have rejected my advances towards you. I always thought we would be great together. We were at one time, so long ago. So, I will help you only if you swear to become mine. Do you need to think about it?"

Tarsula watched as The Gate Keeper roamed the grounds looking for her. She laid down behind a pile of ash and sticks watching him. She didn't need to think about it, she Chanted back swiftly. "Yes, Ramill I will be yours. When can you get to the east coast?"

"I'll leave immediately. I just need to pack a few things, and I will be on my way. Relax my love, I'm coming to get you."

"Thank you Ramill, I knew I could count on you. Remember the book is outside a large oak tree that I split, it's there sitting on a rock. You are a supreme warlock and should have no problem with the incantations. I'll Chant you the address of the castle, let me know when you get there. Hurry please!"

"I'm on my way, Tarsula."

Ramill grabbed a duffel bag and packed it full, all the while thinking about the past. He remembered his first meeting with Tarsula. They were both very young and sexually attracted to each other. Tarsula envied his powers, a high-ranking warlock surpassing all others in the realm of black magic. His power turned her on. Their sexual antics were uninhibited, enduring through the centuries as they were both immortal. Ramill's feelings for her grew and his passion for her was never ending. However, Tarsula grew apart from him, wanting other men, younger men. As time went on, all that was left was friendship, but he always wanted more. Ramill grinned, he zipped up his bag, as Tarsula Chanted the address of the castle over to him. He was a man on a quest, now she would finally be his. The cock in his pants started to stiffen as he remembered her, quickly calling a cab to take him to the airport.

* * *

The two-week honeymoon was over. Kayla and Peter drove to the airport on a rainy Sunday to pick up Sam and Mary. Kayla was grateful her run as Boss Lady was over, but she was proud of herself for doing a good job.

"Are you okay? Peter asked. Seeing a weird look on Kayla's face.

"Oh Yeah, I hope they took loads of pictures."

"I'm sure they did." Peter grinned.

"Oh!" Kayla placed her hand on her abdomen. "The babies are kicking up a storm."

"Are you alright?" Peter asked, concerned.

"Yeah, the babies are restless today." Kayla placed her hand on her belly and rubbed it, in a circular motion hoping it would calm them down.

Pulling into the visitors parking lot, the airport was extremely busy. They walked into the terminal and waited at the gate for Sam and Mary's plane to arrive, watching as others scurried past them. Kayla's attention was drawn to the far side of the terminal. Her eyes caught sight of Mary, as Peter waved his hands in the air, to let them know they were there. The four of them ran towards each other, a hug fest ensued.

"So, tell us all about it." Peter asked.

"Well, I can only tell you about the G- rated parts." Sam replied, as Mary slapped his shoulder gently, laughing and slightly blushing.

"How was it running the café for two weeks Kayla?" Sam asked, eager to hear her answer.

"Well, I think I did okay, I received the title of Boss Lady." Kayla answered chuckling.

"Boss Lady, well I knew you had it in you." Sam replied, smiling.

"By the way Walter says congrats." Kayla mentioned, grinning.

"Good old Walter, we go back aways. He always gives me a break on beef and chicken. Anyhow, even though the honeymoon was fantastic, I'm ready to get back to work. I missed the café. Thanks for handling things for me Kay."

"Sure thing. Oh!" Kayla let out a cry of discomfort.

"Are you okay?" Sam asked, looking at her worried.

"Yeah, the babies are rough housing in here." Kayla replied, touching her belly. "I swear, sometimes it feels like they're wrestling."

"That's good. It sounds like you're going to have two strong babies on your hands." Mary stated, taking hold of Sam's hand and looking at him lovingly.

"Well, I have news." Peter announced. I've asked Kayla to marry me before the babies get here. She said yes, but wanted to wait until you guys got back."

"That's wonderful!" Sam said, beaming. "That means a lot to me, that you wanted to wait. Just give us the date and time and we'll be there."

The rest of the ride home was a day by day account of their time in Italy. Reaching their destination Peter helped Sam with the bags. As Mary and Kayla continued their conversation on Italy's most delicious foods.

"Speaking of food." Mary said, collecting her belongings from the back seat. Sam and I would love both of you to come over for dinner? What do you say?"

"We would love that. Thank you, Mary."

"It's the least we can do, after all you ran the café for two weeks, that had to be challenging."

"Actually Mary, it wasn't that bad, after the first week I kind of had it together."

"Good going." Mary said, as she exited the car. "Let us know what night works for you guys."

Peter came back picking up the rest of the bags, as Mary followed behind him. Kayla waited by the car leaning up against it. The parking spot gave her a complete view of the building's courtyard. She smiled as a group of kids played, kicking around a soccer ball. Standing there, her eyes settled on a small child much younger than the other kids. He had tousled red hair and an endearing plaid shirt, seemingly distant from the other children.

The sun finally made an appearance, shining brightly into Kayla's eyes. Opening the car door to retrieve her sunglasses, putting them on, she glanced back across the courtyard. Her eyes scanned the open area in search of the small boy, but he was nowhere to be found. He must have gone home, Kayla thought, as Peter came back.

* * *

Ramill had landed and rented a car at the airport. He had written the address for the castle, on a piece of paper, tucked into the right pocket of his jeans. The plan was, to check into his hotel and then make his way over to the castle later that night, cloaked in the shadow of darkness. If everything went smoothly, he would be making love to her this evening. A broad smile appeared on his bearded face.

* * *

Tarsula's stomach was growling in need of nourishment. Still very much alive, all her human needs still needed to be fulfilled. Like eating and sleeping, both of which she needed, but hardly got. Food was scarce, and she was afraid to close her eyes, always needing to be aware of her surroundings. Sitting on a pile of ash and kindle, the smell of food wafted through the air. Standing up, she followed the scent. Hiding behind a large boulder Tarsula watched, as trays of food were being brought up to Mantus. Her mouth watered at the sight of it all, slowly making her way to the staircase which led to Mantus's domain. Tarsula waited and watched as all of Mantus's minions came back down with empty trays. Climbing slowly, hiding herself behind erns and statues, making her way upwards. Reaching the top, a massive table came into view covered in an abundance of delicious dishes. A roast chicken was the closest thing to her. She looked around, afraid to leave her hiding place. However, the need for something to eat became too great for her to ignore. Tarsula ran towards it, pulling it off the table, only to be met by Lucifer. A two headed monster of a dog, that growled at her with two muzzles, all turned up in a threatening snarl.

Tarsula had to think fast. Breaking off both chicken legs, she slowly and with great care approached Lucifer, holding them out for him to feed upon, which he did savagely. She backed away from him, never taking her eyes away from this giant canine. Lucifer suddenly ran towards her, as she tried to get away, certain that her life was about to end. Instead, the massive heads pushed Tarsula underneath Mantus's enormous table.

"Lucifer!" Mantus yelled. "What the fuck are you doing there?" He kicked the dog with his enormous hooved foot. Lucifer whimpered and laid down, as Tarsula watched from her hiding spot beneath the table, eating what remained of the chicken. Thinking surely, Lucifer could have given her away and made her presence known, but he remained vigilant and quiet.

After some time, Mantus got up from the table, his stomach was full. Walking past Lucifer, one more hard kick was in order, as he walked away laughing. Tarsula crawled out from her hiding spot. She patted Lucifer on his heads and gave him what was left of the chicken, she didn't eat. Splitting it into two equal parts, then slowly she backed away and descended the staircase, sight unseen.

* * *

In the darkness, Ramill found his way to Danmore Castle, parking at the bottom of the private road. He took out a flashlight from his duffel bag and walked along the tree line reaching the top of the hill. Standing there, Chanting to Tarsula that he had arrived. The Chant came through loudly, as Tarsula found a secluded spot, to try and hide herself.

"Ramill, go to the bottom of the meadow. There you will find a tree with a large X, that will be your point of entry. Walk straight ahead through the woods, keep moving forward. It may take a few minutes, until you reach the oak tree that's split in two."

"Okay love." Ramill walked quickly, as he searched for the tree with the large X. Finding it, he moved steadily onward, until stopping at the sight of the giant oak which stood before him. "I see the tree Tarsula! Where is the book?"

"It should be there Ramill, I left it on a rock. Do you see it?"

Ramill looked around, moving his flashlight around the giant tree. "I see it! I've got it Tarsula it's here!"

"Fantastic! Now, I have to get to the Gate of Human Suffering. Stay put, I have to find the key to the gate. If I can't find it, I will have to climb it. I'll Chant you back when I've made my escape, please be patient and wait for my instruction."

"I will my love, no worries. I'm going to cloak myself, so I won't be seen standing here." Ramill placed the notebook back on the rock, reaching down he ran his hands along the tops of his shoes. Working his way up his legs and over the rest of his body, becoming completely invisible.

Tarsula ran, hiding herself amongst the debris and bones which covered the ground. Arriving at The Gate of Human Suffering. She looked everywhere hoping to find the key but then remembered the Gate Keeper wore it around his neck. There was nothing else she could do; she had to climb up and over it. Tarsula grabbed onto body parts as she ascended the gate of arms, legs, and torsos. As she grabbed hold of a young man's muscular thigh, she looked up. His body was still intact, but totally fixed to the wrought iron, as she climbed upwards. He looked down at her, handsome and young, just Tarsula's type. Her head came to rest between his toned thighs. Tarsula smiled, giving his cock a few quick strokes. She wanted to continue with the hand job, but she needed to get out of there. The moans and groans of sexual gratification was music to Tarsula's ears. I've still got it, Tarsula thought, as she continued to climb up the gate. Leaving the poor guy with his semi hard on, and no way to relieve himself. "Come back here!" He yelled after her. "You bitch! You fucking cunt!"

"I've been called worse," she said. Throwing her legs over the top of the gate, she made her way down on the other side, holding onto bodies once again. Then finally landing onto the ground of ash and bugs, as an alarm sounded around her.

Tarsula Chanted to Ramill, to cross over into the astral plane. Ramill got the Chant, which came in as a blood shattering scream. Holding the book, he read the notes Tarsula had written. He easily tore the earthly plane, allowing him to cross into the astral. Still invisible, searching for the golden rope, he saw Michael and many others. He also saw a horned beast, which he gathered was Hegate. Tarsula had described him once or twice.

Tarsula hid herself behind a row of dead trees. "Ramill, do you see the golden rope? Ramill, can you hear me?"

"Yes Tarsula, I am looking. I see it! Do I make the tear here?"

" Yes, tear the ground there and send me down the rope, hurry." Ramill made the tear, as he kicked the rope into position. Looking around, to be sure, no one saw the rope moving. "Tarsula I will cloak the rope but only here in the astral plane, above the tear, you will be able to see it down below."

"Do it now! I'm running to you." The Gate Keeper spotted her, running after her quickly. She could see the golden rope being thrown down in the distance. She ran as fast as she could, but The Gate Keeper was faster. He grabbed the back of her shirt, but

Tarsula was able to free herself from his grip, running away franticly. The Gate Keeper lunged at her, this time getting a firm hold of her leg. Tarsula screamed. Try as she might, she could not escape, he began dragging her back to hell.

"No! No! Please I can't go back there!"

"Oh, you are going back, and the punishment will be great. I can't wait to tell Mantus, that your war on earth failed, he will not be pleased. You can't imagine what waits for you Tarsula," as The Gate Keeper laughed uncontrollably.

Tarsula tried to grab on to something, anything that would hold her. She kicked and screamed, begging and crying. Suddenly out of nowhere, came the hound of hell Lucifer, he ran over attacking The Gate Keeper. Lucifer wanted to help Tarsula, repaying her for the kindness that she had shown him. The giant canine knocked him to the ground, which made him lose his hold on Tarsula's leg. Lucifer tore into The Gate Keeper's flesh, huge pieces of his snake like neck were torn off, as the two headed beast continued to tear into him. A river of green sticky substance ran from The Keeper's neck with every bite, as the vicious onslaught continued.

Tarsula made it to the golden rope in front of her, she Chanted as she took hold of it. "Pull me up Ramill! Pull me up now!" Ramill brought the rope up cloaking it, as it entered the astral plane. Tarsula who now stood in front of him, was also invisible, cloaked with Ramill's spell. She quickly mended the tear in the astral plane, as Ramill slowly kicked the rope back to where he had found it, making it visible once again. He reached out his hands trying to feel for Tarsula's body, as a hand grabbed hold of his. They simply walked back into the earthly plane closing the tear, and then through the split oak tree. They were back together once again.

CHAPTER TWENTY-THREE

LOVE NEVER DIES

Mary had decided to finally empty out the suitcases from their honeymoon. They had been sitting in the bedroom, on the floor for a while. She gathered up all the dirty clothes, bringing them into the laundry room. Then, walking back into the bedroom Mary saw that her closet door was open. That's funny, she thought, I don't remember opening it. Closing the empty suitcase, she stood on her tippy toes, trying to place it back on the top shelf of her closet. Wanting to get it into position, a cardboard box fell, hitting the floor and spilling its contents. It contained photos and mementos from past years, that were now scattered across the bedroom rug. Old pictures of mom and dad, when they were young and in love. Aunts and uncles, along with cousins she had long since lost touch with. There were also photos of her childhood pet. A black lab called Inky, who stood proudly next to her as a child. Mary smiled, looking at the picture of herself. Remembering how much she loved Inky, and how inseparable they were. Gathering all of the photos, she placed them back into the cardboard box. Putting it back in the closet, next to her suitcase and left the room. However, there was one photo, which remained on the rug. It had fallen slightly underneath the bed unseen and faced down.

* * *

Ramill and Tarsula walked hand in hand, no longer invisible, to the bottom of the hill. Ramill kissed her cheek, as Tarsula kept thanking him for saving her. She searched for her car, which was no longer parked where she had left it, the day of Sam's and Mary's wedding. Apparently, the car had been towed or stolen. Ramell placed his arm around her shoulder and escorted her to his car. She got in as Ramill walked around to the driver's side. Sitting down beside her, he began. "I'm so happy we are back together. I was shocked when I got your Chant, it has been a while."

"Well, I knew I could count on you Ramill. I thought, if anyone could save me, it would be you."

Ramill smiled. "Shall we go back to my hotel room?" He asked hesitantly, not sure of what Tarsula's answer would be. After all, she had just escaped from one hellish adventure, literally.

"Sure Ramill," Tarsula responded. She remembered their past so long ago, when sex with him, was more than gratifying. She wondered if he could still satisfy her sexually. "One more thing Ramill, I need to pick up my clothes and belongings at the hotel, where I had been staying. Also, I am in desperate need of a shower." Ramill nodded his head yes. Seeing that she was a mess and covered in dirt, also her clothes were torn here and there, coming apart at the seams.

* * *

Sam and Mary had a planned date night. They were going to the Manchester Cinema which was showing the latest sci-fi movie. They had been waiting months, for it to arrive in their small-town theater. Finding a parking spot, they walked inside. Getting their tickets, they moved quickly to the concession stand. Loading up on snacks and drinks, then walking through the lobby, looking for theater room number four. Going in and walking up a slight ramp, the lines of chairs came into view. They climbed up the dark steps, wanting to sit farther away from the screen. Mary found the row she wanted to be in, they made their way to the middle and sat down.

The room became dark, as the trailers started to show,

loud and intriguing, along with a public message to respect other moviegoers around you. Mary's attention was drawn away from the screen for a moment. Her eyes fell upon a young child, standing under the exit sign. Was he looking at her? Did he have on a plaid shirt? She couldn't see his facial features or the color of his hair, but a cold chill ran up her arms. Squinting, her eyes, it did not allow her to see any better.

"Shit!" Sam said quietly, spilling his drink. Mary turned to him, taking a napkin and helping him clean himself off. Looking back, the child was gone. Mary looked at Sam, ready to say something but remained silent. Telling herself to relax, no point in bringing it up when the child was gone. Perhaps, he had sat down with his parents or his family had walked out.

Mary stood up, placing her drink in the cupholder. "I'll be right back Sam, I need to use the ladie's room. She slowly walked down the stairs, opening the exit door which led out into the parking lot. Looking around quickly there was no sign of him. Sam was watching her from his chair, wondering what the hell was she doing! Mary walked down the ramp to the door of the lobby. She glanced up and down, there were lots of children, but none of them had on a plaid shirt. Walking back inside the theater, she was met by Sam, carrying their drinks and snacks. "What's going on Mary? What are you doing?"

"I'll tell you later, come on, let's go watch the movie."

* * *

Walking into his hotel room, Ramill placed Tarsula's belongings on a desk. Taking out a night shirt from her bag and going into the bathroom, she felt a second shower was needed.

Ramill called down to room service and ordered a few entrees, not sure what Tarsula would like. Fish, beef, and pasta were all ordered for tonight's dinner. Along with a bottle of wine and a cookie plate, he remembered how obsessed she was with sugar.

After her second shower, Tarsula felt more like herself again. She walked back into the room, wearing just her night shirt. Ramill smiled, looking at her up and down.

"I've called room service; I thought you might be hungry." he remarked.

"Yes, I am actually, they don't feed you well in hell," she answered.

"I also ordered a cookie plate; I remembered your sweet tooth," a smile crossed his chiseled face.

"Yes", Tarsula answered him timidly. "You remembered. We do have quite a past, you and I. We used to be good together."

"We still can be good together Tarsula. With my powers and yours, who knows what kind of stuff we could get into." Ramill sat down at a small table. Tarsula walked over to him, lifting up her night shirt over her thighs as she straddled his lap, kissing him. Tarsula could feel Ramill's cock becoming erect on the inside of her left thigh.

There was a knock on the door, as someone called out. "Room Service!" Tarsula stood up, opening the door, as a man carted in the food. Ramill tipped him, closing the door and locking it. Reaching for a cookie, her hand was stopped by Ramill. He took her hand placing it on his erect cock, then releasing himself from the confinement of his pants. Tarsula grinned, she had forgotten how large his member was. She sat down on the bed, as he stood blatantly before her. He placed himself into her mouth, as Tarsula gave him head remembering the things that sent him over the edge. Ramill held her head gently, as she pleased him orally. Pushing her back onto the bed, he laid on top of her. His cock found its place between her thighs. Ramill's moans and groans were turning her on. She wrapped her legs around him, bringing him deeper into her. He fucked her, enjoying the position for a while, but then told her to get on her knees. Tarsula knew, what was coming next, she spread her ass cheeks for him. He had been the first one, to introduce her to anal sex, and she had learned to enjoy this taboo act. It had become part of her sexual routine. His cock was definitely wet enough, as he slowly fucked her ass. Tarsula groaned as his cock slid in and out of her, again and again. Tarsula brought her hand down to her pussy and fingered her clit. Ramill couldn't hold back any longer, coming inside her. Withdrawing he took a tissue and wiped himself off, but Tarsula wasn't done yet.

She told him to go into the bathroom and wash himself thoroughly. Taking off her night shirt she stood before him naked, as he walked back into the room. Ramill walked over to her fondling her tits. He sucked her nipples, gently licking and biting them. His hand traveled down to her pussy, fingering her. He could feel her wetness, as his dick took on a life of its own, once again. Tarsula laid down on the bed, spreading her legs.

Ramill professed his love for her, telling her she was beautiful and how he had never stopped thinking about her, through all the years they were apart. He climbed onto the bed, still singing his praises for her. However, Tarsula wasn't in the mood for sweet nothings in her ear. She wanted hard core sex and wasn't interested in romantic bedroom talk. "Oh no Ramill," she said, pushing him gently with her hand. "Reverse the position." Tarsula got on top, aligning her pussy with Ramill's mouth. "That's it Ramill." Tarsula moaned, as he licked her aggressively. Tarsula grinned, well that's one way to shut him up, she thought.

* * *

After the movie was over, Sam and Mary sat in the car talking about it. The actors, the storyline, what they liked or didn't like about it. Sam's curiosity was getting the better of him, until he finally asked. "Who were you looking for Mary?" She was hoping he wasn't going to bring it up, not really having any answers for him. Who was she looking for? That was the question. Who was this young child, she saw in Italy and now here? Not even able to describe him, except for the fact, he had red hair and wore plaid shirt. Never seeing his features, never getting close enough, to see facial details.

"Sam, this is going to sound strange, but I think I keep seeing a boy. The boy, that the woman in Italy saw, hanging around our table. Then seeing him again, the next day, running around with

215

a small dog outside the restaurant, DeFalco's. Now I'm seeing him here. I don't know how, but I swear it's him. Red hair, plaid shirt, he was looking right at me. The thing is, every time I look for him, he runs away from me. Almost like he is playing a game of some sort."

"Mary, let's try to think logically about this. How old is this boy?"

"Six, maybe seven, I'm not sure."

"Okay, so you think a six-year-old child followed us from Italy and is now stalking you?"

"Well, that sounds crazy when you say it like that Sam."

"Yet, that's what you're saying Mary. Come on think about it, it doesn't make sense right?"

"I guess so." Mary had to admit Sam had a point, to think otherwise would be insanity. She decided to change the subject. "Want to get some burgers, my treat?"

"Sure, you had me at my treat," answered Sam, laughing.

They made their way to Eddie's, an all night diner, serving customers 24 hours a day. Sam opened the door for Mary as they walked inside. Kayla and Peter were having a bite to eat. Seeing them walk in, Peter got up and asked them over to their table. They sat together in a booth, as Sam talked about the movie they had just seen.

"Sounds like you both enjoyed it." Peter remarked, sipping on his milkshake.

"Yeah, except for Mary's wild imagination." Sam added.

Mary gave Sam a look of surprise. She couldn't believe, he would bring it up to Peter and Kayla. Now everyone would think she was losing her mind.

"Her imagination, what do you mean Sam?" Kayla inquired.

Mary chimed in. "I keep seeing this child. I saw him in Italy and now I am seeing him here, there are you happy Sam?" Everyone could tell, Mary was pissed off.

The waitress came over to take their food order. "Two cheeseburgers both medium rare with fries," Sam ordered.

"And to drink?"

"Two diet colas no lemon, please." Mary replied.

"Mary, what did this child look like? I'm just curious," asked Kayla

"He's young, around six maybe, with red hair, wearing a plaid shirt. I can never see his features, he is always too far away." Kayla looked down at the table, unsure if she should tell Mary about the boy in the courtyard that day. He seemed to fit the description, would mentioning it make her freak out? Maybe it was just a coincidence. I don't want to upset her, Kayla thought, yet maybe I should tell her? At least Mary would know it's not her imagination.

"Mary, I just want to tell you something. I don't want to upset you, but I think I saw the child you are referring to, standing in the courtyard of your building." A look of confusion came across Mary's face.

"You saw him, Kayla? Did he say anything to you?" Mary inquired, hoping Kayla wasn't making this up, only to make her feel better.

"No, he was too far away. I only noticed him because he was so much smaller than the other kids. Also, the way he was dressed, standing there, he seemed out of place to me." Kayla looked over at Sam, who looked stunned. Was this a real thing? A child following his wife around, but how? Why?

Peter bit into his chicken sub, he was deep in thought. An idea came into his head, but he didn't want to tell the others, not yet. It was too far-fetched, even for him. However, it could make sense if someone were to believe in that sort of thing. He took a sip of his milkshake and looked at Kayla. She could tell Peter's mind was busy, like he wanted to say something, but was holding back for some reason. The silence at the table was broken by Sam, asking Kayla if she had ever seen that boy come into the café?

"No Sam, not that I can remember."

"Mary, when you see him, is he always alone?" Peter asked.

"Well, the first time he was brought to my attention, was in

Italy. I didn't see him at all, but the woman in the ladie's room apparently did. She saw him hanging around our table, thinking he could have been our grandson. She described him to me. The next time I did see him, outside a restaurant where we stopped for lunch, and then tonight. I saw him in the movie theater, he was alone standing under the exit sign."

"Did you say, he was alone when you saw him, Kayla?" Sam asked, rubbing the back of his neck trying to think.

"Yeah, like I said, he was just standing there, off to the side by himself." Kayla answered. "This is so strange. If any of us see him again, maybe we should try to talk to him. What do you think Mary?"

"Yes, that sounds like a good idea, Kayla. I've got to say this whole thing is weird. It frightens me a little. Still, I'm glad you spoke up, at least now I know I'm not losing my mind." Mary remarked.

When dinner was over they said their goodbyes. Sam hit the horn twice as they drove away. Kayla fastened her seatbelt and looked at Peter. "Okay, what were you thinking and not saying? I know you wanted to say something, but for some reason you remained silent. So, let's hear it." Kayla asked.

"I wanted to wait until we were alone. I mean, I know you have an open mind. I'm not sure about Sam or Mary and this is just a theory. Remember when Mary died and Kranthar brought her back.? What if, something came back with her?"

"Something? Like a spirit? I mean, I guess it could be possible. So, why this boy and why Mary?" Kayla asked, looking for answers.

"I don't know, like I said, it's just a theory." The ride home was exceptionally quiet, as they both tried to figure out what was happening. Kayla thought ghosts, why not. We've been through some crazy stuff in this town lately. Things nobody would believe, even if we told them. Kayla looked out her side window, into the darkness. She felt uneasy; wondering what was going to happen next?

* * *

The next day Sam got to work early as usual but wasn't feeling his best. He hardly slept thinking about Mary and the boy in the plaid shirt. He busied himself, getting things ready for the morning rush. The bell above the door chimed as Kayla walked in.

"Good morning, Sam."

"Good morning Kay, how are you feeling this morning? Only a few more months to go." Sam turned to her and smiled.

"I'm okay, but you look tired. Did you have a rough night?"

Sam stopped what he was doing and leaned over the counter. "I keep thinking about that boy, the one in the plaid shirt. I keep trying to think if I ever saw him come into the café. You're sure you never saw him before, right?"

"Just that one time, in the courtyard. I only saw him once, outside your building. I'm sure it's not the same boy Mary saw in Italy. How could it be, right?" Kayla placed her hand on Sam's shoulder and said. "Lots of people wear plaid shirts." Sam nodded his head and continued with what he was doing.

Max came rushing in with his gym bag in tow. "Hey guys, what's going on? He said, running his fingers through his perfectly styled hair. "I got my hair cut last night. Jeanna said, it was getting too long. What do you think guys?" Max asked, turning his head this way and that. Kayla looked over at Sam, who just shook his head and continued working.

"Your hair looks great Max." Kayla answered

"Yeah right, I think so too. Max responded, checking himself out in a stainless-steel napkin holder. He removed his gym bag off his shoulder, placing his keys on the counter. Throwing his gym bag in the storage room, he got an apron off the shelf, placing it over his head. Coming back to pick up his keys, they were gone. "Kayla did you see where I put my keys? I thought I left them right here on the counter."

"Nope, check your bag."

"I know I put them right here! Where the hell could they have gone?" Kayla scanned the tables, finding them on a table near the front door.

"Here they are Max, you must have put them down not realizing it."

"No Kayla, I didn't put them there."

"Good morning, lady and gents!" Emily announced, running in with seconds to spare. "Not Late!" she yelled.

"You will never change!" Max yelled, at Emily in an annoyed voice.

"He misplaced his keys." Kayla informed her.

"So, he's taking it out on me? Shit!" Emily replied.

CHAPTER TWENTY-FOUR

BENNY

Mary had the day off from her desk job at the hospital. Getting dressed in her most comfortable clothes, she planned on doing a thorough cleaning around the house. Removing her vacuum from the hall closet, she started with the dining room. Making her way around, vacuuming under all the furniture, picking up the dust bunnies. Traveling down the hallway, keeping the vacuum on a high setting, Mary used a special attachment for cleaning the baseboards. Next, she entered their bedroom dusting the furniture and vacuuming the plush carpeting under her feet. Then realizing, she couldn't remember the last time she had vacuumed under the bed. Getting on her knees, some boxes needed to be removed which were stored there. As she dragged out the first box, a photograph emerged with it. Picking it up and turning it over Mary gasped, bringing her hand up to her mouth. It was a picture of her son, who had died many years ago. He had been in a horrific accident at the young age of five. All of her memories came flooding back, as she studied the photograph and remembered that tragic day.

Stepping outside with her son Benny, on a beautiful summer morning. The task at hand, was to give her lovely front garden some much needed T.L.C. Getting all her gardening tools from the shed, she watched Benny closely as he played with a beach ball, throwing it up and trying to catch it. She smiled watching, as he entertained himself. Putting on her gardening gloves, she started with pulling the weeds from the flower beds. Once that was done, it was time to feed and water. Mary looked over at Benny, who had now changed from a beach ball to a baseball. Making her way back to the shed to get the plant fertilizer, she heard a car coming to a screeching halt. Running outside, she looked in the front yard of the house for Benny. Where was he? Panic set in, as she looked around frantically. Mary's gaze fell onto the street, where a small group of people had gathered. Walking into the crowd of onlookers, Mary fell to her knees, as someone dialed 911. She held Benny in her arms praying to God not to take him, but I guess God was busy that day, he died on the way to the hospital.

Now, staring at the black and white photo, she remembered his curly red hair and his favorite plaid shirt. Was this the child she was seeing, was it Benny? Mary sat down on the bed, as tears ran down her face. She held the photo tightly in her hand, trying to come to some conclusion. A thought came to her. Sam told me I had died that day, I passed away in my sleep. A heart attack, but I was brought back by some miracle. Maybe Benny came back with me? Would that be possible? I know some people believe in ghosts, Mary thought. She looked at the photo once more, having a plenitude of emotions running through her. Wondering if she should tell Sam, never mentioning Benny to him before? It was so long ago, a lifetime ago. He knew she was married once, and that her husband passed away a few years ago. Never telling him about the son she once had. Mary stood up, photograph in hand and placed it in the top drawer of her dresser. This is crazy she thought, closing the drawer and continued with her cleaning.

* * *

At the end of the day, it was time to close the café. The patio lights came on, as everyone was packing it in. They all walked out together to their individual cars, hugging each other and saying goodnight. Sam watched as his group pulled away, all of them honking their horns as they drove past him.

As Emily drove up Courtlin, she noticed a small boy running through a parking lot, towards a woman who was waiting by her car, the woman crouched down telling him to come to her. "Come here baby, come on sweetie." Emily smiled, that must be his mom, cute kid. I wish I had his energy she thought, as she drove past them. The woman then bent down picking up her Jack Russell puppy, that had gotten off his leash. "Let's go home baby, my little sweetie." She said, placing her dog in the back seat, starting her car and exiting the parking lot.

Sam got into his car, getting in and fastening his seatbelt, he pulled out of his parking space. He couldn't wait to get home and see Mary. Especially since she had the day off, and had promised to make him his favorite dinner, of steak and homemade mashed potatoes with gravy. Stopping at a light he turned on the radio, to chill out. Immediately, he felt something, a very light kicking on the back of his seat. It was constant, almost in time to the music that was playing. It felt like something a kid would do, just to get on your nerves. Sam looked in his rear-view mirror, the back seat was empty. Yet, the ongoing kicking continued. Turning around in his seat, he checked the floor. Perhaps someone was hiding back there, he could find nothing. As the light changed, he turned off the radio, the kicking suddenly stopped. Did I just imagine that? He started to drive, still looking in the rear-view mirror. He felt like an idiot, allowing his imagination to get the better of him.

* * *

Later, that evening Emily, Simon, Max and Jeanna were meeting at the Pier House for dinner. After much coaxing from Jeanna, Max finally opened his wallet, ready to splurge a little. As they walked inside, the large dining room glowed with a romantic touch of candlelight. Soft music played, from overhead speakers mounted on the ceiling. They were seated at a table in the middle of the room, one of the few tables that remained unoccupied. The plates, glasses, and silverware shone with an amber glow, as a waiter came over to present them with the wine list and menus.

"We'd like to order the house wine." Max told the waiter, handing him back the wine list.

"Will that be the house red, or white?"

"White, ladies?" Max asked, as Emily and Jeanna nodded their heads with approval.

"Hey Jeanna, look long tablecloths." Max remarked, with a sexy grin. Jeanna just smiled and shook her head.

"What's that all about? Long tablecloths?" asked Emily.

"I'll tell you later, Em. Max thinks he's funny." Jeanna answered, remembering the night at their favorite restaurant Anthony's.

* * *

Ramill and Tarsula sat in the hotel room, exhausted, from their on going sexual antics. Ramill was hungry and in need of a change of scenery. "Let's go out to eat tonight. The food is okay at the hotel, but I feel like going someplace nice, special and expensive. Know any place like that, Tarsula my love?"

"There is one place that comes to mind it's called The Pier House. I've been there once just for drinks. It was pretty busy that night, the food is probably good even though the atmosphere is a little dark for my taste."

"I think we should give it a try, sounds romantic." In Ramill's mind, he had them sitting at a table by candlelight, sipping expensive wine and looking into each other's eyes.

"Okay, but I need to disguise myself. I'm not sure if the police are still looking for me."

"The police? What have you been up to my darling Tarsula?" She went on to explain the fiasco with Michael and Kayla. How they had kidnapped her and locked her a room against her will. "Michael needed to have her for his own. He was hell bent on possessing her." Tarsula informed him.

Ramill smiled. "As a man, I can understand Michael's obsessive behavior. I mean, a man infatuated, will do almost anything for the woman he loves. Even reaching into hell to bring her back," he said, kissing Tarsula gently on her hand. Tarsula beamed, she had found her partner in crime.

* * *

After a delicious dinner, Sam had decided to ask Mary what was going on. She wasn't her usual cheerful self; he could tell something was bothering her tonight.

"Are you alright sweetheart? You seem to have something on your mind, what is it?" Sam asked.

"I wasn't going to tell you, but I can't stop thinking about it. I want to show you something." Mary went to get the photo she had stashed in the top drawer of her dresser. Walking over to Sam, she handed it to him. "I think this is the boy I've been seeing." Sam looked at the picture, he could tell the photograph was old, bent at the top and creased down the side.

"Who is this?" Sam asked, looking at Mary waiting for an answer.

"It's my son. He died as a child a long time ago, in a horrible car accident. He had red hair, like his dad. That plaid shirt was his favorite, I remember now, what a fuss he would make when I threw it in the wash."

"Mary, why didn't you ever tell me you had a son? I'm so sorry that happened to him."

" I've been thinking. Maybe he came back with me, that time I died briefly. I mean, why wouldn't a child want to be with his mother, especially, as young as he was."

"What? Come on Mary. You think this is the boy you've been seeing?" Sam asked, staring at the picture.

"Maybe, his name was Benny." Sam put his arms around Mary holding her tight. As Mary softly cried. Sam tried to wrap his mind around what she had just said. Was this the ghost of her child? Did he really feel someone kicking the back of his seat in his car tonight? The hair on his arms stood up, as he wondered if ghosts really existed and if they did, how do you send them back?

* * *

225

Tarsula and Ramill had arrived at the Pier House. She had disguised herself, as a thirty-year-old attractive woman, with auburn hair. As they were escorted through the dining room, on their way to one of the side rooms, Tarsula's eyes grew wide. Noticing Max first, then Jeanna, Emily and Simon sitting at a table enjoying themselves. She remembered Max, and the fun that was had, in the bathroom at Michael's christmas party. A wicked smile crossed her face, as they sat down. Ramill looked over at her, he could see the wheels in her mind were turning. He placed his hand on hers, asking what she was thinking. Tarsula smiled. "Let's have a little fun tonight. What do say, Ramill?"

Ramill gave her a sinister look. "What do you have in mind, my love." Tarsula needed time to think. She reached into her handbag pulling out a small book. It contained what Tarsula called party tricks. Looking through the pages one stood out to her. She turned the book around pointing to a page, showing it to Ramill. He laughed, in an ominous fashion. Tarsula whispered what her plan was, Ramill whispered back. "Yes, but not just their food, everyone's."

"Everyone in the restaurant?" Tarsula's grin widened, "I'm not sure I am powerful enough for that trick."

"I am my darling." Ramill took the book, he rubbed his hands together. The overhead lighting began to flicker, dimmed, and then went out. The speakers above their heads, that had been piping out soft music became quiet. Everyone looked around startled, wanting to know what was going on. The only light that remained was coming from a single candle on each table. Then a scream could be heard, as a woman pushed back her chair, letting it fall to the floor. It made a loud bang echoing through the dining room. Her entrée of mouthwatering whole trout started to flip around on her plate. The pasta dishes were coiling around within their bowls, moving and crawling out onto the tablecloths, resembling worms or small snakes. Max, Jeanna, Emily and Simon looked around wanting to know what was happening. Max looked down at his lobster tacos.

The shell, which contained the delicious lobster meat had turned into an ugly mouth, flapping moving up and down, chewing on the lobster meat within it. The group jumped up and stood away from their table. Emily screamed, as her half chicken moved its leg and flapped its wing. Simon stood up looking down at his plate, his flounder stuffed with crab meat, was unrolling itself. The crab meat was moving, across the table and onto the floor, it moved like tiny ants. Jeanna watched as the shrimp on her plate moved their tails, wiggling to and fro, jumping and frolicking around. All hell broke loose as the diners watched their food scurrying away. Screams and cries echoed through the Pier House. Suddenly, all the lights came back on, the food on the table looked perfectly normal. Nothing was moving, the food sat on the plate pristine, ready to be enjoyed. A hush came over the crowd, some people left, while others sat back down. Max, Jeanna, Emily and Simon looked at each other, not sure what to do. Max sat down first, looking at his tacos. He picked one up examining it, then took a bite, it tasted delicious. Simon looked at his flounder all rolled up, neat and tidy, as if nothing had happened. He poked at it with his fork. Picking up a piece he popped it into his mouth, buttery and flavorful. The girls stared at each other, looking around everything seemed back to normal. They sat back down hesitantly but couldn't bring themselves to take a bite of their food. "What the fuck just happened?" Jeanna asked, upset and looking for answers.

"Maybe some kind of mass hypnosis, I was at a carnival once, where some guy hypnotized a large group of people. They were clucking like chickens, for Christ's sake! Come on ladies the food is good, there's nothing wrong with it," Max proclaimed, as he continued to eat his tacos. Emily looked at Simon, who was enjoying his stuffed flounder. Looking around, a large group of people had left. However, the ones that remained looked like they were enjoying their food. Jeanna picked up a shrimp and shook it. With no movement detected, she took a bite. Finding it yummy, she smiled at Emily and dipped it into her cocktail sauce. Emily called the waiter over asking for a doggy bag and then ordered a large salad. She couldn't get the moving chicken out of her mind and could not bring herself to take a bite.

Tarsula covered her mouth, it was hard to control her laughter. Ramill looked down at his meal, his crab cakes were delectable. "That was fantastic Ramill." Tarsula acknowledged, cutting into her steak.

"Anything for you, my wonderful Tarsula."

* * *

Back at the condo, Sam sat on the sofa still looking at the picture of Benny. As Mary sat down beside him, he handed her the picture. "I think we need to show this to Kayla", he said.

"Yes, since she is the only other person that saw him." Mary concurred.

"I'll bring it to the café tomorrow. I'll show it to her, let's see what she says."

"Okay, thank you." Mary placed the picture down on the coffee table. She was trying her best not to show emotion. However, inside she was freaking out. Sam put his arm around her, rubbing her shoulder, as they watched the ten o'clock news together.

* * *

Kayla was very late getting home, she had to run some errands, as well as dealing with the traffic, which was unbearable. Peter had cooked a meal of baked ziti and garlic bread, which he had kept warm for her. She could smell it walking through the front door. He came over to her, giving her a kiss and a warm embrace. Walking into the kitchen she was met with a fantastic surprise….

Willie had come for a visit. He was sitting on a piece of garlic bread, trying to lick the butter and garlic off of it. He looked up at Kayla as she walked in. Flying up to her shoulder, his small clawed hand touched her cheek, as a black toothy smile appeared, on his little brown face. "Kay la, Willie return!" he said.

"Willie, I'm so happy to see you! I've missed you so much."

Kayla held out her hand as Willie flew onto it. "When did he get here?" she asked Peter.

"He was here when I got home, sitting on the living room rug. He must have come in through the mail slot, as usual."

Willie flew down to Kayla's extended belly. He puffed out his cheeks, making his face look much rounder and full, as he touched her stomach. "I think he just called you fat!" Peter said, laughing.

Kayla placed her hand on her abdomen. "No Willie, babies! Understand?" He just looked at her confused. Kayla had a thought, she ran and got her book called, Being Pregnant and What to Expect. Turning to the section, stages of pregnancy, she showed it to Willie. "Babies inside Willie. I'm going to be a mom and Peter is going to be a dad." She turned to the back of the book, were it showed a woman holding her newborn. "See, Willie baby. Babies inside, two."

Willie thought for a moment then blurted out, "babies hide!"

"Yes, babies hide, in here." Kayla responded, touching her roundness and laughing.

After dinner it was time to relax. Peter and Kayla made themselves comfortable on the sofa in the living room. Willie landed on Kayla's protruding belly listening, placing his large pointy ear against it. His head bobbed up and down, as his tiny clawed foot tapped in unison. It was as if he was keeping time to a song. However, Kayla soon realized he was listening to the babies' heartbeats. No need for a stethoscope, apparently voyeur pixies have extraordinary hearing. She caressed Willie's head, with her pinky finger ever so gently. Watching him, fall asleep as his eyes started to close. Kayla took a corner of a throw blanket and covered his small body. Looking over at Peter he was grinning, as they enjoyed their evening together.

* * *

Kayla woke up the next morning with a smile on her face, remembering sweet Willie. He went back to Zadoc, a beam of light had picked him up, late in the evening. Placing her feet on the floor, she looked down at them, they were swollen again. She would definitely need to wear her sandals today. Pushing herself off the bed, wanting to stick it out for at least one more week, trying to work for as long as possible. Not wanting to leave Sam short of help, anyway, she didn't feel sick just uncomfortable. Kayla told herself to hold on, her due date was getting close, in September.

Peter sat up in bed watching her struggle. "Why don't you stay home, Sam would understand."

"It's okay Peter. I feel alright to work, I'll just wear my sandals. I told Sam I would work for as long as I could. Anyway, he tells me to leave, if he sees I'm getting tired."

"Alright just don't overdo it." Peter got up taking her in his arms, he couldn't wait to be a father. He often wondered who the babies would look like. He was anxious and excited, knowing the babies would be there soon.

* * *

In the morning, Sam got out of bed knowing the café would be very busy today. Now that it was summer, sunny and warm. The outside tables were always filled, so if others wanted to eat, they would have to make their way inside. He called out to Mary, going into the kitchen to put on the coffee. Mary woke up putting on her slippers and robe, then strolled into the kitchen to make breakfast.

"So, Sam don't forget about the photo today." Mary reminded him.

"I won't, I'm going to get to the café early. Usually, Kayla gets there ahead of Max and Emily. I just want to show it to her first. No sense getting Emily and Max involved."

"Good idea Sam."

Sam was ready to leave for work. He walked into the living room to retrieve the photograph that was left on the coffee table last night, it wasn't there. Looking around on the floor and under the sofa, he found nothing. Where the hell was it? Sam called out to Mary.

"What's up?"

"Mary, I thought you left the photo on this table last night. It's not here!"

"It has to be, I remember placing it right here on this table." They both searched again, coming up empty handed.

"Listen, we'll look more tonight, I should get going." Sam walked into the front hallway to pick up his wallet and keys. There sitting in the middle of his bifold, was the black and white photo of Benny. Sam looked at it stunned, not believing what he was seeing. Mary walked over to him, placing her hand over her mouth, when she saw it. "How is this possible Sam? I know I didn't put that there, and I know for a fact that you didn't." Sam didn't know how to respond to her.

He quickly picked up his wallet with the picture, placing them into his pants pocket. Giving Mary a kiss and a hug he headed out. Telling her he would call her later, and not to worry. Mary slowly walked back into the living room, looking around. Was she really alone? Or was Benny in some dark corner hiding from her? She called out his name, as a chill went through her body, looking around. This train of thought has got to stop, she told herself. This wasn't the time to flip out, she needed to get ready for work.

CHAPTER TWENTY-FIVE
A BLAST FROM THE PAST

The traffic was decent as Sam made his way to the café. Parking his car he walked to his bright yellow building. Once inside, he started to get things ready for the morning rush. Moments later, Kayla arrived, saying a fast good morning to him, before quickly walking to the bathroom. Sitting down relieving herself, she closed her eyes hoping these frequent bathroom trips would soon come to an end, once the babies were born. After washing her hands, Kayla greeted Sam properly.

"Good morning, Sam. How are you?" Sam handed her the picture of Benny.

"Is this the child you saw that day in the courtyard?" he asked.

"This is an old picture, Sam. The shirt looks similar, but I couldn't see his face really. Who is this?"

"It's Mary's son. He died when he was five, in a car accident."

The bell above the door sounded as Max came in saying. "Good morning, all." He walked towards the back, putting on an apron and waited for someone to say something. Max looked at Sam and Kayla, trying to figure out the expressions on their faces, as Emily came running in out of breath. "Sorry I'm late!"

Max walked over taking the photo, Sam held in his hand. "Who's the kid?" he asked Sam. Emily walked over curious, wanting to see what everyone was looking at.

"What's going on?" she asked, as Max handed her the photograph. "Hey, I saw this kid. Well, it looked like him, but it couldn't be right? I mean, this is an old picture. Who is he Sam?"

"You said, you saw him?" asked Sam.

"I said, I saw a kid that looked like him. He had the same tousled hair, red if I remember correctly and a similar styled shirt," replied Emily.

"Where did you see him Em?" Kayla inquired.

"I saw a small boy last night when we were all leaving, he was running around the parking lot on Courtlin. There was a woman calling out to him, I thought it was his mom, so I kept on driving. Who is he anyway?"

"He was Mary's son", Sam answered hesitantly. He wasn't sure he wanted to bring Emily and Max into what he thought was happening, but now he had no choice.

"Mary's son! He would be old right now. Come on guys, this is an old picture!" Emily shook her head, how could they think she had seen this boy. "Have you both lost your mind?" Emily walked away putting on an apron and started to fill the salt and pepper shakers. While Max smiled, walking back to the kitchen, to prep for the morning crowd. Kayla put her hand on Sam's shoulder, as Sam looked down at the photograph, wondering if he had in fact lost his mind.

Kayla walked over to Max, she wanted to know where his head was at. "Hey Max, do you believe in ghosts?"

"Ghosts? After last night, I'm not sure what I believe in anymore."

"What do you mean, Max?"

"I know you're aware that, Jeanna and I went with Emily and Simon, to the Pier House last night. I swear there had to be a hypnotist having dinner there. I mean everyone's food started moving around on their plates. Then as quickly as it started, everything was back to normal. Emily wouldn't eat her chicken; she took it home and ordered a salad. He must have sent out some kind of mass hypnosis, letting people believe their food was coming alive, probably thinking it was funny."

"What! Max, I wouldn't mention this to Emily but, do you think Michael and Tarsula are back in town? That just sounds like something she would do, messing with people's minds."

Max swallowed hard. "I don't know Kay. What's with the picture Sam was showing us this morning? Does he really think it's the ghost of Mary's dead son?"

"Well, I did see the child myself, hanging outside Mary's and Sam's condo, also Mary saw him when they were in Italy. Remember when…." She paused for a moment almost saying Kranthar, but corrected herself. "Remember when Peter brought her back, she was dead for a while, maybe he came back with her."

"I don't know." Max replied, continuing to chop up peppers and onions. "I just hope, that fucking weird shit isn't going to start happening again." The bell chimed above the door; the morning rush was about to begin.

* * *

Later that day, Mary's shift was over at the hospital. Walking to her car the soft breeze of summer blew through her hair, soft and gentle. Going through the parking lot, she stopped quickly in her tracks. As a car pulled out right in front of her, nearly hitting her. Apparently, they didn't see her. "Jesus Christ!" She said out loud, giving the driver a pissed off look. Standing there, a small hand found its way into hers. Feeling its chubby palm and small fingers, Mary jumped back, as the small hand fell away. She wasn't expecting this gentle touch. Was it just her imagination? Getting into her car, she just sat there for a moment, thinking about what had just happened. Finally composing herself, Mary started her car. Still slightly shaken up, opening the window trying to clear her mind with some fresh air. Her tears began to fall, thinking about the child she had lost, so long ago.

* * *

The group gathered after finishing the day. Kayla placed her feet up on a chair, as they all sat down together. "So, I want to have a conversation." Sam began, "about this child some of us have been seeing. We all know that Mary had passed away and was brought back to the world of the living. I think Mary's son was brought back with her."

"You mean like a ghost, Sam?" Emily asked.

"Yes, like a ghost Emily." Sam answered. "Mary saw him in Italy and then again at the movie theater here in town. Kayla saw him in the courtyard of our building and Emily, you saw him in the parking lot last night." Sam looked over at Emily. "Don't freak out Em, or let your imagination run wild, as you are known to do." Emily looked down at her feet, knowing Sam had a point. Did she actually see a ghost? Emily tried to remain calm.

Everyone jumped, as someone started pounding on the door of the café. Sam got up, moving the shade to one side, he saw Mary standing there looking very upset. He quickly unlocked the door, as she fell into his arms, crying and trying to compose herself. "I felt him Sam, I could feel his small hand holding mine." Sam held her in his arms, locking the front door again. Walking her to the table, Emily rushed to get her some water.

"Tell us what happened Mary." Kayla asked, in a calm, quiet voice. Mary tried to stay calm as she explained what happened in the parking lot of Saint Paul's. Sam got up and got the bottle of scotch in need of a drink. He poured a drink for all of them, as Max looked at Kayla. She could read his mind, he was thinking, fucking, weird, shit, is starting to happen again. "I think I know someone who can help us." Kayla blurted out. "I met her on our vacation in the Bahamas. Her name is Jilly Williams. She knew I was having twins, way before I did, I think I still have her card somewhere. If Jilly can't help us, she might know someone who can." Kayla remarked.

Getting home, Kayla went into her bedroom closet pulling out the beach bag she had on vacation. Dumping out its contents, the card Babette had given her fell onto the bed. She dialed the number immediately. "Hello." It sounded like her, her Jamaican accent stood out.

"Hello, is this Jilly Williams?"

"Yes, and who are you?"

"My name is Kayla Conrad. You read my tarot cards a while ago. I don't know if you remember me? You told me I was having twins, and you were right."

"Yes, I do remember you. If I remember correctly, you ran out in the middle of your reading."

"Yeah, sorry about that. Would you know anything about ghosts?" There was dead silence on the line. "Hello, Jilly."

"I'm here, ghosts are all around us, they are very close by. They do not ascend to someplace in the sky. I believe, they can walk among us, if they so choose."

Kayla felt a chill, continuing with the conversation. "I have a friend who briefly crossed over, but they were able to bring her back. We think she came back with an attachment, her son, who died as a child a very long time ago."

"I see, that would be my sister Babette's specialty, she is a talented medium. Would you like her number?"

"Yes please, I met her once at an airport, she gave me your card."

"I hope she can help you. Where do you live?"

"I'm on the east coast, near New York."

"Well, you're in luck, my sister lives in Mendham, New Jersey. Do you know it?"

"Yes, I think so, I appreciate your help Jilly. I'm sorry I ran out on you."

CHAPTER TWENTY-SIX

HEGATE AND BABETTE

Hegate would spend the day placing souls into newborn babies. He watched as Detective Roberts approached him. "Thank-you Hegate, for letting me have my revenge on Michael, watching him turn to dust was a pleasure."

"You're welcome. You know he is here, waiting to descend into the bowels of hell."

"Great, that's where he belongs Hegate."

"Unlike you detective, you will ascend shortly, or would you rather be reborn? Give it another shot at life? I'm placing souls today in newborns. I know you helped Kayla escape from Michael's grasp. She will be giving birth soon, to a son. I can place your soul in her baby. What do you think, Detective Roberts?"

"I'm not sure I want to go back just yet. Do I have to?"

"No, you have free will. I just thought since you know her and that she would be a doting, loving mother, you would enjoy that. Better her, than a woman who doesn't give a shit. Know what I mean?"

"Yeah. What's the alternative Hegate?"

"I can send you to heaven, you absolutely qualify. Though you may find it a bit boring. Having anything you desire at your whim. Relaxing day, after day, after day. That can get monotonous after a while. Are you sure you wouldn't want to give it another go? Get back into law enforcement, try to make a difference in the world? Once you leave here, there's no turning back."

Detective Roberts thought for a moment. "Maybe I should go back. I do love law enforcement, and quite frankly heaven sounds a bit dull, as you described it. Alright Hegate, I'll give it another shot. Place my soul into Kayla's boy, she is a lovely woman. I will be proud to be her son."

"Good choice Roberts, you won't have to wait long only a few more weeks." Hegate smiled, as Detective Roberts walked away. Hegate let out a laugh, it came from deep within his gut. He could hardly contain himself thinking about it. Michael's soul would be placed in Kayla's daughter, while Detective Roberts soul would be placed in her son. That's priceless Hegate thought, laughing loud and hard, how do I come up with this shit!

* * *

Kayla and Sam had scheduled a meeting with Babette at her home in Mendham. Sam drove thinking it would be best if Mary didn't know what they were up to. He would fill her in later, once they had more information. Kayla looked out her side window impressed with the town. "I guess mediums make good money, look at these houses Sam."

"Yeah, she must be talented, the real deal to afford all of this."

"This is it Sam! Pull into the driveway."

The house was set way off the road. As they got closer, the large home came into view. It was a massive ranch. Surrounded by trees and many pots containing a variety of flowers. The colors popped against the white stone house. It had a terracotta roof, which had a warm glow to it, thanks to the afternoon sun. This house reminded Kayla of homes she had seen in a magazine, tucked away in the French countryside, breathtaking to look at.

Getting out of the car, the graveled driveway crunched beneath their feet as they walked. Kayla rang the doorbell, as they looked around and waited. The door opened as Babette stood in front of them wearing a brightly colored sundress. Loosely fitted and comfortable, her hair was wrapped in the same glorious fabric as her dress.

"Good afternoon, won't you both come in," she greeted them with her lovely Jamaican accent. "Get out of the afternoon sun, it's a hot one today." Babette remarked, as a pleasing smile came across her face.

"Thank you for seeing us Babette, this is Sam." Kayla smiled, as she introduced him.

Babette reached out to shake his hand "So, my sister Jilly tells me you're in need of my help. Let's go in and sit down. I have a fresh pitcher of Sorrel tea in the fridge. I make it with hibiscus buds, then I add fresh ginger, sugar, and let it chill overnight. I serve it over ice with a splash of soda water and a squirt of lime juice. It's very refreshing on hot days like this." Babette glanced over at Kayla. "However, child, in your condition it may not be safe. Maybe some plain decaf iced tea would be more suitable. How does that sound? You must be due soon?"

"Yes, in a few weeks. I've never heard of Sorrel tea, it sounds delicious, but some decaf tea would be better I suppose. Thank you."

Sam grinned, as Babette went to get the drinks they looked around the home. The rooms were extremely large, almost too large for one person. Although the walls were soft beige in color, she made up for it, adorning the rooms with brightly colored furniture and patterns.

Babette put the tray of drinks down on the table before them. "Here we are, your first taste of Sorrel tea!" Sam took a sip, smiled and said, "it's very good, cool, refreshing." Babette grinned, as she handed Kayla the glass of decaffeinated iced tea.

"Alright, now let us get down to business." Babette was ready to hear all the details, "tell me everything?"

Sam began, "this all started on our trip to Italy. Where we first heard about him and then began to see this small boy." Babette quickly held up her hand, and Sam interpreted the gesture as, be quiet. Babette closed her eyes. Kayla and Sam just looked at each other waiting. Suddenly Babette's eyes popped open, "go on" she said.

Sam continued. "When we got back to the U.S. Kayla saw him and also Emily, she works with us. The thing that has me worried is, he reached out and touched my wife, Mary. She said, she could feel his tiny hand in hers."

"I see him, in my mind's eye, young, very young. He has on a plaid shirt, cute, with red hair."

"YES!" Kayla screamed, then quickly apologized, not being able to hold back her excitement. "I'm so sorry, but that's amazing. Amazing, right Sam?"

Sam just nodded his head yes. He was stunned; she could actually see him? "Why is he here?" Sam asked.

"There was a rip in the vail, he came over with someone. Maybe someone who had passed on briefly and was brought back. Know anyone like that?"

Kayla nodded her head yes "we do" she replied, looking at Sam who had tears in his eyes.

"Tell me." Babette needed the whole story. Sam began; he told her that Mary had passed away briefly from a heart attack but was brought back. Babette listened intently and then asked. "How long was she gone for?"

"We're not sure, she died in her sleep. We think the boy is her son Benny. He died at the age of five, a car accident."

"He's not evil, but a sweet spirit, playful. I think he just wants to be with his mom. Yet, you are right, this is not where he belongs. I will try a cleansing ritual."

"You think our house needs cleansing?" Sam asked.

"No, not your house. Your wife. We need to break the bond between them. It can be difficult, to separate a child from its mother. Do you think Mary would participate in a séance without question?"

"I think so." Sam replied, looking over at Kayla.

"Good, let's set a date and time. Bring as many people with you as possible. It's good to have an abundance of life energy around, since the portal is open."

"The portal?" Kayla asked, thinking of the closet Detective Roberts came out of, floating in front of her as a mist.

"Yes, Miss Kayla, to the other side." Babette stood up to get her appointment book.

* * *

On the drive back home, Sam turned to Kayla and asked. "Have you ever attended a séance, Kay?"

"No, but there's a first time for everything. You?"

"Absolutely not. What do you think Mary will say?" asked Sam.

"I'm not sure. Does she have an open mind?" Kayla questioned.

"She should, with everything that's been going on lately. Do you think we should ask the rest of the group Max, Jeanna, Emily and Simon?"

Kayla thought for a moment. "Well, Babette did say, to bring as many people as possible. So, yes, I think we should include them.

When they arrived at Kayla 's house, he dropped her off and continued on his way home. Kayla walked up the front stairs, as Peter opened the front door. "How did it go? What did she say?"

"Give me a second Peter, let me take my sneakers off." Kayla kicked the sneakers off her swollen feet and took a seat on the sofa. "Okay so, I think she's the real deal, she could actually see him, Benny I mean."

"Wait a minute, she could see him Kay?"

"Yeah, she described him, his plaid shirt, his red hair. We didn't tell her anything. She thinks Benny crossed over with Mary, when Kranthar brought her back."

"You didn't say anything about Kranthar, right?"

"Of course not, Peter. For the simple fact, that Sam thinks you brought Mary back, not a Seeker."

"So, what is Babette going to do? How do we send him back?"

Kayla looked at him with a slight grin on her face. "Feel like attending a séance?"

* * *

Sam parked his car near the courtyard, trying to figure out what to tell Mary. A séance Sam thought should be interesting, but I'm not sure how Mary is going to react. Stepping into the elevator Sam pushed the button for the third floor. The doors started to close, but then stopped halfway, as if someone wanted to get on from the lobby. Holding his hand against the door, he stuck out his head. Not seeing anyone, he released the door, letting it close easily. The elevator rode up to the first floor as the doors opened again. What the hell is happening? Sam thought, as he stuck out his head and looked down the corridor, not a soul in sight. The doors closed, opening on the second floor, once again Sam stuck his head out and had a look around, nothing. Finally arriving on the third floor, the doors opened. Stepping off the elevator, he heard a child laughing behind him. Sam turned to see a small boy standing there, wearing a plaid shirt with tousled red hair. The child smiled at him as the doors closed. Sam tried to keep the doors open, but he wasn't quick enough. Did I just see that, Sam thought? He had to calm down and compose himself before seeing Mary. Walking down the long corridor, his mind was buzzing. Should he tell Mary what had just taken place? His thoughts were, I think I should keep quiet. I don't want to upset her, more than she already is. Getting to his door, he took a few deep breaths, before walking inside. Mary was sitting at the dining room table, working on a puzzle she had started months ago, she called out to him. "How was work?" she asked, looking up from the puzzle.

Sam tried to hide the fact that he was shaken up, so he answered. "Good, great, how was your day?" Yet, in his mind he was thinking. Hey Mary, guess what? I just saw your dead son in the elevator. Yeah, he was pressing all the buttons, so we had to stop on every floor.

"Good, great, nothing out of the ordinary." Mary replied. "I've asked Kayla and Peter to come for dinner one night. Jesus, trying to get four people's schedules to jive is almost impossible."

"Everyone is busy these days. I'm going to wash up for dinner."
Sam walked down the hallway and into the bathroom. He washed
his hands and face, still thinking about the elevator. Was his mind
playing tricks on him? Mary called out to him from the kitchen.
"Dinner's almost ready Sam!"

"I'll be right there!" He walked into the bedroom to change
his clothes. Putting on some jeans and a clean tee shirt he heard a
noise behind him. A low sounding thump, as if something had hit the
ground hard. He looked around, as a baseball rolled out from under
the bed. Sam picked it up, turning it over in his hand, to get a better
look. It was old, worn and torn in places. The leather had taken on a
pale-yellow patina. Walking into the kitchen, he showed it to Mary.
"Is this yours?"

Mary stopped what she was doing, as Sam watched the color
drain from her face. "It looks like the baseball Benny had. He
was playing with it the day he…… well you know." Sam placed
the ball on the counter and then sat down. You could hear a pin
drop as Mary served the meal. They both looked at each other
apprehensively, till Sam suddenly spoke up. "How do you feel about
séances?"

CHAPTER TWENTY-SEVEN

THE SÉANCE

The group gathered outside Babette's home. Everyone was pretty much on time, except for Simon and Emily, who were running late. The front door opened as Babette ushered them in. "We're still waiting for two more people." Sam announced, as they walked inside.

"Alright, but no reason to stand outside in the dark, please make yourselves at home." She acknowledged, showing them into the living room, where they settled down on the sofa and brightly colored chairs. Babette gathered the supplies that would be needed for tonight's séance. Holy water, white candles, and of course Benny's baseball. Sam had contacted her about the ball and was told, in no uncertain terms, that he needed to bring it. The doorbell rang, it was Emily and Simon. Babette escorted them in, to join the group. "So, is this everyone?" she asked, looking around the room.

"Yes, we're all here now." Sam answered. Looking at Emily with that expression of late again as usual, on his face.

"Very good, shall we all go into the back room and take a seat at the table." The group stood up and followed Babette into a large room. They all sat down at a massive round table; a giant light fixture hung above their heads. Babette retrieved the holy water. Walking around them she placed the holy water on each person's forehead in the sign of a cross, while saying something under her breath, that no one could hear or would probably understand. She placed her hands on Mary's shoulders. Babette closed her eyes reciting a prayer in some foreign language. Next, she placed the white candles in the middle of the table and lit them, then she positioned Benny's baseball there and dimmed the lights. She took a seat telling everyone to join hands. "This is the chain of everyone's life force. No matter what you hear or see, do not break the chain. Do all of you understand?" Everyone nodded in agreement. "I'm going to ask for complete silence while I channel." A silence of uncertainty fell around the room. Kayla looked at Sam, while Sam looked at Mary. Emily and Jeanna just looked at everyone, not knowing what to expect next and getting a little frightened by the whole situation. An uneasy quiet took over, as Babette closed her eyes. She tilted her head to one side, as if she was listening to someone. A cool breeze cascaded through the room; the curtains started to move, billowing outward. The light fixture above the table began to move, ever so slightly. A few of the candles on the table went out, as their smoke swirled around them, eventually moving upward towards the ceiling. A child's cry was heard, coming from somewhere within the room. "I see you Benny, I know you are here!" Babette cried out. Some tears trickled down Mary's face. Sam looked at Mary wanting to comfort her but was afraid to break the chain of hands, Babette continued. "Come forward Benny, your mom is here. Did you follow her back to the earthly plane?" Total silence, everyone around the table waited for a reply. Their hearts pounding in their chests. Then, through the darkness came the voice of a child, "Ma ma". Mary cried out loud "Benny!" The baseball in the center of the table started to bounce up and down.

Emily screamed, trying to get up, but Simon held her hand tightly, telling her not to move. "We can't break the chain Em, sit down!" he yelled. Then the voice of the child once again, "Ma ma."

Mary yelled out into the darkness. "I'm here Benny! I'm here! I love you!"

Babette spoke up, "he knows your here, but...."

"What?" Mary asked, with panic in her voice.

Babette took a breath, "he's lost."

"What do you mean he's lost? Can't he go back the way he came in?" Sam asked.

"He's so young, and has traveled to far into the earthly plane, to find the opening back," Babette answered.

"What should we do Babette? We can't just leave him here." Kayla asked, looking for guidance.

They could hear Benny starting to cry very loudly. As Mary screamed into the darkness. "Help him Babette! Help my boy!"

"I don't know where the portal is! I don't know where to send him!" Babette answered loudly. "I'm asking spirits to come forward and help me!"

"Ma ma!" The backs of everyone's chairs were being pushed. The girls screamed as they felt their chairs moving.

"Nobody break the chain!" Babette screamed.

Then from the darkness, a voice called out. "Benny, my boy." Mary knew that voice, it was the voice of her late husband, Grant.

"Grant?" Mary shouted. A smile came to Babette's face. "Yes Mary, he is here."

"Dad dy!" The group then gasped, as two strong ghostly hands came out of the darkness, grabbing the small and transparent hands of a child. Then a voice cut through the room "Mary, I have him." Then dead silence. Until…. Babette spoke. "Another spirit is coming through, the portal is closing, speak quickly spirit!" Babette shouted out.

"S a m m y."

"Rose, Rose!" Sam was beside himself, as tears ran down his face. The familiar voice, was his deceased wife, Rose. She was the only one, to ever call him Sammy and get away with it. To him that was a name for a kid, not a grown man. Anyone who called him Sammy would be corrected at once, except for her.

"The portal is closed." Babette stood up slowly and turned the lights on in the room. Everyone around the table just sat there, in a state of shock. Until Peter's voice broke the silence. "Hey guys the baseball is gone! Where did it go?"

"The baseball was not a part of this world, it went back with Benny, to his." Babette answered calmly.

As the group pulled themselves together, Sam walked over to Babette, still weeping from hearing his deceased wife's voice "I can't thank you enough for all that you've done. You are truly gifted, what do I owe you?"

"There is no charge, when a child is involved. He was lost and couldn't find his way back to the portal, that's all. It happens sometimes, with children who cross over. They want to remain where people are familiar to them, and a mother and child, well that's the strongest bond of all." Sam smiled and turned to walk away but was stopped by Babette's hand on his shoulder. "Your Rose is pretty, I could see her in my mind's eye. Dark hair, big brown eyes, a small beauty mark on her left cheek, a wonderful smile, just lovely."

"Yes, that's my Rose," was all Sam could manage to say, as his tears fell. Mary walked over to him. They wrapped their arms around each other crying and emotionally drained.

The group left Babette's house shaken, over what they had just witnessed. Was it true then, that we never really die, just transition into another realm? After tonight, that was the group's opinion. They all witnessed it up close and personal. Ghostly hands coming out of the darkness, and voices from the past. They would be foolish, to think anything different. Getting into their cars, they made their way down the long driveway. While Babette looked out her front window smiling and sipping on a glass of Sorrel tea.

* * *

Tarsula sat at a small table in the hotel room watching Ramill sleep. She was bored and had decided to go down to the bar, located in the hotel's lobby. A wicked and cunning grin formed across her face. She ran to her carpet bag and lifted out the bottle which contained The Beauty is in the Eye of the Beholder spray. This spray made all men see her, as their most sexual desire. The epitome of what beauty was in their eyes. Each man saw a different woman, his ideal sexual partner. Tall and thin or curvy and voluptuous, blonde, brunette, or redhead. The girl next door with a natural kind of beauty, to a highly made-up fashion model, her make-up and hair done to perfection. Tarsula sprayed herself generously from her feet to the top of her head, while saying the incantation. She took a room key from Ramill's coat pocket and took the elevator down to the lobby. She laughed, Ramill will never catch me cheating on him, she thought. He will probably see me as some redhead, with big boobs and an ass that won't quit. I could fuck a guy right in front of him, and he would have no clue it was me.

Walking across the lobby to the Tap Room Bar, the eyes of men were upon her. Each man lost in his own sexual fantasy. Making her way to the corner of the room she sat down and waited. The bartender walked over to her, placing a bowl of peanuts in front of her. "What can I get you lovely lady?"

Tarsula gave him the once over thinking, I'm not impressed or attracted to him, "white wine please."

"Listen, my name is Ted, I get off in about" …. Ted looked over at the clock. "Thirty minutes, would you like to have dinner with me?"

"No thank you Ted, I'm waiting for someone."

"Aren't we all." Ted replied, in a hopeless voice, being rejected once again. When her wine was brought over, she sipped it slowly. Scanning the bar for any sight of a suitable sexual partner. She watched the door as a few businessmen paraded past her, all of them smiling and gawking at her. Tarsula had decided to call it a night, until her eyes became fixated on two gentlemen that had just walked in. An older guy with salt and pepper hair, along with a much younger version of himself. The resemblance was uncanny, Tarsula thought they must be father and son. The older gentleman's shirt was fitted hugging his muscles tightly, he seemed to be in great shape, for a man his age. Not usually Tarsula's type, but there was a certain rugged look to him, that she found very appealing. The younger guy was blonde and on the thin side, not at all a sexual turn on for her. So, drinking her last bit of wine, she sashayed over to the bar where they were both sitting. It took a few moments for them to notice her; they smiled cordially at Tarsula. Both making it obvious, they were attracted to whatever kind of woman they were each seeing. The two men turned towards each other, having a quiet conversation amongst themselves. The younger of the two got up and left, leaving the older one walking over to her.

"I'm Kent, and you are?"

"Whoever you want me to be." Tarsula responded.

"Good answer." Kent chuckled. "Can I buy you another?" He asked, as his eyes roamed the body of a thin Asian beauty.

* * *

Ramill woke up, his eyes looked around the room, calling out to Tarsula. He got up looking into the bathroom, no sign of her. He checked the pocket of his jacket, one of the room keys was missing. Ramill dressed quickly taking his room key and the elevator down. He frantically looked around the lobby and a small gift shop, finally spotting her, sitting at the bar with some strange guy. Tarsula watched Ramill, she wondered what kind of girl he was seeing, as he walked over to her. Taking a seat next to her at the bar, he took hold of Tarsula's hand. A look of shock appeared on Tarsula's face. So much for true love! How can he be so horny and so unfaithful? Tarsula's anger started to mount, if he tries to leave with me, I will pack up my shit. He will never see me again. Ramill turned to Tarsula and looked deeply into her eyes. "Why didn't you wake me up Tarsula? I would have come down for a drink with you."

What just happened? A look of shock spread across her face. At that moment Tarsula realized that she was the woman of Ramill's most sexual desire. He saw her, not some picture perfect sex goddess. "Ramill, do you see me?" she asked.

"Yes, of course. What kind of question is that?" Ramill smiled at her. "Was I supposed to see someone else?"

"No." For the first time in a long time Tarsula felt loved, and desired. She threw her arms around Ramill kissing his lips. Taking his hand, she pulled him away from the bar. "Let's go back to the room. I know you are well rested." Tarsula said in his ear. "That's good cause you're going to need your strength. I'm going to fuck your brains out." Ramill smiled, as they waited for the elevator.

The bartender walked over to Kent, asking him to pay for his bar tab. "Do I owe you for the drink I brought the young lady, she never drank it?"

"Yeah, sorry dude. If I poured it, you pay for it, it's that simple," the bartender grinned. "Nice piece of ass though, sorry you missed out."

Ramill opened the door to their hotel room. Walking in he placed his arms around Tarsula's waist. "Come back to the west coast with me. I have a large home, way too big for me. There's really nothing left for you here, now that Michael is gone. What's keeping you here Tarsula?" She thought for a moment and realized he was right. Her vindictive nature almost got her banished to hell forever, if it wasn't for Ramill, she would still be there. Tarsula's eyes teared up as she looked at his face. "Yes Ramill, you are right. There is nothing left for me here in this town. Besides, I need a change of scenery, a new place to explore."

"I can make you happy Tarsula. We were happy once; we can be again. Pack your things, we can get on a flight tonight." Ramill kissed her lips, exploring her mouth with his tongue. For the first time in a long time, Tarsula finally felt protected and safe in the arms of a man.

CHAPTER TWENTY-EIGHT

KAYLA TURNS ON THE WATER WORKS

Peter and Kayla arrived at Sam and Mary's condo for dinner. It was a long time coming, as everyone's schedule eventually aligned. Wine and cake in hand, they waited outside their door, and were quickly greeted by Sam. He escorted them in, taking the cake from Kayla's hands. Mary yelled out from the kitchen. "Hey guys, just give me a minute, I'm taking the roast out of the oven!"

"Come on in and sit down. Peter, it feels like forever since I've seen you. You haven't been dropping by the café lately." Sam remarked, placing some glasses on the table.

"Yeah sorry, I've been really busy with school activities. I think I've taken on more than I should have." Peter replied, looking over at Kayla.

"Don't feel bad Sam. I'm pregnant with his babies, and I hardly see him." Peter shook his head, he just knew she was going to say something about his long hours at school.

Mary walked out carrying a large platter of roasted potatoes and vegetables. She placed it down next to a beautifully cooked roast. Sam brought over a basket of bread and started to fill all the wine glasses, except Kayla's. She would have a tall glass of pomegranate juice over ice instead. The food was delicious, if Mary had any talent at all, it was her cooking. After dinner, they sat in the living room while Sam made the coffee, to go with the cake Kayla and Peter had brought. Mary was telling them a funny story about something that happened at the front desk of the hospital when……

"Ohoooo!" Kayla bent over in pain. Everyone stopped what they were doing and came over to her. "I need to use the bathroom, Owwww!" Kayla yelled, as Peter helped her stand, again she cried out in pain. "I think I'm having contractions! Take me to the hospital Peter!" Sam got his keys, as Mary ran to get her purse. Sam would drive, since he was paying for a parking space that was very close to the front entrance of the building. Everyone got into the elevator as a gush of pale-yellow fluid ran down between Kayla's legs onto the elevator's floor. "So sorry about the elevator guys!" Kayla apologized, as another contraction began.

"Don't worry sweetheart," Sam answered. "That's what I'm paying overpriced HOA fees for." They finally arrived in the lobby, as another contraction bent Kayla over in pain. Sam picked her up and carried her to his car. Peter got on his phone and asked Sergeant Daniels for a police escort, saying they were still quite far away from the hospital, and in need of assistance. Daniels got into his car, turning on the police siren, trying to get to them, as quickly as possible. He picked up his two-way radio and explained the situation reporting their location, along with the license plate number of Sam's car.

A scream came from the backseat. "Drive faster, the baby's coming!" Kayla screamed. Sam put the petal to the metal, while Peter kept telling Kayla to breathe. Police sirens could be heard behind them. Sam looked into his rearview mirror. "Should I stop and pull over!" A resounding "No" was yelled from inside the car. A police trooper pulled alongside Sam's car, telling them to follow him. He would get them to the hospital as quickly and as safely as possible. Another scream of excruciating pain came from Kayla. "I can feel the baby it's coming!" Peter lifted up Kayla's sun dress and removed her panties. He could see the top of the baby's head

crowning. "Jesus Christ, it's coming, I can see the top of its head!"
Then Kayla felt the need to push, and just like that, the first baby
arrived into the world.

* * *

Meanwhile, on the astral plain Hegate was getting his souls
ready. He knew one of Kayla's children had already arrived onto the
earthly plain. He needed to make haste, grabbing hold of Michael
he asked. "Are you ready Michael?" Michael just nodded his head,
a dark orb surrounded by a deep orange light, exploded from
Michael's chest. Michael's body pixelized and blew away, as Hegate
held the dark orange orb, rolling it between his massive hands. He
watched it becoming smaller and smaller then, disappearing into
nothingness.

* * *

Kayla's baby girl cried loudly, screaming. Moving her small
arms back and forth through the air, as if having a temper tantrum,
as she received her father's soul. Sam pulled into the hospital's
emergency parking lot. The police opened the back door as Mary
and Sam looked on. She had given birth to a strikingly beautiful
baby girl. One of the police officers ran in to get a doctor, who cut
the cord, wrapping her in a blanket and running her inside to be
checked out. Soon, the next baby came into view, only this one
was breech. Peter could almost see its foot. Another gut-wrenching
scream came from Kayla's lips, she wanted to push. Peter started to
scan her, looking below the surface of her skin, he yelled out to her.
"No Kayla! Don't push! Just breath!" The doctor wanted to remove
her from the vehicle. "Leave her!" Peter shouted at the doctor to
let her be. Peter could see what was happening, he had an idea.
Dropping his head to his chest, a ribbon of light ran up his body. He
placed his hand near Kayla's vagina, as his light rope entered her.
Those standing close by had no idea what was truly going on. No
one could actually see what he was doing. Scanning he could see the
babies' legs, he gently took hold of them with his light rope, turning
him back into the correct position. He continued to scan and noticed

253

the baby's umbilical cord was wrapped around its neck. Very gently, he used his light to remove the cord, bringing it over the baby's head, and away from its neck. Then and only then did he give Kayla the command to push. She gave it all she had, out came his son, head first. The baby's cry was loud and strong, as everyone cheered!

* * *

Hegate looked at Detective Roberts, are you ready. "Yes, Hegate, I'm ready." Hegate extracted a globe of light from the detective's body. His orb was pristine, pure white light. He held it in his hands watching it get smaller and smaller. Looking up he saw Detective Roberts wave good-bye, as his body disappeared into nothingness. Kayla's son, suddenly grew quiet and calm. A serene expression formed on his small round face, as he received the soul of Detective Roberts.

Sergeant Daniels arrived just as they were taking Kayla out of the backseat and into the hospital. Peter filled him in on what had just happened. He reached out, putting his arms around Peter congratulating him.

Kayla and her babies were brought up to the maternity ward and checked over. Her sundress was removed and replaced with a hospital gown, as the babies were brought over to the nursery.

* * *

A day later, Max and Jeanna, along with Mary and Sam came walking into Kayla's hospital room. Emily and Simon were the last to arrive. Emily ran over to Kayla hugging her tightly, holding two large teddy bears, one pink, one blue. "Hey there Momma!" Emily was overcome with emotion. "We saw the babies they are beautiful. Your baby girl is breathtaking. I can't imagine what she'll look like as she grows. You guys are going to have your hands full with that one."

"Thanks for the warning, Em." Peter smiled. Everyone took turns holding the babies. They talked about different names to call them, who the babies looked like, that kind of thing. After some time had passed, Peter could see Kayla was getting tired. "Listen guys,

254

maybe we should all go downstairs and give Kayla a chance to rest. What do you say?" asked Peter.

"Yes, let's all go down to the cafeteria, Kay's been through a lot. Come on, I'm buying." Sam declared.

* * *

The nurses gathered around the new babies, that had just arrived. One of them picked up Kayla's daughter, calling the other nurses over. "Have you ever seen a more beautiful newborn? Just look at her." Yes, they were all in agreement, she was truly gorgeous. Then Kayla's baby girl opened her eyes. "Do her eyes look strange to you? The color looks different in each eye." One of the nurses remarked, as the other nurses came over to take a look. "Maybe, but as you know, it takes time for the baby's eye color to adjust. Another nurse remarked, "yes maybe they'll stay blue, dark hair and blue eyes, now that's a perfect combination."

* * *

Everyone had returned back to Kayla's room, to say goodbye and found Kayla fast asleep. "Listen guys, I think we should leave. We can come back tomorrow." Emily stated. They decided to leave, letting Kayla get the sleep she so deserved. Peter walked out with them. After a while, he returned to the room and saw that Kayla was now awake. "Hey baby." Peter whispered. "How are you feeling? I stopped by the nursery. I spoke to one of the nurses, they're going to bring the babies in here soon. So, we can bond with them, any ideas for names yet? I wanted to name my son after my dad however, Zadoc doesn't quite work for me."

"Yeah, me either." Kayla chuckled. "We need a good strong name. How about Jaden? I've always liked that name."

"How about Nathan? It's an English name, it means protection." Peter remarked.

"Nathan La' Sogian, it kind of has a ring to it, and I like what the name stands for. Your mom will be happy, since La' Sogian is her last name." Kayla added.

255

"Well, my dad, being who he is, doesn't have a last name. They don't use them there, I don't know why." When Peter was born, he took his mom's last name. Everyone thought she was a single mom, with a dead-beat boyfriend, who didn't want anything to do with being a father.

Two nurses came into the room with the babies, both of them in rolling bassinets. Both babies were sporting a pink or blue knitted cap. Nathan was removed from his bassinet and handed to Peter.

"Time to think about girl names." Kayla remarked, as she was handed her beautiful daughter. The nurses were leaving but first asked if Peter would be staying the night? "We have cots, we can bring one in. Most men stay, it keeps the family together and insures strong bonding with the babies."

"Well, if that's the case I would love to stay. Thank you." The nurses smiled, as they took their leave. "Okay, let's look up some names." Peter took his phone out of his pocket and scrolled girl names. "Let's see we have, Abigail, Amanda, Amelia."

"No, start with the names beginning with E." Kayla suggested.

"So, we have Eleanor, Elizabeth, Ella." Kayla stopped him immediately.

"Ella, I love that name, what is the meaning behind it?" Peter looked it up, while Kayla waited for an answer.

"It means, light or beautiful fairy woman, but it can also mean goddess." Peter smiled. "All of those descriptions suit her. What do you think, Kay?"

"I think we just named our kids. Nathan and Ella La' Sogian, I love it! What do you think?"

"Good choices. So, momma Kayla, I have one more question for you."

"Oh yeah, what's that?" Kayla looked up from Ella.

"When are we getting married?" Peter bent down and kissed her tenderly.

"ASAP Peter, ASAP." Peter sat down on the bed next to Kayla, as they held their new babies in their arms. This was one of those moments in life to be cherished forever. Peter was beside himself with happiness. Kayla was already thinking about her upcoming nuptials to him. She looked at her children with love in her eyes, remembering a time not so long ago. When Peter had come over, to help her put up a Christmas tree. She remembered telling him back then that they made a good team. Smiling to herself she realized, the team just got bigger.

Kayla woke up the next morning, on the first day of Autumn. Looking over at Peter he was sound asleep. His left leg dangling over the edge of the cot, as he quietly snored. Kayla got up slowly to check on the babies. Everyone was sound asleep, except for her. She walked to the window and looked outside. Some of the trees were beginning to show signs of color. It brought a smile to her face, knowing she was finally, in her favorite time of year.

* * *

Zadoc and Kranthar approached the front desk of Saint Paul's Hospital. "Salutations, we are here to see the grandest of my children." Mary looked somewhat confused as to what was being asked. Kranthar continued, "his son just had twins." Mary thought, maybe he's from another country and not sure of the proper English.

"Oh, your grandchildren, got it. Some dear friends of mine also just had twins. Fraternal twins, a boy and a girl. What is the name of the mom?" asked Mary.

"Kayla Conrad," replied Zadoc.

"Wait a minute, I know them, they are also my friends. So, you must be Peter's dad, small world isn't it? What are your names?"

"I am Zadoc, and this is my comrade Kranthar."

"Are those your first names or last?" Mary smiled, looking up at them.

"Last? We are never last, always first." Kranthar informed her.

"Okay." A look of confusion crossed Mary's face, as she quickly called for Gloria to hold down the fort. She was going to escort Zadoc and Kranthar to Kayla's room, on the maternity floor.

"Okay gentleman, if you will both follow me, I will show you to

257

Kayla's room."

Walking along the corridors Kranthar was lagging behind. He was curious about all the different rooms, and what was going on in them. Zadoc noticed some double doors, which were decorated with cartoon animals. "Where do those doors go?" he asked.

"Oh, that's the children's ward. If you'll both follow me, please." They waited for the elevator, as Zadoc and Kranthar looked at each other, not believing there were so many sick children, that they needed their own ward of this hospital place. On their planet, the young never got sick. People were constantly scanned. If there was a problem, it would be dealt with quickly and thoroughly. Never giving the problem, a chance to progress.

Walking off the elevator Mary said. "Here we are, if you'll follow me." They walked into the room just as Peter was waking up.

"Dad!" Peter walked over to them, giving them both a huge hug. They approached Kayla, who stood up slowly as Zadoc and Kranthar embraced her. "Thank you, Mary." Peter said, as Mary left the room, she had to get back to the front desk.

"Salutations! Let's have a look at my grandest of children." Kayla and Peter laughed.

"Alright." Peter picked up his son smiling. "I love the baseball caps you're both wearing, it's a nice touch, Peter complimented his father. This is Nathan, his name means protection. He's ten minutes younger than our baby girl Ella. He handed Nathan to Zadoc, who lost no time scanning the baby from head to toe.

"An extremely healthy little guy. Good job Kayla. Oh, by the way Willie sends his best regards. I will send him down to you soon. I know he wants to meet these little ones." A huge smile appeared on Kayla's face, as well as a tear formed in her eye. She always got emotional when Willie was mentioned, her love for him was immense. They had been through a lot together; she couldn't wait to see him again.

Zadoc placed Nathan back in his bassinet and picked up Ella. He scanned her up and down, then suddenly stopped. Did he just see something? He started again, scanning her, then he spoke. "She is also healthy, but there may be one imperfection. I mean, she is very young, so we will have to see."

Kayla and Peter came running over looking at their beloved daughter. "What is it dad? What do you see?"

"Her eyes are healthy, however there may be a color variation between the two. I've noticed a difference in their pigmentation. I'm sure it will be fine, human eyes need time to adjust. Otherwise, she is good in every way." They stayed for a little while longer but then decided to leave. Both of them were curious about the children's ward, they needed to see it for themselves.

Peter looked over at Kayla with both confusion and hurt in his eyes. A different eye color? One blue, one brown with a touch of gold, is that right Kayla? This can't be happening right now! He thought, are these children even mine? He felt like someone just stabbed him in the chest with a knife.

Kayla just looked at him, not really knowing what to say, that was all in the past. She no longer wanted or had any feelings for Michael, other than hate. "I'm so sorry Peter, when I was with Michael I was still confused. I hadn't made up my mind, as to who I wanted to be with. Please forgive me."

A few tears fell down Peter's face. However, he loved her more than life itself and he loved the babies. Even though he only knew them for a short time, they were a family now. If Ella was part of Michael, she was also a part of Kayla. It wasn't Ella's fault, her father was some ungodly creature. He would love the three of them, regardless of what happened in the past. Peter would look towards the future now, a future together. He reached out for Kayla who ran into his arms. "Thank you Peter." That was all she said, as they held each other tightly and cried softly.

CHAPTER TWENTY-NINE
ZADOC AND KRANTHAR

Zadoc and Kranthar walked around the hospital opening closed doors and looking into rooms. They took the elevator up and down numerous times thinking it was fun, especially when the doors opened and closed by themselves. They walked into a room whose door was ajar; a guy was mopping the floor. They both walked inside, as he smiled at them. "Good afternoon," he said, greeting them and then walking out. Rows of metal lockers stood before them, all locked up tight. Towards the back of the room Kranthar noticed some white coats hanging on hooks. "Look Zadoc, people wear these here, it must be some kind of dress code. Shall we?" Zadoc nodded his head yes, they put them on as they walked out into the corridor.

"We need to find the children's ward, I need to know what that's all about." They took the elevator to the second floor in search of the doors, with animals. Finding them they walked in, shocked by what they encountered. Many rooms of young children, some hooked up to machines, with tubes going in and out of them. While others were sitting in chairs with wheels. They also noticed a few of the children had their legs or arms bandaged up. Standing in the hallway, a child's voice called out to them. "Hello." After a moment, the child called out again. "Hello." They both turned to see a small girl lying in a bed, with many tubes going in and out of her small and fragile body. Zadoc and Kranthar walked over to her bedside. "Are you doctors?" she asked. Zadoc and Kranthar didn't know how to respond. "My mommy and daddy are in the chapel praying, I think I'm very sick." She was laying down weak and very pale, most of her hair was gone, as she put on a knitted cap. Kranthar and Zadoc looked at each other, as Kranthar gently closed the door to the room, Zadoc started to scan her.

"Something is wrong with her blood, it's effecting her organs." He said, dropping his chin to his chest. "Close your eyes dear, and don't be afraid. You're going to feel a burning sensation, but don't worry you're going to be okay." The child closed her tired eyes, as a line of pure white light circled around her small body, extremely bright. Kranthar took a blanket and covered the small window in the door, to keep the light contained within the room. The light moved faster and faster around her tiny frame; a small whimper could be heard from the child's mouth. Zadoc brought the light back into his fingers. He told her not to worry, everything was going to be okay now, he smiled down at her holding her hand. Then they quickly stepped back into the corridor. "So," Kranthar said, "how many can we save today?"

"As many as possible, without being noticed." Zadoc grinned.

* * *

Later that evening Sam was picking up Mary at the hospital. He wanted to see the babies and then go out to dinner. Picking her up at the front desk, he said hi to Gloria, as they both made their way to the elevators, waiting. Something was happening in the children's ward, doctors and nurses were running in. Parents were coming out crying, with prayers coming from their lips. What was happening? They walked over to the double doors; Mary grabbed a nurse she knew and asked. "Betty, what is going on?" Betty turned to her with tears streaming down her face. "The children are healed! It's a miracle from God!"

"Which children Betty?"

"ALL OF THEM!" Even the most severe cases of cancer,

totally gone! The children that have broken bones are being x-rayed as we speak. It's a miracle, Mary! We just can't understand how this could be possible!" Betty walked away, telling the other nurses and doctors what was going on.

Sam and Mary got on the elevator, looking at each other in disbelief. As the doors were closing, a group from the local news ran by them towards the children's ward.

Kayla and Peter could hear people running through the hall and lots of commotion happening. Mary and Sam walked into the room. "Do you know what's happening Sam?" Kayla asked.

"One of the nurses downstairs said, the children on the second floor were healed by some kind of divine intervention. It's crazy down there, the doctors and nurses are running everywhere. The news also showed up to get the story." Peter looked at Kayla, knowing full well his dad and Kranthar were responsible for this. He didn't have a doubt in his mind, he knew the people of earth had such a long way to go, to even come close to the extraterrestrials on my father's planet. Peter smiled, just thinking about it, he felt a sense of pride knowing that he was part of this highly intelligent society.

"So, how are the babies today?" Sam asked. He looked down at Nathan, sleeping in his bassinet.

"Want to hold him, Sam?"

"No, I don't want to wake him." Sam walked over to Ella. "She is the most beautiful baby girl." Sam acknowledged with tears in his eyes. Ella opened her eyes as Mary walked over.

"Would you like to hold her, Mary?"

"May I? It's been some time since I've held a baby in my arms." Kayla picked her up, placing her in Mary's arms. "Kayla she is so beautiful, it's almost uncanny. I mean I have seen lots of babies, but they can't compare with Ella. I know girls are supposed to take after their dads, but I'm sorry to say Peter, I only see Kayla in her. However, Nathan has your coloring and your dark curly hair."

"That's alright Mary, her looks might change as she grows older." Peter replied, but in his mind he was thinking. That's because her father is a blood sucking vampire, with two different colored eyes. Looking down at the baby girl, that he once thought was his, a sadness overcame him.

* * *

On the second floor, a news reporter first on the scene was handed a microphone. "John Montgomery here. I am on the second floor of Saint Paul's Hospital. A miraculous transformation has taken place here, in the children's ward of this hospital. From small things to stage four Leukemia." The reporter announced, his voice cracking and doing his best to hold back his emotions. He waved to a young couple, asking them to step forward in front of the camera. "Mr. and Mrs. Garcia, please in your own words, tell us what happened with your daughter, Maria."

"Well, she was in stage four of Acute Myeloid Leukemia, the doctors had given her less than a year to live." The woman was doing her best to get her words out. "The doctors were amazed she was sitting up in her bed and her color looked good, so they took some blood. It came back negative, her bone marrow was checked with no sign of the disease, it was totally gone. We prayed in the chapel earlier today, the lord must have heard us." Suddenly the woman broke down and cried uncontrollably, quickly comforted by her husband.

"So, there you have it folks. Wait a moment, doctor, can we have a word please!" A doctor in charge of the children's wing stepped forward. "We don't understand what is happening here. There's a boy who came in with a broken arm, we just did an x-ray. Somehow his bones have shifted back into alignment, his arm was healed, like his cast had been on for months! All I can say is, miracles have taken place in Saint Paul's today." The doctor walked away, scratching his head. John Montgomery looked directly into the camera. "So, that's it for now folks. Do you believe in miracles? I have to say I am starting to. Back to you Claire, at the station."

* * *

Sam and Mary were leaving the hospital, trying to maneuver

around the chaos that was happening around them. Reporters and doctors running past them, all trying to figure out what was going on. In the lobby, Mary looked over at Gloria, who was surrounded by people, all trying to get their children into the children's ward and news reporters looking to get a story. Sam grabbed Mary's hand as they exited out to the parking lot. They were met with a chaotic traffic jam. People were looking for a parking space, while news vans were double parked needing to report the story. When they got to their car it was surrounded by vehicles, people with sick children, and news reporters from different stations. There was no chance in hell of leaving. Pandemonium had set in! Sam got on his cell phone and called Max. He wanted him to pick them up, down the block from the hospital.

Max picked up his phone. "Hey Sam, it's a little late for a call, what's going on?" Sam went on to explain the situation to him. "That's some crazy shit!" Max responded. "I've got to get dressed, give me ten and I'll be on my way."

Sam put his arm around Mary as they walked out of Saint Paul's parking area, and down the street. Standing on the corner in front of the town's post office, the line to get into the hospital's parking lot was growing, cars were lining up waiting. Sam put his arm around Mary, as they walked further down the street. He knew Max would be caught in this mess and wanted to get as far away from the hospital as possible. Three blocks away now he called back Max. "Hey Max, we are in front of the hardware store on Clark Ave. pick us up there."

"Okay Sam, I'm on my way."

* * *

Kayla looked out the window of her hospital room. "What the hell is going on down there? Peter come and take a look at this!" Peter walked over to the window and looked down. A sea of cars and people running every which way. Different news stations, with reporters trying to report the story in the middle of the parking lot. Some people were getting out of their cars, carrying their sick children in their arms, just abandoning their cars in the middle of traffic. Peter closed his eyes and shook his head, knowing that his father was responsible for all of this mayhem. He knew his father's intentions were good, but now realized why his mom was so insistent, to have his gifts remain hidden when he was a child.

Meanwhile, the reporter John Montgomery found his way to Maria Garcia's room. Her parents were packing up her things, she would soon be heading home. John walked in quietly, with his camera guy in tow. "Excuse me but, might I have a word with your daughter. I think it's important that people get the real story here, from the lips of a child. A child who experienced the miracle." Mr., and Mrs. Garcia just looked at each other, then Maria spoke. "There were two men in the hallway, I said hello to them and they walked into my room."

"What did they look like?" John asked, holding the microphone in front of her.

"They were very tall and pale, and they were wearing baseball caps, but I think they were bald. I thought they were doctors, cause they had on white coats. They spoke softly to me, in a gentle way. One of them came over to my bed, he told me to close my eyes and not to be afraid. I felt a burning sensation go through my body. I remember him telling me that everything was going to be okay now and not to worry. They smiled at me and then left the room." John motioned to his camera guy to cut the feed. He got his story, it would be sent out through the air waves, as soon as they got back to the station.

* * *

Max pulled his car over as Sam and Mary got in. "What the hell is going on Sam?" Sam looked over at Jeanna, and grinned.

"Have you eaten yet? Let's go to the diner on Sutton, my treat. What do you say?"

"Sounds good, hungry Jeanna?" Max asked.

"Yeah actually, I'm in the mood for pancakes." Jeanna replied, looking over at Mary and smiling.

"Thanks for picking us up Max. We couldn't get our car out of the hospital's parking lot. Some insane stuff went down in the children's ward tonight. All the kids were healed, from broken bones to cancer."

"What the hell are you talking about Sam?" Inquired Max.

"Don't worry, I'm sure it will be on the news tonight. They're calling it a miracle. I'm not sure if miracles happen in this day and age. Or, how all the kids on that floor were healed, but they were, somehow, they were."

Arriving at the diner they got out of the car and walked into a brightly lit atmosphere. Neon signs that advertised burgers and shakes hung on the walls, as red pleather booths, bordered both sides of the establishment. The floor beneath their feet was a black and white checkerboard pattern, as were the stool seats that stood along the counter. A waitress seated them at a booth, near the windows. Leaving them menus and a perfect view of the T.V. Usually a game would be playing, but not tonight. Tonight, the whole town was buzzing with what happened at Saint Paul's this evening.

Sam, Mary, Max, and Jeanna watched the T.V. screen intently, as doctors and nurses told their stories. A few of the children also spoke up, talking about two men who spoke kindly to them. Assuring them that they would be just fine, and not to worry.

Max watched, as two police cars pulled into the parking lot. Sam looked out the window and saw Sergeant Daniels exit his patrol car and make his way to the door. Upon walking in Daniels noticed Sam immediately. He excused himself, as the other patrol men followed a waitress to a booth. Daniels walked over to them, "Sam, Max, Ladies, how is everyone doing tonight?"

"Hey sergeant, any ideas as to what happened at the hospital tonight?" Sam asked. "According to the news, some miracles took place, is that true?"

"Well Sam, I don't know much about miracles, but from what I've heard, something remarkable did happen there tonight. I've never seen this town in such a frenzy, people were bringing in their sick family members by the carloads. It was a total chaotic state of affairs." Suddenly everyone's attention was drawn to the television screen as a small child spoke. "There were two men in the hallway, I said hello to them and they walked into my room."

The reporter responded. "What did they look like?"

"They were very tall and pale and they were wearing baseball caps, but I think they were bald. I thought they were doctors, cause they were wearing white coats. They spoke softly to me, in a gentle way. One of them came over to my bed, he told me to close my eyes and not to be afraid. I felt a burning sensation go through my body. I remember him telling me that everything was going to be okay now and not to worry. They smiled at me and then left the room."

A news anchor cut in. "Well, there you have it folks. Were they people with strong healing abilities or angels sent from God? We will probably never know, I can tell you one thing though. Whoever the parents are, of the children that were healed tonight, they will be eternally grateful. So, from channel 15 news center, good night and have a pleasant tomorrow."

Sergeant Daniels said his goodbyes and went to join his fellow officers. The description kept going around his head. Maria was describing the Seekers, no doubt about it. Tall, pale and bald. Speaking softly and in a caring way. Were they in the hospital to see Peter and Kayla? Maybe Zadoc wanted to see his newborn grandchildren? It had to be him, there was no other explanation. Daniels reached into his pocket and took hold of his crystal, it instantly felt warm in his hand. Was that a sign from Zadoc that he had guessed right. Daniels placed his food order and took a seat with the other officers. A small grin began to form on the sergeant's face, as he thought about his friend, on some distant planet out there in the universe.

* * *

The next morning some peace had returned to Saint Paul's hospital ever so slowly. There were no more miraculous healings. The press and news vans were slowly exiting the parking lot. Peter had taken an Uber early in the morning, back home to pick up his car with the baby seats. Everyone was going home today and he was excited. After the babies had been fed. Kayla's breakfast was brought in, on a tray and placed on a table beside the bed, just as Peter walked in. "Hey hon, you really left early this morning, way before I woke up. Where did you go?" Kayla asked.

"I took an Uber to go home and pick up my car with the baby seats."

"Oh, that's right the baby seats, I totally forgot about those. Good thinking Peter."

"Okay, well thank God these babies have one responsible parent."

CHAPTER THIRTY

A HOMETOWN WEDDING

It was the peak of fall in mid-October, the foliage had turned to the brilliant colors of red, gold, and burnt orange. The most perfect time to have a wedding, at least that's what Kayla thought. Unfortunately, so did lots of other couples apparently, all the venues in the town were booked solid. Until, Sam came up with a fantastic idea. He would close down the café and have the wedding there. The café was definitely big enough to hold friends and family, so why not? Sam had arranged for the Justice of the Peace to come in, and Flowers by Brian was contacted to do the flowers and the wedding décor. Family and friends were invited along with the regular customers, that knew Kayla well. A day of celebration was about to transpire.

A huge banner was hung outside of Perk Up entitled WISH KAYLA AND PETER WELL. SIGN THIS BANNER WITH YOUR BEST WISHES! A black magic marker was clipped to the side of it, where the people of the town could sign it and write their congratulations to the happy couple.

Tables and chairs were being set up on the patio, while an arch of flowers and fall leaves was constructed for the couple to stand under and recite their wedding vows. Emily and Simon arrived first, go figure, this was a day she would never be late for. Max and Jeanna arrived going straight to the banner, writing a few loving words. Sam and Mary were busy inside helping the caterers set things up.

Soon the town's people started to gather and take their seats, including Tina Abruzzi and her husband Dominick. Kayla and Tina never lost touch, after that day she helped her escape from Michael. She had become a close friend.

Sergeant Daniels and his wife Bonnie arrived, still arguing over his lack of organization and his inability to manage time.

Kayla and Peter made their appearance, toting the babies in their carriers. Emily and Simon ran over to them, quickly followed by Max and Jeanna. Kayla lifted Ella out of her carrier and gave her to Emily to hold, then Nathan was handed over to Max.

Kayla laughed, the expression on Max's face was absolute terror. "Don't be afraid to hold him Max," Jeanna said. "It's great practice for when we have ours one day." For some reason that comment, didn't have a relaxing effect on Maxwell.

The Justice of the Peace took his place under the archway, as Peter, and Sam stood alongside him. The officiant raised his hands, asking everyone to please stand. The Wedding March was softly played over the speakers, that were placed here and there amongst the bushes unseen.

Kayla walked towards the archway, her off- white chiffon dress flowed behind her as she walked. She gazed out over the crowd of friends and family as tears ran down her face. Feeling like the luckiest woman in the world. However, two family members were missing, Zadoc and Willie. She wanted them there so badly but knew it would be too risky if anyone were to see Willie. They would probably try to catch him, and God knows, what would happen to him then. Looking over in the front row, there sat Emily holding baby Ella and Max holding baby Nathan, still unsure if he was holding him correctly. Kayla watched as Jeanna repositioned Max's arms one more time, cradling Nathan's head.

Kayla took her spot alongside Peter, as The Honorable Edward J. Taylor began. "Everyone please take your seats. Friends, family, we are here to witness the love of Kayla Jenn Conrad and Peter La'Sogian on this beautiful autumn day. Starting with promises and hope for a bright future. A day filled with wishes, for the best life has to offer. Love is a wonderful thing, if you find the right person. To go through the ups and downs of our day-to-day lives with. I've known Sam Anderson for years, and he believes these two will last the test of time. So, today is the day to celebrate their love. Let's begin, shall we."

"Peter La' Sogian, do you take Kayla to be your lawfully wedded wife. To love and to cherish, in sickness and in health, forsaking all others from this day forward. Till death do you part?" Peter looked at Kayla and smiled, he then glanced at the front row, seeing Emily and Max holding his children, he answered. "I do."

"And do you Kayla Jenn Conrad, take Peter to be your lawfully wedded husband. To love and to cherish, in sickness and in health, forsaking all others from this day forward. Till death do you part?" Kayla looked at Sam and then Peter, so sure this was the best decision she would ever make. "I do."

"So, now that you have committed yourselves. I will, let you both recite the wedding vows you wrote to each other. Peter, if you would be so kind to go first."

"Kayla, it is not difficult to see why any man would be enamored with you. You are beautiful inside and out. From the moment I saw you, my heart beat a little faster. I never in my wildest dreams thought that one day you would be mine. I am so thankful for you and our children, and I look forward to a lifetime of happiness with you." Peter somehow made it through his vows, even though his voice cracked with emotion every now and again.

Kayla looked over at the officiant, who nodded his head, to say that it was her turn. "Peter, it took me a while to realize all of your remarkable qualities. Your kindness and love that you have for me and now our children, mean the world to me. I feel safe in your arms, and I know you will always be there for me in good times and bad, always putting me and our children first. You are a man of great character, and I will love you forever."

"So now, may we have the rings please" After the rings were exchanged the officiant turned to Peter and Kayla and said. "It is my greatest pleasure, by the power that has been vested in me and in front of all these witnesses, that I pronounce you husband and wife. Peter you may kiss your bride." Peter held Kayla tightly in his arms and kissed her lips, as the crowd cheered.

Champagne bottles were being popped open, and the speakers were turned up. The chairs were pushed over to the side, as heat lamps were brought out. The patio now became the dance floor.

Kayla and Peter danced their first dance holding each other and their babies. Kayla was beyond happy. This was the family she had always dreamt about having.

Max held onto Jeanna, running his hands up and down her back. They then joined Peter and Kayla on the dance floor. Holding Jeanna close, Max kissed her neck and whispered sweet nothings in her ear.

Emily and Simon were eating hors d'oeuvres, and dancing like no one was watching. She laughed, as Simon spun her around and dipped her.

Sam and Mary only danced the slow songs, because of Sam's two left feet and Mary wasn't fond of getting her toes stepped on.

Sergeant Daniels and his wife Bonnie had stopped their bickering, long enough to have one romantic dance together. Daniels wondered if Zadoc and the Seekers knew what was going on this evening? He reached into the pocket of his sport jacket, touching his crystal, which suddenly grew warm in his hand. As the day slowly faded into night, the lights around the patio came on, just as they always did at Perk Up, but tonight was different. No one was afraid of walking to their cars or wondering what was waiting for them, lurking in the shadows. The air felt light and weightless, like a spell had been lifted off the town. Suddenly, fireworks shot through the night sky, but in a way that no one had ever witnessed before. Instead of them shooting from the ground up, they were falling down from the sky above. Peter smiled at Kayla, a nice wedding gift Dad, he thought. Daniels looked up at the sky with Bonnie, he also had the feeling Zadoc was sending them his well wishes. Everyone else couldn't figure it out, some thought the fireworks were being thrown off a plane, to explode in the night sky. The reception lasted until the early morning hours. People were saying goodbyes and still talking about the fireworks, that nobody could quite understand.

Kayla and Peter needed to leave. It had been a long day and night, looking at their babies in their carriers sound asleep. Emily, Simon and Jeanna helped them take stuff to their car, as Max stayed on helping Sam take down the banner. Max took a moment as he tried to read some of the things people wrote. Some people just wrote congratulations, while others left poems or quotes of undying love. Some of the stuff made him laugh out loud. Then, one signature jumped out at him. It wasn't written in black magic marker like all the others, it was written in bright red, it said. LOVE YOUR LITTLE GIRL! SHE'S LOVELY! SHE REMINDS ME OF SOMEONE I ONCE KNEW! That was it, no name as to who wrote it, just those three sentences at the bottom right corner of the banner. Sam undid the ties on his side, as Max untied his, the banner fell down and was rolled up neatly, securing it with an orange ribbon.

* * *

Arriving home, Kayla and Peter brought the babies in, placing their carriers on the sofa. Peter made a few more trips to the car to unload. As Kayla walked into the kitchen a large beam of light caught her eye. Azulon, Kranthar, and Zadoc waved and smiled at her, through the window of the kitchen door.

Kayla opened the door and welcomed them inside. "Did you see our show of lights? That was my idea." Azulon announced all proud of himself, as Peter walked into the kitchen, so happy to see his dad standing before him.

"Salutations my dear boy, we watched your day from above. Kayla, I have a surprise for you."

Kayla smiled, wondering what the surprise could be. Zadoc pulled back his robe and Willie came flying out, straight onto Kayla's shoulder. "K a y l a, Willie return." He called out her name and rubbed his small brown face against her cheek.

"Willie!" Kayla started to cry; she loved him so much. This was the best wedding gift anyone could ever give her. "Willie come, would you like to see the babies?" Everyone walked out into the living room, as Willie flew around the babies excitedly.

Kayla softly held Willie in her hand, as she introduced her babies to him. "This is Nathan my son, and Ella my daughter." Willie smiled, exposing his black toothy grin. He flew around them landing on both of them occasionally, tilting his head and looking at them sweetly.

"We wanted to be in attendance at your nuptials but, it would have been too dangerous for Willie to attend, I do believe." said Kranthar.

"We do understand, Kranthar. No worries." Peter acknowledged, knowing it was best to keep Willie hidden.

Kayla added. "I am so happy and grateful to see him. Thank you for bringing Willie to us." Kayla watched as Willie hovered above the babies, landing on the edge of their carriers. He saw that Nathan's blanket had fallen down somewhat. He flew to it, placing it lovingly back up around Nathan's neck, and smiled.

"Dad," Peter said. "I know it was you and Kranthar who wreaked havoc at the hospital that night. What were you both thinking? I know your intentions were good, but an entire floor of kids cured? This town went into a state of hysterics. Please don't do anything like that again, alright?"

"Yes, we understand, we thought we were helping. So many sick children, why so many?" Zadoc asked.

"I don't know." Peter responded. Unfortunately, that was a question only God knew the answer to.

"Well." Zadoc announced. "Peter, Kayla we should take our leave now. Willie looked at Kayla and said, "Willie return!" Kayla gently kissed Willie's face, as he flew over to Zadoc landing in the inside pocket of his robe.

"May we use your yard to ascend?" Azulon inquired.

"Of course." Peter replied. After the hugs and goodbyes were done. Everyone stepped outside, as a large beam of light shot down from the night sky, they were gone in seconds.

* * *

The next morning Kayla woke up to the smell of toast and coffee. Since they were still both on maternity leave, Peter wanted to surprise her with a good breakfast. "Something smells good," Kayla remarked, as she walked into the kitchen.

"I hope you like it, I made all your favorites. Pancakes with butter and syrup. Freshly squeezed orange juice, not from the carton. Scrambled eggs with sausage and a full pot of regular coffee. No more decafe!" Peter grinned.

"Thanks so much sweetie. I forgot to tell you I'm having a play date with Emily and Dino in a few days."

"Wow! Emily and Dino?" Peter questioned.

"Well, she thought it would be a good idea to have Dino get use to the babies. Just in case we would want her and Simon to babysit one night."

"Oh, okay got it." Peter smiled. "I guess it's always good to know you have a backup, if you ever need one."

"Yep." That was all Kayla answered back, as she continued to feed herself, the breakfast that Peter lovingly made her.

* * *

Later that day Peter left for school. Even though he was still on maternity leave, there was a conference meeting he wanted to attend. He liked being informed on whatever was happening at the school.

While Peter was away, Kayla went to see her friends at Perk Up. She piled her twins into the double seated stroller and made her way down Courtlin, stepping inside the bell chimed.

"Hey!" Sam yelled, running over to her and helping her with the door. "How are my god babies doing today?"

"Fine." Kayla answered, giving him a kiss on the cheek. Emily served her customers and then ran over to her. "Hey Em, busy today?"

"Always, I can't wait till you come back to work. It's not the same here without you,"

"I agree," Max said, as he ran over for a kiss and hug. "Hey Kay, do you have a moment? I want to show you something."

"You two go ahead, I'll watch the babies." Sam announced, he loved spending time with them. Watching the expressions on their little faces change or even just watching them sleep, totally relaxed and calm.

"Jesus Max, where the hell are you taking me?" Kayla asked. Max was bringing her down the cellar stairs.

"This is your banner from your wedding day." Max answered. "I want you to see something that I thought was weird." Max slowly untied the banner, opening it up just enough for Kayla to see the lower right corner of it. "There, read it, and let me know your thoughts."

The first thing Kayla noticed, was that it was signed in bright red, not black like the other signatures. After reading it Kayla looked up at Max. "It mentions only Ella, she reminded them of someone that they knew. Are you thinking, what I'm thinking Max?" They both spoke up at once, as if they were joined by one mind, together they said. "TARSULA!"

"Max, there is also something I want to tell you. Ella is Michael's daughter. I tried to hide it, but she may have his eyes."

"You mean two different colors?"

"Yes, it's nothing definite yet. I mean baby's eyes change as they get older, but it's very possible."

"Kay, does Peter know?"

"We talked about it a little, so yeah, he knows."

"Do you think that's why Tarsula would come back? Does she know that Ella, is Michael's daughter?"

"Yes, she does. Anyway, we don't even know if it was Tarsula who signed the banner. Let's not get ahead of ourselves." Yet in Kayla's mind, she had the feeling it had to be her, who else would sign those words in bright red ink.

CHAPTER THIRTY-ONE

THE PLAY DATE

The time for jackets and scarves had arrived, as the wind blew cold. Emily showed up right on time with Dino. Kayla greeted her at the door. "Hey Dino!" Kayla picked him up giving him loads of kisses on his Italian Greyhound face. Dino loved getting kisses, turning his head just so; he was definitely a lover not a fighter.

Kayla set the baby carriers on the rug in the living room, as Dino approached them cautiously. He sniffed Ella and Nathan trying to get their scent. Then he licked Nathan's face, which made Nathan smile and giggled. Both girls laughed, Dino and the babies were going to be the best of friends. "Shall we get going?" Emily asked. "I wish it was just a tad warmer out there, but as long as we bundle up, we should all be fine." Emily helped Kayla place the babies in the back seat of the car, while Dino sat in the front seat on Emily's lap.

They were going to Sunset Park, a huge park with a variety of trees dressed in autumn colors. A walking trail meandered around a substantial lake. It was a favorite spot for runners, who ran around the lake getting in their daily exercise. As they walked along the path, Dino walked ahead of them on his leash, trying to find the perfect stop to mark, while Kayla and Emily took in the beautiful colors of fall. After once around the lake, Kayla settled down on a park bench, while Emily and Dino went to grab a couple of coffees. A raven black as coal, flew onto a tree branch above her, watching. It had been keeping a close eye on them, the moment they entered the park. Being fixated on Kayla's two babies, wondering which one was Michael's. It needed a closer look, maybe there would be some kind of resemblance that would give it away. It flew off the branch and nestled itself, on the back of the bench Kayla was sitting on. "Oh, hello there." Kayla greeted the raven; she always greeted animals that came close to her. She was a true animal lover and sometimes enjoyed their company more than people. The raven side stepped closer to her and the babies. It looked down at the child in the front seat of the stroller, it's dark curly hair and olive complexion, gave the raven some clues as to who the father was. In the blink of an eye, it jumped off the back of the bench and onto baby Nathan. Kayla jumped up in a panic, screaming and trying to scare it away. Each time her hands got close enough, they were aggressively pecked at. Emily and Dino were coming back with the coffee, he broke loose from Emily's grip on the leash. He ran towards the babies, jumping at the raven, ready to attack and kill. Dino managed to get its left wing into his mouth. However, the raven was fast and scratched Dino's face with its taloned foot. He released it and was now whimpering from the scratch on his sweet Greyhound face. Emily took a napkin holding it onto the scratch to stop the bleeding. "What the fuck Kay! What the hell was that?"

Kayla was extremely shaken up. "That raven came out of nowhere, is Dino okay?" Kayla reached down and petted his head. "Thank God you were here Dino." Nathan was crying, Kayla removed him from the stroller, just to make sure he was alright, and then looked over at Ella who was sleeping soundly unaware of what had just occurred.

"Let's get out of here, it's too cold anyway. Are you alright Kay? Do you want me to drive?"

"I'm alright Em, thank you." Kayla placed Nathan back into the stroller, as Emily picked up Dino carrying him back to the car.

Kayla was nervous. Between the banner Max had shown her, and now this raven thing. Her mind was racing. She knew deep in her soul, only one person could be responsible for this sort of thing, that fucking witch, TARSULA!

* * *

Tarsula flew back to her car. Her left arm now showed the markings of Dino's teeth. "Fucking dogs, they should all be killed off the face of the earth!" Tarsula was pissed, driving back to her hotel room. Wanting desperately to see Michael's child, she had to come back to this shithole of a town. Ramill tried to persuade her not to, but it fell on deaf ears. Once Tarsula had her mind set on something, common sense went out the window. Her eyes turned red as blood, as she drove. I wonder, she thought, if there's a way to take the baby girl. After all she is Michael's daughter, he was like a son to me. It's only right that I should have her, to raise as my own. I could teach her the old ways, bring her back with me to Ramill's house in California. No one would ever think of looking for her there. "I heard her call the baby Ella." Tarsula said, talking to herself out loud. "Shit! That name would have to be changed. Ella sounds so fragile and dainty. This child of mine would have to have a strong and powerful name. A name that says, Don't Fuck with Me!" Tarsula smiled, possessed by the devil himself, she started to laugh out loud. She was insane with insidious intent.

* * *

Arriving home, everyone went inside. Kayla went to the bathroom to get some peroxide and antibiotic cream for Dino's face. He had saved the day, the least she could do was clean up his battle wound. Emily held his face as Kayla cleaned the cut, he whimpered at first, but he was fine once the antibiotic ointment was applied. Dino scurried away and laid down on the sofa, between the two babies. It was as if he knew something was happening and he wanted to protect them.

"Emily, I'm worried that Tarsula might be back in town, if she ever left that is. Max showed me a signature on the bottom of our wedding banner. Someone signed it in red, mentioning Ella. It said,

279

how she reminded them of someone they once knew. Then today at the park, it seems that raven wanted to harm only Nathan."

"Kay, maybe you're reading too much into all of this. However, I do think we should keep a watchful eye on Ella, for sure. Kay, can I ask you a question?"

"Yeah, what is it?"

"Is Ella Michael's daughter?"

"Yes, she is. Sometimes when I look at her eyes, in a certain light, they seem to have a slight variation in color. Peter already knows, yet he is still willing to raise her as his own. God, I love him." Emily took a deep breath, she reached out and took Kayla into her arms.

"Don't worry Kay," Emily said. Tarsula doesn't stand a chance between the two of us. I will protect my God babies at all costs. Right Dino!" Dino looked at her and barked in agreement.

CHAPTER THIRTY-TWO

THE FALL FESTIVAL ARRIVES

The time for the Fall Festival had arrived, happening every year near the end of October. Food stands and tables were arranged and set up in the center of town. The rides once again, were being trucked in from across the country, as loads of games were being constructed in one area, just in case you had money to throw away. All the stores in town were decorated for fall and Halloween including Perk Up. Sam wasted no time this year decorating the café. He used the same items Emily and Kayla had purchased from Tilly's last year, which cost him a small fortune. Emily and Max stayed one night to help him decorate the place, since Kayla was still out on maternity leave.

Emily picked up her cell phone, she badly wanted Kayla and Peter to go with her and Simon to the festival.

Peter picked up Kayla cell, since she was busy feeding the babies. "Hey Em, how are ya?"

"I'm good. Where's Kay?"

"Feeding the babies. Want to leave her a message or I can have her call you back?"

"So, are you guys going to the Fall Festival this year? I mean, we go every year."

"I don't think so Em, with the babies and all, it may be a little too much."

"Can we come over? I bought you guys something that might

change your mind."

"Sure, you can come over, but I don't think it will change how we feel."

"We'll be right over," Emily quickly hung up. "Hey Simon, come on we're going to Kayla's house!"

* * *

Peter answered the door, as Simon and Emily walked in, she handed him two gifts. "What's this Em? It's not my birthday."

"It's not for you, it's for my God babies." Emily smiled at him, walking over to Kayla giving her a hug.

"What is it Em?" Kayla asked curiously.

"Well, open them," the gifts were unwrapped with care. "They're baby harnesses, to put the babies in and strap them to your body. Nothing could be safer than that, one for each of you. No excuse now not to attend the Fall Festival." Kayla and Peter just shook their heads and smiled.

"So Peter, what are we going to wear?" Kayla asked. "Let's all put our heads together and think of four great costumes."

"Does this mean you're going?" Emily inquired. Even though she knew the answer was a resounding, yes.

* * *

Zadoc gathered two of his best Seeker and comrades, Kranthar and Azulon. "I'm sending you both down to my son's town. They are having some kind of party, where the entire town is involved. Let's call it a case study, on what the humans call fun."

Kranthar raised his hand. "Do we wear our long coats and hats to blend in?"

"Not tonight Kranthar, you may go as you are." Kranthar and Azulon just looked at each other.

"As we are?" questioned Azulon.

"Yes, it is a party. A party, where humans dress up in strange costumes. For some reason, this is fun for them, why I do not know. However, you must keep your light force hidden, dim it way down."

282

"We will Zadoc. When do we leave?" Kranthar asked.

"As soon as possible, I have to recalculate our navigation system. I must search for an isolated area to land. I hope this night will enlighten you both." Zadoc said, smiling.

* * *

Kayla was getting the costumes ready for the Fall Festival. This year would be better and different from all of the years before, because now they would go together as a family. Peter and Kayla would go as pirates. She would wear a short black skirt and a white billowy blouse, with ruffles gathered around the wrists. A red scarf tied around her head, and black boots, she felt sexy wearing it. Peter's outfit was black jeans, a red shirt, leather vest, and an eye patch over his right eye. Along with a fake beard, they had purchased from a Halloween store, he felt like a dork. Kayla searched everywhere for costumes that the babies could wear. All she could find was a couple of orange onesies. They would both go as pumpkins, she already had the orange knitted caps for them. She only needed to add a felt stem and some green leaves. Feeling bad, that she had to dress them alike, but they would have a lifetime exploring their own individual personalities.

Emily was prepared this year for the festival. Not like last year, when she had waited until the last minute. Her costume this year would be a sexy nurse. She would wear a nurse's uniform a few inches above her knees, form fitting, with white fish net stockings and a nurse's cap to complete the look. Emily tried to persuade Simon to dress as a doctor, but he had his mind set on the persona of a devil. Wearing a red shirt, black blazer and pointy tip boots. He strapped on a headband which allowed two horns to protrude from his forehead, as well as a belt with a red pointy tail, that came out from underneath his jacket.

Jeanna's outfit was a sexy teacher, wearing dark framed glasses. She pulled her attire from her closet. It consisted of a blue pleated mini skirt, white dress shirt and black necktie. She would wear her hair up in a bun. On her feet she would wear black and white saddle shoes. Max was going as a police officer. Sergeant Daniels lent him a uniform, promising to give it back when the night was over. Max was teasing Jeanna, wanting to use it in their sexual foreplay. Saying, he would only keep her out of jail, if she would satisfy him with sexual favors. Typical Max!

Sam and Mary would also attend together this year; both dressed as clowns. Mary did up their faces in clown makeup, and they would wear some old suits that Sam had in the back of his closet. Mary had sewn a huge flower on each of the suit's lapels. Sam's suit was very big on Mary, which made the outfit even better. Everyone was ready for their night of fun.

* * *

Zadoc had made his final adjustments to the navigation system, they were getting ready to beam down. "You can wear your robes, but keep your light source turned off." Zadoc instructed them once again.

Willie was close by, listening to everything that was being said. He knew something special was happening on Earth and also knew Kranthar and Azulon were heading there. "Willie Hide!" He said to himself, as he flew into the inside pocket of Kranthar's robe.

Azulon and Kranthar walked into the launch room. Putting on their robes, which provided extra protection from the elements, as they traveled downward on a beam of light.

"Are you both ready?" inquired Zadoc.

"Yes, our light sources are turned off." Azulon acknowledged.

"Good, guarded travels to you both," Zadoc announced. Within seconds they were gone, heading towards Earth.

* * *

Everyone was meeting at the café, this was the plan so they could enjoy the night together. Sam and Mary were the first to arrive. They waited inside for the group, having coffee and donuts. Sam kept a watchful eye outside, as the group assembled. They were laughing and commenting on each other's costumes. "Alright is everyone ready?" Sam clapped his hands together, as the group walked into the crowds of people.

The first thing that hit them was the smell of all the festival food choices. It carried through the air making everyone's mouth water, which made everyone want to indulge. Feeding their bellies with any of the numerous choices that could be had. They made their way to Gino's food stand, all deciding on some Italian food to start off the night. A few of the options were meatball subs, pizza, sausage and peppers, along with many other delicious cuisine choices.

As Kayla walked past Tommy's Hardware and Rosie's Hair Salon, memories of the alleyway between the buildings came back to haunt her. Visions of having sex with Michael returned to her. She closed her eyes for a second and then looked down at her daughter Ella. There was no doubt, that she was Michael's. Her eyes were starting to ever so slightly, show their difference in color. She looked over at Peter as they walked, who gave her a smile and a kiss on the cheek. It's funny how life turns out sometimes, she thought. As they waited in line to order their food, people were commenting on how beautiful Ella was. In her mind she remembered Michael, and how irresistible he was to her. Would Ella grow up with those same qualities, being so desired by others? The thought of it, scared her to death.

Peter broke her train of thought, asking her what she wanted to eat. "Want to get a foot long meatball sub, we can split it?"

"Yeah, that sounds good." Kayla answered, as she thought about how far her life had come in one single year.

* * *

Kranthar and Azulon landed behind a building unseen. Their purple robes were warm to the touch, from the friction of traveling on the beam of light. Willie wanted to get out of Kranthar's inside pocket. He slowly climbed out, making his way to the back of his robe and exiting downward near his feet, unseen. "Willie hide." He said to himself, as he flew above the crowds, hiding himself here and there amongst the games and rides. At one point he got hungry and landed inside, of Mac's Burgers. A gentleman had just sat down with his food, there was ketchup on the table, but he wanted mustard. He walked away leaving his meal unattended for a moment. Willie swopped down, pulling the all beef patty from the bun, then flew to the roof of the stand to enjoy it. The man came back with mustard in hand, when he removed the bun, he was shocked. There was lettuce and tomato but nothing else.

Kranthar and Azulon were taking notes, mentally. A young guy made a comment as he walked by them. "Cool alien costumes," they heard him say.

"Great tidings to you." Azulon answered. The guy turned to his girlfriend and said. "I guess they are trying to stay in character, you know, like they are real extraterrestrials."

"How ridiculous, like anyone would believe that!" she responded.

Azulon stopped walking and watched as a game was being played. The object of the game was to throw a baseball and knock down as many milk jugs as possible, with one throw. You needed to knock down at least six stacked jugs, to win a prize. They watched as a guy struggled to knock down two. He was starting to feel inadequate, as his girlfriend started to lose interest, calling him a loser. "You can't hit anything!" Azulon heard her say. "You should just give up and take me home. I don't even know why I came here with you, I must have been desperate!" Paying no attention to her, the guy paid for one more bucket of balls. On the first throw nothing. Nothing was hit on the second, or the third. He had one more ball, it was now or never. He threw it with all his might. Azulon used his telekinetic ability, to knock down not only six jugs, stacked in a pyramid form, but the entire stand of twenty four milk jugs. They came crashing down, as everyone looked on and cheered. The guys girlfriend, who ten seconds ago was bad mouthing him, suddenly was hugging and kissing him, as she jumped up and down with excitement.

"WINNER, WINNER, CHICKEN DINNER!" Yelled, the

game attendant. "You are eligible for three stuffed animals or one gaint teddy bear."

Azulon took a mental note. Humans only show affection, when they get what they want. Interesting, he thought.

* * *

Willie suddenly spotted Kayla, he wanted to fly to her, but she was surrounded by people. He had been told on all visits to Earth, he should remain hidden. He followed the group, hiding in different booths. He slid between folded tee shirts, hid among stuffed animals, dove headfirst into the pocket of a jean jacket that was hanging, waiting to be sold. When he couldn't find anything to hide in, he crawled under the stands themselves.

Kayla and Peter made their way to the Ferris Wheel, while the others walked to the haunted house. They got into the small encloser as the doors were closed behind them, they started to move upwards. The ride would stop and go, giving everyone a view of the entire celebration below. Willie flew into the cab that they were sitting in. "Kay la!" he said all proud of himself, for surprising her, he landed on Peter's knee.

"Oh my God, Willie! What are you doing here? How did you get here?" Kayla was happy to see him but was afraid that he would be noticed.

Willie looked up at her and smiled. "Willie hide, Willie return, Willie follow." Kayla picked him up gently and placed him in the side pocket of Ella's baby harness.

"Willie stay in there and hide. Understand?"

"Willie hide!" he repeated.

"Jesus Kay, where did he come from?" Peter questioned.

"I don't know, but at least we have him now, he's safe."

Stepping off the Ferris Wheel the group got back together. Nathan started to fuss. "I think he needs a change." Peter announced.

"Hey Peter, Sam is buying beers, come on!" Max yelled.

"It's alright, give Nathan to me." Kayla removed Ella from her body, strapping her onto Emily. "You don't mind do you Em?"

"Are you kidding? I'm in heaven, I just wish she was mine." Emily remarked, looking lovingly at Ella. Kayla excused herself going into one of the stores she knew had a bathroom and changing table, using it before when she had to change Ella. Not even thinking, that Willie was still in the side pocket of Ella's harness, fast asleep.

As the group walked away, Emily waited patiently for her to return. Kissing Ella's head and whispering sweet words of love to her God child. Standing there she heard Simon calling out to her. "Emily! Emily! Come here quick! Emily! Help me! The sound was coming from an alleyway between two buildings.

"Oh my God!" Emily ran to him, down the alley only to be met by Tarsula.

"So, we meet again Emily, I mean you no harm. I just want the baby, Ella. She is Michael's offspring after all, she belongs with me!"

"Go fuck yourself, Tarsula! She turned to run, but Tarsula acted quickly, putting Emily into a deep sleep by touching her head. Tarsula gently laid her onto the ground unhooking Ella from her, unaware that Willie was now awake and knew everything that was happening. Tarsula held the baby in her arms and ran.

Kayla came out of the store looking for Emily, where the hell was she? She called out to her, "Emily! Emily!" No response, Kayla was in a panic, as the group came back together. "I can't find Emily!" Now crying hysterically. "She has Ella!" Then Willie came flying over to Kayla, flying into the pocket of her blouse, he only had to say four words to her. "TARSULA RETURN! FOLLOW WILLIE!"

"Oh my God, Peter! It's Tarsula I think she has Ella!" Kayla yelled out. Willie flew out of her pocket, ahead of the group, no one saw him take flight, except for Kayla. Willie could see the crowd from above, flying past Kranthar and Azulon. He stopped momentarily in front of them, then continued to fly quickly, going after Tarsula.

"Did I just see Willie?" Kranthar asked. They watched as Kayla, Peter and their group of friends ran past them. "Come

Azulon, something is happening, they may need our help."

* * *

Tarsula left the fairgrounds with baby Ella, as Willie spotted her from above. He flew down, straight at her. Willie screamed "TAR SU LA!" He stretched out his tiny arms, his claws ready to strike. He tore at her eyes and face. She dropped Ella, as Azulon and Kranthar approached. Azulon reacted quickly, using his light rope to cradle Ella, letting her land softly onto the ground. Tarsula was screaming. "I can't see that little flying fuck gouged my eyes!" The group gathered round her, Tarsula's eyes were bleeding, she could hardly see and probably would end up blind. Willie flew into the side pocket of Ella's harness. He let out a deep breath, knowing that Ella was safe now and smiled.

Kranthar and Azulon took hold of Tarsula's arms. "Come with us," they told her. We are medics working the festival, we will address your eyes." They both looked at Kayla and Peter, and then smiled, as Peter strapped Ella's harness onto his body. "Don't worry Peter, she will not trouble you again." Kranthar informed him.

Tarsula was still screaming, "I can't see, what the fuck! I'm going to kill that fucking pixie!" The group looked at each other, wondering what the hell she was ranting about. "Pixie? What's a pixie?" questioned Max.

Peter heard a small voice coming from his harness. "Peeeter." He looked down, as Willie looked up at him from the side pocket of Ella's harness, giving him a huge smile.

"Thank you Willie." Was all Peter could muster, until he broke down and cried. He now realized how special this five inch tall pixie truly was. He had saved his daughter, for which he would be eternally grateful.

Kranthar reached into the side pocket of Ella's harness. He held Willie gently in his hand, being careful to keep him hidden from the others. He placed him in the inside pocket of his robe, and then escorted Tarsula away, still screaming that she would kill Willie, if given the chance. However, Kayla and Peter knew Zadoc would

289

never let that happen.

* * *

Emily woke up in an alley, as a crowd gathered around her. Getting off the ground, she brushed herself off, then quickly realized she no longer had Ella strapped to her body. Panic set in, as she ran through the crowds of people. She started to cry, unsure where the baby was, where had Tarsula taken her? What would she tell Kayla and Peter? Emily became hysterical, running. Then she stopped, seeing the group before her, she ran to them. Seeing two harnesses she exhaled, as a sigh of relief washed over her. "Oh thank God!" Emily cried. Simon ran to her, taking her into his arms. Kayla and Peter walked over to her, as Emily looked at Nathan and Ella. Both were asleep, unharmed. "Kay, I saw Tarsula, she tried to take Ella!"

"It's okay Em. I don't think we need to worry about Tarsula anymore." Emily wiped the tears off her face, as they all called it a night. The group left the festival, grateful that the babies were fine. Peter thought of Willie and smiled, if it wasn't for him, Lord knows what would have happened to Ella.

* * *

Kranthar and Azulon were ready to beam up, standing in an isolated part of the fairgrounds. Tarsula was still fussing. They asked her to remain calm, they were taking her to a medical facility, for her eyes. Kranthar relaxed his mind, telepathically he spoke to Zadoc. "We are ready to ascend. Please move the navigation system for us to approach, the planet Lorna first."

"Why, Lorna? That planet is so isolated and barren. It is filled with the awful people we have abducted in the past. The ones with criminal minds, unconscionable killers, and the worst of mankind. It would be hard to survive there for very long." Zadoc commented.

"Yes Zadoc, we know. We need to drop something off there, the witch named Tarsula. She tried to take your grandest child Ella, for her own," remarked Kranthar.

Zadoc, grew angry quickly. "How can anyone take a child from its rightful parents. I am resetting the navigation system. When approaching Lorna, just throw her down within the beam, do not land yourselves, then continue for home."

"Oh Zadoc, one more thing, we have Willie with us." Kranthar looked inside the pocket of his robe, as Willie looked up at him and smiled.

"Willie?" Zadoc questioned.

"Yes, he must have hid himself in one of our robes. He probably was in need of seeing Kayla and your grandest children. He saved Ella from Tarsula."

Zadoc shook his head and smiled. A tear fell down Zadoc's face, as the love for Willie grew much stronger, than it already was.

CHAPTER THIRTY-THREE

FOOTBALL AND CAKE

The guys were all getting together on a Sunday afternoon, to watch football at Peter's house Sam was the first to arrive, with a tray full of buffalo chicken wings. He was greeted with a hug from Peter, with Nathan in his arms. The next to arrive was Max, carrying a few cases of beer and a duffel bag slung over his shoulder, which contained chips and dips. Simon was the last to arrive, everyone was thinking that Emily's lack of punctuality was rubbing off on him. He held in his hand a large charcuterie board, containing different cheeses and deli meats. Peter had set up a table in the living room to accommodate all of the food and drinks. He walked into the kitchen, taking out pasta salad and potato salad from the fridge, that Kayla had made the night before. The T.V. was turned on, as the four of them got into the game. They yelled at their team, it didn't matter if they were winning or losing. Giving each individual football player some pointers, like there was a chance in hell they would be heard. Nathan was sitting quietly on Peter's lap, watching, just like one of the guys.

Since the guys were together, the ladies decided to have some fun on their own. They would all meet at a new establishment in town called Sweet Delights. The assortment of cakes, pies and pastries would make anyone's mouth water. The décor inside felt light and fresh, with the colors of pink, mint green and white. The ladies arrived one at a time, first in the door was Kayla with Ella strapped to her chest. Followed by Mary, Jeanna and always late Emily.

"This place is lovely." Mary said, declaring her approval. "I love the colors, it's very inviting."

"Yes, it is nice," Emily agreed. "And look at all the cakes, I want a slice from all of them."

"Me too!" Jeanna chimed in. "I have to control myself, since we postponed the wedding and I already bought my dress. I can't gain any weight, if I still want to fit into it."

Kayla smiled. "Well ladies, I don't have anything to fit into, so let's get us some cake! Along with some coffee of course."

They all walked to the lighted glass case, containing the mouthwatering treats. Before it was all said and done, sixteen slices were served at the table along with coffee and tea.

"Christ, I think we ordered too much." Emily announced, licking her lips.

" I don't think so," remarked Mary. "Now we can try a little of everything, except for little Ella. Poor thing, she's still too young for rich foods."

Everyone dove in, the table was deep in conversation as a stranger entered, making his way to the case and deciding what to buy. Twelve large pastries were carefully placed in a pink box and tied up with white string. He turned, seeing the ladies laughing and having a wonderful time. He walked over to them, looking down at Ella.

"Hello ladies, what a beautiful little girl. What's her name?"

Kayla looked up at him ready to place a piece of cake into her mouth. "Ella."

"Ella, what a lovely name. I'm new to the neighborhood and haven't met many people yet. I suppose meeting people takes time," he said, smiling kindly.

"Well, I'm Emily, that's Jeanna, this is Mary, and that lovely lady is Kayla, Ella's mom." Emily announced, making the introductions.

"Nice meeting all of you, have a great afternoon." The stranger turned to leave, as Emily shouted from across the bakery.

"What's your name sir?"

He turned and grinned. "My name, it's Ramill, I'm sure I'll see you all again. Good day ladies."

EPILOGUE

Kranthar and Azulon were approaching the planet, Lorna. They were ready to deploy Tarsula, sending her down on a navigational beam of light, Azulon turned to Kranthar. "Should we restore her eyesight? At least give her a fighting chance, against those that inhabit that forsaken place."

Kranthar agreed. "Yes, alright but make it fast, we are nearly at the point of drop off.

Tarsula stood in a tunnel of light, upset and trying to get out. She couldn't see a damn thing, thanks to Willie.

Azulon went to her, placing his hands against the cylinder of light. His light rope entered the tube encapsulating her, spinning and turning around her body and head. Tarsula shrieked even louder, as she felt her skin burning, then suddenly became quiet. Azulon retracked his light rope, as she brought her hands up to her face. She could see again, everything was crystal clear. Tarsula started to laugh, overcome with gratitude that her eyesight had been restored, then just like that she was dropped. She let out a bone chilling scream and landed on an open field. "Where the fuck am I?" Tarsula looked around. "Is this Earth?" In the distance she could see others moving towards her. As the crowd got closer, she asked, "what town is this?"

A man stepped forward away from the group. "Do you mean what planet?" he answered, with an evil smirk on his unshaven face. Tarsula looked over at the crowd and became frightened, not sure what they were planning to do to her. Thinking fast, she placed a protective bubble around herself, happy she could still use her magical powers. She tried to Chant for Ramill, with no reply, now realizing she was on her own, Tarsula sat on the ground and cried. Sitting there looking out into the crowd of people, searching for one kind face, that might be willing to help her. One of the men reached for her but only got so far, being blocked by something unseen. He tore at it with his hands, tried to break it with a rock, took out his knife and stabbed at it, but it remained intact. "Who are what are you, he asked"? Never encountering anything like this protective bubble, Tarsula had placed around herself.

"My name is Tarsula, I'm a witch with great powers. I wasn't sure what your intentions were, so I cast a protective shield around myself."

The man with the unshaven face smiled. "A protective shield? Your powers could come in handy around here. We are always fighting with another group of shit heads on this planet. If you join us and use your powers against them, I will see to it that you are not harmed. What do you say Tarsula?"

"What planet is this?" Tarsula had thought she was back on Earth.

" This is Lorna, we were all thrown here, because of our wicked ways, by some fucking aliens."

" Aliens?" Her first thought went to Peter, is that what he was, a fucking alien? Tarsula looked at the man that stood before her. "It's hard for me to trust others. If I take down my protective shield, you must promise me that I will remain safe."

"I promise. My name is Cain, I am the leader of this group of misfits. I was going to kill you at first, I have no need for a slightly older female. Since, I am not sexually attracted to you, and I didn't think you would do well in a battle. Yet, this changes everything, if you will use your powers against the others, I would be crazy to let anything happen to you. Do what I ask and stand with us, you have my word, no harm will come to you."

Tarsula stood up, "do I have a choice?" she asked, looking at Cain.

"No, not really. I'm afraid it's my way or nothing."

Closing her eyes she took down the bubble around herself. Cain stepped closer, placing his arm around her shoulder. "I think you and I will become good friends, so tell me Tarsula, what other talents do you possess?"

A faint smile formed on Tarsula's face. Maybe this place won't be so bad after all, she thought, as a slight bloom of red began to blossom within her eyes, once again.

www.ingramcontent.com/pod-product-compliance
Lightning Source LLC
Chambersburg PA
CBHW032351310726
48973CB00007B/1954